Joseph Barber Lightfoot, Pope Clement I

S. Clement of Rome

an appendix containing the newly recovered portions

Joseph Barber Lightfoot, Pope Clement I

S. Clement of Rome
an appendix containing the newly recovered portions

ISBN/EAN: 9783337335496

Printed in Europe, USA, Canada, Australia, Japan

Cover: Foto ©Andreas Hilbeck / pixelio.de

More available books at **www.hansebooks.com**

S. CLEMENT OF ROME.

Cambridge:
PRINTED BY C. J. CLAY, M.A.
AT THE UNIVERSITY PRESS.

S. CLEMENT OF ROME.

AN APPENDIX

CONTAINING THE

NEWLY RECOVERED PORTIONS.

WITH

INTRODUCTIONS, NOTES, AND TRANSLATIONS.

BY

J. B. LIGHTFOOT, D.D.

LADY MARGARET'S PROFESSOR OF DIVINITY, CAMBRIDGE,
CANON OF ST PAUL'S.

London:
MACMILLAN AND CO.
1877

PREFACE.

THE present volume will hardly need many words by way of explanation. The discovery of Bryennios, who a little more than a year ago was enabled to publish for the first time the two Epistles of S. Clement entire, has suggested to recent editors a revision and completion of their work. To this end I might have followed the course pursued by Hilgenfeld and by Gebhardt and Harnack, and have superseded my former volume by a new edition. On the whole however it seemed to me more advisable to issue an Appendix. I thought that in this way I should better consult the convenience of those who possessed my edition; while at the same time there would be a certain advantage in summing up and discussing the results of conjectural criticism, as seen in the light of recently discovered facts, with greater freedom than would have been possible, if I had undertaken an entirely new edition. The present part of the work therefore appears as a supplement to my edition of S. Clement's Epistles published in 1869, and is paged continuously with it. A general title page and a table of contents are added, which are intended to be prefixed to the whole volume.

This Appendix was commenced soon after the copies of Bryennios' edition reached England in February of last year;

but various causes have delayed its completion. More especially the discovery of the Syriac Version about the end of
June stayed my hand: for it was obviously important to
include, not only a discussion of those broader questions which
the appearance of these epistles in such a form suggested, but
also a complete account of the various readings exhibited in
this text. This in itself, with the necessary pressure of other
work, was a task of some months; and it involved a recasting
of certain portions which had been already completed. Lastly,
when the text and notes were already in type, though not
struck off, the new editions of Hilgenfeld and of Gebhardt and
Harnack appeared; and it was necessary to take account of
their labours. I am glad to have had the advantage of testing
my results by theirs. These causes, added to the necessary
hindrances of professional and other duties, have delayed the
publication of this Appendix several months later than I had
at first contemplated.

In a review of my edition which appeared soon after its
publication, in the Göttingen *Gelehrte Anzeigen*, signed with
the well-known initials H. E., disappointment was expressed
that it contained no discussion of the question who was the
writer of the First Epistle. At the time I had deliberately
excluded this subject, as I had then a project of a history
of Early Christian Literature, where such an investigation would
have found a place. But this project has long since been
abandoned, and the question is therefore discussed in the present
volume (p. 257 sq.). Some time after these sheets were struck
off, I found with satisfaction that M. Renan, in the *Journal
des Savants*, January 1877, maintained, as I have done, the
Jewish origin of the writer, and on substantially the same
grounds. Though this seems at present to be an unfashionable
view, I venture to hope that, when the phenomena of the

epistle are more carefully considered, it will find general acceptance.

No apology will, I trust, be needed for attempting to add another to the existing translations of these epistles. Such an attempt finds its justification in the fact that considerable portions will appear now for the first time in an English dress and that elsewhere conjectural readings have been displaced by the ascertained text.

It remains for me to fulfil the pleasant task of acknowledging my obligations to friends who have aided me in the course of the work. My thanks are due, among others, to the authorities of the British Museum, more particularly to Mr Bond the Keeper, and Mr E. M. Thompson, the Assistant Keeper of the Manuscripts, for their unfailing courtesy and assistance, whensoever I have troubled them: to Signor Ignazio Guidi of Rome, for his kindness in consulting and transcribing from MSS in the Vatican Library—a kindness which I appreciate the more because I had no claims whatever upon it; to Dr Hort, to whom I owe several valuable suggestions even in places where his name is not directly mentioned; to Professor Wright, who has taken much trouble in supplying me with information respecting some Oriental MSS; to Mr Van-Sittart, who has extended to this work the supervision for which I have been indebted to him on former occasions and has corrected the proof sheets of a considerable portion of the volume; and especially to Mr Bensly, whose name I have had occasion to mention many times in the course of the work, and whose aid has been invaluable to me in all that relates to the Syriac Version.

TRINITY COLLEGE,
April 13th, 1877.

THE DOCUMENTS.

CLEM.

THE DOCUMENTS.

A PERIOD of nearly two centuries and a half has elapsed since the Epistles of S. Clement of Rome were first published from the Alexandrian MS, now in the British Museum, but then belonging to the King's Library. On the title page of the *Editio princeps*, which appeared in 1633, the editor, Patrick Young, speaks of the text as taken ' ex laceris reliquiis vetustissimi exemplaris Bibliothecæ Regiæ.' In this mutilated condition the two epistles remained till the other day. The First Epistle had lost one leaf near the end, while the surviving portion occupied nine leaves, so that about a tenth of the whole had perished (see above pp. 23, 166). The Second Epistle ended abruptly in the middle, the last leaves of the MS having disappeared. It is now ascertained that the lost ending amounted to a little more than two-fifths of the whole. Moreover the MS in different parts is very much torn, and the writing is blurred or obliterated by time and ill usage, so that the ingenuity of successive editors has been sorely exercised in supplying the lacunæ.

After so long a lapse of time it seemed almost beyond hope, that the epistles would ever be restored to their entirety. Yet within the last few months they have been discovered whole in two distinct documents. The students of early patristic literature had scarcely realized the surprise which the publication of the complete text from a Greek MS at Constantinople had caused, when it was announced that the University of Cambridge had procured by purchase a MS containing the two epistles whole in a Syriac Version. Of these two new authorities for the text I proceed to give an account.

15—2

I.

At the close of the last year a volume was published at Constantinople, bearing the title:

Τοῦ ἐν ἁγίοις πατρὸς ἡμῶν Κλήμεντος ἐπισκόπου Ῥώμης αἱ δύο πρὸς Κορινθίους ἐπιστολαί. Ἐκ χειρογράφου τῆς ἐν Φαναρίῳ Κωνσταντινουπόλεως βιβλιοθήκης τοῦ Παναγίου Τάφου νῦν πρῶτον ἐκδιδόμεναι πλήρεις μετὰ προλεγομένων καὶ σημειώσεων ὑπὸ Φιλοθέου Βρυεννίου μητροπολίτου Σερρῶν κ.τ.λ. Ἐν Κωνσταντινουπόλει, 1875.

['The Two Epistles of our holy father Clement Bishop of Rome to the Corinthians; from a manuscript in the Library of the Most Holy Sepulchre in Fanar of Constantinople; now for the first time published complete, with prolegomena and notes, by Philotheos Bryennios, Metropolitan of Serræ. Constantinople, 1875.]

This important MS is numbered 456 in the library to which it belongs. It is an 8vo volume, written on parchment in cursive characters, and consists of 120 leaves. Its contents, as given by Bryennios, are as follows:

fol. 1—32   Τοῦ ἐν ἁγίοις Ἰωάννου τοῦ Χρυσοστόμου σύνοψις τῆς παλαιᾶς καὶ καινῆς διαθήκης ἐν τάξει ὑπομνηστικοῦ[1].

fol. 33—51b   Βαρνάβα ἐπιστολή.

fol. 51b—70a   Κλήμεντος πρὸς Κορινθίους Α'.

fol. 70a—76a   Κλήμεντος πρὸς Κορινθίους Β'.

fol. 76a—80   Διδαχὴ τῶν δώδεκα Ἀποστόλων.

fol. 81—82a   Ἐπιστολὴ Μαρίας Κασσοβόλων πρὸς τὸν ἅγιον καὶ ἱερομάρτυρα Ἰγνάτιον ἀρχιεπίσκοπον Θεουπόλεως Ἀντιοχείας.

fol. 82a—120a   Τοῦ ἁγίου Ἰγνατίου Θεουπόλεως Ἀντιοχείας

        πρὸς Μαρίαν

        πρὸς Τραλλιανούς

        πρὸς Μαγνησίους

        πρὸς τοὺς ἐν Ταρσῷ

        πρὸς Φιλιππησίους περὶ βαπτίσματος

        πρὸς Φιλαδελφεῖς

        πρὸς Σμυρναίους

        πρὸς Πολύκαρπον ἐπίσκοπον Σμύρνης

---

[1] This is doubtless the same work which is printed in Montfaucon's edition of S. Chrysostom, VI. p. 314 sq. Bryennios says that the treatise in this MS contains only the Old Testament and ends with Malachi. Montfaucon stops short at Nahum, apparently because his MSS failed him there.

πρὸς Ἀντιοχεῖς
πρὸς Ἥρωνα διάκονον Ἀντιοχέα
πρὸς Ἐφεσίους
πρὸς Ῥωμαίους.

The genuine Epistle of Clement is headed Κλήμεντος πρὸς Κορινθίους Αʹ; the so-called Second Epistle likewise has a corresponding title, Κλήμεντος πρὸς Κορινθίους Βʹ. At the close of the Second Epistle is written, Στίχοι χ. ῥητὰ κʹε. At the end of the volume is the colophon; Ἐτελειώθη μηνὶ Ἰουνίῳ εἰς τὰς ιαʹ. ἡμέραν Γʹ. Ἰνδ θʹ. ἔτους ϛφξδʹ. χειρὶ Λέοντος νοταρίου καὶ ἀλείτου. The date A.M. 6564 is here given according to the Byzantine reckoning, and corresponds to A.D. 1056, which is therefore the date of the completion of the MS.

It is strange that this discovery should not have been made before. The Library of the Most Holy Sepulchre at Constantinople is attached to the Patriarchate of Jerusalem in that city, and therefore has something of a public character. It has moreover been examined more than once by learned men from Western Europe. A catalogue of its MSS, compiled in 1845 by Bethmann, appeared in Pertz *Archiv der Gesellsch. f. ältere deutsche Geschichtkunde* IX. p. 645 sq.; but it does not mention this volume (see *Patr. Apost. Op.* I. i. p. xii, Gebh. u. Harn., ed. 2). Some years later, in 1856, M. Guigniant read a report of the contents of this library before the French Academy of Inscriptions, which is published in the *Journal Général de l'Instruction Publique* 1856, XXV. p. 419; and again this MS is unnoticed. M. Guigniant seems to have attended chiefly to classical literature, and to have made only the most superficial examination of the Christian writings in this collection: for he says, somewhat contemptuously, that these MSS 'unfortunately comprise little besides Homilies, Prayers, Theological and Controversial Treatises, written at times not very remote from our own,' with more to the same effect (as quoted in the *Academy*, May 6, 1876). Again, two years later, the Rev. H. O. Coxe, the Librarian of the Bodleian, visited this Library and wrote a report of his visit (*Report to H. M. Government on the Greek MSS in the Libraries of the Levant*, pp. 32, 75, 1858), but he too passes over this volume in silence. A serious illness during his stay at Constantinople prevented him from thoroughly examining the libraries there.

This MS is designated I (Ἱεροσολυμιτικός) by Bryennios, and by Hilgenfeld after him. But this designation is misleading, and I shall therefore call it C (Constantinopolitanus) with Gebhardt and Harnack.

Facsimiles of C are given by Bryennios at the end of his volume. The contractions are numerous and at first sight perplexing. It systematically ignores the ι subscript or adscript with a single exception, ii. § 1 τῆι θελήσει (p. 147); and, if Bryennios has in these particulars reproduced it faithfully in his own text[1], it also universally omits before consonants the so-called ν ἐφελκυστικόν which appears in the Alexandrian MS, and writes οὕτω under the same circumstances, when the older MS has οὕτως. It is written with a fair amount of care throughout, so far as regards errors of transcription. In this respect it contrasts favourably with A, which constantly betrays evidence of great negligence on the part of the scribe. But, though far more free from mere clerical errors, yet in all points which vitally affect the trustworthiness of a MS, it must certainly yield the palm to the Alexandrian. The scribe of A may be careless, but he is guileless also. On the other hand the text of C shows manifest traces of critical revision, as will appear in the sequel.

But, notwithstanding this fact, which detracts somewhat from its weight, it still has considerable value as an authority. More especially it is *independent* of A; for it preserves the correct reading in some instances, where A is manifestly wrong. I pass over examples of slight errors where one scribe might blunder and another might correct his blunder (e. g. § 1 ξένοις A, ξένης C; § 2 ἐστερνισμένοι A, ἐνεστερνισμένοι C; § 3 ἀπεγαλάκτισεν A, ἀπελάκτισεν C; § 25 διανεύει A, διανύει C; § 35 φιλοξενίαν A, ἀφιλοξενίαν C). These are very numerous, but they prove nothing. Other instances however place the fact of its independence beyond the reach of doubt: e.g. § 2 μετ' ἐλέους (μετελαιουσ) A, which is read μετὰ δέους in C, where no divination could have restored the right reading; § 3 κατὰ τὰς ἐπιθυμίας αὐτοῦ τῆς πονηρᾶς A, where critics with one accord have substituted τὰς πονηράς for τῆς πονηρᾶς without misgiving, thus mending the text by the alteration of a single letter, but where the reading of C shows that the words τῆς καρδίας have dropped out in A after ἐπιθυμίας; § 21 διὰ τῆς φωνῆς A, where C has διὰ τῆς σιγῆς, as the sense demands and as the passage is quoted by Clement of Alexandria; § 34 προτρέπεται (προτρεπετε) οὖν ἡμᾶς ἐξ ὅλης τῆς καρδίας ἐπ' αὐτῷ μὴ ἀργοὺς μήτε παρειμένους εἶναι ἐπὶ πᾶν ἔργον ἀγαθόν, where some critics have corrected ἐπ' αὐτῷ in various ways, while others, like myself, have preferred to retain it and put a slightly strained meaning on it (see the note p. 113), but where C solves the difficulty at once by inserting πιστεύοντας after ἡμᾶς and thus furnishing a government for ἐπ' αὐτῷ; § 37, where ευεικτικως, or whatever may be the reading of A (see p. 121)

---

[1] This however may be doubted. Hilgenfeld (p. xix) calls attention to the fact, that in § 33 Bryennios in his note gives ἐστήρισεν as the reading of C before a consonant.

could not have suggested ἐκτικῶς which appears in C. It follows from these facts (and they do not stand alone) that C is not a lineal descendant of A, and that the text which they have in common must be traced back to an archetype older than the 5th century, to which A itself belongs.

On the other hand, the *critical revision*, to which I have already referred, as distinguishing the text of C when compared with that of A, and thus rendering it less trustworthy, betrays itself in many ways.

(1) C exhibits *harmonistic* readings in the quotations. Thus in § 4 it has τῷ Κυρίῳ for τῷ Θεῷ in Gen. iv. 3 in accordance with the LXX; and again ἄρχοντα καὶ δικαστὴν for κριτὴν ἢ δικαστὴν in Exod. ii. 14, also in accordance with the LXX (comp. also Acts vii. 27). In § 13 it gives τοὺς λόγους for τὰ λόγια in Is. lxvi. 2 in conformity with the LXX. In § 22 again it has τὸν ἐλπίζοντα for τοὺς ἐλπίζοντας in Ps. xxxii. 10 after the LXX. In § 33, having before spoken of justification by faith and not by works, Clement writes τί οὖν ποιήσωμεν, ἀδελφοί; ἀργήσωμεν ἀπὸ τῆς ἀγαθοποιΐας; as read in A: but this sentiment is obviously suggested by Rom. vi. 1 sq., τί οὖν ἐροῦμεν; ἐπιμένωμεν τῇ ἁμαρτίᾳ κ.τ.λ., and accordingly C substitutes τί οὖν ἐροῦμεν for τί οὖν ποιήσωμεν. In § 34 Clement quotes loosely from Is. vi. 3 πᾶσα ἡ κτίσις, but C substitutes πᾶσα ἡ γῆ in accordance with the LXX and Hebrew. Later in this chapter again Clement gives (with some variations) the same quotation which occurs in 1 Cor. ii. 9, and C alters it to bring it into closer conformity with S. Paul, inserting ἃ before ὀφθαλμὸς and substituting τοῖς ἀγαπῶσιν for τοῖς ὑπομένουσιν, though we see plainly from the beginning of the next chapter that Clement quoted it with τοῖς ὑπομένουσιν. In § 35, in a quotation from Ps. l. 16 sq., C substitutes διὰ στόματος for ἐπὶ στόματος so as to conform to the LXX. In § 36, where A reads ὄνομα κεκληρονόμηκεν, C has κεκληρονόμηκεν ὄνομα with Heb. i. 4. In § 47 for αὐτοῦ τε καὶ Κηφᾶ τε καὶ Ἀπολλώ, C substitutes ἑαυτοῦ καὶ Ἀπολλώ καὶ Κηφᾶ, which is the order in 1 Cor. i. 12. Though A itself is not entirely free from such harmonistic changes, they are far less frequent than in C.

(2) Other changes are obviously made from *dogmatic* motives. Thus in ii. § 9 we read Χριστὸς ὁ Κύριος ὁ σώσας ἡμᾶς, ὢν μὲν τὸ πρῶτον πνεῦμα, ἐγένετο σάρξ κ.τ.λ. This mode of speaking, as I have pointed out in my notes (p. 202), is not uncommon in the second and third centuries: but to the more dogmatic precision of a later age it gave offence, as seeming to confound the Second and Third Persons of the Holy Trinity. Accordingly C substitutes λόγος for πνεῦμα, 'Jesus Christ, being first Word, became flesh,' thus bringing the statement into

accordance with the language of S. John. Again, in § 30 of the genuine Epistle, τοῖς κατηραμένοις ὑπὸ τοῦ Θεοῦ, the words ὑπὸ τοῦ Θεοῦ are omitted in C, as I suppose, because the scribe felt a repugnance to ascribing a curse to God; though possibly they were struck out as superfluous, since they occur just below in the parallel clause τοῖς ηὐλογημένοις ὑπὸ τοῦ Θεοῦ. Again in § 12 'Ραὰβ ἡ πόρνη, C reads 'Ραὰβ ἡ ἐπιλεγομένη πόρνη, the qualifying word being inserted doubtless to save the character of one who holds a prominent place in the Scriptures. Under this head also I am disposed to classify the various reading in § 2, τοῖς ἐφοδίοις τοῦ Θεοῦ ἀρκούμενοι, where C reads τοῦ Χριστοῦ for τοῦ Θεοῦ; but this is a difficult question, and I reserve the discussion of it till the proper place. In § 14 too the substitution of αἱρέσεις for ἔριν is probably due to an orthodox desire to give definiteness to Clement's condemnation of the factious spirit.

(3) But more numerous are the *grammatical* and *rhetorical* changes, i.e. those which aim at greater correctness or elegance of diction. These are of various kinds. (*a*) The most common perhaps is the substitution of a more appropriate tense, or what seemed so, for a less appropriate: e.g. § 1 βλασφημεῖσθαι for βλασφημηθῆναι; § 7 ἱκετεύοντες for ἱκετεύσαντες; § 12 λελάληκας for ἐλάλησας, ἐγενήθη for γέγονεν (see the note in the addenda); § 17 ἀτενίσας for ἀτενίζων; § 20 προσφεύγοντας for προσπεφευγότας; § 21 ἀναιρεῖ for ἀνελεῖ; § 25 τελευτήσαιτος for τετελευτηκότος, πληρουμένου for πεπληρωμένου; § 35 ὑποπίπτει for ὑπέπιπτεν; § 40 προσταγεῖσι for προστεταγμένοις; § 44 ἐστὶν for ἔσται, πολιτευσαμένους for πολιτευομένους; § 49 δέδωκεν for ἔδωκεν; § 51 στασιασάντων for στασιαζόντων; § 53 ἀναβάντος for ἀναβαί[νοντος]; ii. § 4 ὁμολογήσωμεν for ὁμολογῶμεν; ii. § 7 φθείρων for φθείρας; ii. § 8 ποιήσῃ for ποιῇ and βοηθεῖ for βοηθήσει. (*b*) The omission, addition, or alteration of connecting particles, for the sake of greater perspicuity or ease: e.g. § 8 γὰρ omitted; § 12 ὅτι... καὶ inserted; § 16 δὲ omitted; § 17 ἔτι δὲ omitted, and again δὲ inserted; § 30 τε...καὶ inserted; § 33 δὲ substituted for οὖν; § 65 (59) καὶ omitted before δι᾽ αὐτοῦ; ii. § 2 δὲ omitted; ii. § 3 οὖν omitted; ii. § 7 οὖν omitted; ii. § 10 δὲ substituted for γάρ. (*c*) The substitution of a more obvious preposition for a less obvious: e.g. § 4 ἀπό for ὑπό (twice), § 9 ἐν τῇ λειτουργίᾳ for διὰ τῆς λειτουργίας, § 11 εἰς αὐτὸν for ἐπ᾽ αὐτόν, § 44 περὶ τοῦ ὀνόματος for ἐπὶ τοῦ ὀνόματος. (*d*) An aiming at greater force by the use of superlatives: § 2 σεβασμιωτάτῃ for σεβασμίῳ, § 33 παμμεγεθέστατον for παμμέγεθες. (*e*) The omission of apparently superfluous words: e.g. § 1 ἀδελφοί, ὑμῶν; § 4 οὕτως; § 7 εἰς (after διέλθωμεν); § 8 γὰρ (after ζῶ); § 11 τοῦτο; § 15 ἀπό; § 19 τὰς...γενεάς (τοὺς being substituted); § 21 ἡμῶν; § 30 ἀπό; § 38 [ἤτω]

καί (if this mode of supplying the lacuna in A be correct), where the meaning of the words was not obvious (see the note in the addenda); § 40 ὁ before τόπος; § 41 μόνη; § 44 ἄνδρες (with the insertion of τινες in the preceding clause); ii. § 7 αὐτῶν; ii. § 8 ἐν before ταῖς χερσίν (with other manipulations in the passage which slightly alter the sense); ii. § 8 μετανοίας: and (though much less frequently) the insertion of a word; e.g. § 14 τὸν before ἀσεβῆ; § 33 ἀγαθοῖς (but conversely ἀγαθῆς is absent from C but present in A in § 30); ii. § 1 τοῦ before μὴ ὄντος; ii. § 8 ἔτι. (f) Alterations for the sake of an easier grammatical construction or a more obvious sense: e.g. § 2 τῶν πλησίον for τοῖς πλησίον; § 4 τὸ πρόσωπον for τῷ προσώπῳ; § 15 ἔψεξαν αὐτὸν for ἐψεύσαντο αὐτόν; § 20 ἐπ' αὐτῆς for ἐπ' αὐτήν; ii. § 3 τῆς ἀληθείας boldly substituted for ἡ πρὸς αὐτόν on account of the awkwardness; ii. § 9 ἀπολάβητε for ἀπολάβωμεν. (g) The substitution of orthographical or grammatical forms of words, either more classical or more usual in the transcriber's own age: e.g. § 6 ὀστῶν for ὀστέων, § 15 εὐλόγουν for εὐλογοῦσαν, § 38 εἰσήλθομεν for εἰσήλθαμεν, § 57 προείλοντο for προείλαντο, §§ 4, 6 ζῆλον for ζῆλος, § 13 τύφον for τύφος, ἐλεεῖτε for ἐλεᾶτε, § 20 ὑγίειαν for ὑγείαν, § 33 ἀγάλλεται for ἀγαλλιᾶται, § 37 χρᾶται for χρῆται (but conversely, ii. § 6 χρῆσθαι for χρᾶσθαι), § 39 ἐναντίον for ἔναντι, § 40 ὑπερτάτῃ for ὑπερτάτῳ, § 53 Μωσῆ for Μωϋσῆ (and similarly elsewhere), § 50 ταμιεῖα for ταμεῖα (ταμια), § 65 (59) ἐπιπόθητον for ἐπιποθήτην, ii. § 2 ἐκκακῶμεν for ἐγκακῶμεν, ii. § 5 ἀποκτένοντας (sic) for ἀποκτέννοντας, ii. § 7 πείσεται for παθεῖται, ii. § 12 δύο for δυσί, δήλη for δῆλος. So too ἐρρίζωσεν ἐρρύσατο, φυλλορροεῖ, for ἐξερίζωσεν, ἐρύσατο, φυλλοροεῖ; πρᾶος, πραότης, for πραΰς, πραΰτης; etc. And again C has commonly ἑαυτοῦ etc. for αὐτοῦ etc., where it is a reflexive pronoun. In many such cases it is difficult to pronounce what form Clement himself would have used (see pp. 25, 26); but the general tendency of the later MS is obvious, and the scribe of A, being nearer to the age of Clement than the scribe of C by about six centuries, has in all doubtful cases a prior claim to attention. (h) One other class of variations is numerous; where there is an exchange of simple and compound verbs, or of different compounds of the same verb. In several cases C is obviously wrong; e.g. § 20 παραβάσεως for παρεκβάσεως, μεταδιδόασιν for μεταπαραδιδόασιν; while other cases do not speak for themselves, e.g. § 7 ἐπήνεγκε for ὑπήνεγκεν, § 12 ἐκκρεμάσῃ for κρεμάσῃ, § 16 ἀπελθόντες for ἐλθόντες, § 25 ἐγγεννᾶται for γεννᾶται, § 37 τελοῦσι for ἐπιτελοῦσιν, § 43 ἠκολούθησαν for ἐπηκολούθησαν, § 55 ἐξέδωκαν for παρέδωκαν, ii. § 1 ἀπολαβεῖν for λαβεῖν, ii. § 12 ἐρωτηθεὶς for ἐπερωτηθείς, but the presumption is in favour of the MS which is found correct in the crucial instances. (i) Again there are two or three instances where C substitutes the active voice for the middle; § 8 ἀφέλετε for ἀφέλεσθε, § 23 ἐπιδείκνυσι for ἐπιδείκνυνται, § 43 ἐπέδειξε for ἐπεδείξατο, and in all these the middle seems to be correct: while conversely in § 38, ἐντρεπέσθω the reading of C must be substituted for the soloecistic ἐντρεπέτω which stands in A.

In some passages, where none of these motives can be assigned, the variations are greater, and a deliberate change must have 'been made on the one side or the other. In these cases there is frequently little or no ground for a decision between the two readings from internal evidence; e.g. § 1 περιστάσεις for περιπτώσεις, § 5 ἔριν for φθόνον (where however ἔριν may be suspected as an alteration made to conform to the expression ζῆλον καὶ ἔριν just below), § 6 κατέσκαψε for κατέστρεψεν, § 8 ψυχῆς for καρδίας, § 28 βλαβερᾶς (sic) for μιαρᾶς, § 35 πονηρίαν for ἀνομίαν, § 51 ἄνθρωπον for θεράποντα, § 55 ὑπομνήματα for ὑποδείγματα. But elsewhere the judgment must be given against C; e.g. § 32 τάξει for δόξῃ, § 33 προετοιμάσας for προδημιουργήσας, § 41 προσευχῶν for εὐχῶν, § 47 ἀγάπης for ἀγωγῆς (possibly an accidental change), § 53 δεσπότης for θεράπων, § 56 Κύριος for δίκαιος, ii. § 1 πονηροὶ for πηροί, ii. § 10 ἀνάπαυσιν, ἀνάπαυσις, for ἀπόλαυσιν, ἀπόλαυσις: while in no such instance is A clearly in the wrong; for I do not regard § 41 εὐχαριστείτω A, εὐαρεστείτω C, as an exception. And generally of the variations it may be said that (setting aside mere clerical errors, accidental transpositions, and the like) in nine cases out of ten, which are at all determinable, the palm must be awarded to A[1].

[The above account of the relation of C to A was written before the discovery of the Syriac Version; and it has received the strongest confirmation from this latter authority. It will be seen in the sequel that in nearly every case which is indeterminable from internal evidence S throws its weight into the scale of A.]

It will be unnecessary to give examples of the usual clerical errors, such as omission from homoeoteleuton, dropping of letters, and so forth. Of these C has not more than its proper share. Generally it may be said that this MS errs in the way of omission rather than of insertion. One class of omissions is characteristic and deliberate. The scribe becomes impatient of copying out a long quotation, and abridges it, sometimes giving only the beginning or the beginning and end, and sometimes mutilating it in other ways (see §§ 18, 22, 27, 35, 52). A

---

[1] This estimate of the relative value of A and C agrees substantially with those of Harnack (*Theolog. Literaturz.*, Feb. 19, 1876, p. 99) and of Gebhardt (ed. 2, p. xv). Hilgenfeld takes a different view, assigning the superiority to C (ed. 2, p. xx).

characteristic feature of this MS also is the substitution of ὑμεῖς, ὑμῶν, etc., for ἡμεῖς, ἡμῶν, etc. I say characteristic; because, though the confusion of the first and second persons plural of the personal pronoun is a very common phenomenon in most MSS owing to itacism, yet in this particular case it is far too frequent and too·one-sided to be the result of accident. The motive is obvious. When read aloud, the appeals in the letter gain in directness by the substitution of the second person.

Instances will be given in the addenda which show how at some stage in its pedigree the readings of C have been influenced by the uncial characters of a previous MS from which it was derived : see §§ 2, 21, 32, 40, 43.

From the list of contents given above (p. 224) it will have appeared that the interest of this MS does not end with Clement. What may be the value of the *Doctrina Duodecim Apostolorum* remains to be seen; but a new authority for the Greek of Barnabas will be a great gain, more especially in the earlier part where we are altogether dependent on the very corrupt text of א. And, though from the order of the Ignatian Epistles and the space occupied by them it is clear that this MS gives the Long Recension, yet here again another authority, belonging (as we may hope) to a different family from those already known, will be a welcome acquisition. The editor promises to publish the Barnabas and Ignatius shortly (p. viii).

But in addition to the absolute gain of this discovery in itself, the appearance of the volume which I have been discussing is a happy augury for the future in two respects.

In the first place, when a MS of this vast importance has been for generations unnoticed in a place so public as the official library of a great Oriental prelate, a hope of future discoveries in the domain of early Christian literature is opened out, in which the most sanguine would not have ventured to indulge before.

Secondly, it is a most cheering sign of the revival of intellectual life in the Oriental Church, when in this unexpected quarter an editor steps forward, furnished with all the appliances of Western learning, and claims recognition from educated Christendom as a citizen in the great commonwealth of literature.

II.

A few months. after the results of this important discovery' were given to the world, a second authority for the complete text of the two epistles came unexpectedly to light.

The sale catalogue of the MSS belonging to the late Oriental scholar M. Jules Mohl of Paris contained the following entry.

'1796. Manuscrit syriaque sur parchemin, contenant le N. T. · (moins l'Apocalypse) d'apres la traduction revue par Thomas d'Héraclée. ...Entre l'épître de S. Jude et l'épître de S. Paul aux Romains, se trouve intercalée une traduction syriaque des deux épîtres de S. Clément de Rome aux Corinthiens.'

It was the only Syriac MS in M. Mohl's collection.

The Syndicate of the Cambridge University Library, when they gave a commission for its purchase, were not sanguine enough to suppose that the entry in the catalogue would prove correct. The spurious Epistles on Virginity are found in a copy of the Syriac New Testament immediately after the Epistle of S. Jude taken from the Philoxenian version (see above, p. 15); and it was therefore concluded that the two epistles in question would prove to be these. It seemed incredible that such a treasure as a Syriac version of the Epistles to the Corinthians, forming part of a well known collection, should have escaped the notice of all Oriental scholars in France. It was therefore a very pleasant surprise to Mr Bensly, into whose hands the MS first came after its purchase, to discover that they were indeed the Epistles to the Corinthians. He at once announced this fact in a notice sent simultaneously to the Academy and the Athenæum (June 17, 1876), and began without delay to prepare for the publication of this version.

To Mr Bensly's volume, which will probably appear shortly after my own, I must refer my readers for a fuller account of this unique MS and the version which it contains. It will be sufficient here to give those facts which are important for my purpose.

The class mark is now *Add. MSS* 1700 in the Cambridge University Library. The MS is parchment, 9½ inches by 6½, written in a current hand; each page being divided into two columns of from 37 to 39 lines. It contains the Harclean recension of the Philoxenian version of the New Testament; but, like some other MSS of this recension, without the asterisks, obeli, and marginal readings. The books are arranged as follows :

1. The Four Gospels. These are followed by a history of the Passion compiled from the four Evangelists.

2. The Acts and Catholic Epistles, followed by the Epistles of S. Clement to the Corinthians.

3. The Epistles of S. Paul, including the Epistle to the Hebrews, which stands last.

At the beginning of the volume are three tables of lessons, one for each of these three divisions.

Quite independently of the Clementine Epistles, this volume has the highest interest; for it is the only known copy which contains the whole of the Philoxenian (Harclean) version, so that the last two chapters of the Epistle to the Hebrews, with the colophon following them, appear here for the first time.

At the end of the fourth Gospel is the well-known subscription, giving the date of the Philoxenian version A.D. 508, and of the Harclean recension A.D. 616; the latter is stated to be based in this part of the work on three MSS (see White's *Sacr. Evang. Vers. Syr. Philox.* pp. 561 sq., 644 sq., 647, 649 sq.; Adler *Nov. Test. Vers. Syr.* p. 45 sq.; *Catal. Cod. MSS Orient. Brit. Mus.* I. p. 27, no. xix, ed. Forshall). The history of the Passion, which follows, and which was compiled for lectionary purposes, is found also in other MSS (see White l. c. p. 645, Adler l. c. p. 63).

In the second division the colophon which follows the Epistle of S. Jude is substantially the same with that of the Oxford MS given by White (*Act. Apost. et Epist.* I. p. 274). The Catholic Epistles are followed immediately on the same page by the Epistles of Clement, the Epistle of S. Jude with its colophon ending one column, and the First Epistle of Clement beginning the next. This latter is headed :

ܟܬܒܐ ܩܬܘܠܝܩܝ ܕܩܠܡܝܣ ܬܠܡܝܕܗ
ܕܦܛܪܘܣ ܫܠܝܚܐ ܕܠܘܬ ܥܕܬܐ ܕܩܘܪܢܬܝܐ.

The Catholic Epistle of Clement the disciple of Peter the Apostle to the Church of the Corinthians.

At the close is written :

ܫܠܡܬ ܐܓܪܬܐ ܩܕܡܝܬܐ ܕܩܠܡܝܣ : ܐܝܬܝܗ̇ܬ
ܡܝܢ ܬܠܐ ܩܘܪܢܬܝܐ ܡܢ ܪܗܘܡܝ.

Here endeth the First Epistle of Clement, that was written by him to the Corinthians from Rome.

Then follows:

ܕܝܠܗ ܕܗ̇. ܕܝܠܗ ܐܓܪܬܐ ܕܬܪ̈ܬܝܢ ܠܘܬ ܩܘܪܢܬܝܐ.

Of the same the Second Epistle to the Corinthians.

At the close of the Second Epistle is

ܫܠܡܬ ܐܓܪܬܐ ܕܬܪ̈ܬܝܢ ܕܩܠܝܡܝܣ. ܕܠܘܬ ܩܘܪܢܬܝܐ.

Here endeth the Second Epistle of Clement to the Corinthians.

This subscription with its illumination ends the first column of a page; and the second commences with the introductory matter (the capitulations) to the Epistle to the Romans.

At the close of the Epistle to the Hebrews, and occupying the first column of the last page in the volume, is the following statement:

ܐܬܟܬܒ ܟܬܒܐ ܗܢܐ ܕܦܘܠܘܣ ܫܠܝܚܐ
ܘܐܬܦܚܡ. ܡܢ ܨܚܚܐ ܗ̇ܘ ܕܟܬܝܒ ܗܘܐ ܒܡܒܘܓ
ܡܕܝܢܬܐ: ܗ̇ܘ ܕܐܦ ܗܘ̣ ܐܬܦܚܡ ܗܘܐ ܡܢ
ܨܚܚܐ ܕܐܝܬ[ܘܗܝ] ܗܘܐ ܒܩܣܪܝܐ ܡܕܝܢܬܐ
ܕܦܠܣܛܝܢܐ: ܒܝܬ ܟܬܒ̈ܐ ܕܩܕܝܫܐ ܦܡܦܝܠܘܣ:
ܕܟܬܝܒ ܗܘܐ ܒܟܬܒܬ ܐܝܕܗ. ∴

This book of Paul the Apostle was written and collated from that copy which was written in the city of Mabug (Hierapolis); which also had been collated with (from) a copy that was in Cæsarea a city of Palestine in the library of the holy Pamphilus, and was written in his own handwriting, etc.

After this follows another colophon, which occupies the last column in the MS, and begins as follows:

ܥܡܠ ܕܝܢ ܗܢܐ ܐܘ ܒܝܬ ܫܘܡܠܝܐ ܕܟܬܒܐ ܗܢܐ
ܦ̇ܠܓܐ ܫ̈ܢܐ ܕܐܘܢܓܠܝܘܢ: ܘܕܦ̈ܪܟܣܝܣ ܕܫ̈ܠܝܚܐ
ܘܢ̈ܝܚܐ: ܘܐܓܪ̈ܬܐ ܬܪ̈ܬܝܢ ܕܩܠܝܡܝܣ: ܥܡ ܫܠܡܘܬܐ
ܕܦܘܠܘܣ ܫܠܝܚܐ: ܐܝܟ ܬܘܪܓܡܐ ܕܬܐܘܣܒܐ
ܚܕܬܐ. ܒܫܢܬܐ ܗܝ ܕܐܠܦ ܘܐܪܒܥܡܐܐ

Now this life-giving book of the Gospel and of the Acts of the Holy Apostles[1], and the two Epistles of Clement, together with the teaching of Paul the Apostle, according to the correction of Thomas of Heraclea, received its end and completion in the year one thousand four hundred and eighty one of the Greeks in the little convent of Mar Saliba, which is in the abode of the monks on the Holy Mountain of the Blessed City of Edessa. And it was written with great diligence and irrepressible love and laudable fervour of faith and at the cost of Rabban Basil the chaste monk and pious presbyter, who is called Bar Michael, from the city of Edessa, so that he might have it for study and meditation spiritual and useful both of soul and of body. And it was written by Sahda the meanest of the monks of the same Edessa.

The remainder of this colophon, which closes the volume, is unimportant.

The year 1481 of the era of the Seleucidae corresponds to A.D. 1170.

On the last page of each quire, and on the first page of the following quire, but not elsewhere, it is customary in this MS to give in the upper margin the title of the book for the time being. This heading, in the case of the First Epistle of Clement, is

[1] Under the title 'Acts' the writer here evidently includes the Catholic Epistles. At the beginning and end of the table of lessons for the second division it is used as a designation for the whole division, comprising the Clementine as well as the Catholic Epistles.

ܪܕܝܬܐ ܕܩܠܡܝܤ ܠܘܬ ܩܘܪܢܬܝܐ ܩܕܡܝܬܐ.

The First Epistle of Clement to the Corinthians.

In the case of the Second Epistle no occasion for any such heading arises.

The Epistles of Clement are divided into lessons continuously with the Acts and Catholic Epistles, which constitute the former part of the same division. They are as follows :

94. 26th Sunday after the Resurrection ; Inscr. Ἡ ἐκκλησία κ.τ.λ.
95. 27th Sunday after the Resurrection ; § 10 Ἀβραὰμ ὁ φίλος κ.τ.λ.
96. 34th Sunday after the Resurrection ; § 16 Ταπεινοφρονούντων γὰρ κ.τ.λ.
97. 35th Sunday after the Resurrection ; § 16 Ὁρᾶτε, ἄνδρες ἀγαπητοί κ.τ.λ.
98. 36th Sunday after the Resurrection ; § 19 Τῶν τοσούτων οὖν κ.τ.λ.
99. 37th Sunday after the Resurrection ; § 21 Τὸν Κύριον Ἰησοῦν κ.τ.λ.
100. The Funeral of the Dead ; § 26 Μέγα καὶ θαυμαστὸν κ.τ.λ.
101. 38th Sunday after the Resurrection ; § 30 Ἁγίου [Ἁγία] οὖν μερὶς κ.τ.λ.
102. 39th Sunday after the Resurrection ; § 33 Τί οὖν ποιήσωμεν κ.τ.λ.
103. 28th Sunday after the Resurrection ; § 50 Αἱ γενεαὶ πᾶσαι κ.τ.λ.
104. 29th Sunday after the Resurrection ; § 52 Ἀπροσδεής, ἀδελφοί, κ.τ.λ.
105. 30th Sunday after the Resurrection ; § 56 Βλέπετε, ἀγαπητοί κ.τ.λ.
106. 31st Sunday after the Resurrection ; § 59 Ἐὰν δέ τινες κ.τ.λ.
107. 32nd Sunday after the Resurrection ; § 62 Περὶ μὲν τῶν ἀνηκόντων κ.τ.λ.
108. The Mother of God ; ii. § 1 Ἀδελφοί, οὕτως κ.τ.λ.
109. 33rd Sunday after the Resurrection ; ii. § 5 Ὅθεν, ἀδελφοί, κ.τ.λ.
110. 25th Sunday after the Resurrection ; ii. § 19 Ὥστε, ἀδελφοὶ καὶ ἀδελφαί, κ.τ.λ.

These rubrics, with the exception of the numbers (94, 95, etc.), are imbedded in the text[1], and therefore cannot be a later addition. The numbers themselves are in the margin, and written vertically.

I have been anxious to state carefully all the facts bearing on the relation of the Clementine Epistles to the Canonical Books of the New Testament in this MS, because some questions of importance are affected

---

[1] With the exception of the last rubric, which is itself in the margin, having apparently been omitted accidentally.

by them. As the result of these facts, it will be evident that, *so far as regards the scribe himself*, the Clementine Epistles are put on an absolute equality with the Canonical writings. Here for the first time they appear, not at the close of the volume, as in A, but with the Catholic Epistles—the position which, as I pointed out (p. 12), is required on the supposition of perfect canonicity. Moreover no distinction is made between them and the Catholic Epistles, so far as regards the lectionary. Lastly, the final colophon renders it highly probable that the scribe himself supposed these epistles to have been translated with the rest of the New Testament under the direction of Philoxenus and revised by Thomas of Heraclea.

But at the same time it is no less clear that he was mistaken in this view. In the first place, while each of the three great divisions of the New Testament, the Gospels, the Acts and Catholic Epistles, and the Pauline Epistles, has its proper colophon in this MS, describing the circumstances of its translation and revision, the Clementine Epistles stand outside these notices, and are wholly unaccounted for. In the next place the translation itself betrays a different hand, as will appear when I come to state its characteristic features; for the Harcleo-Philoxenian version shows no tendency to that unrestrained indulgence in periphrasis and gloss which we find frequently in these Syriac Epistles of Clement. Thirdly, there is no indication in any other copies, that the Epistles of Clement formed a part of the Harcleo-Philoxenian version. The force of this consideration however is weakened by the paucity of evidence. While we possess not a few MSS of the Gospels according to this version, only one other copy of the Acts, Catholic Epistles, and Pauline Epistles is known to exist[1]. Lastly, the table of lessons, which is framed so as to include the Clementine Epistles, and which therefore has an intimate bearing on the question, seems to be unique. There is no lack of Syriac lectionaries and tables of lessons, whether connected with the Peshito or with the Philoxenian (Harclean) version, and not one, I believe, accords with the arrangement in our MS; though on this point it is necessary to speak with reserve, until all the MSS have been examined. These facts show that the

[1] This is the Ridley MS, from which White printed his text, now in the Library of New College, Oxford. It contains the Gospels, Acts, Catholic Epistles, and Pauline Epistles, as far as Heb. xi. 27. Separate books however and portions of books are found elsewhere; e.g. Acts i. 1—10 (*Catal. Cod. Syr. Bibl. Bodl.* no. 24, p. 79, Payne Smith) James, 2 Peter, 1 John (*Catal. of Syr. Manusc. in the Brit. Mus.* no. cxxi. p. 76, Wright); 2 Peter, 2, 3 John, Jude, in an Amsterdam MS. (see above, p. 15); besides lessons scattered about in different lectionaries.

Clementine Epistles must have been a later addition to the Harclean New Testament. What may have been their history I shall not venture to speculate, but leave the question to Mr Bensly for further discussion. I will only add that the Syriac quotations from these epistles found elsewhere (see above, pp. 185 sq., 200 sq.) are quite independent of this version, and sometimes even imply a different Greek text. This fact however does not help us much; for they occur in collections of extracts, which we should expect to be translated, wholly or in part, directly from the Greek.

As a rendering of the Greek, this version is (with notable exceptions which will be specified hereafter) conscientious and faithful. The translator has made it his business to reproduce every word of the original. Even the insignificant connecting particle τε is faithfully represented by ܕܝܢ. The several tenses too are carefully observed, so far as the language admitted: e. g. an imperfect is distinguished from a strictly past tense. To this accuracy however the capabilities of the Syriac language place a limit. Thus it has no means of distinguishing an aorist from a perfect (e. g. § 25 τελευτήσαντος or τετελευτηκότος, § 40 προστεταγμένοις or προσταγεῖσι), or a future tense from a conjunctive mood (e. g. § 16 τί ποιήσομεν or τί ποιήσωμεν). And again in the infinitive and conjunctive moods it is powerless to express the several tenses (e. g. § 1 βλασφημηθῆναι and βλασφημεῖσθαι, § 13 στηρίζωμεν and στηρίξωμεν).

So far it is trustworthy. But on the other hand, it has some characteristics which detract from its value as an authority for the Greek text, and for which allowance must be made.

(i) It has a tendency to run into paraphrase in the translation of individual words and expressions. This tendency most commonly takes the form of double renderings for a word, more especially in the case of compounds. Examples of this phenomenon are: § 1 περιπτώσεις *lapsus et damna*; § 6 παθοῦσαι *patientes et tolerantes*; § 15 μεθ' ὑποκρίσεως *cum assumptione personarum et illusione*; § 19 ἐπαναδράμωμεν *curramus denuo* (*et*) *revertamur*, ἀτενίσωμεν *videamus et contemplemur*; § 20 τῶν δεδογματισμένων ὑπ' αὐτοῦ *quæ visa sunt Deo et decreta sunt ab illo*, παρεκβαίνει *exit aut transgreditur*, διέταξεν *mandavit et ordinavit*; § 25 παράδοξον *gloriosum et stupendum*, ἀνατρεφόμενος *nutritus et adultus*, γενναῖος *fortis et firmus*; § 27 ἀναζωπυρησάτω *inflammetur denuo et renovetur*; § 30 ὁμόνοιαν *consensum et paritatem animi*; § 34 παρειμένους *solutos et laxos*, κατανοήσωμεν *contemplemur et videamus*; § 44 ἐλλογίμων *peritorum et sapientium* (a misunderstanding of ἐλλόγιμος, which is repeated in § 62); § 50 φανερωθήσονται *revelabuntur et cognoscentur*; § 58 ὑπακούσωμεν *audiamus et respondeamus*; § 59 ἀρχέγονον *caput* (*prin-*

cipium) et creatorem; ii. § 2 ὁ λαὸς ἡμῶν *congregatio nostra et populus,* στηρίζειν *sustentare et stabiliret;* § 4 ἀποβαλῶ *educam et projiciam foras;* § 11 ἀνόητοι *stulti et expertes mente;* § 13 μετανοήσαντες ἐκ ψυχῆς *revertentes et ex corde pœnitentes* (comp. § 15), θαυμάζουσιν *obstupescunt et admirantur;* § 14 αὐθεντικὸν *idcam et veritatem;* § 18 τῶν εὐχαριστούντων *eorum qui confitentur et accipiunt gratiam (gratias agunt);* § 19 ἀγανακτῶμεν *cruciemur et murmuremus;* with many others. Sometimes however the love of paraphrase transgresses these limits and runs into great excesses: e.g. § 21 μὴ ἀποτακτεῖν ἡμᾶς ἀπὸ τοῦ θελήματος αὐτοῦ *ne rebellantes et deserentes ordinem faciamus aliquid extra voluntatem ejus;* § 53 ἀνυπερβλήτου *exaltatae et super quam non est transire;* § 55 πολλοὶ βασιλεῖς καὶ ἡγούμενοι λοιμικοῦ τινος ἐνστάντος καιροῦ *multi reges et magnates de principibus populorum siquando tempus afflictionis aut famis alicujus instaret populo;* ii. § 3 παρακούειν αὐτοῦ τῶν ἐντολῶν *negligemus et spernemus mandata ejus dum remisse agimus neque facimus ea* (comp. § 6, where ἐὰν παρακούσωμεν τῶν ἐντολῶν αὐτοῦ is translated *si avertimus auditum nostrum a mandatis ejus et spernimus ea*); with many other instances besides.

(ii) The characteristic which has been mentioned arose from the desire to do full justice to the Greek. The peculiarity, of which I have now to speak, is a concession to the demands of the Syriac. The translation not unfrequently transposes the order of words connected together: e.g. § 30 ταπεινοφροσύνη καὶ πραΰτης; § 36 ἄμωμον καὶ ὑπερτάτην, ἀσύνετος καὶ ἐσκοτωμένη. This transposition is most commonly found where the first word is incapable of a simple rendering in Syriac, so that several words are required in the translation, and it is advisable therefore to throw it to the end in order to avoid an ambiguous or confused syntax (the Syriac having no case-endings). Thus in the instances given ταπεινοφροσύνη is *humilitas cogitationis,* and ἄμωμος, ἀσύνετος, are respectively *quae sine labe, quae sine intellectu.* Where no such reason for a transposition exists, it may be inferred that the variation represents a different order in the Greek: e.g. § 12 ὁ τρόμος καὶ ὁ φόβος, § 18 τὰ χείλη...καὶ τὸ στόμα, ii. § 15 ἀγάπης καὶ πίστεως, ii. § 17 προσέχειν καὶ πιστεύειν. Sometimes this transposition occurs in conjunction with a double or periphrastic rendering, and a very considerable departure from the Greek is thus produced: e.g. § 19 ταῖς μεγαλοπρεπέσι καὶ ὑπερβαλλούσαις αὐτοῦ δωρεαῖς *donis ejus abundantibus et excelsis et magnis decore;* § 64 (58) τὸ μεγαλοπρεπὲς καὶ ἅγιον ὄνομα αὐτοῦ *nomen ejus sanctum et decens in magnitudine et gloriosum.*

To the demands of the language also must be ascribed the constant repetition of the preposition before several connected nouns in the

Syriac, where it occurs only before the first in the Greek. The absence of case-endings suggested this repetition for the sake of distinctness.

In using the Syriac Version as an authority for the Greek text, these facts must be borne in mind. In recording its readings therefore all such variations as arise from the exigencies of translation or the peculiarities of this particular version will be passed over as valueless for my purpose. Nor again will it be necessary to mention cases where the divergence arises simply from the pointing of the Syriac, the form of the letters being the same: as e.g. the insertion or omission of the sign of the plural, *ribui*. A more remarkable example is § 39, where we have ܟܣܪ̈ܐ *ἔργων* in place of ܟܣܪ̈ܐ *παίδων*. Experience shows that even the best Syriac MSS cannot be trusted in the matter of pointing. In all cases where there is any degree of likelihood that the divergence in the Syriac represents a different reading, the variation will be mentioned, but not otherwise. Throughout the greater part of the epistles, where we have two distinct authorities (A and C) besides, these instances will be very rare. In the newly recovered portion on the other hand, where A fails us, they are necessarily more frequent; and here I have been careful to record any case which is at all doubtful.

Passing from the version itself to the Greek text, on which it was founded, we observe the following facts:

(i) It most frequently coincides with A, where A differs from C. The following are some of the more significant examples in the genuine Epistle: § 1 ἡμῖν...περιπτώσεις A S, καθ' ἡμῶν...περιστάσεις C; § 2 ὁσίας A S, θείας C; *ib.* μετ' ἐλεοῦς (ελαιους) A S, μετὰ δέους C; *ib.* σεβασμίῳ A S, σεβασμιωτάτῃ C; § 4 βασιλέως Ἰσραὴλ A S, om. C; § 5 φθόνον A S, ἔριν C; § 6 κατέστρεψεν A S, κατέσκαψε C; § 7 ἐν γὰρ A S, καὶ γὰρ ἐν C; § 8 ὑμῶν A S, τοῦ λαοῦ μου C; § 9 διὰ τῆς λειτουργίας A S, ἐν τῇ λειτουργίᾳ C; § 10 τῷ Θεῷ A S, om. C; § 13 ὡς κρίνετε κ.τ.λ., where A S preserve the same order of the clauses against C; § 14 ἔριν A S (so doubtless S originally, but it is made ἔρεις by the diacritic points), αἱρέσεις C; § 15 ἐψεύσαντο A S, ἔψεξαν C; § 19 τὰς πρὸ ἡμῶν γενεὰς βελτίους A S, τοὺς πρὸ ἡμῶν βελτίους C; § 23 πρῶτον μὲν φυλλοροεῖ A S, om. C; § 25 ἐπιπτὰς A S, om. C; § 28 μιαρὰς A S, βλαβερὰς C; *ib.* ἐκεῖ ἡ δεξιά σου A S, σὺ ἐκεῖ εἰ C; § 30 ἀπὸ τοῦ Θεοῦ A S, τοῦ Θεοῦ C; *ib.* ἀγαθῆς A S, om. C; *ib.* ὑπὸ τοῦ Θεοῦ A S, om. C; § 32 δόξῃ A S, τάξει C; § 33 ποιήσωμεν A S, ἐροῦμεν C; § 34 ἡ κτίσις A S, ἡ γῆ C; § 35 ὁ δημιουργὸς καὶ πατὴρ κ.τ.λ. A S, where C has a different order; *ib.* τὰ εὐάρεστα καὶ εὐπρόσδεκτα αὐτῷ A S, τὰ ἀγαθὰ καὶ εὐάρεστα αὐτῷ καὶ εὐπρόσδεκτα C; § 39 ἄφρονες καὶ ἀσύνετοι κ.τ.λ. A S, where C transposes and omits words; § 43 αὐτὰς A S, αὐτὸς C; § 47 αὐτοῦ [τε] καὶ Κηφᾶ κ.τ.λ., where the order of the names is the same in AS, but different in C; *ib.* μεμαρτυρημένοις...δεδοκιμασμένῳ παρ' αὐτοῖς AS, δεδοκιμασμένοις... μεμαρτυρημένῳ παρ' αὐτῶν C; *ib.* ἀγωγῆς AS, ἀγάπης C; § 51 θεράποντα τοῦ Θεοῦ AS, ἄνθρωπον τοῦ Θεοῦ C; *ib.* Αἰγύπτου AS, αὐτοῦ C; § 53 θεράπων AS, δεσπότης C; § 55 ὑποδείγματα AS, ὑπομνήματα C: § 56 δίκαιος AS, Κύριος C; § 65 (59) καὶ δι' αὐτοῦ AS, δι' αὐτοῦ C. The so-called Second Epistle furnishes the following examples among others: § 1 πηροὶ AS, πονηροὶ C; § 3 καὶ οὐ προσκυνοῦμεν αὐτοῖς AS, om. C; *ib.* ἡ πρὸς αὐτὸν AS, for which C substitutes τῆς ἀληθείας; § 9 πνεῦμα AS, λόγος C (see p. 227); § 10 ἀπόλαυσιν, ἀπόλαυσις AS, ἀνάπαυσιν, ἀνάπαυσις C; § 11 μετὰ ταῦτα AS, εἶτα C.

(ii) On the other hand there are some passages, though comparatively few, in which S agrees with C against A. Examples of these are: § 2 τοῦ Χριστοῦ CS, τοῦ Θεοῦ A; § 3 τῆς καρδίας αὐτοῦ CS, om. A; § 4 ἄρχοντα καὶ δικαστὴν CS, κριτὴν ἢ δικαστὴν A; § 8 ψυχῆς CS, καρδίας A; § 12 ἡ ἐπιλεγομένη πόρνη CS, ἡ πόρνη A; *ib.* τὴν γῆν CS, τὴν [πό]λιν A; *ib.* ὅτι...καὶ CS, om. A; § 15 διὰ τοῦτο CS, om. A; § 21 σιγῆς CS, φωνῆς A; *ib.* ἀναιρεῖ CS, ἀνελεῖ A; § 22 τὸν δὲ ἐλπίζοντα CS, τοὺς δὲ ἐλπίζοντας A; § 25 ἐγγεννᾶται CS, γεννᾶται A; § 33 προετοιμάσας CS, προδημιουργήσας A; § 34 πιστεύοντας, CS, om. A; *ib.* ἃ ὀφθαλμὸς CS, ὀφθαλμὸς A; *ib.* Κύριος CS, om. A; *ib.* ἀγαπῶσιν CS, ὑπομένουσιν A; § 35 διὰ στόματος CS, ἐπὶ στόματος A; § 38 τημελείτω CS, where A has μητμμελειτω; *ib.* the words [ἤτω] καὶ omitted in CS, but found in A; § 40 δέδοται CS, δέδεται A; § 41 εὐαρεστείτω CS, εὐχαριστείτω A; § 52 Αἰγύπτῳ CS, γῇ Αἰγύπτου A; § 56 ἔλαιον CS, ἔλεος (ελαιος) A. In the Second Epistle the examples of importance are very few: e.g. § 8 ποιήσῃ (ποιῇ) σκεῦος ταῖς χερσὶν αὐτοῦ καὶ διαστραφῇ CS, ποιῇ σκεῦος καὶ ἐν ταῖς χερσὶν αὐτοῦ διαστραφῇ A; *ib.* ἀπολάβητε CS, ἀπολάβωμεν A.

Of these readings, in which CS are arrayed together against A, it will be seen that some condemn themselves by their harmonistic tendency (§§ 4, 22, 34, 35); others are suspicious as doctrinal changes (§ 12 ἐπιλεγομένη); others are grammatical emendations of corrupt texts (§ 38), or substitutions of easier for harder expressions (§ 12 ὅτι...καὶ, 21 ἀναιρεῖ); others are clerical errors, either certainly (§ 40) or probably (§ 41): while in the case of a few others it would be difficult from internal evidence to give the preference to one reading over the other (§§ 25, 33, 52). There are only three places, I think, in the above list, in which it can be said that CS are certainly right against A. In two of these (§§ 3, 34 πιστεύοντας) some words have been accidentally omitted in A; while the third (§ 21 σιγῆς for φωνῆς) admits no such explanation.

(iii) The independence of S, as a witness, will have appeared from the facts already stated. But it will be still more manifest from another class of examples, where S stands alone and either certainly or probably or possibly preserves the right reading, though in some cases at least no ingenuity of the transcriber could have supplied it. Such instances are: § 7 τῷ πατρὶ αὐτοῦ, where C has τῷ πατρὶ αὐτοῦ τῷ Θεῷ, and A apparently τῷ Θεῷ [καὶ πατρ]ὶ αὐτοῦ; § 15 where S supplies the words omitted by homœoteleuton in AC, but in a way which no editor has anticipated; § 18 ἐλαίῳ for ἐλέει (ελαιει), but this is perhaps a scribe's correction; § 22 πολλαὶ αἱ θλίψεις κ.τ.λ. supplied in S, but omitted by AC because two successive sentences begin with the same words: § 35 διὰ πίστεως S, where A has πίστεως and C πιστῶς; § 36 εἰς τὸ φῶς where AC insert θαυμαστὸν [αὐτοῦ] in accordance with 1 Pet. ii. 9; § 43 ὡσαύτως καὶ τὰς θύρας, where AC read ῥάβδους to the injury of the sense, and some editors emend ὡσαύτως ὡς καὶ τὰς ῥάβδους, still leaving a very awkward statement; § 46 πόλεμός (πόλεμοί) τε, where S adds καὶ μάχαι, an addition which the connecting particles seem to suggest, though it may have come from James iv. 1; ib. ἵνα τῶν ἐκλεκτῶν μου διαστρέψαι, where AC have ἵνα τῶν μικρῶν μου σκανδαλίσαι, though (for reasons which I have stated in the addenda) I cannot doubt that S preserves the original reading; § 48 ἵνα...ἐξομολογήσωμαι, where A has ἐξομολογήσωμαι (without ἵνα) and C. ἐξομολογήσομαι; ii § 1 οἱ ἀκούοντες ὡς περὶ μικρῶν [ἁμαρτάνουσιν, καὶ ἡμεῖς] ἁμαρτάνομεν, where the words in brackets are omitted in AC owing to the same cause which has led to the omissions in §§ 15, 22; ii § 3, where S alone omits ἐνώπιον τῶν ἀνθρώπων and μου, which are probably harmonistic additions in AC; ii § 7 θέωμεν, where AC have the corrupt θῶμεν. These facts show that we must go farther back than the common progenitor of A and C for the archetype of our three authorities.

But beside these independent readings S exhibits other peculiarities, which are not to its credit.

(i) The Greek text, from which the translation was made, must have been disfigured by not a few errors; e.g. § 2 ἑκόντες for ἄκοντες, ἰδίᾳ for ἴδια; § 8 εἰπὼν for εἶπον; § 9 τελείους for τελείως; § 11 κρίσιν (?) for κόλασιν; § 14 θεῖον (ΘΕΙΟΝ) for ὅσιον (ΟCΙΟΝ); § 17 ἀτενίσω (?) for ἀτενίζων; § 20 δικαιώσει for διοικήσει, διὰ for δίχα, ἄνεμοί τε σταθμῶν (?) for ἀνέμων τε σταθμοὶ, συλλήψεις (?) for συνελεύσεις; § 21 θείως (ΘΕΙΩC) for ὁσίως (ΟCΙΩC); § 24 κοιμᾶται νυκτὸς ἀνίσταται ἡμέρας (?) for κοιμᾶται ἡ νὺξ ἀνίσταται ἡ ἡμέρα, ξηρὰν διαλύεται for ξηρὰ καὶ γυμνὰ διαλύεται; § 33 ἐκοιμήθησαν for ἐκοσμήθησαν; § 35 ὑποπίπτοντα for ὑπέπιπτεν (ὑποπίπτει) πάντα (some letters having dropped out); § 36 διὰ τοῦτο for διὰ τούτου several times, θανάτου for τῆς ἀθανάτου (the τῆς having been absorbed in the termination of the preceding δεσπότης); § 37 ὕπαρχοι (?) for ἔπαρχοι; § 39 καθαιρέτης (?) for καθαρός, ἔπεσον αὐτοῦ for ἔπαισεν αὐτούς; § 40 ἰδίοις τόποις for ἴδιος[ὁ]τόπος; § 42 κενῶς for καινῶς; § 45 μιαρῶν, ἀδίκων for μιαρὸν, ἄδικον; § 50 εἰ μὴ add. ἐν ἀγάπῃ from just below; § 51 δὲ ἑαυτῶν omitted, thus blending the two sentences together; § 59 ἀνθρώπων (ανων) for ἐθνῶν, εὑρετὴν for εὐεργέτην, ἐπιστράφηθι for ἐπιφάνηθι, ἀσθενεῖς (?) for ἀσεβεῖς; § 60 χρηστὸς for πιστὸς; § 62 ᾗ δι' ὧν for ἥδιον, ἔδει μέν for ἤδειμεν; ii. § 2 τὰ πρὸς inserted before τὰς προσευχὰς (.ταπροστασπρος-); § 5 παροιμίαν for παροικίαν, ποιῆσαν (?) for ποιήσαντας; § 6 οὗτοι for [οἱ τοι]οῦτοι [δίκαιοι], the letters in brackets having been omitted; § 9 ἔλθε (ἦλθε) for ἐλ[εύσεσ]θε, again by the dropping of some letters; § 10 προδότην for προοδοιπόρον, perhaps owing to a similar mutilation; § 11 πιστεύσωμεν διὰ τὸ δεῖν for δουλεύσωμεν διὰ τοῦ μή; § 16 πατέρα δεχόμενον for παραδεχόμενον (πρα for παρα-); § 17 προσευχόμενοι for προσερχόμενοι (?), εἰδότες for ἰδόντες; § 19 τρυφήσουσιν for τρυγήσουσιν. There are occasionally also omissions, owing to the recurrence of the same sequence of letters, homœoteleuton, etc. : e.g. § 12 καὶ ἐλπίζουσιν (?), § 14 οἱ δὲ παρανομοῦντες κ.τ.λ., § 58 καὶ προστάγματα, § 59 τοὺς ταπεινοὺς ἐλέησον, ii. 6 καὶ φθοράν; but this is not a common form of error in S.

(ii) Again S freely introduces glosses and explanations. These may have been derived from the Greek MS used, or they may have been introduced by the translator himself. They are numerous, and the following will serve as examples: § 10 τοὺς ἀστέρας, add. τοῦ οὐρανοῦ; § 19 τοῦ Θεοῦ for αὐτοῦ, God not having been mentioned before in the same sentence; § 25 τοῦ χρόνου, add. τῆς ζωῆς; ib. οἱ ἱερεῖς explained οἱ τῆς Αἰγύπτου; § 42 παραγγελίας οὖν λαβόντες, add. οἱ ἀπόστολοι; § 43 τῶν φυλῶν, add. πασῶν τοῦ Ἰσραήλ; § 44 τὴν ἀνάλυσιν, add. τὴν ἐνθένδε; § 51 φόβου, add. τοῦ Θεοῦ; § 62 τόπον, add. τῆς γραφῆς; § 63 μώμου, add. καὶ σκανδάλου; ii 6 ἀνάπαυσιν, add. τὴν ἐκεῖ; ib. τὸ βάπτισμα, add. ὃ ἐλάβομεν; § 8 βαλεῖν, followed by a long explanatory gloss; ib. ἐξομολογήσασθαι, add. περὶ τῶν ἁμαρτιῶν; § 9 ἐκάλεσεν, add. ὢν ἐν τῇ σαρκί; § 12 ὑπό τινος, add. τῶν ἀποστόλων; § 13 τὸ ὄνομα, add. τοῦ Κυρίου in one place and τοῦ Χριστοῦ in another; § 14 ἐκ τῆς γραφῆς τῆς λεγούσης, altered into ex iis de quibus scriptum est; ib. τὰ βιβλία, add. τῶν προφητῶν; ib. ὁ Ἰησοῦς ἡμῶν, an explanatory clause added; § 17 ἔσονται, add. ἐν ἀγαλλιάσει; § 19 τὸν ἀναγινώσκοντα ἐν ὑμῖν, add. τὰ λόγια (or τοὺς λόγους) τοῦ Θεοῦ.

(iii) Again: we see the hand of an emender where the original text seemed unsatisfactory or had been already corrupted; e.g. § 14 ἐξεζήτησα τὸν τόπον κ.τ.λ., altered to agree with the LXX; § 16 τῆς μεγαλωσύνης omitted; ib. πάντας ἀνθρώπους substituted for τὸ εἶδος τῶν ἀνθρώπων, in accordance with another reading of the LXX; § 17 κακοῦ changed into πονηροῦ πράγματος, in accordance with the LXX; § 20 τά substituted for τούς...μάζους, the metaphor not being understood by or not pleasing the corrector; § 21 τοῦ φόβου omitted; § 30 Ἁγία substituted for Ἁγίου, the latter not being understood; § 33 κατὰ διάνοιαν omitted for the same reason; § 35 σε omitted, and τὰς ἁμαρτίας σου substituted, in accordance with a more intelligible but false text of the LXX; § 38 the omission of μή before τημελείτω, and of [ἤτω] καί before μὴ ἀλαζονευέσθω (see above p. 228 sq.); § 40 the omission of ἐπιτελεῖσθαι καί (see p. 245); § 44 ἐπὶ δοκιμήν, an emendation of the corrupt ἐπιδομήν; § 45 τῶν μὴ ἀνηκόντων, the insertion of the negative (see the addenda); ib. the insertion of ἀλλὰ before ὑπὸ παρανόμων and ὑπὸ τῶν μιαρὸν (μιαρῶν) κ.τ.λ., for the sake of symmetry; § 59 the alteration of pronouns and the insertion of words at the beginning of the prayer, so as to mend a mutilated text (see below p. 246); § 62 the omission of εἰς before ἐνάρετον βίον, and other changes, for the same reason; ii § 3 ἔπειτα δὲ ὅτι substituted for ἀλλά, to supply an antithesis to πρῶτον μέν; § 4 ἀγαπᾶν [τοὺς πλησίον ὡς] ἑαυτούς, the words in brackets being inserted because the reciprocal sense of ἑαυτούς was overlooked; § 12 αὐτοῦ for τοῦ Θεοῦ, because τοῦ Θεοῦ has occurred immediately before; § 13 the substitution of ἡμᾶς...λέγομεν for ὑμᾶς...βούλομαι, from not understanding that the words are put into the mouth of God Himself; § 14 the omission of ὅτι, to mend a mutilated text; § 17 the omission of ἐν τῷ Ἰησοῦ owing to its awkwardness.

There are also from time to time other insertions, omissions, and alterations in S, which cannot be classed under any of these heads. The doxologies more especially are tampered with.

In such cases, it is not always easy to say whether the emendation or gloss was due to the Syrian translator himself, or to some earlier Greek transcriber or reader. In one instance at all events the gloss distinctly proceeds from the Syrian translator, or a Syrian scribe: § 1, where the Greek word στάσις is adopted with the explanation *hoc autem est tumultus.* This one example suggests that a Syrian hand may have been at work more largely elsewhere.

THE inferences which I draw from the above facts are the following:

(1) In A, C, S, we have three distinct authorities for the text. Each has its characteristic errors, and each preserves the genuine text in some passages, where the other two are corrupt.

(2) The stream must be traced back to a very remote antiquity

before we arrive at the common progenitor of our three authorities. This follows from their mutual relations.

(3) Of our three authorities A (if we set aside merely clerical errors, in which it abounds) is by far the most trustworthy. The instances are very rare (probably not one in ten), where it stands alone against the combined force of CS. Even in these instances internal considerations frequently show that its reading must be accepted notwithstanding.

Its vast superiority is further shown by the entire absence of what I may call *tertiary* readings, while both C and S furnish many examples of these. Such are the following. In § 8 (1) διελεγχθῶμεν the original reading; (2) [δι]ελεχθῶμεν A, its corruption; (3) διαλεχθῶμεν CS, the corruption emended. In § 15 (1) Ἄλαλα κ.τ.λ. S, the full text; (2) some words omitted owing to homœoteleuton, A; (3) the grammar of the text thus mutilated has been patched up in C by substituting γλῶσσα for γλῶσσαν, and making other changes. In § 21 (1) εἰς κρίμα πᾶσιν ἡμῖν A; (2) εἰς κρίματα σὺν ἡμῖν C, an accidental corruption; (3) εἰς κρίματα (or κρίμα) ἡμῖν S, the σὺν being discarded as superfluous. In § 30 Ἁγίου οὖν μερίς A; (2) Ἁγία οὖν μερίς S, a corruption or emendation; (3) Ἁγια οὖν μέρη C, a still further corruption or emendation. In § 35 (1) the original reading διὰ πίστεως S; (2) πίστεως A, the preposition being accidentally dropped; (3) the emendation πιστῶς C. In § 38 (1) μὴ ἀτημελείτω, the original reading; (2) μὴ τημελείτω (written apparently μητημμελειτω) A, the α being accidentally dropped; (3) τημελείτω CS, the μὴ being omitted to restore the balance, because the words now gave the opposite sense to that which was required. In § 39 ἔπαισεν αὐτοὺς C, or ἔπεσεν αὐτούς, as by a common itacism it is written in A; (2) ἔπεσεν αὐτοῦ, the final σ being lost in the initial σ of the following σηρός; (3) ἔπεσον αὐτοῦ S, a necessary emendation, since a plurality of persons is mentioned in the context. In § 40 (1) ἐπιμελῶς ἐπιτελεῖσθαι καὶ οὐκ εἰκῇ...γίνεσθαι, presumably the original text; (2) ἐπιτελεῖσθαι καὶ οὐκ εἰκῇ...γίνεσθαι AC, the word ἐπιμελῶς being accidentally omitted owing to the similar beginnings of successive words; (3) οὐκ εἰκῇ... γίνεσθαι S, the words ἐπιτελεῖσθαι καὶ being deliberately dropped, because they have now become meaningless. In § 44 (1) the original reading, presumably ἐπιμονήν; (2) the first corruption ἐπινομήν A; (3) the second corruption ἐπιδομήν C; (4) the correction ἐπὶ δοκιμήν S. In § 45 (1) the original reading τῶν μιαρὸν καὶ ἄδικον ζῆλον ἀνειληφότων C; (2) τῶν μιαρῶν καὶ ἄδικον ζῆλον ἀνειληφότων A, an accidental error; (3) τῶν μιαρῶν καὶ ἀδίκων ζῆλον ἀνειληφότων S, where the error is consistently followed up. In § 48 (1) ἵνα εἰσελθών...ἐξομολογήσωμαι S with Clem. Alex.; (2) εἰσελθών...ἐξομολογήσωμαι A, ἵνα being accidentally dropped; (3) εἰσελθών...ἐξομολογήσομαι C, an emendation suggested by the omission. In § 59, where A is wanting, (1) the original text, presumably ὀνόματος αὐτοῦ. [Δὸς ἡμῖν, Κύριε,] ἐλπίζειν ἐπὶ τὸ...ὄνομά σου κ.τ.λ.; (2) the words in brackets are dropped out and the connexion then becomes ἐκάλεσεν ἡμᾶς...εἰς ἐπίγνωσιν δόξης ὀνόματος αὐτοῦ, ἐλπίζειν ἐπὶ τὸ...ὄνομά σου, as in C, where the sudden transition from the third to the second person is not accounted for; (3) this is remedied in S by substituting αὐτοῦ for σου and making similar alterations for several lines, till at length by inserting the words ' we will say' a transition to the second person is effected. In § 62 in like manner (1) the original text had presumably εἰς ἐνάρετον βίον...διευθύνειν [τὴν πορείαν αὐτῶν]; (2) the words in brackets were omitted, as in C; (3) a still further omission of εἰς was made, in order to supply an objective case to διευθύνειν, as in S. In ii. § 1 (1) ποῖον οὖν C; (2) ποιουν A, a corruption; (3) ποῖον S. In ii. § 14 (1) the original reading, presumably ὅτι τὰ βιβλία...τὴν ἐκκλησίαν οὐ νῦν εἶναι...[λέγουσιν, δῆλον]; (2) the words in brackets are accidentally omitted, as in C; (3) this necessitates further omission and insertion to set the grammar straight, as in S. In some of these examples my interpretation of the facts may be disputed; but the general inference, if I mistake not, is unquestionable.

The scribe of A was no mean penman, but he put no mind into his work. Hence in his case, we are spared that bane of ancient texts, the spurious criticism of transcribers. With the exception of one or two harmonistic changes in quotations, the single instance wearing the appearance of a deliberate alteration, which I have noticed in A, is τῆς φωνῆς for τῆς σιγῆς (§ 21); and even this might have been made almost mechanically, as the words τὸ ἐπιεικὲς τῆς γλώσσης occur immediately before.

(4) Of the two inferior authorities S is much more valuable than C for correcting A. While C alone corrects A in one passage only of any moment (§ 2 μετὰ δέους for μετ' ἐλέους), S alone corrects it in several. In itself S is both better and worse than C. It is made up of two elements, one very ancient and good, the other debased and probably recent: whereas C preserves a fairly uniform standard throughout.

(5) From the fact that A shares both genuine and corrupt readings with C, C with S, and S with A, which are not found in the third authority, it follows that one or more of our three authorities must give a mixed text. It cannot have been derived by simple transcription from the archetype in a direct line, but at some point or other a scribe must have introduced readings of collateral authorities, either from memory or by reference to MSS. This phenomenon we find on the largest scale in

the Greek Testament; but, wherever it occurs, it implies a considerable circulation of the writing in question.

(6) We have now materials for restoring the original text of Clement very much better than in the case of any ancient Greek author, except the writers of the New Testament. For instance the text of a great part of Æschylus depends practically on one MS of the 10th or 11th century; i.e. on a single authority dating some fifteen centuries after the tragedies were written. The oldest extant authority for Clement on the other hand was written probably within three centuries and a half after the work itself; and we have besides two other independent authorities preserving more or less of an ancient text. The youngest of these is many centuries nearer to the author's date, than this single authority for the text of Æschylus. Thus the security which this combination gives for the correctness of the ultimate result is incomparably greater than in the example alleged. Where authorities are multiplied, variations will be multiplied also; but it is only so that the final result can be guaranteed.

(7) Looking at the dates and relations of our authorities we may be tolerably sure that, when we have reached their archetype, we have arrived at a text which dates not later, or not much later, than the close of the second century. On the other hand it can hardly have been much earlier. For the phenomena of the text are the same in both epistles; and it follows therefore, that in this archetypal MS the so-called Second Epistle must have been already attached to the genuine Epistle of Clement, though not necessarily ascribed to him.

(8) But, though thus early, it does not follow that this text was in all points correct. Some errors may have crept in already and existed in this archetype, though these would probably not be numerous; e.g. it is allowed that there is something wrong in ii. § 10 οὐκ ἔστιν εὑρεῖν ἄνθρωπον οἵτινες κ.τ.λ. Among such errors I should be disposed to place § 6 Δαναΐδες καὶ Δίρκαι, § 20 κρίματα, § 40 the omission of ἐπιμελῶς before ἐπιτελεῖσθαι, § 44 ἐπινομήν, § 51 διά τινος τῶν τοῦ ἀντικειμένου, and perhaps also § 48 the omission of ἤτω γοργὸς (since the passage is twice quoted with these words by Clement of Alexandria), together with a few other passages.

And it would seem also that this text had already undergone slight mutilations. At the end of the First Epistle we find at least three passages where the grammar is defective in C, and seems to require the insertion of some words; § 59 ὀνόματος αὐτοῦ...ἐλπίζειν ἐπὶ τὸ ἀρχέγονον κ.τ.λ, § 60 ἐν πίστει καὶ ἀληθείᾳ...ὑπηκόους γενομένους, § 62 δικαίως διευθύνειν...ἱκανῶς ἐπεστείλαμεν. Bryennios saw, as I think correctly, that in all these places this faulty grammar was due to accidental omissions. Subsequent editors have gone on another tack; they have attempted to justify the grammar, or to set it straight by emendations of individual words. But, to say nothing of the abrupt transitions which still remain in the text so emended, the fresh evidence of S distinctly confirms the view of Bryennios; for it shows that these same omissions occurred in a previous MS from which the text of S was derived, though in S itself the passages have undergone some manipulations. These lacunæ therefore must have existed in the common archetype of C and S. And I think that a highly probable explanation of them can be given. I find that the interval between the omissions § 59, § 60, is $35\frac{1}{2}$ or 36 lines in Gebhardt ($37\frac{1}{2}$ in Hilgenfeld), while the interval between the omissions § 60, § 62 is 18 lines in Gebhardt (19 in Hilgenfeld). Thus the one interval is exactly twice the other. This points to the solution. The archetypal MS comprised from 17 to 18 lines of Gebhardt's text in a page. It was slightly frayed or mutilated at the bottom of some pages (though not all) towards the end of the epistle, so that words had disappeared or were illegible. Whether these same omissions occurred also in A, it is impossible to say; but, judging from the general relations of the three authorities and from another lacuna (ii. § 10 οὐκ ἔστιν εὑρεῖν ἄνθρωπον οἵτινες κ.τ.λ.) where the same words or letters are wanting in all alike, we may infer that they did so occur. Other lacunæ (e.g. ii. § 14 ἀλλὰ ἄνωθεν κ.τ.λ.) may perhaps be explained in a similar way.

THE EPISTLE OF S. CLEMENT

TO THE

CORINTHIANS.

THE EPISTLE OF S. CLEMENT

CORINTHIANS.

THE discovery of the documents which I have described must necessarily have the highest interest for students of early Christian history. Independently of the absolute value of the contents of these newly recovered portions in themselves, no such addition has been made to our knowledge of the earliest Christian literature for the last two centuries. The later decades of the first half of the seventeenth century were rich in acquisitions of this kind. The two Epistles of Clement were first published in 1633; the Ignatian Epistles in their earlier and more authentic form in Latin by Ussher in 1644, in Greek by Voss in 1646; the Epistle of Barnabas by Menard in 1645. From that time to the present generation some accessions have been made to the literature of the subapostolic ages, but these have been inconsiderable compared with the treasure thus accumulated within a few years towards the middle of the seventeenth century.

Like the period just mentioned, the last thirty years have been rich in discoveries. During this time we have seen the publication of the work of Hippolytus on Heresies by E. Miller in 1851, which has thrown a flood of light on the history of the Church and the reception of the Canon during the second century and the early years of the third; of the Syriac Ignatius by Cureton in 1845, and more fully in 1849, which (even though it should ultimately be accepted only as an abridgment of the original text) is yet of the highest value for the criticism of this early writer; of the lost ending of the Clementine Homilies by Dressel in 1853, of which the chief interest consists in the indisputable quotations from the Gospel of S. John; of the Syriac Fragments of Melito and other early Christian writers by Cureton in 1855; of the Codex Lipsiensis and the accompanying transcript by Anger in 1856, and the Codex Sinaiticus by Tischendorf in 1862, thus giving for the first time the beginning of the Epistle of Barnabas and the greater part of the Shepherd of Hermas in the original Greek; and now at length, in 1875, of the two Epistles of Clement complete by Bryennios, since supplemented by the discovery of a Syriac Version of the same.

Among all these recent acquisitions the last is unique. In point of historical importance indeed it must yield the palm to the work of Hippolytus. But the recovery of only a few pages of Christian litera-ture which certainly belong to the first century, together with several others which can hardly be placed later than about the middle of the second, must in the paucity of documents dating from this period invest it with the highest interest. Under these circumstances, it is not unnatural that we should endeavour to estimate the gain which has accrued to us from the accession of this treasure.

The newly recovered portion of the first or genuine Epistle of Clement consists, as I have said (p. 223), of about one-tenth of the whole. It stands immediately before the final prayer, commendation of the bearers, and benediction, which form the two brief chapters at the close of the epistle. It contains an earnest entreaty to the Co-rinthians to obey the injunctions contained in the letter and to heal their unhappy schisms; an elaborate prayer which extends over three long chapters, commencing with an invocation and ending with an intercession for rulers and governors; and then another appeal of some length to the Corinthians, justifying the language of the letter and denouncing the sin of disobedience. The subject is not such as to admit of much historical matter; but the gain to our knowledge not-withstanding is not inconsiderable.

1. In the first place we are enabled to understand more fully the secret of Papal domination. This letter, it must be premised, does not emanate from the bishop of Rome, but from the Church of Rome. There is every reason to believe the early tradition which points to S. Clement as its author, and yet he is not once named. The first person plural is maintained throughout, 'We consider,' 'We have sent.' Accordingly writers of the second century speak of it as a letter from the community, not from the individual. Thus Dionysius, bishop of Corinth, writing to the Romans about A D. 170, refers to it as the epistle 'which you wrote to us by Clement (Euseb. *H. E.* iv. 23)': and Irenæus soon afterwards similarly describes it; 'In the time of this Clement, no small dissension having arisen among the brethren in Corinth, the Church

in Rome sent a very sufficient letter to the Corinthians urging them to peace (iii. 3. 3).' Even later than this, Clement of Alexandria calls it in one passage 'the Epistle of the Romans to the Corinthians' (*Strom.* v. 12, p. 693), though elsewhere he ascribes it to Clement. Still it might have been expected that somewhere towards the close mention would have been made (though in the third person) of the famous man who was at once the actual writer of the letter and the chief ruler of the Church in whose name it was written. Now however that we possess the work complete, we see that his existence is not once hinted at from beginning to end. The name and personality of Clement are absorbed in the Church of which he is the spokesman.

This being so, it is the more instructive to observe the urgent and almost imperious tone which the Romans adopt in addressing their Corinthian brethren during the closing years of the first century. They exhort the offenders to submit 'not to them, but to the will of God' (§ 56). 'Receive our counsel,' they write again, 'and ye shall have no occasion of regret' (§ 58). Then shortly afterwards : 'But if certain persons should be disobedient unto the words spoken by Him (i. e. by God) through us, let them understand that they will entangle themselves in no slight transgression and danger, but we shall be guiltless of this sin' (§ 59). At a later point again they return to the subject and use still stronger language ; 'Ye will give us great joy and gladness, if ye render obedience unto the things written by us through the Holy Spirit, and root out the unrighteous anger of your jealousy, according to the entreaty which we have made for peace and concord in this letter ; and we have also sent unto you faithful and prudent men, that have walked among us from youth unto old age unblameably, who shall be witnesses between you and us. And this we have done, that ye might know, that we have had and still have every solicitude, that ye may speedily be at peace (§ 63).' It may perhaps seem strange to describe this noble remonstrance as the first step towards papal aggression. And yet undoubtedly this is the case. There is all the difference in the world between the attitude of Rome towards other Churches at the close of the first century, when the Romans as a community remonstrate on terms of equality with the Corinthians on their irregularities, strong only in the righteousness of their cause, and feeling, as they had a right to feel, that these counsels of peace were the dictation of the Holy Spirit, and its attitude at the close of the second century, when Victor the bishop excommunicates the Churches of Asia Minor for clinging to a usage in regard to the celebration of Easter which had been handed down to them from the Apostles, and thus foments instead of healing dissensions (Euseb. *H. E.* v. 23, 24). Even this second stage has carried the power of Rome only a very small step in advance towards the pretensions of a Hildebrand or an Innocent or a Boniface, or even of a Leo; but it is nevertheless a decided step. The substitution of the bishop of Rome for the Church of Rome is an all important point. The later Roman theory supposes that the Church of Rome derives all its authority from the bishop of Rome, as the successor of S. Peter. History inverts this relation and shows that, as a matter of fact, the power of the bishop of Rome was built upon the power of the Church of Rome. It was originally a primacy, not of the Episcopate, but of the Church. The position of the Roman Church, which this newly recovered ending of Clement's Epistle throws out in such strong relief, accords entirely with the notices in other early documents. A very few years later—from ten to twenty—Ignatius writes to Rome. He is a staunch advocate of episcopacy. Of his six remaining letters, one is addressed to a bishop as bishop; and the other five all enforce the duty of the Churches whom he addresses to their respective bishops. Yet in the letter to the Church of Rome there is not the faintest allusion to the episcopal office from first to last. He entreats the Roman Christians not to intercede and thus by obtaining a pardon or commutation of sentence to rob him of the crown of martyrdom. In the course of his entreaty he uses words which doubtless refer in part to Clement's Epistle, and which the newly recovered ending enables us to appreciate more fully; 'Ye never yet,' he writes, 'envied any one,' i.e. grudged him the glory of a consistent course of endurance and self-sacrifice, 'ye were the teachers of others (οὐδέποτε ἐβασκάνατε οὐδενί· ἄλλους ἐδιδάξατε, § 3).' They would therefore be inconsistent with their former selves, he implies, if in his own case they departed from those counsels of self-renunciation and patience which they had urged so strongly on the Corinthians and others. But, though Clement's letter is apparently in his mind, there is no mention of Clement or Clement's successor throughout. Yet at the same time he assigns a primacy to Rome. The Church is addressed in the opening salutation as 'she who hath the presidency (προκάθηται) in the place of the region of the Romans.' But immediately afterwards the nature of this supremacy is defined. The presidency of this Church is declared to be a presidency of love (προκαθημένη τῆς ἀγάπης). This then was the original primacy of Rome—a primacy not of the bishop but of the whole Church, a primacy not of official authority but of practical goodness, backed however by the prestige and the advantages which were necessarily enjoyed by the Church of the metropolis. The reserve of Clement in his epistle harmonizes also with the very modest estimate of his dignity implied in the language of one who appears to' have been a younger contemporary, but who wrote (if tradition can be trusted) at a somewhat later date. Thou shalt therefore, says the heavenly Shepherd to Hermas, 'write two little books,' i.e. copies of this work containing the revelation, 'and thou shalt send one to Clement and one to Grapte. So Clement shall send it to the cities abroad, for this charge is committed unto him, and Grapte shall instruct the widows and the orphans ; while thou shalt read it to this city together with the presbyters who preside over the Church (Herm. *Vis.* ii. 4).' And so it remains till the close of the second century. When, some seventy years later than the date of our epistle, a second letter is written from Rome to Corinth during the episcopate of Soter (about A.D. 165—175), it is still written in the name of the Church, not the bishop, of Rome ; and as such is acknowledged by Dionysius of Corinth. 'We have read your letter' (ὑμῶν τὴν ἐπιστολήν), he writes in reply to the Romans. At the same time he bears a noble testimony to that moral ascendency of the early Roman Church which was the historical foundation of its primacy ; 'This hath been your practice from the beginning ; to do good to all the brethren in the various ways, and to send supplies (ἐφόδια) to many Churches in divers cities, in one place recruiting the poverty of those that are in want, in another assisting brethren that are in the mines by the supplies that ye have been in the habit of sending to them from the first, thus keeping up, as becometh Romans, a hereditary practice of Romans, which your blessed bishop Soter hath not only maintained, but also advanced,' with more to the same effect[1].

2. Another point of special interest in the newly recovered portion of Clement's Epistle is the link of connexion which it supplies with the earlier history of the Roman Church. In the close of the epistle mention is made of the bearers of the letter, two Romans, Claudius Ephebus and Valerius Bito, who are sent to Corinth with Fortunatus—

[1] Euseb. *H. E.* iv. 23. Harnack (p. xxix. ed. 2) says that this letter of Dionysius 'non Soteris tempore sed paullo post Soteris mortem (175—180) Romam missa esse videtur.' I see nothing in the passage which suggests this inference. On the contrary the perfect tenses (διατετήρηκεν, ἐπηύξηκεν), used in preference to aorists, seem to imply that he was living. The epithet μακάριος, applied to Soter, confessedly proves nothing : for it was used at this time and later not less of the living than of the dead (e. g. Alexander in Euseb. *H. E.* vi. 11). Eusebius himself, who had the whole letter before him, seems certainly to have supposed that Soter was living, for he speaks of it as ἐπιστολὴ...ἐπισκόπῳ τῷ τότε Σωτῆρι προσφωνοῦσα.

the last mentioned being apparently a Corinthian (though this is not clear), and perhaps the same who is named in S. Paul's First Epistle (xvi. 17). In the newly discovered portion these delegates are described in the words which I have already quoted, as 'faithful and prudent men who have walked among us from youth unto old age unblameably (ἄνδρας πιστοὺς καὶ σώφρονας ἀπὸ νεότητος ἀναστραφέντας ἕως γήρους ἀμέμπτως ἐν ἡμῖν).' Now the date of this epistle, as determined by internal and external evidence alike, is somewhere about the year 95; and, as old age could hardly be predicated of men under sixty at least, these persons must have been born about the year 35 or earlier. Thus they would be close upon thirty years of age when S. Paul first visited Rome (A.D. 61—63). They must therefore have had a direct personal knowledge of the relations between the two Apostles S. Peter and S. Paul (supposing that S. Peter also visited the metropolis, as I do not doubt that he did), and of the early history of the Roman Church generally; for the description obviously implies that they had been brought up in the Christian faith from their youth. If we couple this notice with the fact that in an earlier passage of the epistle these two Apostles are held up together as the two great examples for the imitation of the Christian, we see a new difficulty in the way of the Tübingen theory, which is founded on the hypothesis of a direct antagonism between the teaching of the two Apostles, and supposes an entire dislocation and discontinuity in the early history of the Christian Church, more especially of the Church of Rome. To this theory the Epistle of Clement, the one authentic document which has the closest bearing on the subject, gives a decided negative.

3.　But the notice of these persons also suggests some remarks on the *personnel* of this epistle.

Strange as it may appear, every fresh investigation seems to point more definitely to the conclusion that a chief stronghold of Christianity in Rome during the earliest ages was the imperial palace itself. The passage in S. Paul's Epistle to the Philippians (iv. 22) will be remembered at once. The members of 'Cæsar's household' are the only Roman Christians singled out specially as sending salutations to their Philippian brethren. I have endeavoured to show elsewhere that these were apparently no recent converts, but that the long list of salutations in the Epistle to the Romans probably contains some names of slaves or freedmen belonging to the palace of the Cæsars (*Philippians* p. 169 sq.). It has also been pointed out in an earlier part of the present work (p. 170) that the names of these two delegates mentioned by S. Clement,

Claudius and Valerius, suggest some connexion with the imperial household. This becomes still more probable, now that we know them to have been old men in the closing years of the first century. On the supposition that they were freedmen or children of freedmen, they would probably have obtained their names somewhere about the time when a Claudius was seated on the imperial throne with a Valeria as his consort (A.D. 41—48). Thus, when S. Paul wrote from Rome to Philippi (about A.D. 62), they would be young men in the prime of life; their consistent course would mark them out as the future hope of the Church in Rome; they could hardly be unknown to the Apostle; and their names (among many others) would be present to his mind when he dictated the words, 'They that are of Cæsar's household salute you.'

But, if we see ground for assigning the bearers of Clement's letter to the imperial household, there is at least equal reason for inferring such a connexion in the case of the writer himself. The Neronian persecution, whatever else it had done, had not permanently checked the progress of the Gospel either in Rome at large or within the precincts of the imperial household. If Christianity was strong in the palace under the Claudian dynasty, its strength had increased manifold under the Flavian. The 'deadly superstition,' no longer content with the slaves, freedmen, and retainers of the Cæsars, had laid hands on the Cæsars themselves. I have discussed elsewhere (*Philippians* p. 22 sq.) the notices respecting Flavius Clemens and Flavia Domitilla his wife. Flavius Clemens was the emperor's cousin-german; he was colleague of Domitian in the consulship; and his children had been designated by Domitian as successors to the imperial throne; when he was suddenly put to death by the emperor for his profession of Christianity. Flavia Domitilla was not only allied to the emperor by marriage: she was also his blood-relation, the daughter of his own sister; and, when her husband was put to death, she herself was banished to one of the islands [1].

But the evidence of the spread of Christianity in the Flavian household does not stop here. Among the early burial places of the Roman Christians was one called the *Cœmeterium Domitillæ*. This has been identified beyond question by the investigations of de Rossi with the catacombs of the Tor Marancia near the Ardeatine Way. With characteristic patience and acuteness the eminent archæologist has traced the

---

[1] I have given reasons elsewhere for rejecting the opinion that *two* persons of this name, the wife and the niece of Fl. Clemens, suffered for their Christian profession; see *Philippians* p. 22 sq. (ed. 4), where the divergences in the authorities are explained.

early history of this cemetery; and it throws a flood of light on the matter in question [1]. Inscriptions have been discovered which show that these catacombs are situated on an estate once belonging to the Flavia Domitilla who was banished on account of her faith. Thus one inscription records that the plot of ground on which the cippus stood had been granted to P. Calvisius Philotas as the burial place of himself and others, EX . INDVLGENTIA . FLAVIAE . DOMITILL[AE] (Orelli-Henzen *Inscr.* no. 5422). Another monumental tablet is put up by one Tatia in the name of herself and her freedmen and freedwomen. This Tatia is described as [NV]TRIX . SEPTEM . LIB[ERORVM] . DIVI . VESPA-SIAN[I] . [ET] . FLAVIAE . DOMITIL[LAE] . VESPASIANI . NEPTIS, and the sepulchre is stated to be erected EIVS . BENEFICIO, i.e. by the concession of the said Flavia Domitilla, to whom the land belonged (Orelli-Henzen *Inscr.* no. 5423). A third inscription runs as follows...FILIA . FLAVIAE . DOMITILLAE......[VESPASI]ANI . NEPTIS . FECIT . GLYCERAE . L . ET......[POST]ERISQVE . EORVM . etc. (*Corp. Inscr. Lat.* VI. no. 948)[2]. This last indeed was not found on the same site with the others, but was embedded in the pavement of the Basilica of San Clemente in Rome: but there is some reason for thinking that it was transferred thither at an early date with other remains from the Cemetery of Domitilla. Even without the confirmation of this last monument however the connexion of this Christian cemetery with the wife of Flavius Clemens is established beyond any reasonable doubt. And recent excavations have supplied further links of evidence. This cemetery was approached by an above ground vestibule, which leads to a hypogæum, and to which are attached chambers, supposed to have been used by the custodian of the place and by the mourners assembled at funerals. From the architecture and the paintings de Rossi infers that the vestibule itself belongs to the first century. Moreover the publicity of the building, so unlike the obscure doorways and dark underground passages which lead to other catacombs, seems to justify the belief that it was erected under the protection of some important personage and during a period of quiet such as intervened between the death of

[1] De Rossi's investigations will be found in the *Bulletini di Archeologia Cristiana* 1865, pp. 17 sq., 33 sq., 41 sq., 89 sq.; 1874, pp. 5 sq., 68 sq., 122 sq.; 1875, pp. 5 sq., 46 sq.; comp. *Roma Sotterranea* I. p. 186 sq., 266 sq.

[2] The lacunæ in the inscription may be filled up in more ways than one; but

this uncertainty does not affect the main point. It matters little for our purpose, whether the *Flaviæ Domitillæ* of this inscription is identified with the wife of Clemens or with her mother, the daughter of Vespasian. The name *Flavia Domitilla* was inherited from her grandmother, the wife of Vespasian; Sueton. *Vespas.* 3.

Nero and the persecution of Domitian. The underground vaults and passages contain remains which in de Rossi's opinion point to the first half of the second century. Here also are sepulchral memorials, which seem to belong to the time of the Antonines, and imply a connexion with the Flavian household. Thus one exhibits the monogram of a FLAVILLA; another bears the inscription φλ. CABEINOC . ΚΑΙ . ΤΙΤΙΑΝΗ . ΑΔΕΛΦΟΙ; a third, φλ. ΠΤΟΛΕΜΑΙΟC . ΠΡ . ΚΑΙ ΟΥΛΠΙ . ΚΟΝΚΟΡΔΙΑ. As regards the second, it will be remembered that the father of FL Clemens and brother of Vespasian bore this very name T. Flavius Sabinus[1]; and de Rossi therefore supposes that we have here the grave of actual descendants (grandchildren or great grandchildren) of this Flavius Sabinus, through his son Flavius Clemens the Christian martyr[2]. In illustration of the name Titiane again, he remarks that three prefects of Egypt (A.D. 126, A.D. 166, A.D. 215 or 216) bore the name Flavius Titianus, and that the wife of the emperor Pertinax was a Flavia Titiana. We may hesitate to accept these facts as evidence that the persons in question were actual descendants of the imperial house; but if not, the names will at all events point to some freedmen or retainers of the family. Moreover, connected with this same cemetery was the cultus of one S. Petronilla, who was reputed to have been buried here, and in whose name a basilica was erected on the spot at the close of the fourth century[3]. This virgin saint

[1] Borghesi (*Œuvres* III. p. 372 sq.) has shown that this T. Flavius Sabinus was prefect of the city during the Neronian persecution. He is described as a man of a gentle disposition (Tac. *Hist.* iii. 65 'mitem virum abhorrere a sanguine et cædibus,' and again 'Sabinus non insultans et miseranti propior,' *ib.* 75 'innocentiam justitiamque ejus non argueres ...in fine vitæ alii segnem, multi moderatum et civium sanguinis parcum credidere'); and it is pleasant to think with de Rossi (*Bull. di Archeol. Crist.* 1865, p. 18, 1875, p. 66) that the conduct of the Christian martyrs at this crisis gave the first impulse towards Christianity in his family. In the epithet 'segnis' we are reminded of the description which Suetonius (*Domit.* 15) gives of his son Fl. Clemens, 'contemptissimæ inertiæ.' For the bearing of this description on his Christianity see *Philippians* p. 22.

[2] The two sons of Fl. Clemens, when they were designated successors to the throne, assumed the names Vespasianus and Domitianus by order of Domitian; they were then little children; Sueton. *Domit.* 15. We hear nothing of them afterwards, but on the fall of the Flavian dynasty they would retire into private life and probably drop their assumed names. In A.D. 262 we read of one Domitian, a successful general, 'qui se originem diceret a Domitiano trahere atque a Domitilla;' Trebell. Poll. *Tyr. Trig.* 12.

[3] The sarcophagus of this Petronilla was removed from the Cemetery of Domitilla to the Basilica of S. Peter by Paul I (A.D. 757—767). For the recent discovery of the Basilica of S. Petronilla and of another memorial of her

was in legendary story designated the daughter of S. Peter. Some modern critics have sought to explain this designation by a spiritual fatherhood, just as this same Apostle speaks of his 'son Marcus' (1 Pet. v. 13). But the legend obviously has arisen from the similarity of names, *Petros, Petronilla;* and thus it supposes a natural relationship. The removal of her sarcophagus to the Vatican in the eighth century, and the extraordinary honours there paid to her, are only explicable on this supposition. Of this personage de Rossi has given a highly probable account[1]. It had been remarked by Baronio that the name Petronilla is connected etymologically not with *Petros,* but with *Petronius* (he might have added *Petro*); and de Rossi calls attention to the fact that the founder of the Flavian family was one T. Flavius Petro, a native of Reate, the grandfather of the two brothers, T. Flavius Sabinus the prefect of the city and T. Flavius Vespasianus the emperor[2]. This Petronilla therefore, whom the later legend connects with S. Peter, may have been some scion of the Flavian house, who, like her relations Fl. Clemens and Fl. Domitilla, became a convert to Christianity. Even the simple fact of a conspicuous tomb bearing the name *Petronilla* would have been a sufficient starting-point for the legend of her relationship to S. Peter in an age when the glorification of that Apostle was a dominant idea.

I have given an outline of the principal facts which de Rossi has either discovered or emphasized, and of the inferences which he has drawn from them, so far as they bear on my subject. He has also endeavoured to strengthen his position by other critical combinations; but I have preferred to pass them over as shadowy and precarious. Even of those which I have given, some perhaps will not command general assent. But the main facts seem to be established on grounds which can hardly be questioned; that we have here a burial place of Christian Flavii of the second century; that it stands on ground which once belonged to Flavia Domitilla; and that it was probably

cultus within the Cemetery of Domitilla, together with the sepulchre of SS. Nereus and Achilles, see *Bull. di Archeol. Crist.* 1874, pp. 5 sq., 68 sq., 122 sq., 1875, p. 5 sq. See also below p. 262, note 1.

[1] *Bull. di Archeol. Crist.* 1865, p. 22. De Rossi seems still to attach weight to the opinion that this Petronilla was a spiritual daughter of S. Peter: but he himself has deprived this hypothesis of its *raison d'être* by pointing out the true derivation of the name. The spiritual relationship is a mere invention of modern critics, following Baronio (*Ann.* 69, § xxxiii). To this writer it is offensive that a daughter should have been born to S. Peter after his call to the Apostleship; and he argues against the natural relationship accordingly. The old legend had no such scruple.

[2] Sueton. *Vespas.* 1.

granted by her to her dependents and coreligionists for a cemetery. There is reason for believing that in the earliest ages the Christians secured their places of sepulture from disturbance under the shelter of great personages, whose property was protected by the law during their life time, and whose testamentary dispositions were respected after their death[1].

But if the Flavian household was the stronghold of Christianity in Rome at this time, what light does this fact throw on the authorship of our letter? Who was this Clemens bishop of Rome, so famous a name in later legend, and (as we may infer) so important a personage in contemporary Christian history? One answer is obvious. S. Paul, writing to the Philippians (iv. 3), mentions with commendation a certain Clemens. Origen therefore identified this person with the bishop of Rome, just as he identified the Hermas saluted in the Roman Epistle with his namesake the author of the Shepherd; and in both points he is followed by later writers. But his opinion does not appear to be based on any tradition. Moreover the Clemens saluted by S. Paul was apparently a Philippian; and, as the name is not uncommon, all ground for the identification disappears[2]. Others again in recent times have supposed that the bishop of Rome and writer of the letter was none other than Flavius Clemens, the cousin of Domitian, who was put to death for his faith[3]. It may be confidently affirmed however that, if the bishop of Rome had been the nearest male relative to the reigning emperor and the father of the boys whom Domitian had already designated as his successors to the throne, the fact would have been paraded in the earliest annals of Christianity and could not have passed into oblivion. Others again have conjectured that he was a less conspicuous scion of the imperial family. Thus de Rossi makes him the son of a brother of Fl. Clemens[4], herein following the Acts of SS. Nereus and Achilles. These acts however are confessedly a spurious production[5];

[1] De Rossi *Bull. di Archeol. Crist.* 1864, p. 25 sq., *Rom. Sotter.* I. p. 102 sq.

[2] See *Philippians* p. 166 sq., for a fuller discussion of this question.

[3] Of recent editors, Hilgenfeld is very decided in identifying Clement the consul with Clement the bishop; p. xxxii sq. (ed. 2), comp. *Zeitschr. f. Wiss. Theol.* 1869, p. 232 sq. Harnack leans to this opinion, but speaks with hesitation; p. lxii sq. (ed. 2).

[4] *Bull. di Archeol. Crist.* 1865, p.

20 sq.

[5] *Acta Sanct. Rolland.* Maii III. p. 4. Nereus and Achilles are there represented as the chamberlains (*eunuchi*) of S. Domitilla the Virgin, and as having been martyred at the same time with her. On the other hand the inscription which Damasus placed in this Cemetery of Domitilla implies that they were soldiers of the tyrant, who refused to be the instruments of his cruelty and resigned their military honours: *Bull. di Archeol.*

there is no reason to think that they had any other basis of fact besides the cultus of SS. Nereus and Achilles and of S. Petronilla[1] in connexion with the Cemetery of Domitilla; and no such nephew of Fl. Clemens is mentioned elsewhere. Moreover this solution is open to the same objections as the last, though not in the same degree. Again, Ewald conjectures that he was a son of Fl. Clemens, and appeals to the *Homilies* and *Recognitions* for support[2]; but for this conjecture there is even less to be said. These Clementine writings do indeed regard Clement the bishop as a distant relative of the Roman emperor[3], not however of Domitian, but of Tiberius; while the names given in the story to his father, mother, and brothers—Faustus, Mattidia, Faustinus, Faustinianus—are borrowed from the imperial family of later sovereigns, Hadrian and the Antonines. This romance therefore is valueless as evidence; and at most it can only be taken to imply a tradition that our Clement was somehow or other connected with the household of the Caesars. Nor indeed is Ewald's theory consistent with

Crist. 1874, p. 20 sq. Whether the legend of these martyrs was founded on fact or not, it is impossible to say. The discovery of a monumental stone with their names in the Cemetery of Domitilla would be a sufficient starting-point for the story in the fourth and later centuries, when martyrdoms were the favourite subjects for romance. There is reason for believing that gravestones have been largely instrumental in such fictions.

[1] The Acts of S. Petronilla are incorporated in those of SS. Nereus and Achilles (see also *Act. SS. Bolland.* Maii xxxi, VII. p. 413 sq., this being her own day). So far as I can see, the legend of S. Petronilla is due to the combination of two elements: (1) The story mentioned by S. Augustine as related in some apocryphal writings of the Manicheans, that S. Peter miraculously healed his daughter (whose name is not given) of the palsy (*c. Adim.* 17, *Op.* VIII. p. 139). This story seems to be suggested by the incident related in Mark i. 29 sq., Luke iv. 38 sq. (2) The discovery of a sarcophagus in the cemetery of the Christian Flavii bearing the name of Petronilla. When this tomb was transferred to the

Vatican by Paul I, a Church adjoining the Basilica of S. Peter was built for its reception. It seems to have been inscribed AVRELIAE . PETRONILLAE . FILIAE . DVLCISSIMAE (see *Bull. di Archeol. Crist.* 1865, p. 46). The first word however is elsewhere given as AVREAE, and possibly it may have been somewhat obliterated by time. The identification with S. Peter's daughter would naturally arise out of this inscription, which was even believed to have been engraved by the Apostle's own hand.

[2] *Gesch. des V. Israel* VII. p. 296 sq.

[3] *Hom.* xii. 8, where Clement says, τῷ ἐμῷ πατρὶ ὡς καὶ συντρόφῳ αὐτὸς Καῖσαρ συγγενίδα προσηρμόσατο γυναῖκα, ἀφ' ἧς τρεῖς ἐγενόμεθα υἱοί... ἡ μὲν οὖν μήτηρ μου Ματτιδία ἐλέγετο, ὁ δὲ πατὴρ Φαῦστος, τῶν δὲ ἀδελφῶν καὶ αὐτῶν ὁ μὲν Φαυστῖνος ἐκαλεῖτο ὁ δὲ Φαυστινιανὸς ἐλέγετο (comp. iv. 7, xiv. 6, 10). The parallel passage in the *Recognitions* (vii. 8) is 'patri, utpote propinquo suo et una educato, nobilis adaeque familiae Caesar ipse junxit uxorem' etc. Ewald supposes that this Faustus and Mattidia are intended to represent Flavius Clemens and Flavia Domitilla.

history or chronology. The sons of Flavius Clemens were yet children destined to the imperial purple at the very time when our Clement presided over the Church of the metropolis.

But the theory which identifies the writer of the epistle with the cousin of Domitian seems to me to be open to still graver objections. Is it possible to conceive this letter as written by one, who had received the education and who occupied the position of Flavius Clemens; who had grown up to manhood, perhaps to middle life, as a heathen; who was imbued with the thoughts and feelings of the Roman noble; who about this very time held the most ancient and honourable office in the state in conjunction with the emperor; who lived in an age of literary dilettantism and of Greek culture; who must have mixed in the same circles with Martial and Statius and Juvenal, with Tacitus and the younger Pliny; and in whose house Quintilian lived as the tutor of his sons, then designated by the emperor as the future rulers of the world?[1] Would not the style, the diction, the thoughts, the whole complexion of the letter, have been very different? It might not perhaps have been less Christian, but it would certainly have been more Classical—at once more Roman and more Greek—and less Jewish, than it is.

The question, whether the writer of this epistle was of Jewish or Gentile origin, has been frequently discussed and answered in opposite ways. The special points, which have been singled out on either side, will not bear the stress which has been laid upon them. On the one hand, critics have pleaded that the writer betrays his Jewish parentage, when he speaks of 'our father Jacob,' 'our father Abraham' (§§ 4, 31); but this language is shown to be common to early Christian writers, whether Jewish or Gentile (see p. 44). On the other hand, it has been inferred from the order 'day and night' (§§ 2, 20, 24) that he must have been a Gentile; but examples from the Apostolic writings show that this argument also is quite invalid (see p. 39). Or again, this latter conclusion has been drawn from the mention of 'our generals' (§ 37), by which expression the writer is supposed to indicate his position as 'before all things a Roman born'[2]. But this language would be equally

[1] Quintil. *Inst.* iv. Procem. 'Quum vero mihi Domitianus Augustus sororis suae nepotum delegaverit curam,' etc. Sueton. *Domit.* 15 'Flavium Clementem ...cujus filios *etiam tum parvulos* successores palam destinaverat.' The rhetorician seems to have been indebted to the father of his pupils for the highest honours; Auson. *Grat. Act. ad Gratian.* 31 'Quintilianus, consularia per Clementem ornamenta sortitus, honestamenta nominis potius videtur quam insignia potestatis habuisse.'

[2] Ewald *Gesch. d. V. Israel* VII. p. 206.

appropriate on the lips of any Hellenist Jew who was a native of Rome. Setting aside these special expressions howéver, and looking to the general character of the letter, we can hardly be mistaken, I think, in regarding it as the natural outpouring of one whose mind was saturated with the knowledge of the Old Testament. The writer indeed, like the author of the Book of Wisdom, is not without a certain amount of Classical culture (§§ 20, 25, 33, 37, 38, 55); but this is more or less superficial. The thoughts and diction alike are moulded on 'the Law and the Prophets and the Psalms.' He is a Hellenist indeed, for he betrays no acquaintance with the Scriptures in their original tongue: but of the Septuagint Version his knowledge is very thorough and intimate. It is not confined to any one part, but ranges freely over the whole. He quotes profusely, and sometimes his quotations are obviously made from memory. He is acquainted with traditional interpretations of the sacred text (§§ 7, 9, 11, 31). He teems with words and phrases borrowed from the Greek Bible, even where he is not directly quoting it. His style has caught a strong Hebraistic tinge from its constant study. All this points to an author of Jewish or proselyte parentage, who from a child had been reared in the knowledge of this one book[1].

Jews were found in large numbers at this time among the slaves and freedmen of the great houses, even of the imperial palace[2]. I observe this very name Clemens borne by one such person, a slave of the Cæsars, on a sepulchral monument; D.M. CLEMETI. CAESARVM. N. N. SERVO. CASTELLARIO. AQVAE. CLAVDIAE. FECIT. CLAVDIA. SABBATHIS. ET. SIBI. ET. SVIS (Orelli *Inscr.* 2899): for his nationality may be inferred from the name of his relative Sabbathis, who sets up the monument. And elsewhere there is abundant evidence that the name at all events was not uncommon among the dependents of the Cæsars about this time. Thus we read in a missive of Vespasian, DE. CONTROVERSIA .... VT. FINIRET. CLAVDIVS. CLEMENS. PROCVRATOR. MEVS. SCRIPSI. EI (Murat. MXCI. 1). In another inscription we have, EVTACTO. AVG. LIB. PROC. ACCENSO. DE. LAT. (*sic*) A. DIVO. VESPASIANO. PATRI. OPTIMO. CLEMENS. FILIVS

---

[1] This conviction of a Judaic authorship is strengthened in my mind every time I read the epistle. On the other hand Harnack says (p. lxiii, ed. 2), 'rectius ex elegante sermonis genere et e cc. 37, 55, judices eum nobili loco natum fuisse patria Romanum': and Ewald (l. c.) argues (I think, somewhat perversely) that the length of the writer's quotations from the Old Testament shows that the book was novel to him. But in fact the direct quotations are only a very small part, and the least convincing part, of the evidence.

[2] See *Philippians* p. 14.

(*ib*. DCCCXCIX. 2); in another, CLEMENS . AVG . AD . SVPELECT . (*ib*. CMXVII. 10); in another D . M . SEDATI . TI . CL . SECVNDINI . PROC . AVG . TABVL . CLEMENS . ADFINIS (*ib*. CMXV. 9); in another, PRO . SALVTE . T . CAESARIS . AVG . F . IMP . VESPASIANI . TI . CLAVDIVS . CLEMENS . FECIT (*Corp. Inscr. Lat.* VI. no. 940); in another, T . VARIO . CLEMENTI . AB . EPISTVLIS . AVGVSTOR., this last however dating in the reign of M. Aurelius and L. Verus A.D. 161—169 (*ib*. III. no. 5215); while in another, found in the columbarium of the Freedmen of Livia and therefore perhaps belonging to an earlier date than our Clement, we read IVLIA . CALLITYCHE . STORGE . CLAVDI . EROTIS . DAT . CLEMENTI . CONIVGI . CALLITYCHES (*ib*. MCCCLIV. 7). I venture therefore to conjecture that Clement the bishop was a man of Jewish parentage, a freedman or the son of a freedman belonging to the household of Flavius Clemens the emperor's cousin. It is easy to imagine how under these circumstances the leaven of Christianity would work upwards from beneath, as it has done in so many other cases; and from their domestics and dependents the master and mistress would learn their perilous lessons in the Gospel. Even a much greater degree of culture than is exhibited in this epistle would be quite consistent with such an origin; for amongst these freedmen were frequently found the most intelligent and cultivated men of their day. Nor is this social status inconsistent with the position of the chief ruler of the most important Church in Christendom. A generation later Hermas, the brother of bishop Pius, speaks of himself as having been a slave (*Vis.* i. 1); and this involves the servile origin of Pius also. At a still later date, more than a century after Clement's time, the papal chair was occupied by Callistus, who had been a slave of one Carpophorus an officer in the imperial palace (Hippol. *Hær.* ix. 12). The Christianity which had thus taken root in the household of Domitian's cousin left a memorial behind in another distinguished person also. The famous Alexandrian father, who flourished a century later than the bishop of Rome, bore all the three names of this martyr prince, Titus Flavius Clemens. He too was doubtless a descendant of some servant in the family, who according to custom would be named after his patron when he obtained his freedom[1].

---

[1] This conjunction of names occurs also in an inscription found at Augsburg, T . FL . PRIMANO . PATRI . ET . TRAIAN . CLEMENTINAE . MATRI . ET . T . FL . CLEMENTI . FRATRI (*Corp. Inscr. Lat.* III. no. 5812), where the name *Traiana* is another link of connexion with the imperial household. Compare also T . FLAVIVS . LONGINVS ..ET . FLAVI . LONGINVS . CLEMENTINA . MARCELLINA . FIL[I] (*ib*. no. 1100); MATRI . PIENTISSIMAE . LVCRETIVS . CLEMENS . ET . FL . FORTVNATVS . FILI (*ib*. no.

The imperial household was henceforward a chief centre of Christianity in the metropolis. Irenæus writing during the episcopate of Eleutherus (circ. A.D. 175—189), and therefore under M. Aurelius or Commodus, speaks of 'the faithful in the royal court' in language which seems to imply that they were a considerable body there (iv. 30. 1). Marcia, the concubine of this last-mentioned emperor, was herself a Christian, and exerted her influence over Commodus in alleviating the sufferings of the confessors (Hippol. *Hær.* l. c.). At this same time also another Christian, Carpophorus, already mentioned, whose name seems to betray a servile origin, but who was evidently a man of considerable wealth and influence, held some office in the imperial household. A little later the emperor Severus is stated to have been cured by a physician Proculus, a Christian slave, whom he kept in the palace ever afterwards to the day of his death: while the son and successor of this emperor, Caracalla, had a Christian woman for his foster-mother (Tertull. *ad Scap.* 4). Again, the Christian sympathies of Alexander Severus and Philip, and the still more decided leanings of the ladies of their families, are well known. And so it continued to the last. When in an evil hour for himself Diocletian was induced to raise his hand against the Church, the first to suffer were his confidential servants, the first to abjure on compulsion were his own wife and daughter[1].

4. Bearing these facts in mind, we turn to the *persecution* of the Christians under Domitian. And here the close connexion, not only of Christianity, but (as it would appear) of the bearers and the writer of the letter, with the imperial household serves to explain the singular reserve which is maintained throughout this epistle. The persecutor and the persecuted met face to face, as it were. They mixed together in the common affairs of life; they even lived under the same roof.

5844). The name FLAVIVS . CLEMENS occurs also in another inscription (Murat. CDXCIV. 4), along with many other names which point to the household of the Cæsars, though at a later date. So too *C.I.L.* III. no. 5783. Comp. also D . M . C . VALERIO . CLEMENTI . C . IVLIVS . FE-LIX . ET . FLAVIA . HEREDES (Murat. MDV. 12).

This last inscription illustrates the connexion of names *Valerius* and *Clemens* which appears in our epistle. Of this phenomenon also we have other examples: e.g. a memorial erected C . VALERIO . C .

F . STEL . CLEMENTI by the DECVRIONES . ALAE . GETVLORVM . QVIBVS . PRAEFVIT . BELLO . IVDAICO . SVB . DIVO . VESPASIANO . AVG . PATRE (Orelli, no. 748), found at Turin. This Valerius Clemens therefore was a contemporary of our Clement. For other instances of the combination Valerius Clemens see *Corp. Inscr. Lat.* III. no. 633, 2572, 6162, 6179, Muratori MCDXV. 1, MDLXIV. 12. So too Valerius Clementinus *C.I.L.* III. no. 3524, and Valeria Clementina, *ib.* 2580.

[1] Mason *Persecution of Diocletian* p. 121 sq.

Thus the utmost caution was needed, that collisions might not be provoked. We can well understand therefore with what feelings one who thus carried his life in his hand would pen the opening words of the letter, where he excuses the tardiness of the Roman Church in writing to their Corinthian brethren by a reference to 'the sudden and repeated calamities and reverses' under which they were suffering (§ 1). Not a word is said about the nature of these calamities; not a word here or elsewhere about their authors. As the text has been hitherto supplied, these sufferings are represented as past, τὰς [γενομ]ένας ἡμῖν, 'which befel us.' But one of our newly discovered authorities gives a present tense, 'which are befalling us' (γινομένας for γενομένας) ; and this seems on the whole better suited to the general tenour of the letter. There is no indication anywhere that the fears of the Roman Christians had ceased. On the contrary, after referring to the victims of the Neronian persecution, it is said significantly, 'We are in the same lists, and the same struggle awaits us' (§ 7)[1]. The letter therefore was probably written while the Church was still at the mercy of the tyrant's caprice, still uncertain when and where the next blow might fall. However this may be, it could hardly have been penned before the two most illustrious members of the Church, the patron and patroness of the writer (if my hypothesis be correct), had paid the one by his death, the other by her banishment, the penalty of their adherence to the faith of Christ; for these seem to have been among the earliest victims of the emperor's wrath. Flavius Clemens was consul A. D. 95, and he appears to have suffered immediately after the close of the year[2]. In September of the year following the tyrant himself was slain. The chief conspirator and assassin was one Stephanus, a freedman, the steward of Domitilla. He is even said to have struck the blow with the name of Flavius Clemens on his lips, as if he were the avenger of his master's death[3]. If this be so, the household of this earliest of

[1] This interpretation however must not be pressed. The words may refer to the Christian course generally, and need not have any special reference to the endurance of persecution.

[2] Suetonius (*Domit.* 15) says that Domitian put him to death 'tantum non in ipso ejus consulatu.' On the other hand, Dion Cassius (lxvii. 16) speaks of him as ὑπατεύοντα at the time. Clinton supposes that he was executed in the year 95, to which as consul he gave his name,

but 'after he had abdicated the consulship.'

[3] All our authorities are agreed in representing this person as the chief assassin : Suet. *Domit.* 7 'Stephanus Domitillæ procurator et tunc interceptarum pecuniarum reus consilium operamque tulit etc'; Dion Cass. lxvii. 15, 16, μετὰ Στεφάνου ἀπελευθέρου...ὁ Παρθένιος...τὸν Στέφανον ἐρρωμενέστερον τῶν ἄλλων ὄντα εἰσέπεμψε κ. τ. λ.; Philostr. *Vit. Apoll.* viii. 25 Στέφανος τοίνυν ἀπελεύθερος τῆς

Christian princes must have contained within its walls strange diversities of character. No greater contrast can be conceived to the ferocity and passion of these bloody scenes which accompanied the death of Domitian, than the singular gentleness and forbearance which distinguishes this letter throughout. In no respect is this ἐπιείκεια, to which beyond anything else it owes its lofty moral elevation, more conspicuous than in the attitude of these Roman Christians towards their secular rulers, whom at this time they had little cause to love. In the prayer for princes and governors, which appears in the newly recovered close of the epistle, this sentiment finds its noblest expression: 'Guide our steps to walk in holiness and righteousness and singleness of heart, and to do such things as are good and well-pleasing in Thy sight, and in the sight of our rulers.' 'Give concord and peace to us and to all that dwell on the earth...that we may be saved, while we render obedience to Thine Almighty and most excellent Name, and to our rulers and governors upon the earth. Thou, O Lord and Master, hast given them the power of sovereignty through Thine excellent and unspeakable might, that we, knowing the glory and honour which Thou hast given them, may submit ourselves unto them, in nothing resisting Thy will. Grant unto them therefore, O Lord, health, peace, concord, stability, that they may administer the government which Thou hast given them without failure. For Thou, O heavenly Master, King of the ages, givest to the sons of men glory and honour and power over all things that are upon the earth. Do Thou, Lord, direct their counsel according to that which is good and well-pleasing in Thy sight, that, administering in peace and gentleness, with godliness, the power which Thou hast given them, they may obtain Thy favour' (§§ 60, 61). When we remember that this prayer issued from the fiery furnace of persecution after experience of a

---

γυναικὸς κ. τ. λ. (he has just before mentioned the wife of Flavius Clemens). The motives of his act however are differently represented. The language of Suetonius suggests that he did it to extricate himself from a charge of embezzlement. Dion Cassius says that he was only the instrument of a general conspiracy in the household, to which even the empress Domitia herself was suspected to have been privy, and that the conspirators acted in self-defence, as Domitian was believed to entertain designs against their

lives. Philostratus connects the act directly with the death of Clemens, saying of Stephanus, εἴτε τὸν τεθνεῶτα [Κλήμεντα] ἐνθυμηθεὶς εἴτε πάντας, and represents him as addressing Domitian thus, οὐ τέθνηκεν ὁ πολεμιώτατός σοι Κλήμης, ὡς σὺ οἴει, ἀλλ' ἔστιν οὗ ἐγὼ οἶδα, καὶ ξυντάττει ἑαυτὸν ἐπὶ σέ. These words have a strange ring, when we remember that this Clemens was a Christian. Stephanus himself was killed in the fray which ensued.

cruel and capricious tyrant like Domitian, it will appear truly sublime —sublime in its utterances, and still more sublime in its silence. Who would have grudged the Church of Rome her primacy, if she had always spoken thus?

5. The mention of this intercession for rulers leads to the consideration of another point of importance, the *liturgical* character of this newly recovered portion. The whole epistle may be said to lead up to the long prayer or litany, if we may so call it, which forms a fit close to its lessons of forbearance and love. Attention is directed to it at the outset in a few emphatic words: 'We will ask with fervency of prayer and supplication that the Creator of the universe may guard intact the number of His elect that is numbered throughout the whole world, through His beloved Son Jesus Christ' (§ 59). The prayer itself extends to a great length, occupying some seventy lines of an ordinary octavo page. Moreover it bears all the marks of a careful composition. Not only are the balance and rhythm of the clauses carefully studied, but almost every other expression is selected and adapted from different parts of the Old Testament.

This prayer or litany begins with an elaborate invocation of God arranged for the most part in antithetical sentences. Then comes a special intercession for the afflicted, the lowly, the fallen, the needy, the wanderers, the hungry, the prisoners, and so forth. After this follows a general confession of sins and prayer for forgiveness and help. This last opens with an address, evincing the same deep sense of the glories of Creation, which is one of the most striking characteristics in the earlier part of the epistle: 'Thou through thine operations didst make manifest the everlasting fabric of the world, etc.' (§ 60). It closes, as the occasion suggests, with a prayer for unity: 'Give concord and peace to us and to all that dwell on the earth, as Thou gavest to our fathers, etc.' After this stands the intercession for rulers, which I have already quoted. The whole closes with a doxology.

It is impossible not to be struck with the resemblances in this passage to portions of the earliest known liturgies. Not only is there a general coincidence in the objects of the several petitions, but it has also individual phrases, and in one instance a whole cluster of petitions[1], in common with one or other of these. Moreover, this litany in S. Clement's Epistle begins with the declaration, 'We will ask with fervency of prayer and supplication' (ἐκτενῆ τὴν δέησιν καὶ

---

[1] See the parallel from *Liturg. D. Marc.* p. 21, in the note on § 59 τοὺς ἐν θλίψει κ. τ. λ.

ἱκεσίαν ποιούμενοι); and the expression reminds us that this very word, ἡ ἐκτενής, was the designation given to a corresponding portion in the Greek ritual, owing to its peculiar fervency[1]. We remember also that the name of S. Clement is especially connected with a liturgy incorporated in the closing books of the Apostolic Constitutions, and the circumstance may point to some true tradition of his handiwork in the ritual of the Church. Moreover, this liturgy in the Constitutions, together with the occasional services which accompany it, has so many phrases in common with the prayer in S. Clement's epistle, that the resemblances cannot be accidental. But no stress can be laid on this last fact, seeing that the writers alike of the earlier and later books of the Apostolic Constitutions obviously had Clement's epistle in their hands.

What then shall we say of this litany? Has S. Clement here introduced into his epistle a portion of a fixed form of words then in use in the Roman Church? Have the extant liturgies borrowed directly from this epistle? Or do they owe this resemblance to some common type of liturgy, founded (as we may suppose) on the prayers of the Synagogue, and so anterior even to Clement's epistle itself? The origin of the earliest extant liturgies is a question of high importance; and with the increased interest which the subject has aroused in England of late years, it may be hoped that a solution of the problems connected with it will be seriously undertaken; but no satisfactory result will be attained, unless it is approached in a thoroughly critical spirit and without the design of supporting foregone conclusions[2]. Leaving this question to others for discussion, I can only state the inference which this prayer of S. Clement, considered in the light of probabilities, suggests to my own mind. There was at this time no authoritative written liturgy in use in the Church of Rome: but the prayers were modified at the discretion of the officiating minister. Under the dictation of habit and experience however these prayers were gradually assuming a fixed form. A more or less definite order in the petitions, a greater or less constancy in the individual expressions, was already

---

[1] See *Apost. Const.* vii. 6—10, where the deacon invites the congregation again and again to pray ἐκτενῶς, ἔτι ἐκτενῶς, ἔτι ἐκτενέστερον. Comp. *Liturg. S. Chrys.* p. 122 (ed. Neale) τὴν ἐκτενῆ ταύτην ἱκεσίαν προσδέξαι.

[2] Such an investigation must include a careful study of the prayers of the Synagogue with a view to ascertaining their antiquity. Some of the parallels to S. Clement's prayer which will be noticed below in the Addenda are strongly suggestive of a connexion.

perceptible. As the chief pastor of the Roman Church would be the main instrument in thus moulding the liturgy, the prayers, without actually being written down, would assume in his mind a fixity as time went on. When therefore at the close of his epistle he asks his readers to fall on their knees and lay down their jealousies and disputes at the footstool of grace, his language naturally runs into those antithetical forms and measured cadences which his ministrations in the Church had rendered habitual with him when dealing with such a subject. This explanation seems to suit the facts. The prayer is not given as a quotation from an acknowledged document, but as an immediate outpouring of the heart; and yet it has all the appearance of a fixed form. This solution accords moreover with the notices which we find elsewhere respecting the liturgy of the early Church, which seem to point to forms of prayer more or less fluctuating even at a later date than this[1].

6. Again fresh light is thrown on the *doctrinal teaching* of S. Clement by this discovery. The genuineness of the passage relating to the Holy Trinity, quoted by S. Basil as from Clement (see above p. 168), was questioned by many. The hesitation was due chiefly to the assumption that this very definite form of words involved an ana-chronism; and it was partially justified by the fact that several spurious writings bearing the name of Clement were undoubtedly in circulation in the fourth century when Basil wrote. The passage however has a place in the genuine epistle; and though, as S. Basil says, it is expressed ἀρχαϊκώτερον, i.e. with a more primitive simplicity than the doctrinal statements of the third and fourth century, yet it is much more significant in its context than the detached quotation of this

---

[1] Justin *Apol.* i. 67 (p. 98 E) καὶ ὁ προεστὼς εὐχὰς ὁμοίως καὶ εὐχαριστίας, ὅσῃ δύναμις αὐτῷ, ἀναπέμπει. We cannot indeed be certain from the ex-pression ὅσῃ δύναμις itself that Justin is referring to unwritten forms of prayer, for it might express merely the fervency and strength of enunciation; though in the passage quoted by Bingham (*Christ. Ant.* xiii. 5. 5) from Greg. Naz. *Orat.* iv. § 12 (I. p. 83) φέρε, ὅσῃ δύναμις, ἁγνισά-μενοι καὶ σώματα καὶ ψυχὰς καὶ μίαν ἀναλαβόντες φωνήν κ. τ. λ., the ὅσῃ δύνα-μις has a much wider reference than to the actual singing of the Song of Moses, as he takes it. But in connexion with its context here, it certainly suggests that the language and thoughts of the prayers were dependent on the person himself: as e. g. in *Apol.* i. 55 (p. 90) διὰ λόγου καὶ σχήματος τοῦ φαινομένου, ὅσῃ δύναμις, προτρεψάμενοι ὑμᾶς κ. τ. λ. (comp. i. 13, p. 60). This is forty or fifty years after the date of Clement's letter. In illustration of ὅσῃ δύναμις Otto refers to Tertullian's phrase (*Apol.* 39), quoting it however incorrectly, 'Ut quisque...de proprio ingenio potest, provocatur in me-dium Deo canere.' The force of ὅσῃ δύναμις may be estimated from its occur-rences in Orig. *c. Cels.* v. 1, 51, 53, 58, viii. 35.

father would have led us to infer. 'As God liveth,' writes Clement,
'and the Lord Jesus Christ liveth, and the Holy Ghost, (who are) the
faith and the hope of the elect, so surely etc.' The points to be observed here are twofold. *First;* for the common adjuration in the Old
Testament, 'as the Lord (i. e. Jehovah) liveth,' we find here substituted
a form which recognizes the Holy Trinity. *Secondly;* this Trinity is
declared to be the object or the foundation of the Christian's faith
and hope. On the other hand, our recently discovered authorities
throw considerable doubt on the reading in an earlier passage of the
epistle (§ 2), where the Divinity of Christ is indirectly stated in the
almost patripassian language of which very early patristic writings
furnish not a few examples. Where Clement speaks of 'His sufferings'
(τὰ παθήματα αὐτοῦ), our new authorities agree in substituting 'Christ'
(τοῦ Χριστοῦ), as the person to whom the pronoun refers, in the place
of 'God' (τοῦ Θεοῦ) which stands in the Alexandrian MS. This various
reading will be discussed in its proper place.

7. Lastly; the discovery of the Syriac Version throws some light
on the *canonical reception* of the epistle. Not without some hesitation,
I expressed an opinion in the earlier part of this work (p. 21) that a
Syrian Christian would probably understand by the two Epistles of
Clement the spurious letters in praise of Virginity. I am still disposed
to think that this was the case in the fourth and fifth centuries, to which
I was referring. But our MS shows that at a later date the Epistles
to the Corinthians were not only known to the Syrian Church but also
treated by some persons as strictly canonical. With the evidence
which is now before us we are able to trace the following stages in
their progress towards full canonicity.

(1) The genuine Epistle of Clement was read from time to time
on Sundays in the Church of Corinth to which it was addressed (see
above pp. 3, 11). Our information on this point relates to about
A.D. 170. This reading however did not imply any canonicity; for
Dionysius bishop of Corinth, to whom we are indebted for the information, tells us at the same time that his Church purposes doing
the same thing with a second letter of the Roman Church which they
had only just received when he wrote (Euseb. *H. E.* iv. 23).

(2) This practice was extended from the Church of Corinth to
other Christian communities. Eusebius, in the first half of the fourth
century, speaks of this epistle as 'having been publicly read in
very many Churches both formerly and in his own time' (*H. E.* iii. 16
ἐν πλείσταις ἐκκλησίαις ἐπὶ τοῦ κοινοῦ δεδημοσιευμένην πάλαι τε καὶ καθ'
ἡμᾶς αὐτούς).

(3) For convenience of reading, it would be attached to MSS of the New Testament. But, so far as our evidence goes, this was not done until two things had first happened. (*a*) On the one hand, the Canon of the New Testament had for the most part assumed a definite form in the MSS, beginning with the Gospels and ending with the Apocalypse. (*b*) On the other hand, the so-called Second Epistle of Clement had become inseparably attached to the genuine letter, so that the two formed one body. I shall endeavour to give an explanation of this attachment, when I come to speak of the Second Epistle. Hence, when we find our epistle included in the same volume with the New Testament, it carries the Second Epistle with it, and the two form a sort of *appendix* to the Canon. This is the case with the Alexandrian MS in the middle of the fifth century, where they stand after the Apocalypse, i. e. after the proper close of the sacred volume—thus occupying the same position which in the earlier Sinaitic MS is occupied by other apocryphal matter, the Epistle of Barnabas and the Shepherd of Hermas.

(4) It was an easy stage from this to include them among the Books of the New Testament, and thus to confer upon them a patent of canonicity. Uncritical transcribers and others would take this step without reflexion. This is done by the scribe of A in his table of contents (see above, p. 22 sq.).

It is interesting to observe, though the fact seems to have been overlooked, that the treatment in the Alexandrian MS exactly accords with the language of the 85th Apostolical Canon as read in the Coptic Churches. The Books of the New Testament are there given as 'The Four Gospels......the Acts of us the Apostles; the two Epistles of Peter; the three of John; the Epistle of James, with that of Judas; the fourteen Epistles of Paul; the Apocalypse of John; the two Epistles of Clement which ye shall read aloud[1].' Here the several divisions

---

[1] The Coptic form of the Apostolical Canons is preserved in both the great dialects of the Egyptian language. The Thebaic is found in a MS recently acquired by the British Museum, *Orient.* 1320. I shall give an account of this MS (which has not been noticed hitherto) in the Addenda to this volume, for it throws another ray of light on the dark question of the history of the *Apostolical Constitutions.* The Memphitic is published by Tattam in the volume entitled '*The Apostolic Constitutions or Canons of the Apostles in Coptic,*' London 1848. This Memphitic version however was not made directly from the Greek, but is a very recent and somewhat barbarous translation from the previously existing Thebaic Version. The concluding words of the clause quoted stand in the Thebaic ⲦⲈⲚⲦⲈⲚⲈⲠⲒⲤⲦⲞⲖⲎⲠⲎⲖⲎⲘⲎⲤ · ⲈⲦⲈⲦⲚⲈⲞⳅⲞⲦⲢⲒⲂⲞⲖ, which I have translated in the text; in the Memphitic, as given by Tattam (p. 211), ϯⲂϯ ⲚⲈⲠⲒ-

of the New Testament occur in the same order as in A, though the Catholic Epistles are transposed among themselves[1]; moreover the Clementine Epistles are placed after the Apocalypse, as in that MS; and, as a reason for adding them, it is stated that they were to be read publicly[2].

(5) Their canonicity being assumed, it remained to give practical effect to this view, and to place them in a position consistent with it. In other words, they must be transferred from the appendix to the body of the New Testament. The only known document, which has actually taken this step, is our Syriac Version, where they are attached to the Catholic Epistles. The date of this MS (A.D. 1170) throws some light on the matter.

It has been observed above (p. 12), that the general silence about the Epistles of S. Clement in the older discussions on the Canon of Scripture seems to show that their claims to canonicity were not considered serious enough to demand refutation. In the 85th and last of the Apostolical Canons however the case is different. If the existing Greek text of this Canon may be trusted, this document not only admits them to a place among the Scriptures, but ranges them with the Catholic Epistles. The list of the New Testament writings runs as follows; 'Four Gospels,......; of Paul fourteen Epistles; of Peter two Epistles; of John three; of James one; of Jude one; of Clement two Epistles; and the Constitutions (διαταγαί) addressed to you the bishops, through me Clement in eight books, which ought not to be published to

ϲⲧⲟⲗⲏ ⲛ̄ⲁⲕⲗⲏⲙⲏⲥ ⲉⲧⲉⲧⲉⲛⲟⲩⲟⲧ ⲅ̄ⲓ ⲉⲃⲟⲗ, which he renders 'the two Epistles of Clemens, which you read out of.'

In the Arabic Version of this Canon, Brit. Mus. *Add.* 7211, fol. 22 b (dated A.D. 1682), in like manner the 14 Epistles of S. Paul are followed by the Revelation, and the Revelation by the 'Two Epistles of Clement, and they are one book.' After this comes the clause about the Apostolic Constitutions, substantially the same as in the Greek Canon. This is an Egyptian MS. In the Carshunic MS, *Add.* 7207, fol. 27 b (A.D. 1730), which is of Syrian origin, the Apocalypse is omitted, so that the Epistles of Clement are mentioned immediately after the 14 Epistles of St Paul. Here again follows

a clause relating to the eight books of the Apostolic Constitutions.

[1] The order of the Catholic Epistles among themselves is the same also in the Greek 85th Canon. It may have been determined either by the relative importance of the Apostles themselves, or by the fact that the Epistles of S. James and S. Jude were accepted as canonical in the church from which the list emanated, at a later date than 1 Peter and 1 John.

[2] The clause about reading aloud seems to refer solely to the Epistles of Clement. At least this restriction is suggested by the connexion, as well as by comparison with a somewhat similar clause relating to Ecclesiasticus which closes the list of the Old Testament writings. But on this point there must remain some uncertainty.

all (ἃς οὐ χρὴ δημοσιεύειν ἐπὶ πάντων), owing to the mystical teaching in them (διὰ τὰ ἐν αὐταῖς μυστικά) ; and the Acts of us the Apostles[1].' Some doubt however may reasonably be entertained whether the words Κλήμεντος ἐπιστολαὶ δύο are not a later interpolation. In the first place, the form is somewhat suspicious. As these Clementine letters range with the Catholic Epistles, we should not expect a repetition of ἐπιστολαί; and, as Clement is the reputed author of the Canons, we should expect ἐμοῦ Κλήμεντος, so that the obvious form would be 'Of me Clement two[2].' On this point however I should not lay any stress, if the external evidence had been satisfactory. But the subsequent history of this Canon tends to increase our suspicions. The Trullan Council (A.D. 692) in its 2nd Canon adopts 'the 85 Canons handed down to us in the name of the holy and glorious Apostles,' adding however this caution; 'But seeing that in these Canons it hath been commanded that we should receive the Constitutions (διατάξεις) of the same holy Apostles, (written) by the hand of Clement, in which certain spurious matter that is alien to godliness hath been interpolated long ago by the heterodox to the injury of the Church, thus obscuring for us the goodly beauty of the divine ordinances, we have suitably rejected such Constitutions, having regard to the edification and safety of the most Christian flock, etc.[3]' Here no mention is made of the Epistles of Clement; and therefore, if the Trullan fathers found them in their copy of the 85th Apostolical Canon, they deliberately adopted them as part of the Canonical Scriptures. The Canons of this Trullan Council were signed by the four great patriarchs of the East. The Council itself was and is regarded by the Eastern Church as a General Council[4].

---

[1] Ueltzen *Const. Apost.* p. 253.

[2] Beveridge (*Synod.* II. ii. p. 40) remarks on the difference between the mention of Clement in the two cases. He argues from it that different persons are meant.

In the Syriac copy, Brit. Mus. *Add.* 14,526 fol. 9a (a MS of the VIIth cent., and probably written soon after A.D. 641; see Wright's *Catalogue* p. 1033) it is 'of me Clement two Epistles.' In another Syriac copy, *Add.* 12,155, fol. 205b (apparently of the VIIIth cent.; *ib.* pp. 921, 949) the scribe has first written 'of me Clement,' and has corrected it 'of him Clement' (ܟܢ altered into ܩܢ). This seems to be a different translation

from the former. The Canon in question is the 81st in the former, the 79th in the latter. A third Syriac MS *Add.* 14,527 (about the XIth cent.; *ib.* p. 1036) follows the last as corrected and reads 'of him Clement.' I owe these facts to the kindness of Prof. Wright, who also investigated the readings of the Æthiopic, Carshunic, and Arabic MSS for me, as given elsewhere in my notes, pp. 274, 278. In the Syriac MS from which Lagarde has published his text (*Rel. Jur. Eccl. Ant. Syr.* 1856 p. ܩ) the form exactly follows the Greek, 'Of Clement two Epistles.'

[3] Bevereg. *Synod.* I. p. 158.

[4] The Trullan or Quinisextine Council

From this time forward therefore the Epistles of Clement would become an authoritative part of the New Testament for the Christians of the East. How comes it then, that not a single MS of the Greek Testament among many hundreds written after this date includes them in the sacred volume? But this is not all. About the middle of the eighth century John of Damascus gives a list of the New Testament Scriptures (*de Fid. Orthod.* iv. 17, *Op.* I. p. 284, Lequien). It ends: 'Of ·Paul the Apostle fourteen Epistles; the Apocalypse of John the Evangelist; the Canons of the Holy Apostles by the hand of Clement' (κανόνες τῶν ἁγίων ἀποστόλων διὰ Κλήμεντος). Here is no mention of Clement's Epistles. But one MS, Reg. 2428, which exhibits interpolations elsewhere, inserts a mention of them, reading the last sentence κανόνες τῶν ἁγίων ἀποστόλων καὶ ἐπιστολαὶ δύο διὰ Κλήμεντος, where the very form of the expression betrays the insertion. This interpolation is significant; for it shows that there was a disposition in some quarters to introduce these epistles into the Canon, and that ancient documents were tampered with accordingly[1]. Again, in the Stichometria attached to the *Chronographia* of Nicephorus, patriarch of Constantinople (†A.D. 828), though itself perhaps of an older date, the Epistles of Clement are not placed among the undoubted scriptures, nor even among the disputed books of the Canon, among which the Epistle of Barnabas and the Gospel of the Hebrews have a place, but are thrown into the Apocrypha[2]. Again, a little later we have the testimony of another patriarch of Constantinople, the great Photius, who died towards the close of the ninth century. In his edition of the *Nomocanon*[3] (Tit. iii. cap. ii, *Op.* IV. p. 1049 sq., ed. Migne) he mentions the 85th Apostolical Canon as an authority on the subject of which it treats. Yet elsewhere he not only betrays no suspicion that these Clementine Epistles are canonical, but speaks in a manner quite inexplicable on this hypothesis. In one passage

was commonly called the 'Sixth' Council by the Greeks, being regarded as a supplement to that Council; Hefele *Conciliengeschichte* III. p. 299. The 7th General Council (the Second of Nicæa, A.D. 787) adopted both the Apostolical Canons themselves and the Canons of the Trullan Council as a whole (see Hefele *ib.* p. 443); and thus they were doubly confirmed as the law of the Greek Church.

[1] Harnack (*Præf.* xli, ed. 2) seems disposed to accept καὶ ἐπιστολαὶ δύο as

part of the genuine text, though he speaks hesitatingly. But seeing that this MS stands alone and that it is, as Lequien says, 'interpolatus varie' in other parts, the spuriousness of these words can hardly be considered doubtful.

[2] Westcott *Canon* p. 552 sq. (ed. 4), Credner *Zur Gesch. des Kanons* p. 97 sq.

[3] On the relation of the *Nomocanon* of Photius to earlier works of the same name, see Hergenröther *Photius* III. p. 92 sq.

of his *Bibliotheca* (Cod. 113) he incidentally repeats the statement of Eusebius (without however mentioning his name), that the First Epistle was at one time 'considered worthy of acceptance among many, so as even to be read in public' (παρὰ πολλοῖς ἀποδοχῆς ἠξιώθη ὡς καὶ δημοσίᾳ ἀναγινώσκεσθαι), whereas 'the so-called Second Epistle is rejected as spurious' (ὡς νόθος ἀποδοκιμάζεται). In another (Cod. 126) he records reading the two epistles, apparently for the first time; he treats them exactly in the same way as the other books of which he gives an account; he criticizes them freely; he censures the First, not only for its faulty cosmography, but also for its defective statements respecting the Person of Christ; he complains of the Second, that the thoughts are tumbled together without any continuity; and he blames both in different degrees for quoting apocryphal sayings 'as if from the Divine Scripture.' Moreover, his copy of these Clementine Epistles was not attached to the New Testament, but (as he himself tells us), was bound up in a little volume with the Epistle of Polycarp[1].

For these reasons it may be questioned whether the Clementine Epistles were included in the Greek catalogue of the 85th Apostolic Canon, as ratified by the Trullan Council[2], though they are found in

[1] It is true that the procedure of the Trullan Council in this respect was very loose. It confirmed at the same time the Canons of the Councils of Laodicea and Carthage, though the Canons of Carthage contained a list of the Canonical books not identical with the list in the Apostolical Canons, and this may also have been the case with the Laodicean Canons (see Westcott *Canon* p. 434, ed. 4). But these Canons were confirmed *en bloc* along with those of other Councils and individual Fathers; and no indication is given that their catalogues of scriptural books came under review. On the other hand not only are the Apostolical Canons placed in the forefront and stamped with a very emphatic approval, but their list of scriptural books is made the subject of a special comment, so that its contents could not have been overlooked. The difficulty however is not so much that the Trullan Council should

have adopted these Clementine Epistles into their Canon carelessly, as that (if they had done this) the fact should have been ignored for several centuries.

[2] This inference will seem the more probable, when it is remembered that the list of the New Testament writings in the 85th Apostolical Canon occurs in several other forms, in which the Clementine Epistles are differently dealt with.

(i) The Egyptian form has been given already (p. 273). Here the Apocalypse is inserted, and the two Clementine Epistles are thrown to the end. No mention is made of the Apostolic Constitutions.

(ii) Harnack (Præf. p. xlii, ed. 2) has given another form of this Greek list which was copied by Gebhardt from a Moscow MS of the 15th century, Bibl. S. Synod. cxlix, fol. 160 b, where the New Testament writings are enumerated as follows; τῆς δὲ καινῆς διαθήκης βιβλία δ'. ἐπιστολαὶ Πέτρου β'. Ἰωάννου τρεῖς. Ἰακώ.

Syriac copies of an earlier date. But in the 12th century the case is different. At this date, and afterwards, the Greek canonists no longer pass them over in silence. Alexius Aristenus, œconomus of the Great Church at Constantinople (c. A. D. 1160), repeats this list of the 85th Canon, expressly naming 'the two Epistles of Clement,' and mentioning the rejection of the Constitutions by the Trullan Council (*Bevereg. Synod.* I. p. 53); and more than a century and a half later, Matthæus Blastaris (c. A. D. 1335, *Syntagma* B. 11) interprets the second Trullan Canon as including the Clementine Epistles in the same condemnation with the Constitutions[1]. This is certainly not the case; but it shows to what straits a writer was driven, when he felt obliged to account for the conflict between the current text of the 85th Apostolical Canon and the universal practice of his Church.

It will thus be seen that the only author who distinctly accepts the two Clementine Epistles as canonical is Alexius Aristenus. His

---

βου Ἰούδα μία. Κλήμεντος α'. Παύλου ἐπιστολαὶ ιδ'. The context shows decisively that this Moscow list is taken from the 85th Apostolical Canon. The word εὐαγγελία seems to have been left out after βιβλία by homœoteleuton; and Acts is perhaps omitted from carelessness owing to its position at the end of the list in the Canon itself. The omission of the Second Clementine Epistle is the remarkable feature here.

(iii) The three *Æthiopic* MSS, Brit. Mus. *Orient.* 481 (XVIIth cent.), *Orient.* 796 (about A. D. 1740), *Orient.* 793 (about the same date as the last), after the Apocalypse, name the eight books of the Ordinances of Clement (i. e. the Apostolic Constitutions) and do not mention the Epistles of Clement at all. On the other hand the Æthiopic text of the Canons as printed by W. Fell (*Canones Apostolorum Æthiopice* p. 46, Lips. 1871) repeats the list as it stands in the Coptic (see above, p. 273), ending 'Abukalamsis, i. e. visio Ioannis, duæ Epistolæ Clementis'; and the Æthiopic MS Brit. Mus. *Orient.* 794 (XVth cent.) ends similarly, though the number of Clement's Epistles is not mentioned. Again the independent

list in the MS *Add.* 16,205, (described by Dillmann *Catal. Cod. Æthiop. Brit. Mus.* p. 40), has them, but in a different position, ending '...Epistola Iudæ, Clementis Epistolæ 2, Apocalypsis, Pauli 14.' In other independent lists, *Add.* 16,188 (described by Dillmann l. c. p. 4) and *Orient.* 829, the Epistles of Clement are omitted. On the Æthiopic recensions of the *Apostolic Canons*, and on different Æthiopic lists of the Biblical books, see Dillmann in Ewald's *Jahrbücher*, 1852, p. 144 sq.

An account of Arabic and Carshunic MSS is given above, p. 274.

Generally it may be said that this Canon is altered freely so as to adapt it to the usage of particular Churches. Still the normal Greek form is the best supported, as being confirmed by the Syriac MSS, which are the most ancient of all.

[1] Bevereg. *Synod.* II. ii. p. 56 αἱ δὲ προστίθησι διὰ τοῦ Κλήμεντος δύο ἐπιστολὰς καὶ τὰς ποιηθείσας τούτῳ διατάξεις τῶν ἀποστόλων ὕστερον ὁ τῆς συνόδου δεύτερος κανὼν διέγραψεν, ὡς πολὺ τὸ νόθον πρὸς τὴν αἱρετικὴν καὶ παρέγγραπτον δεξαμένας.

work was written within a few years of the date of our MS (A. D. 1170), and its authority stood very high. It would perhaps be over bold to assume that the influence of Aristenus was felt in a Syrian monastery at Edessa; but at all events the coincidence of date is striking, and seems to show a tendency to the undue exaltation of these Clementine Epistles in the latter half of the twelfth century. . There is no reason however for thinking that our MS represents more than the practice of a very restricted locality, or perhaps of a single monastery. Several other Syriac MSS, either of the Gospels or of Evangelistaries, are in existence, dating not many years before or after this, and written (in some instances) on this same Mountain of Edessa[1]; and if on examination of these it should be found, as seems not unlikely, that the table of lessons in our MS is unique, the fact will not be unimportant in its bearing on the canonicity here ascribed to the Clementine Epistles.

[1] At least in one instance, the Paris MS described by Adler (*Nov. Test. Vers. Syr.* p. 58), of which the date is A. D. 1212 and the place 'Cœnobium Deiparæ, cui cognomen est Hospitium, in monte sancto Edessæ.'

THE NEWLY RECOVERED PORTION

OF

THE EPISTLE OF S. CLEMENT

TO THE

CORINTHIANS.

ALL deviations from the text of C are recorded in the notes, except a few differences of accent and punctuation which are unimportant. The ν ἐφελκυστικὸν however is uniformly inserted, though wanting in C; see above, p. 226.

For the rule which has been observed in recording or omitting to record the deviations of S, see above, p. 240.

ἀνθ᾽ ὧν γὰρ Ηδίκογν νηπίογς, φονεγθήςονται, καὶ
ἐξεταςμὸς ἀςεβεῖς ὀλεῖ· ὁ δὲ ἐμοῦ ἀκούων καταςκηνώςει
ἐπ᾽ ἐλπίδι πεποιθώς, καὶ Ηςγχάςει ἀφόβως ἀπὸ παντὸς κακοῦ.

LVIII. Ὑπακούσωμεν οὖν τῷ παναγίῳ καὶ ἐνδόξῳ
5 ὀνόματι αὐτοῦ, φυγόντες τὰς προειρημένας διὰ τῆς
σοφίας τοῖς ἀπειθοῦσιν ἀπειλάς, ἵνα κατασκηνώσωμεν

2 ἐξετασμὸς ἀσεβῶς ὀλεῖ] *inquisitio impiorum perdit ipsos* S.   3 πεποιθώς]
confidens S, using the same expression which occurs just below (§ 58) as the rendering of πεποιθότες: om. C.   See the lower note.   4 παναγίῳ] S translates as if
ἁγίῳ. In § 35 πανάγιος is fully rendered.   5 φυγόντες] φεύγοντες (?) S.

1. ἀνθ᾽ ὧν κ.τ.λ.] The continuation
of the quotation Prov. i. 32, 33, from
the LXX. See above, p. 167.

2. ἐξετασμός] 'enquiry', 'investigation', i. e. 'trial and judgment',
as in Wisd. iv. 6.   The Hebrew
however is שַׁלְוַת 'security', i. e.
'false confidence'; which the LXX
translators seem either to have misread or to have connected with שָׁאַל
'to ask, enquire'. In the' earlier
part of the verse the LXX departs
widely from the Hebrew.

3. πεποιθώς] This word does not
occur in the great MSS of the LXX
(ℵAB); nor indeed, so far as I know,
is the reading κατασκηνώσει ἐπ᾽ (v. l.
ἐν) ἐλπίδι πεποιθώς found in any MS
of this version, though ἀναπαύσεται
ἐν εἰρήνῃ πεποιθώς appears in place of
it in no. 248 (Holmes and Parsons),
this last being a Hexaplaric reading
(see Field's *Hexapla*, ad loc.). Clem.
Alex. however clearly so quotes it,
Strom. ii. 22 (p. 501 sq.) ἡ πανάρετος
Σοφία λέγει· Ὁ δὲ ἐμοῦ ἀκούων κατασκηνώσει ἐπ᾽ ἐλπίδι πεποιθώς· ἡ γὰρ τῆς
ἐλπίδος ἀποκατάστασις ὁμωνύμως ἐλπὶς
εἴρηται· διὰ [l. διὸ] τοῦ Κατασκηνώσει
τῇ λέξει παγκάλως προσέθηκε τὸ Πεποιθώς; though elsewhere, *Strom.* ii. 8
(p. 449), iv. 23 (p. 632), he has
ἀναπαύσεται ἐπ᾽ εἰρήνης (-νῃ) πεποιθώς.

It is clear that πεποιθώς is genuine
in the text of our Clement; since he
dwells upon it in the beginning of
the next chapter, κατασκηνώσωμεν
πεποιθότες κ.τ.λ.   For other examples
of this manner of emphasizing the
key-word of a quotation see the
Addenda on p. 144, l. 3. From the
manner in which Clem. Alex. begins
his quotation from Prov. i. 33, it may
perhaps be inferred that the passage
of his elder namesake was in his mind.

LVIII. 'Let us therefore obey,
that we may escape these threatened
judgments, and dwell in safety. Receive our counsel, and you will never
have occasion to regret it. As surely
as God liveth, he that performeth
all His commandments shall have
a place among them that are saved
through Jesus Christ, through whom
is the glory unto Him for ever'.

4. παναγίῳ] So also above, § 35.
See the note in the Addenda to
p. 116, l. 3.

5. τῆς σοφίας] Wisdom is represented as the speaker in the passage of Proverbs just quoted. Moreover this name Σοφία was given to
the whole book; see above, p. 165.

6. κατασκηνώσωμεν] 'dwell in peace'.
As the common LXX rendering of
שָׁכַן, for which purpose it was chosen

πεποιθότες ἐπὶ τὸ ὁσιώτατον τῆς μεγαλωσύνης αὐτοῦ
ὄνομα. δέξασθε τὴν συμβουλὴν ἡμῶν, καὶ ἔσται
ἀμεταμέλητα ὑμῖν. ζῆ γὰρ ὁ Θεὸς καὶ ζῆ ὁ Κύριος
Ἰησοῦς Χριστὸς καὶ τὸ πνεῦμα τὸ ἅγιον, ἥ τε πίστις
καὶ ἡ ἐλπὶς τῶν ἐκλεκτῶν, ὅτι ὁ ποιήσας ἐν ταπει-
νοφροσύνῃ μετ' ἐκτενοῦς ἐπιεικείας ἀμεταμελήτως τὰ
ὑπὸ τοῦ Θεοῦ δεδομένα δικαιώματα καὶ προστάγματα,
οὗτος ἐντεταγμένος καὶ ἐλλόγιμος ἔσται εἰς τὸν ἀριθμὸν

1 ὁσιώτατον] S renders as if ὅσιον, but the translator's practice elsewhere in rendering superlatives is so uncertain, that no inference can be drawn as to the reading. 2 ἡμῶν] add. ἀδελφοί[μου] S. 3 καὶ ζῆ] So too S; Basil omits

doubtless in part owing to the similarity of sound (see the note on μωμοσκοπηθέν, § 41), it implies the idea of 'rest, peace'.

3. ἀμεταμέλητα] A somewhat favourite word of Clement, §§ 2, 54. So ἀμεταμελήτως, below. For the plural see Kühner Gramm. II. p. 59 sq.

ζῆ γὰρ κ.τ.λ.] This passage is quoted by S. Basil, de Spir. Sanct. 29 (III. p. 61): see above, p. 168, where the quotation is given. For the form of adjuration ζῆ ὁ Θεὸς...ὅτι, 'As surely as God liveth...so surely', comp. ζῆ Κύριος ὅτι...which occurs frequently in the LXX, e.g. 1 Sam. xx. 3, xxvi. 16, xxix. 6, 1 Kings xxii. 14, 2 Kings v. 20, etc. So too Rom. xiv. 11 ζῶ ἐγώ, λέγει Κύριος, ὅτι ἐμοὶ κ.τ.λ. (where S. Paul is quoting loosely from Is. xlv. 23, combining it however with the ζῶ ἐγὼ κ.τ.λ. of Is. xlix. 18); comp. 2 Cor. i. 18, and see Fritzsche Rom. II. p. 242 sq., III. p. 187. For a similar reference to the Trinity see above, § 46. Here They are described as 'the faith and hope (i.e. the object of faith and hope) of the elect'; for ἥ τε πίστις κ.τ.λ. are obviously in apposition to

the preceding words. For ἐλπίς, meaning 'the object of hope', see the note on Ign. Magn. 11 Ἰησοῦ Χριστοῦ τῆς ἐλπίδος ἡμῶν; comp. 1 Tim. i. 1. On the other hand the sense of πίστις is different in Ign. Smyrn 10 ἡ τελεία πίστις, Ἰησοῦς Χριστός (see the note there).

5. τῶν ἐκλεκτῶν] A favourite word with Clement, §§ 1, 2, 6, 46, 49, 52, 59.

6. μετ' ἐκτενοῦς ἐπιεικείας] The phrase occurs again below, § 62. It is a sort of oxymoron, or verbal paradox, like 'strenua inertia', 'lene tormentum'; for ἐπιείκεια involves the idea of 'concession': comp. 1 Thess. iv. 11 φιλοτιμεῖσθαι ἡσυχάζειν. So Greg. Naz. Orat. iv. 79 (I. p. 116), speaking of Julian's persecution, says ἐπιεικῶς ἐβιάζετο. The substantive ἐπιείκεια occurs also §§ 13, 30, 56: the adjective ἐπιεικής, 1, 21, 29. The frequency of these words aptly indicates the general spirit of the letter: see the note on § 1.

8. ἐλλόγιμος] used here, as in § 57, for those who have a place among the elect of God: see also § 44, 62. Comp. Plato Phileb. 17 E

τῶν σωζομένων διὰ Ἰησοῦ Χριστοῦ, δι' οὗ ἐστιν αὐτῷ
10 ἡ δόξα εἰς τοὺς αἰῶνας τῶν αἰώνων. ἀμήν.

LIX. Ἐὰν δέ τινες ἀπειθήσωσιν τοῖς ὑπ' αὐτοῦ
δι' ἡμῶν εἰρημένοις, γινωσκέτωσαν ὅτι παραπτώσει καὶ
κινδύνῳ οὐ μικρῷ ἑαυτοὺς ἐνδήσουσιν, ἡμεῖς δὲ ἀθῷοι
ἐσόμεθα ἀπὸ ταύτης τῆς ἁμαρτίας· καὶ αἰτησόμεθα,
15 ἐκτενῆ τὴν δέησιν καὶ ἱκεσίαν ποιούμενοι, ὅπως τὸν
ἀριθμὸν τὸν κατηριθμημένον τῶν ἐκλεκτῶν αὐτοῦ ἐν

this second ῇ.　　　Κύριος] twice in S, at the end of one line and the beginning of
the next.　　　7 καὶ προστάγματα] om. S.

οὐκ ἐλλόγιμον οὐδ' ἐνάριθμον.

τὸν ἀριθμόν] As above §§ 2, 35, and below § 59, with the note.

9. τῶν σωζομένων] 'of those that are in the way of salvation', as Luke xiii. 23, Acts ii. 47, 1 Cor. i. 18, 2 Cor. ii. 15. The opposite is οἱ ἀπολλύμενοι, 1 Cor. i. 18, 2 Cor. ii. 15, iv. 3, 2 Thess. ii. 10. Comp. also Clem. Hom. xv. 10, Apost. Const. viii. 5, 7, 8. In the Apost. Const. viii. 5 the words are τὸν ἀριθμὸν τῶν σωζομένων as here.

LIX. 'If any disobey our counsels, they will incur the greatest peril; while we shall have absolved ourselves from guilt. And we will pray that the Creator may preserve intact the number of His elect through Jesus Christ, who called us from darkness to light. Open our eyes, Lord, that we may know Thee, who alone art Holiest of the holy and Highest of the high; who settest up and bringest low; who bestowest riches and poverty, life and death; who art the God of all spirits and of all flesh; whose eye is all-seeing, and whose power is omnipresent; who multipliest the nations and gatherest together Thine elect in Christ. We beseech thee, Lord, assist the needy, the oppressed, the

feeble. Let all the nations know that Thou art God alone, and Jesus Christ is Thy Son, and we are Thy people, the sheep of Thy pasture'.

11. ὑπ' αὐτοῦ] i. e. τοῦ Θεοῦ. In the same way they again claim to be speaking with the voice of God below, § 63 τοῖς ὑφ' ἡμῶν γεγραμμένοις διὰ τοῦ ἁγίου πνεύματος; comp. § 56 μὴ ἡμῖν ἀλλὰ τῷ θελήματι τοῦ Θεοῦ. See also Ign. Philad. 7 τὸ πνεῦμα οὐ πλανᾶται, ἀπὸ Θεοῦ ὄν... ἐλάλουν......Θεοῦ φωνῇ, where a similar claim is made.

12. παραπτώσει] 'fault', 'transgression': Jer. xxii. 21. Comp. Justin Dial. 141 (p. 371). It does not occur elsewhere in the LXX, nor at all in the N.T., though παράπτωμα is common. Polybius uses it several times; comp. also Sext. Empir. adv. Math. i. 210.

13. ἀθῷοι] As above, § 46. For the whole expression, ἀθῷος εἶναι ἀπὸ ἁμαρτίας, comp. Num. v. 31.

15. τὸν ἀριθμὸν κ.τ.λ.] See Rev. vii. 4 sq. The same phrase τὸν ἀριθμὸν τῶν ἐκλεκτῶν αὐτοῦ has occurred already § 2. In one of the prayers in the last book of the Apostolic Constitutions (viii. 22) we have ὁ τὴν τοῦ κόσμου σύστασιν διὰ τῶν ἐνεργουμένων φανεροποιήσας καὶ τὸν ἀριθμὸν

CLEM.　　　　　　　　　　　　　　　19

ὅλῳ τῷ κόσμῳ διαφυλάξῃ ἄθραυστον ὁ δημιουργὸς
τῶν ἁπάντων διὰ τοῦ ἠγαπημένου παιδὸς αὐτοῦ Ἰησοῦ
Χριστοῦ, δι' οὗ ἐκάλεσεν ἡμᾶς ἀπὸ σκότους εἰς φῶς,
ἀπὸ ἀγνωσίας εἰς ἐπίγνωσιν δόξης ὀνόματος αὐτοῦ.

1 ἄθραυστον] add. *Deus* S.   3 Χριστοῦ] add. *Domini nostri* S.   ἡμᾶς]
me S ; but this is doubtless a clerical error in transcribing the Syriac suffix.   5 Δὸς

τῶν ἐκλεκτῶν σου διαφυλάττων, where
the expression here is combined with
another which occurs below (§ 60);
thus clearly showing that the writer
borrows directly or indirectly from
Clement.

1. ἄθραυστον] The word does not
occur in the LXX or N. T. It is
however not uncommon in classical
writers: e.g. Dion Cass. liii. 24
ἄθραυστον καὶ ὁλόκληρον τῷ διαδόχῳ
τὴν πόλιν παρέδωκεν, which passage
illustrates its sense here. Comp.
Apost. Const. viii. 12 διαφυλάξῃς
ἀσείστον.

ὁ δημιουργὸς κ.τ.λ.] The same phrase
occurs above § 26; comp. § 33. For
δημιουργὸς see the note on § 20.

2. τοῦ ἠγαπημένου παιδὸς κ.τ.λ.] So
again lower down in this chapter,
διὰ Ἰησοῦ Χριστοῦ τοῦ ἠγαπημένου
παιδός σου, and Ἰησοῦς Χριστὸς ὁ παῖς
σου. It is worth observing in connexion with the other coincidences,
that these expressions ὁ ἠγαπημένος
(ἀγαπητὸς) παῖς σου, ὁ παῖς σου, occur
several times in the prayers in the
Apost. Const. viii. 5; 14, 39, 40, 41.
Comp. also *Epist. ad Diogn.* 8,
and *Mart. Polyc.* 14, where it is
twice put into the mouth of Polycarp, who was certainly a reader of
Clement's Epistle. This designation is taken originally from Is. xlii. 1,
quoted in Matt. xii. 18 ἰδού, ὁ παῖς
μου ὃν ᾑρέτισα, ὁ ἀγαπητός μου [εἰς]
ὃν εὐδόκησεν ἡ ψυχή μου; where παῖς
is 'servant, minister' (עֶבֶד). Comp.
Acts iii. 13, 26, iv. 27, 30. But the
higher sense of υἱὸς was soon im-

ported into the ambiguous word παῖς :
e.g. *Apost. Const.* viii. 40 τοῦ μονογενοῦς σου παιδὸς Ἰησοῦ Χριστοῦ, *Epist.
ad Diogn.* 8, Iren. iii. 12. 5, 6, etc. ;
and probably *Mart. Polyc.* 14 ὁ τοῦ
ἀγαπητοῦ παιδός σου Ἰησοῦ Χριστοῦ
πατήρ. And so Clement seems to
have used the word here.

3. ἐκάλεσεν κ.τ.λ.] From 1 Pet.
ii. 9 τοῦ ἐκ σκότους ὑμᾶς καλέσαντος εἰς
τὸ θαυμαστὸν αὐτοῦ φῶς. The epithet
θαυμαστὸν which is wanting here is
supplied by § 36 (as read in the
Greek MSS) ἀναθάλλει εἰς τὸ θαυμαστὸν [αὐτοῦ] φῶς, where however
the epithet is omitted in the Syriac
and in Clem. Alex.

4. ἀγνωσίας] ' *stubborn ignorance*',
a stronger word than ἀγνοίας : comp.
1 Pet. ii. 15. It occurs also Job
xxxv. 16, Wisd. xiii. 1, 1 Cor. xv. 34.
See also *Clem. Hom.* ii. 6, iii. 47,
iv. 8, xviii. 13, 18.

εἰς ἐπίγνωσιν δόξης] Comp. *Apost.
Const.* viii. 11 ὁ διὰ Χριστοῦ κήρυγμα
γνώσεως δοὺς ἡμῖν εἰς ἐπίγνωσιν τῆς
σῆς δόξης καὶ τοῦ ὀνόματός σου.
The language of Clement here seems
to be inspired by Ephes. i. 5 sq.

5. ἐλπίζειν] Some words have been
omitted in the Greek MS, as the first
editor has correctly seen. The words
supplied in the text, Δὸς ἡμῖν, Κύριε,
will suffice. The same omission
existed also in the text from which
the Syriac Version was made. In
consequence of this, σου, σε, σε, σου,
ἐπαίδευσας, ἡγίασας, ἐτίμησας, are there
altered to avoid the abrupt transition
from the third person to the second ;

5   [Δὸς ἡμῖν, Κύριε], ἐλπίζειν ἐπὶ τὸ ἀρχεγόνον πάσης
κτίσεως ὄνομά σου, ἀνοίξας τοὺς ὀφθαλμοὺς τῆς καρδίας
ἡμῶν εἰς τὸ γινώσκειν σε, τὸν μόνον ΫΨΙϹΤΟΝ ἐΝ ΫΨΗΛΟΙϹ
ἅΓΙΟΝ ἐΝ ἁΓΙΟΙϹ ἀΝΑΠΑΥΌΜΕΝΟΝ, ΤῸΝ ΤΑΠΕΙΝΟῦΝΤΑ ῦΒΡΙΝ

ἡμῖν, Κύριε] om. C S; see below.   6 ὄνομά σου] nomen ejus sanctum S; see below.
καρδίας] cordium S.   7 σε] eum S.   ὑψηλοῖς] ὑψίστοις C; see the lower note.

and at length words are inserted
before Ἀξιοῦμεν to introduce the
second person. On the recurrence
of lacunæ in our authorities see
above, p. 248. Hilgenfeld gets over
the difficulty in part by substituting
ἄνοιξον for ἀνοίξας: while Gebhardt
and Harnack deny that the text is
either defective or corrupt, and attempt to justify the transition by
such passages as Acts i. 4, xxiii. 22,
etc. (see Winer § lxiii. p. 725). But
the phenomena of our two authorities
show that Bryennios was right.

ἀρχεγόνον] i.e. 'Thy Name which
was the first *origin* of all creation', πάσης κτίσεως being governed
by ἀρχεγόνον. As an active sense
is obviously wanted, it must be
accented ἀρχεγόνον, not ἀρχέγονον,
as by Bryennios: comp. [Aristot.]
de Mund. 6 (p. 399 Bekker) διὰ
τὴν πρώτην καὶ ἀρχαιόγονον αἰτίαν,
where again we should accentuate
ἀρχαιογόνον, for the expression is
synonymous with ὁ πάντων ἡγεμών
τε καὶ γενετώρ which follows immediately after. So too perhaps even
in Clem. Alex. *Strom.* vi. 16 (p. 810)
τὸν ἀρχεγόνον ἡμέραν, for just below
it is defined as πρώτην τῷ ὄντι φωτὸς
γένεσιν: but in Clem. Alex. *Protr.*
5 (p. 56) τὸ πῦρ ὡς ἀρχέγονον σέβοντες
it may be doubtful whether the fire
is regarded as a *principium prin-
cipians* (ἀρχεγόνον), or a *principium
principiatum* (ἀρχέγονον). In Greg.
Naz. *Op.* I. p. 694 we have τὸ
ἀρχέγονον σκότος. The word occurs
also Iren. i. 1. 1 (twice), 1. 5. 2, 1.

9. 3, in the exposition of the Valentinian system, where likewise the
accentuation may be doubtful. It
is not found in the LXX or N. T.
Editors seem universally to accentuate it ἀρχέγονος (see Chandler's
Greek Accentuation § 467); but, I
think, on insufficient grounds.

6. τοὺς ὀφθαλμοὺς κ.τ.λ.] suggested
by Ephes. i. 17 sq. ἐν ἐπιγνώσει αὐτοῦ, πεφωτισμένους τοὺς ὀφθαλμοὺς
τῆς καρδίας ὑμῶν εἰς τὸ εἰδέναι ὑμᾶς
κ.τ.λ. See also above § 36 ἠνεώχθη-
σαν ἡμῶν οἱ ὀφθαλμοὶ τῆς καρδίας.
Comp. *Mart. Polyc.* 2.

7. γινώσκειν κ.τ.λ.] Comp. John
xvii. 3 ἵνα γινώσκωσίν σε τὸν μόνον
ἀληθινὸν Θεόν.

ὕψιστον κ.τ.λ.] From the LXX Is.
lvii. 15 ὁ ὕψιστος ὁ ἐν ὑψηλοῖς κατ-
οικῶν τὸν αἰῶνα, ἅγιος ἐν ἁγίοις
ὄνομα αὐτῷ, ὕψιστος ἐν ἁγίοις ἀναπαυόμενος. So in the prayer *Apost.
Const.* viii. 11 ὕψιστε ἐν ὑψηλοῖς, ἅγιε
ἐν ἁγίοις ἀναπαυόμενε, doubtless taken
from Clement. Similarly the expression ὁ ἐν ἁγίοις ἀναπαυόμενος in
other liturgies, *D. Marc.* pp. 13, 27,
D. Jacob. p. 70 (comp. p. 44), *S.
Chrysost.* p. 118 (ed. Neale).

I have substituted ὑψηλοῖς, as the
reading both of the LXX and of the
Apost. Const. Moreover the Syriac
here translates by the same words,
מרימא במדומא, which render ὕψιστος,
ἐν ὑψηλοῖς, in the Hexaplaric Version
of Is. lvii. 15: thus using two different words. This however is not decisive in itself.

8. τὸν ταπεινοῦντα κ.τ.λ.] From

ὑπερηφάνων, τὸν διαλύοντα λογισμοὺς ἐθνῶν, τὸν ποιοῦντα ταπεινοὺς εἰς ὕψος καὶ τοὺς ὑψηλοὺς ταπεινοῦντα, τὸν πλουτίζοντα καὶ πτωχίζοντα, τὸν ἀποκτείνοντα καὶ ζῆν ποιοῦντα, μόνον εὐεργέτην πνευμάτων καὶ Θεὸν πάσης σαρκός, τὸν ἐπιβλέποντα ἐν ταῖς ἀβύσσοις, τὸν 5 ἐπόπτην ἀνθρωπίνων ἔργων, τὸν τῶν κινδυνευόντων βοηθόν, τὸν τῶν ἀπηλπισμένων cωτῆρα, τὸν παντὸς πνεύματος κτίστην καὶ ἐπίσκοπον, τὸν πληθύνοντα

1 ἐθνῶν] ἀνθρώπων(=ἀν͞ω͞ν) S.   4 ζῆν ποιοῦντα] redimit et vivificat S. εὐεργέτην] εὑρετὴν S.   6 τῶν κινδυνευόντων] illorum qui affliguntur S, but it is probably a loose paraphrase.   10 σε] cum S.   11 σου] ejus S. ἡμᾶς ἐπαίδευσας, ἡγίασας, ἐτίμησας] instruxit nos et sanctificavit nos et honoravit nos S. Ἀξιοῦμεν

Is. xiii. 11 ὕβριν ὑπερηφάνων ταπεινώσω.

1. τὸν διαλύοντα] Probably from Ps. xxxii. 10 διασκεδάζει βουλὰς ἐθνῶν, ἀθετεῖ δὲ λογισμοὺς λαῶν.

2. τὸν ποιοῦντα κ.τ.λ.] Job v. 11 τὸν ποιοῦντα ταπεινοὺς εἰς ὕψος καὶ ἀπολωλότας ἐξεγείροντα, Is. x. 33 ταπεινωθήσονται οἱ ὑψηλοί, Ezek. xxi. 26 ἐταπείνωσας τὸ ὑψηλὸν καὶ ὕψωσας τὸ ταπεινόν, ib. xvii. 24 ἐγὼ Κύριος ὁ ταπεινῶν ξύλον ὑψηλὸν καὶ ὑψῶν ξύλον ταπεινόν. See also Matt. xxiii. 12, Luke xiv. 11, xviii. 14.

3. τὸν πλουτίζοντα κ.τ.λ.] From 1 Sam. ii. 7 Κύριος πτωχίζει καὶ πλουτίζει, ταπεινοῖ καὶ ἀνυψοῖ. Comp. also Luke i. 53.

τὸν ἀποκτείνοντα κ.τ.λ.] Deut. xxxii. 39 ἐγὼ ἀποκτενῶ καὶ ζῆν ποιήσω, 1 Sam. ii. 6 Κύριος θανατοῖ καὶ ζωογονεῖ: comp. 2 Kings v. 7 ὁ Θεὸς ἐγὼ τοῦ θανατῶσαι καὶ ζωοποιῆσαι;

4. εὐεργέτην] Comp. Ps. cxv. 7 ἐπίστρεψον, ψυχή μου...ὅτι Κύριος εὐηργέτησέ σε. So too Liturg. D. Marc. p. 25 ψυχῆς εὐεργέτα.

πνευμάτων κ.τ.λ.] Modified from Num. xvi. 22, xxvii. 16. See also § 62 (58) δεσπότης τῶν πνευμάτων καὶ

κύριος πάσης σαρκός, with the parallels in the note (p. 169). Comp. Liturg. D. Jacob. p. 65 μνήσθητι, Κύριε, ὁ Θεὸς τῶν πνευμάτων καὶ πάσης σαρκός.

5. τὸν ἐπιβλέποντα κ.τ.λ.] Ecclus. xvi. 18, 19, ἄβυσσος καὶ γῆ σαλευθήσονται ἐν τῇ ἐπισκοπῇ αὐτοῦ, ἅμα τὰ ὄρη καὶ τὰ θεμέλια τῆς γῆς ἐν τῷ ἐπιβλέψαι εἰς αὐτὰ τρόμῳ συσσείονται. Comp. Liturg. S. Basil. p. 156 ὁ καθήμενος ἐπὶ θρόνου δόξης καὶ ἐπιβλέπων ἀβύσσους. For the unusual ἐπιβλέπειν ἐν, 'to look into', or 'at', comp. Eccles. ii. 11, 2 Chron. xvi. 9.

τὸν ἐπόπτην κ.τ.λ.] See Ps. xxxii (xxxiii). 13, which passage Clement may perhaps have had in mind, as he has already adopted an earlier verse of the same Psalm in this context. For ἐπόπτης comp. 2 Macc. vii. 35 τοῦ παντοκράτορος ἐπόπτου Θεοῦ, Esther v. 1 τὸν πάντων ἐπόπτην Θεόν.

6. τὸν τῶν κινδυνευόντων κ.τ.λ.] Judith ix. 11 ἐλαττόνων εἶ βοηθός, ἀντιλήπτωρ ἀσθενούντων, ἀπεγνωσμένων σκεπαστής, ἀπηλπισμένων σωτήρ. For ἀπηλπισμένοι comp. Is. xxix. 19, Esth. iv. ad fin. See also Liturg.

ἔθνη ἐπὶ γῆς καὶ ἐκ πάντων ἐκλεξάμενον τοὺς ἀγα-
10 πῶντάς σε διὰ Ἰησοῦ Χριστοῦ τοῦ ἠγαπημένου παιδός
σου, δι᾽ οὗ ἡμᾶς ἐπαίδευσας, ἡγίασας, ἐτίμησας. Ἀξιοῦμέν σε, δέσποτα, ΒΟΗΘΟΝ γενέσθαι κα`ι ἀντιλήπτορα
ἡμῶν. τοὺς ἐν θλίψει ἡμῶν σῶσον· τοὺς ταπεινοὺς
ἐλέησον· τοὺς πεπτωκότας ἔγειρον· τοῖς δεομένοις
15 ἐπιφάνηθι· τοὺς ἀσεβεῖς ἴασαι· τοὺς πλανωμένους τοῦ
λαοῦ σου ἐπίστρεψον· χόρτασον τοὺς πεινῶντας· λύ-

κ.τ.λ.] S prefixes *et dicemus illi cum supplicatione.* 12 σε] so apparently S; om. C.
It seems to be required, as Hilg. and Gebh. have seen. δέσποτα] *Domine bone* S.
13 τοὺς ταπεινοὺς ἐλέησον] om. S, owing to the homœoteleuton. 15 ἐπιφάνηθι]
ἐπιστράφηθι S. ἀσεβεῖς] *aegrotos* (ἀσθενεῖς or νοσοῦντας?) S; see the lower note.

D. *Marc.* p. 17 ἡ ἐλπὶς τῶν ἀπηλπισμένων (comp. *Liturg. S. Basil.*
p. 166), *Act. S. Theodot.* § 21 (in Rui-
nart) 'Domine Jesu Christe, spes
desperatorum'.

8. πνεύματος κτίστην] Zech. xii. 1
Κύριος...πλάσσων πνεῦμα ἀνθρώπου ἐν
αὐτῷ, Is. lvii. 16 πνεῦμα παρ᾽ ἐμοῦ
ἐξελεύσεται, καὶ πνοὴν πᾶσαν ἐγὼ
ἐποίησα. In Amos iv. 13 we have ἐγὼ
...κτίζων πνεῦμα, where it apparently
means 'the wind,' but might easily
be understood otherwise.

ἐπίσκοπον] Job x. 12 ἡ δὲ ἐπισκοπή
σου ἐφύλαξέ μου τὸ πνεῦμα, 1 Pet. ii.
25 τὸν ποιμένα καὶ ἐπίσκοπον τῶν
ψυχῶν ὑμῶν, Wisd. i. 6 ὁ Θεὸς...τῆς
καρδίας αὐτοῦ ἐπίσκοπος ἀληθής. Comp.
Liturg. D. Marc. p. 17 ἐπίσκοπε
πάσης σαρκός.

11. Ἀξιοῦμεν κ.τ.λ.] See the prayer
in the *Apost. Const.* viii. 12 ἔτι
ἀξιοῦμέν σε...ὅπως πάντων ἐπίκουρος
γένῃ, πάντων βοηθὸς καὶ ἀντιλήπτωρ
(with the context), which is evidently
indebted to this passage of Clement.
Comp. Ps. cxviii (cxix). 114 βοηθός
μου καὶ ἀντιλήπτωρ μου εἶ σύ.

13. τοὺς ἐν θλίψει κ.τ.λ.] Compare

the prayer in *Liturg. D. Marc.* p. 21
λύτρωσαι δεσμίους, ἐξελοῦ τοὺς
ἐν ἀνάγκαις, πεινῶντας χόρτασον,
ὀλιγοψυχοῦντας παρακάλεσον,
πεπλανημένους ἐπίστρεψον, ἐσκο-
τισμένους φωταγώγησον, πεπτωκότας
ἔγειρον, σαλευομένους στήριξον, νε-
νοσηκότας ἴασαι......φρουρὸς ἡμῶν
καὶ ἀντιλήπτωρ κατὰ πάντα γενόμενος, where the coincidences are
far too numerous and close to be
accidental.

15. ἀσεβεῖς] Comp. § 3 ζῆλον ἄδικον
καὶ ἀσεβῆ ἀνειληφότας. The reference
in ἀσεβεῖς is not to unbelievers, but
to factious and unworthy members of
the Church. For this word Gebhardt (*Zeitschr. f. Kirchengesch.* p.
307, and ad loc.) conjectures ἀσθενεῖς;
and this may have been the reading
of S. But the occurrence of τοὺς
ἀσθενοῦντας just below is a serious
difficulty, and on this account I have
hesitated about accepting it. It is
not sufficient to answer with Harnack,
'ἀσθενοῦντες animo, ἀσθενεῖς corpore
imbecilles sunt'; for both words are
used indifferently either of physical
or of moral weakness. Supposing

τρῶσαι τοὺς δεσμίους ἡμῶν· ἐξανάστησον τοὺς ἀσθε-
νοῦντας· παρακάλεσον τοὺς ὀλιγοψυχοῦντας· ΓΝώτω-
CAN ἅπαντα τὰ ἔθΝΗ, ὅτι Cύ εἶ ὁ Θεὸc μόΝΟc, καὶ
Ἰησοῦς Χριστὸς ὁ παῖς σου, καὶ Ημεῖς λαόc coy καὶ
πρόΒατα τῆc ΝΟΜῆc coy.   5

LX Cὺ τὴν ἀέναον τοῦ κόσμου σύστασιν διὰ
τῶν ἐνεργουμένων ἐφανεροποίησας· σύ, Κύριε, τὴν
οἰκουμένην ἔκτισας, ὁ πιστὸς ἐν πάσαις ταῖς γενεαῖς,

4 ὁ παῖς σου] add. *dilectus* (ὁ ἠγατημένος) S.   6 Σὺ] add. γὰρ S.   ἀέναον]
ἀένναον C; comp. § 20, where C writes the word in the same way.   τοῦ κόσμου] add
kujus S, as in other passages.   10 ὁ σοφὸς] σοφὸς (om. ὁ) S.   καὶ] om. S.

that ἀσεβεῖς were the original reading, the rendering of S may represent either ἀσθενεῖς (a corruption
of ἀσεβεῖς) or νενοσηκόται (a substitution of a familiar liturgical form, as
appears from *Lit. D. Marc.* p. 21,
quoted above). The Syriac word
here, ܒܝܫܐ, is the same as in the
Peshito Luke ix. 2 ἰᾶσαι τοὺς ἀσθενεῖς (v. l. ἀσθενοῦντας). Comp. Polyc.
Phil. 6 ἐπιστρέφοντες τὰ ἀποπεπλανη-
μένα, ἐπισκεπτόμενοι τοὺς ἀσθενεῖς,
which, so far as it goes, is in favour
of Gebhardt's emendation.
τοὺς πλανωμένους κ.τ.λ.] Ezek. xxxiv.
16 τὸ πεπλανημένον ἐπιστρέψω (where
B has τὸ πλανώμενον ἀποστρέψω).
    1. λύτρωσαι τοὺς δεσμίους] The
reference in this and the neighbour-
ing clauses is doubtless to the victims of the persecution under Domitian; see the note on § 1. The care
of the 'prisoners' naturally occupied
a large space in the attention of
the early Church in the ages of
persecution: comp. Heb. x. 34, xiii. 3,
and see the note on Ign. *Smyrn.* 6.
A prayer for those working 'in the
mines' is found generally in the
early liturgies; comp. *Apost. Const.*
viii. 10 ὑπὲρ τῶν ἐν μετάλλοις καὶ
ἐξορίαις καὶ φυλακαῖς καὶ δεσμοῖς ὄντων

διὰ τὸ ὄνομα τοῦ Κυρίου δεηθῶμεν,
Liturg. D. Marc. p. 17 τοὺς ἐν φυλακαῖς ἢ ἐν μετάλλοις...κατεχομένους πάντας ἐλέησον, πάντας ἐλευθέρωσον, *Lit.
D. Jac.* p. 63 μνήσθητι, Κύριε......
Χριστιανῶν τῶν ἐν δεσμοῖς, τῶν ἐν
φυλακαῖς, τῶν ἐν αἰχμαλωσίαις καὶ
ἐξορίαις, τῶν ἐν μετάλλοις καὶ βασάνοις
καὶ πικραῖς δουλείαις ὄντων πατέρων
καὶ ἀδελφῶν ἡμῶν.
ἐξανάστησον κ.τ.λ.] Comp. 1 Thess.
v. 14 παραμυθεῖσθε τοὺς ὀλιγοψύχους,
ἀντέχεσθε τῶν ἀσθενῶν, quoted by
Harnack.
    2. γνώτωσαν κ.τ.λ.] 1 Kings viii.
60 ὅπως γνῶσι πάντες οἱ λαοὶ τῆς γῆς
ὅτι Κύριος ὁ Θεὸς αὐτὸς Θεὸς καὶ οὐκ
ἔστιν ἔτι, 2 Kings xix. 19 γνώσονται
πᾶσαι αἱ βασιλεῖαι τῆς γῆς ὅτι σὺ
Κύριος ὁ Θεὸς μόνος (comp. Is. xxxvii.
20), Ezek. xxxvi. 23 γνώσονται τὰ ἔθνη
ὅτι ἐγώ εἰμι Κύριος κ.τ.λ. Comp. John
xvii. 3.
    4. ἡμεῖς κ.τ.λ.] From Ps. xcix (c).
2 γνῶτε ὅτι Κύριος αὐτός ἐστιν ὁ Θεός...
ἡμεῖς [δὲ] λαὸς αὐτοῦ καὶ πρόβατα τῆς
νομῆς αὐτοῦ: comp. *ib.* lxxviii (lxxix).
13, xciv (xcv). 7.
    LX. 'Thou didst create all things
in the beginning. Thou that art
faithful and righteous and marvellous
in Thy strength, wise and prudent

δίκαιος ἐν τοῖς κρίμασιν, θαυμαστὸς ἐν ἰσχύϊ καὶ μεγα-
10 λοπρεπείᾳ, ὁ σοφὸς ἐν τῷ κτίζειν καὶ συνετὸς ἐν τῷ
τὰ γενόμενα ἑδράσαι, ὁ ἀγαθὸς ἐν τοῖς ὁρωμένοις καὶ
πιστὸς ἐν τοῖς πεποιθόσιν ἐπὶ σέ, ἐλεῆμον καὶ οἰκτίρμον, ἄφες ἡμῖν τὰς ἀνομίας ἡμῶν καὶ τὰς ἀδικίας καὶ
τὰ παραπτώματα καὶ πλημμελείας. μὴ λογίσῃ πᾶσαν
15 ἁμαρτίαν δούλων σου καὶ παιδισκῶν, ἀλλὰ καθάρισον

12 πιστὸς] mitis (benignus), probably χρηστός, S.　　　15 καθάρισον] καθαρεῖς C;
purifica S. See below.

in Thy creative and sustaining en-
ergy, beneficent and stedfast to them
that put their trust in Thee, merciful
and full of compassion, forgive us
all our offences. Reckon not every
sin against Thy servants : but purify
us with Thy truth and direct our
steps in holiness. Make Thy face to
shine upon us, and protect us with
Thy mighty hand and Thine out-
stretched arm from them that hate
us. Give peace to us and to all the
inhabitants of the earth, as Thou
gavest to our fathers when they
called upon Thee'.

6. Σὺ τὴν ἀένναον κ.τ.λ.] The main
part of this sentence is borrowed in
Apost. Const. viii. 22 (quoted above
on § 59 τὸν ἀριθμόν κ.τ.λ.). Comp.
Wisd. vii. 17 εἰδέναι σύστασιν κόσμου
καὶ ἐνέργειαν στοιχείων.

διὰ τῶν ἐνεργουμένων κ.τ.λ.] i. e.
'didst reveal the inherent constitution
of the world by the succession of
external events'; comp. Rom. i. 20.
The word φανεροποιεῖν is late and
somewhat rare.

8. ὁ πιστὸς κ.τ.λ.] Deut. vii. 9
Θεὸς πιστὸς ὁ φυλάσσων διαθήκην...εἰς
χιλίας γενεάς.

11. ἑδράσαι] Comp. Prov. viii. 25
πρὸ τοῦ ὄρη ἑδρασθῆναι.

ὁ ἀγαθὸς κ.τ.λ.] i. e. 'He is beneficent where His operations can be

seen, and He is trustworthy where
faith takes the place of sight'. The
contrast here is between the things
which are actually seen and the
things which are taken on trust;
comp. Heb. xi. 1 ἔστιν δὲ πίστις...
πραγμάτων ἔλεγχος οὐ βλεπομένων.
For ὁρωμένοις Hilgenfeld has ἐρω-
μένοις; Harnack and Gebhardt read
σωζομένοις, the latter having previously conjectured ὡρισμένοις (*Zeitschr. f.
Kirchengesch.* i. p. 307); Zahn proposes ὁσιουμένοις (*Gött. Gel. Anz.* 1876,
p. 1417). There is no sufficient reason however for questioning the
text. The idea, and in part the language, is taken from Wisd. xiii. 1,
ἐκ τῶν ὁρωμένων ἀγαθῶν οὐκ ἴσχυσαν
εἰδέναι τὸν ὄντα οὔτε τοῖς ἔργοις προ-
σχόντες ἐπέγνωσαν τὸν τεχνίτην. The
language in the latter part of the
sentence is suggested by Ecclus. ii.
10 sq. τίς ἐνεπίστευσε Κυρίῳ καὶ
κατῃσχύνθη ;...διότι οἰκτίρμων καὶ ἐλεή-
μων ὁ Κύριος, καὶ ἀφήσιν ἁμαρτίας.

12. ἐλεῆμον κ.τ.λ.] A very frequent
combination of epithets in the LXX.

15. καθάρισον] This is perhaps the
simplest emendation of καθαρεῖς, the
reading of the MS, which cannot
stand ; καθάρισον having been written
καθάρεισον, and the two last letters
having dropped out. Otherwise we
might read καθάρῃς. Bryennios, Hil-

ἡμᾶς τὸν καθαρισμὸν τῆς σῆς ἀληθείας, καὶ κατεγθγνον
τὰ διαβήματα ἡμῶν ἐν ὁϲιότητι καὶ δικαιοσύνῃ καὶ
ἁπλότητι καρδίας πορεγεϲθαι καὶ ποιεῖν τὰ καλὰ καὶ
εγάρεϲτα ἐνώπιόν ϲου καὶ ἐνώπιον τῶν ἀρχόντων
ἡμῶν. ναί, δέϲποτα, ἐπίφανον τὸ πρόϲωπόν ϲογ ἐφ᾽ 5
ἡμᾶϲ εἰϲ ἀγαθὰ ἐν εἰρήνῃ, εἰϲ τὸ ϲκεπαϲθῆναι ἡμᾶϲ τῇ
χειρί ϲογ τῇ κραταιᾷ καὶ ῥυϲθῆναι ἀπὸ πάϲηϲ ἁμαρ-
τίαϲ τῷ βραχίονί ϲογ τῷ ὑψηλῷ· καὶ ῥῦϲαι ἡμᾶϲ

2 καὶ δικαιοσύνη καὶ ἁπλότητι] om. C; restored by Bensly from S, which has *et
in justitia et in simplicitate*. The omission is due to homœoteleuton. I have
not inserted the prepositions, because it is a common practice of S to repeat
them, where they are not repeated in the Greek; see p. 239.   6 ἐν εἰρήνῃ]
pacis S; but this is probably due to an error of Syriac transcription, since a single
letter (ܠ for ܒ) would make the difference.   12 ὁσίως] S; om. C. This use
of the adverb is characteristic of Clement; otherwise I should have hesitated
to introduce it on such authority.   ὥστε σώ{ζ}εσθαι ἡμᾶς] om. C S; see below.

genfeld, and Gebhardt tacitly retain
καθαρεῖς. For the expression comp.
Num. xiv. 18 καθαρισμῷ οὐ καθαριεῖ
τὸν ἔνοχον, quoted by Bryennios.

1. τῆς σῆς ἀληθείας] See John
xvii. 17 ἁγίασον αὐτοὺς ἐν τῇ ἀληθείᾳ
κ.τ.λ. ; comp. xv. 3.

κατεύθυνον κ.τ.λ.] Ps. xxxix (xl). 3
κατεύθυνε τὰ διαβήματά μου, cxviii
(cxix). 133 τὰ διαβήματά μου κατεύθυνον κατὰ τὸ λόγιόν σου. The phrase
κατευθύνειν τὰ διαβήματα occurs also
Ps. xxxvi (xxxvii). 23, Prov. xx. 24.
The word διαβήματα, 'steps', is rare,
except in the LXX and writers influenced by it.

2. ἐν ὁσιότητι κ.τ.λ.] 1 Kings ix. 4
σὺ ἐὰν πορευθῇς ἐνώπιον ἐμοῦ, καθὼς
ἐπορεύθη Δαυεὶδ, ἐν ὁσιότητι καρδίας.

3. ποιεῖν κ.τ.λ.] Deut. xiii. 18
ποιεῖν τὸ καλὸν καὶ τὸ ἀρεστὸν ἐναντίον
Κυρίου τοῦ Θεοῦ σου: comp. ib. vi. 18,
xii. 25, 28, xxi. 9.

5. ἐπίφανον] Ps. lxvi (lxvii.) 1
ἐπιφάναι τὸ πρόσωπον αὐτοῦ ἐφ᾽ ἡμᾶς :
comp. ib. xxx (xxxi). 18, lxxix (lxxx).

3, 7, 19, cxviii (cxix). 135. See also
Liturg. D. Marc. p. 15.

6. εἰς ἀγαθά] See Jer. xxi. 10
ἐστήρικα τὸ πρόσωπόν μου ἐπὶ τὴν
πόλιν...οὐκ εἰς ἀγαθά ; comp. Amos
ix. 4, Jer. xxiv. 6. For εἰς ἀγαθά see
also Gen. l. 20, Deut. xxx. 9, etc.
Comp. *Liturg. D. Jacob.* p. 63
μνήσθητι...πάντων εἰς ἀγαθόν.

σκεπασθῆναι] For this connexion of
σκεπάζειν comp. Is. li. 16 ὑπὸ τὴν
σκιὰν τῆς χειρός μου σκεπάσω σε
(comp. Wisd. v. 17, xix. 8), Deut.
xxxiii. 27 σκεπάσει σε .. ὑπὸ ἰσχὺν
βραχιόνων ἀενάων : and for the antithetical χειρὶ κραταιᾷ, βραχίονι ὑψηλῷ,
Exod. vi. 1, Deut. iv. 34, v. 15, vii.
19, ix. 26, xi. 2, xxvi. 8, Jer. xxxix
(xxxii). 21, Ezek. xx. 33, 34.

9. τῶν μισούντων κ.τ.λ.] Comp.
Justin. *Apol.* i. 14 (p. 61) τοὺς ἀδίκως
μισοῦντας πείθειν πειρώμενοι, quoted
by Harnack.

11. ἐπικαλουμένων κ.τ.λ.] Ps. cxliv
(cxlv). 8 πᾶσι τοῖς ἐπικαλουμένοις αὐτὸν
ἐν ἀληθείᾳ. For ἐν πίστει καὶ ἀληθείᾳ

ἀπὸ τῶν μισούντων ἡμᾶς ἀδίκως. δὸς ὁμόνοιαν καὶ
10 εἰρήνην ἡμῖν τε καὶ πᾶσιν τοῖς κατοικοῦσιν τὴν γῆν,
καθὼς ἔδωκας τοῖς πατράσιν ἡμῶν, ἐπικαλουμένων σε
αὐτῶν ὁσίως ἐν πίστει καὶ ἀληθείᾳ, [ὥστε σώζεσθαι ἡμᾶς]
ὑπηκόους γινομένους τῷ παντοκράτορι καὶ παναρέτῳ
ὀνόματί σου, τοῖς τε ἄρχουσιν καὶ ἡγουμένοις ἡμῶν
15 ἐπὶ τῆς γῆς.

S renders *et in veritate obedientes fuerunt nomini tuo* etc., thus connecting καὶ
ἐν ἀληθείᾳ with the following clause.   13 παντοκράτορι καὶ παναρέτῳ] The
words are transposed in S, but this does not imply any different Greek text:
see above, p. 239. Also παναρέτῳ is translated as if ἐντίμῳ, מיקרא (see § 3).
But a single letter would make the difference, מיקרא *excellenti.* Elsewhere
בכל יתה is the translation of πανάρετος (see §§ 1, 2, 45, 57); and the translator
might here consider himself excused from the repetition of παν- which occurs in
both words. See also on παναγίῳ above, § 58.

comp. 1 Tim. ii. 7.

13. ὑπηκόους κ.τ.λ.] This might
be a loose accusative, referring to
the datives ἡμῖν τε καὶ πᾶσιν κ.τ.λ.;
comp. Ephes. i. 17, 18 δώῃ ὑμῖν
πνεῦμα σοφίας......πεφωτισμένους
τοὺς ὀφθαλμοὺς κ.τ.λ., Acts xxvi. 3
ἐπὶ σοῦ μέλλων σήμερον ἀπολογεῖσθαι,
μάλιστά γνώστην ὄντα σε κ.τ.λ., and
see Winer § xxxiii. p. 290, § lxiii.
pp. 709 sq., 716, Kühner II. p. 667 sq.
But a double transition, πατράσιν,
ἐπικαλουμένων, γινόμενους, would be
very harsh; and for reasons which
are stated in the introduction (p.
247 sq.), I cannot doubt that some
words have dropped out, such as I
have inserted. Bryennios supplies
καὶ σῶσον ἡμᾶς; Gebhardt reads
ὑπηκόοις γενόμενοις; and Hilgenfeld
alters the whole sentence.

παντοκράτορι] So Hermas *Vis.* iii. 3
τῷ ῥήματι τοῦ παντοκράτορος καὶ ἐν-
δόξου ὀνόματος. At first it had occurred
to me to read παντοκρατορικῷ, as it
occurred to Gebhardt, and as Hilgenfeld actually reads; comp. § 8 τῷ
παντοκρατορικῷ βουλήματι αὐτοῦ. The

omission of -κῷ before καὶ would be
easily explained, especially as the
archetypal MS is shown to have been
mutilated in this neighbourhood. But
the parallel passage from Hermas
quite justifies the reading of the
MS. In the LXX παντοκράτωρ seems
to be always applied directly to God
either as an epithet of Θεὸς or
Κύριος, or independently; and so in
Clement himself, inscr., 2, 32. But
the sense of τὸ ὄνομα, as almost
an equivalent to ὁ Θεὸς (see [Clem.
Rom.] ii. § 13, and the note on
Ign. *Ephes.* 3), explains the excep-
tional usage here and in Hermas.

παναρέτῳ κ.τ.λ.] For this expression
comp. § 45, and for the word πανάρετος the note on § 1.

14. τοῖς τε ἄρχουσιν κ.τ.λ.] The
punctuation, which I have adopted,
was suggested to me by Dr Hort.
It accords with the preceding words
εὐάρεστα ἐνώπιόν σου καὶ ἐνώπιον τῶν
ἀρχόντων ἡμῶν: it disposes of the
superfluous αὐτοῖς (see however § 21,
note): and it throws Σύ into its
proper position of prominence; e. g.

LXI.　Σύ, δέσποτα, ἔδωκας τὴν ἐξουσίαν τῆς βασιλείας αὐτοῖς διὰ τοῦ μεγαλοπρεποῦς καὶ ἀνεκδιηγή-
του κράτους σου, εἰς τὸ γινώσκοντας ἡμᾶς τὴν ὑπὸ
σοῦ αὐτοῖς δεδομένην δόξαν καὶ τιμὴν ὑποτάσσεσθαι
αὐτοῖς, μηδὲν ἐναντιουμένους τῷ θελήματί σου· οἷς δός, 5
Κύριε, ὑγιείαν, εἰρήνην, ὁμόνοιαν, εὐστάθειαν, εἰς τὸ
διέπειν αὐτοὺς τὴν ὑπὸ σοῦ δεδομένην αὐτοῖς ἡγεμονίαν
ἀπροσκόπως. σὺ γάρ, δέσποτα ἐπουράνιε, βασιλεῦ
τῶν αἰώνων, δίδως τοῖς υἱοῖς τῶν ἀνθρώπων δόξαν καὶ
τιμὴν καὶ ἐξουσίαν τῶν ἐπὶ τῆς γῆς ὑπαρχόντων· σύ, 10

5 δὸς] precamur ut des S.

§ 60 Σὺ τὴν ἀέναον κ.τ.λ. and § 61
just below, Σὺ γάρ, δέσποτα κ.τ.λ.
See Athenag. *Suppl.* 1 εὐσεβέστατα
διακειμένους καὶ δικαιότατα πρός τε τὸ
θεῖον καὶ τὴν ὑμετέραν βασιλείαν ;
comp. Theoph. *ad Autol.* i. 11, who
quotes Prov. xxiv. 21 Τίμα, υἱέ, Θεὸν
καὶ βασιλέα κ.τ.λ. The previous editors have all connected the words
τοῖς τε ἄρχουσιν κ.τ.λ. with the following sentence, as apparently does C.

LXI. 'To our earthly rulers, O
Lord, Thou hast given the power,
that we may render them due obedience in entire submission to Thy
will. Therefore grant them health,
peace, stability. For Thou, O
Sovereign of heaven and King of
Eternity, givest honour and authority
to the sons of men upon earth. So
guide their counsels, that they may
administer well the power thus
entrusted to them, and may obtain
Thy favour. O Thou, who alone
art able to do this and far more
than this, we praise thee through
our High-Priest Jesus Christ, through
whom be glory unto Thee for ever'.

1. τῆς βασιλείας] '*of the sovereignty*', i. e. 'of the secular power'.

For the genitive comp. Dan. xi. 20
πράσσων δόξαν βασιλείας, *ib.* 21 ἔδωκεν ἐπ' αὐτὸν δόξαν βασιλείας. The
βασιλεία is the secular as contrasted
with the spiritual power; and, as
such, it is frequently opposed to ἱερωσύνη, e. g. *Apost. Const.* ii. 34 ὅσῳ
ψυχὴ σώματος κρείττων, τοσούτῳ
ἱερωσύνη βασιλείας (comp. vi. 2), *Test.
Duod. Patr.* Jud. 21.

4. ὑποτάσσεσθαι αὐτοῖς κ. τ. λ.]
See 1 Pet. ii. 13, 15 ὑποτάγητε
πάσῃ ἀνθρωπίνῃ κτίσει διὰ τὸν Κύριον...
ὅτι οὕτως ἐστὶν τὸ θέλημα τοῦ Θεοῦ;
comp. Rom. xiii. 2 ὁ ἀντιτασσόμενος
τῇ ἐξουσίᾳ τῇ τοῦ Θεοῦ διαταγῇ ἀν-
θέστηκεν.

5. δὸς κ.τ.λ.] In accordance with
the Apostolic injunctions, Rom.
xiii. 1 sq., Tit. iii. 1, 1 Pet. ii. 13
sq. : comp. Wisd. vi. 1 sq. See also
Polyc. *Phil.* 12. For other passages
in early Christian writers relating to
prayers for temporal rulers, see
Bingham *Ant.* xiii. 10. 5, Harnack
Christl. Gemeindegottesd. p. 218 sq.
(Justin Martyr), p. 378 sq. (Tertullian).
The Apologists naturally lay stress
on the practice, as an answer to the
charge of sedition.

Κύριε, διεύθυνον τὴν βουλὴν αὐτῶν κατὰ τὸ καλὸν καὶ
εὐάρεστον ἐνώπιόν σου, ὅπως διέποντες ἐν εἰρήνῃ καὶ
πραΰτητι εὐσεβῶς τὴν ὑπὸ σοῦ αὐτοῖς δεδομένην ἐξουσίαν ἵλεώ σου τυγχάνωσιν. Ὁ μόνος δυνατὸς ποιῆσαι
15 ταῦτα καὶ περισσότερα ἀγαθὰ μεθ᾽ ἡμῶν, σοὶ ἐξομολογούμεθα διὰ τοῦ ἀρχιερέως καὶ προστάτου τῶν
ψυχῶν ἡμῶν Ἰησοῦ Χριστοῦ, δι᾽ οὗ σοι ἡ δόξα καὶ
ἡ μεγαλωσύνη καὶ νῦν καὶ εἰς γενεὰν γενεῶν καὶ εἰς
τοὺς αἰῶνας τῶν αἰώνων. ἀμήν.

20 LXII. Περὶ μὲν τῶν ἀνηκόντων τῇ θρησκείᾳ ἡμῶν,

14. ἵλεώ σου τυγχάνωσιν] *tranquille compotes fiant auxilii quod* (*est*) *a te* S,
obviously a paraphrase.

6. εὐστάθειαν] 'stability', 'tranquillity', comp. § 65 (59). The word
may mean either 'firmness, steadiness' as a moral quality, or 'stability'
as a material result. The latter seems
to be intended here: comp. 2 Macc.
xiv. 6 οὐκ ἐῶντες τὴν βασιλείαν εὐστα-
θείας τυχεῖν, Wisd. vi. 26 βασιλεὺς
φρόνιμος εὐστάθεια δήμου.

8. ἀπροσκόπως] 'without stumbling', 'without any jar or collision';
as § 20 τὴν λειτουργίαν αὐτῶν ἀπροσ-
κόπως ἐπιτελοῦσιν.

βασιλεῦ τῶν αἰώνων] The phrase
occurs only 1 Tim. i. 17 in the N.T.,
and as a v.l. in Rev. xv. 3 ; but it is
found in the LXX, Tobit xiii. 6, 10 ;
see also *Liturg. D. Jac.* p. 59.
Comp. § 35 πατὴρ τῶν αἰώνων, § 55
Θεὸς τῶν αἰώνων. Here the Eternal
King is tacitly contrasted with the
temporary kings, the βασιλεὺς τῶν
αἰώνων with the βασιλεῖς τοῦ αἰῶνος
τούτου (comp. Ign. *Rom.* 6).

11. διεύθυνον] As above § 20. Otherwise it is not a common word, and
does not apparently occur at all in
the LXX or N.T.

15. μεθ᾽ ἡμῶν] As Luke i. 72
ποιῆσαι ἔλεος μετὰ τῶν πατέρων ἡμῶν,
ib. x. 37, and so probably Acts xiv. 27,
xv. 4 ; comp. Ps. cxviii (cxix). 65
χρηστότητα ἐποίησας μετὰ τοῦ δούλου
σου. It is the Hebraism עִם עָשָׂה.

16. ἀρχιερέως κ.τ.λ.] See the note
on § 36.

17. ἡ δόξα κ.τ.λ.] See the note on
§ 20. It is a favourite form of doxology in Clement.

18. εἰς γενεὰν γενεῶν] i. e. 'the
generation which comprises all the
generations'; as Ps. ci (cii). 24 ἐν
γενεᾷ γενεῶν τὰ ἔτη σου : comp. Ephes.
iii. 21 τοῦ αἰῶνος τῶν αἰώνων. This is
a rare mode of expression, the commoner forms being εἰς γενεὰς γενεῶν
or εἰς γενεὰν καὶ γενεάν, which are
quite different in meaning.

LXII. 'Enough has been said
by us however concerning the things
pertaining to our religion and necessary for a virtuous life. For we have
left no point untouched concerning
faith and repentance and the like,
reminding you that ye ought in all
righteousness to pay your thanksgiving to God, living in harmony
and peace and love; like as our
fathers behaved with all humility
towards God and towards all men.

καὶ τῶν ὠφελιμωτάτων εἰς ἐνάρετον βίον τοῖς θέλουσιν
εὐσεβῶς καὶ δικαίως διευθύνειν [τὴν πορείαν αὐτῶν],
ἱκανῶς ἐπεστείλαμεν ὑμῖν, ἄνδρες ἀδελφοί. περὶ γὰρ
πίστεως καὶ μετανοίας καὶ γνησίας ἀγάπης καὶ ἐγκρατείας καὶ σωφροσύνης καὶ ὑπομονῆς πάντα τόπον 5
ἐψηλαφήσαμεν, ὑπομιμνήσκοντες δεῖν ὑμᾶς ἐν δικαιοσύνῃ καὶ ἀληθείᾳ καὶ μακροθυμίᾳ τῷ παντοκράτορι
Θεῷ ὁσίως εὐαρεστεῖν, ὁμονοοῦντας ἀμνησικάκως ἐν

---

1 καὶ] S; om. C. The clause is translated in S 'et de iis (rebus) scilicet (בית)
quæ in ea (religione), quæ maxime utiles sunt illis qui volunt dirigere vitam (conversationem) excellentia et pietatis et juste, as if the translator had read τῶν ὠφελιμωτάτων δὴ (?) ἐν αὐτῇ ἐνάρετον...διευθύνειν. At all events he must have had a text
which a corrector had emended by striking out or altering εἰς, so as to govern
βίον by διευθύνειν: see above pp. 246, 247. In the Syriac we should probably
read בשפירות for בשפירות, i.e. in pietate (= εὐσεβῶς) for et pietatis.
2 τὴν πορείαν αὐτῶν] om. C S: see below.   4 ἐγκρατείας] על עוויתא super
continentia (as if ὑπὲρ ἐγκρατείας) S, for another preposition (מן de) has been
used before for περί. Perhaps however the insertion of a different preposition is a
mere rhetorical device of the translator; or על may be an accidental repetition of the
first syllable of the following word, as the Syriac forms of the letters would suggest.

And we have done this with the
more pleasure, because we knew that
we were speaking to faithful men,
who had made a diligent study of
God's oracles¹.
20. τῶν ἀνηκόντων] With a dative
as in § 35; see the note on Ign.
Philad. 1. It has a different construction, ἀνήκειν εἰς, in § 45. See the
note there.
τῇ θρησκείᾳ ἡμῶν] Comp. § 45 τῶν
θρησκευόντων τὴν μεγαλοπρεπῆ καὶ
ἔνδοξον θρησκείαν τοῦ ὑψίστου. This
passage explains the force of the
words here: 'that befit men who
serve the one true God'.
1. ἐνάρετον] See the note on
Ign. Philad. 1.
2. διευθύνειν] The MS is obviously defective here; and we must
supply some such words as τὴν

πορείαν αὐτῶν (see § 48), or τὰ διαβήματα (§ 60), or perhaps with Bryennios τὴν βουλὴν αὐτῶν (§ 61). See
the introduction, p. 247 sq.
3. ἱκανῶς ἐπεστείλαμεν] Bryennios
has called attention to the similarity
of language used by Irenæus, when
describing this epistle, iii. 3. 3 ἐπὶ
τούτου οὖν τοῦ Κλήμεντος, στάσεως
οὐκ ὀλίγης τοῖς ἐν Κορίνθῳ γενομένης
ἀδελφοῖς, ἐπέστειλεν ἡ ἐν Ρώμῃ ἐκκλησία ἱκανωτάτην γραφὴν τοῖς Κο-
ρινθίοις.
5. πάντα τόπον κ.τ.λ.] 'we have
handled every topic'; Bryennios adds
by way of explanation, μάλιστα δὲ τῶν
ἁγίων γραφῶν, thus taking πάντα τόπον to mean 'every passage'; and
so it is rendered in the Syriac Version, 'place of Scripture'. In this
sense τύπος occurs above in the ex-

ἀγάπη καὶ εἰρήνη μετὰ ἐκτενοῦς ἐπιεικείας, καθὼς καὶ
10 οἱ προδεδηλωμένοι πατέρες ἡμῶν εὐηρέστησαν ταπει-
νοφρονοῦντες τὰ πρὸς τὸν πατέρα καὶ Θεὸν καὶ κτίστην καὶ πρὸς πάντας ἀνθρώπους. καὶ ταῦτα τοσούτῳ
ἥδιον ὑπεμνήσαμεν, ἐπειδὴ σαφῶς ᾔδειμεν γράφειν
ἡμᾶς ἀνδράσιν πιστοῖς καὶ ἐλλογιμωτάτοις καὶ ἐγκε-
15 κυφόσιν εἰς τὰ λόγια τῆς παιδείας τοῦ Θεοῦ.

We cannot safely infer a different Greek text.　　　5 τόπον] add. scripturæ S.
8 εὐαρεστεῖν] S; εὐχαριστεῖν C. See the same confusion above, § 41. The reading
of S was anticipated by Hilg. and Gebh.　　　9 καθὼς καὶ] καθὼς (om. καὶ) S.
11 Θεὸν καὶ κτίστην] universi creatorem Deum (Θεὸν παγκτίστην?) S; comp. § 19.
12 πρὸς] S; om. C. The authority of S in such a case is valueless in itself (see p. 239),
but the preposition seems to be required here.　　　13 ἥδιον] ᾗ δι' ὧν S, which
translates the clause, et hæc tanto sint (erunt) per ea quæ monuimus. The translator
has had a corrupt text and has translated it word for word, regardless of sense.
ἐπειδὴ σαφῶς ᾔδειμεν γράφειν] quia scilicet manifeste est iis; oportuit enim certe (μὲν)
ut scriberemus S, i.e. ἐπεὶ δὴ σαφῶς ᾗ· δεῖ (or ἔδει) μὲν γὰρ γράφειν κ.τ.λ. Again
a corrupt reading, or rather a false division of the words, has been translated almost verbatim. For the facility with which γὰρ might be omitted or inserted before
γράφω, see Ign. Rom. 7.　　　14 ἐλλογιμωτάτοις] doctis S.

---

pression ἐν ἑτέρῳ τόπῳ, §§ 8, 29, 46.
But this meaning does not seem at
all natural here, where the word is
used absolutely. For τόπος ' a topic,
argument ', comp. e. g. Epict. Diss.
i. 7. 4 ἐπίσκεψίν τινα ποιητέον τῶν
τόπων τούτων, ii. 17. 31 ὅταν τοῦτον
ἐκπονήσῃ...τὸν τόπον, and see other
references in Schweighæuser's index
to Epictetus, s. v. For ψηλαφᾶν
comp. e. g. Polyb. viii. 18. 4 πᾶσαν
ἐπίνοιαν ἐψηλάφα.

8. εὐαρεστεῖν] Doubtless the correct reading, as it explains the subsequent εὐηρέστησαν. For another
example of the confusion of εὐαρεστεῖν, εὐχαριστεῖν, in the authorities,
see § 41.

ἀμνησικάκως] See § 2 ἀμνησίκακοι
(with the note). This word involves
an appeal to the sufferers from the
schisms, who are bidden to harbour
no grudge.

9. μετὰ ἐκτενοῦς κ.τ.λ.] See the
note on § 58, where the same expression occurs.

10. οἱ προδεδηλωμένοι κ.τ.λ.] See
§§ 17, 18, 19; comp. also § 30 ἐδόθη
[ἡ μαρτυρία] τοῖς πάτρασιν ἡμῶν τοῖς
δικαίοις, and § 31 ἀνατυλίξωμεν τὰ
ἀπ' ἀρχῆς γενόμενα· τίνος χάριν ηὐ-
λογήθη ὁ πατὴρ ἡμῶν Ἀβραάμ; κ.τ.λ.
For this use of πατέρες in speaking
of Jewish worthies, see the note on
§ 4.

14. ἐλλογιμωτάτοις] See the note
on § 58 ἐλλόγιμος.

ἐγκεκύφοσιν] Comp. § 53 καλῶς
ἐπίστασθε τὰς ἱερὰς γραφάς, ἀγαπητοί,
καὶ ἐγκεκύφατε εἰς τὰ λόγια τοῦ Θεοῦ,
with the note. For the word ἐγκύπ-
τειν see the note on § 40.

LXIII. Θεμιτὸν οὖν ἐστιν τοῖς τοιούτοις καὶ
τοσούτοις ὑποδείγμασιν προσελθόντας ὑποθεῖναι τὸν
τράχηλον καὶ τὸν τῆς ὑπακοῆς τόπον ἀναπληρώσαντας
προσκλιθῆναι τοῖς ὑπάρχουσιν ἀρχηγοῖς τῶν ψυχῶν
ἡμῶν, ὅπως ἡσυχάσαντες τῆς ματαίας στάσεως ἐπὶ τὸν 5

2 ὑποθεῖναι τὸν τράχηλον] *inclinemus collum nostrum et obediamus* S.   3 ἀναπληρώσαντας...ἡμῶν] *implentes inclinemur illis qui sunt duces animarum nostrarum*

LXIII. 'We ought therefore to
regard so many great examples, and
to bow the neck in submission; that
laying aside all strife we may reach
our destined goal. Ye will make
us happy indeed, if ye obey and
cease from your dissensions in accordance with our exhortation to
peace: And we have sent to you faithful men who have lived among us
unblameably from youth to old age,
to be witnesses between us and you.
This we have done, to show you
how great is our anxiety that peace
may be speedily restored among
you'.

1. Θεμιτόν] The use of this word
seems to be extremely rare, except
with a negative, οὐ θεμιτόν (e. g. Tobit
ii. 13) or ἀθέμιτον (see below).

τοῖς τοιούτοις κ.τ.λ.] § 46 Τοιούτοις
οὖν ὑποδείγμασιν κολληθῆναι καὶ ἡμᾶς
δεῖ κ.τ.λ. For τοιούτοις καὶ τοσούτοις
comp. § 19.

2. προσελθόντας] '*having acceded
to, attended to, assented to, studied*',
as in § 33; comp. 1 Tim. vi. 3 εἴ
τις ἑτεροδιδασκαλεῖ καὶ μὴ προσέρχεται
ὑγιαίνουσιν λόγοις. So we find προσέρχεσθαι ἀρετῇ 'to apply oneself to
virtue', Philo *de Migr. Abr.* 16
(I. p. 449); προσέρχεσθαι τοῖς νόμοις
'to study the laws', Diod. i. 95;
προσέρχεσθαι τῇ σοφίᾳ, τῇ φιλοσοφίᾳ,
'to become a follower of wisdom, of
philosophy', Philostr. *Vit. Ap.* i. 2
(p. 2), iii. 18 (p. 50), comp. LXX
Ecclus. vi. 26 ὁ προσελθὼν αὐτῇ (i. e.

τῇ σοφίᾳ); προσέρχεσθαι φόβῳ Κυρίου
'to give heed to the fear of the Lord',
LXX Ecclus. i. 30; προσέρχεσθαι μη-
δενὶ τῶν εἰρημένων Philo *de Gig.* 9 (I.
p. 267); προσέρχεσθαι τῷ λόγῳ, Orig.
c. Cels. iii. 48. These senses are
derived ultimately from the idea of
'approaching' a person as a disciple'; e. g. Xen. *Mem.* i. 2. 47 ὥνπερ
ἕνεκεν καὶ Σωκράτει προσῆλθον.

ὑποθεῖναι τὸν τράχηλον] '*submit
your neck*', i. e. 'to the yoke';
comp. Ecclus. li. 26 τὸν τράχηλον
ὑμῶν ὑπόθετε ὑπὸ ζυγόν (comp. *ib.* vi.
24, 25), Epictet. *Diss.* iv. 1. 77
παρέδωκας σαυτὸν δοῦλον, ὑπέθηκας
τὸν τράχηλον. So too Acts xv. 10
ἐπιθεῖναι ζυγὸν ἐπὶ τὸν τράχηλον. The
expression is used in a different
sense in Rom. xvi. 4 ὑπὲρ τῆς ψυχῆς
μου τὸν ἑαυτῶν τράχηλον ὑπέθηκαν,
where it means 'laid their neck on
the block', not 'pledged their lives',
as Wetstein and others take it.

3. ἀναπληρώσαντας τόπον] '*to oc-
cupy the place*', '*fulfil the function*';
comp. 1 Cor. xiv. 16 ὁ ἀναπληρῶν
τὸν τόπον τοῦ ἰδιώτου, where the
choice of this elaborate expression
is probably a studied paradox to
bring out the honourable character
of a private station; τόπος denoting
official position or dignity (see above,
§ 40, and the note on Ign. *Polyc.* 1),
while ἰδιώτης implies the opposite of
this. So too here the object may
be to enhance the important *function*
of obedience. See *Clem. Hom.* iii.

προκείμενον ἡμῖν ἐν ἀληθείᾳ σκοπὸν δίχα παντὸς μώμου
καταντήσωμεν. χαρὰν γὰρ καὶ ἀγαλλίασιν ἡμῖν παρέ-
ξετε, ἐὰν ὑπήκοοι γενόμενοι τοῖς ὑφ᾽ ἡμῶν γεγραμμένοις
διὰ τοῦ ἁγίου πνεύματος ἐκκόψητε τὴν ἀθέμιτον τοῦ

S ; ἀναπληρῶσαι C, omitting all the other words. See the lower note.　5 ἡσυ-
χάσαντες] quiescentes et tranquilli S.　6 μώμου] add. et scandalo S.　7 ἀγαλ-
λίασιν] add. magnam S.

60 τὸν ἐμὸν ἀναπληροῦντα τόπον, and comp. Joseph. B. J. v. 2. 5 στρατιώτου τάξιν ἀποπληροῦντα.

4. προσκλιθῆναι κ.τ.λ.] These words are wanting in the Greek MS, and I have restored them by retranslation from the Syriac: see the critical note. The true partisanship is here tacitly contrasted with the false; the rightful leaders with the wrongful. The language is explained by what has gone before; § 14 μυσεροῦ ζήλους ἀρχηγοῖς ἐξακολουθεῖν, § 51 ἐκεῖνοι οἵτινες ἀρχηγοὶ τῆς στάσεως καὶ διχοστασίας ἐγενήθησαν, § 47 διὰ τὸ καὶ τότε προσκλίσεις ὑμᾶς πεποιῆσθαι...προσκλίθητε γὰρ κ.τ.λ., § 50 ἵνα ἐν ἀγάπῃ εὑρεθῶμεν δίχα προσκλίσεως ἀνθρωπίνης ἄμωμοι (comp. § 21 μὴ κατὰ προσκλίσεις). The command to choose the right partisanships here has a parallel in § 45 φιλόνεικοι ἔστε...περὶ τῶν ἀνηκόντων εἰς σωτηρίαν (see the note). The Syriac is נתרכן להנון דאיתיהון מדברנא דנפשתן. For נתרכן I cannot think of any word so probable as προσκλιθῆναι, since רכן is a common translation of κλίνειν, and in § 21 προσκλίσεις is rendered רביונתא דאפי; though προσκλίνεσθαι, πρόσκλισις, are rendered otherwise, but variously, in §§ 47, 50, Acts v. 36, 1 Tim. v. 21. On the other hand מדברנא 'ductores' might be variously rendered. It most commonly represents ὁ ἡγούμενος (§§ 1, 32, 37 in a double rendering, 55, Heb. xiii. 7, 17, 24); but elsewhere ἡγεμών,

καθηγητής, ὁδηγός, etc., even βουλευτής. I have given ἀρχηγός, because it brings out the contrast which Clement seems to have had in his mind. In §§ 14, 51, however, ἀρχηγός is rendered otherwise, רישא, רישנא, and so commonly.

5. στάσεως] Comp. Clem. Hom. i. 4 τῶν τοιούτων λογισμῶν ἡσυχάζειν. This construction follows the analogy of verbs denoting cessation, etc. (see Kühner II. p. 341 sq.). It is unnecessary therefore to read ἡσυχασάσης, as Gebhardt suggests.

6. σκοπόν] Comp. § 6 ἐπὶ τὸν τῆς πίστεως βέβαιον δρόμον καταντήσωμεν, and § 19 ἐπαναδράμωμεν ἐπὶ τὸν ἐξ ἀρχῆς παραδεδομένον ἡμῖν τῆς εἰρήνης σκοπόν, which explains the idea in the writer's mind here. The expression itself is perhaps suggested by Heb. xii. 1 τρέχωμεν τὸν προκείμενον ἡμῖν ἀγῶνα. For σκοπόν comp. Phil. iii. 14.

μώμου] 'fault, defect': see the note on μωμοσκοπηθέν § 41. In the Old Testament it is always a translation of מום 'a blemish'.

7. χαρὰν κ.τ.λ.] As in Luke i. 14 (comp. Matt. v. 12, Rev. xix. 7); see also Mart. Polyc. 18. This combination of words χαρὰ καὶ ἀγαλλίασις does not occur in the LXX.

9. διὰ τοῦ ἁγίου πνεύματος] See the note on § 59 τοῖς ὑπ᾽ αὐτοῦ δι᾽ ἡμῶν εἰρημένοις. Harnack takes these words with ἐκκόψητε, but this does not seem so natural.

ἀθέμιτον] Acts x. 28, 1 Pet. iv. 3 ;

ζήλους ὑμῶν ὀργὴν κατὰ τὴν ἔντευξιν ἣν ἐποιησάμεθα
περὶ εἰρήνης καὶ ὁμονοίας ἐν τῇδε τῇ ἐπιστολῇ. Ἐπέμ-
ψαμεν δὲ καὶ ἄνδρας πιστοὺς καὶ σώφρονας, ἀπὸ νεότητος ἀναστραφέντας ἕως γήρους ἀμέμπτως ἐν ἡμῖν,
οἵτινες καὶ μάρτυρες ἔσονται μεταξὺ ὑμῶν καὶ ἡμῶν. 5
τοῦτο δὲ ἐποιήσαμεν ἵνα εἰδῆτε ὅτι πᾶσα ἡμῖν
φροντὶς καὶ γέγονεν καὶ ἔστιν εἰς τὸ ἐν τάχει ὑμᾶς
εἰρηνεῦσαι.

1 ἔντευξιν] supplicationem et exhortationem S.   3 δὲ καὶ] S; δὲ (om. καὶ) C.
5 οἵτινες καὶ] S; οἵτινες (om. καὶ) C.

and so too 2 Macc. vi. 5, vii. 1, x. 34.

1. ζήλους] See the note on § 4.

ἔντευξιν] This should probably be explained of the 'appeal' to the Corinthians themselves; see the note on [Clem. Rom.] ii. § 19. It might however refer to the foregoing 'prayer' to God for concord; comp. e. g. 1 Tim. ii. 1, iv. 5, Herm. *Mand.* x. 2.

3. ἄνδρας] Claudius Ephebus and Valerius Bito, whose names are given below, § 65 (59). For the bearing of the notice here on the early history of the Roman Church, see the introduction p. 256 sq.

4. γήρους] So Luke i. 36 γήρει (the correct reading), and in several passages in the LXX, e.g. Ps. xci (xcii). 14 γήρει, 1 Kings xiv. 4 γήρους, Ecclus. viii. 6, etc., with more or less agreement in the principal MSS; so also *Clem. Hom.* iii. 43. On this form see Winer *Gramm.* § ix. p. 73 sq., Steph. Thes. *s. v.*, ed. Hase. Our MS has also γήρει above in § 10, where A reads γήρᾳ.

AN ANCIENT HOMILY

COMMONLY CALLED THE

SECOND EPISTLE OF S. CLEMENT.

AN ANCIENT HOMILY

UNKNOWN AUTHOR.

IF the First Epistle of Clement is the earliest foreshadowing of a Christian liturgy, the so-called Second Epistle is the first example of a Christian homily.

The newly recovered ending has set this point at rest for ever. The work is plainly not a letter, but a homily, a sermon. The speaker addresses his hearers more than once towards the close as 'Brothers and sisters' (§§ 19, 20). Elsewhere he appeals to them in language which is quite explicit on the point at issue. 'Let us not think,' he says, 'to give heed and believe now only, while we are being admonished by the presbyters; but likewise when we have departed home, let us remember the commandments of the Lord, etc.' (§ 17). And again a little later he speaks still more definitely; 'After the God of truth, I read to you an exhortation to the end that ye may give heed to the things which are written (i. e. to the scriptures which have just been read), so that ye may save both yourselves and him that readeth in the midst of you' (§ 19). These words remind us of the language in which Justin, who wrote within a few years of the probable date of this homily, describes the simple services of the Christians in his time. 'On the day called Sunday,' he says, 'all remaining in their several cities and districts, they come together in one place, and the memoirs of the Apostles [i. e. the Gospels, as he explains himself elsewhere] or the writings of the Prophets are read, as long as time admits. Then, when the reader has ceased, the president (ὁ προεστώς) in a discourse (διὰ λόγου) gives instruction and invites (his hearers) to the imitation of these good things. Then we all rise in a body and offer up our prayers' (*Apol.* i. 67, quoted in the notes on § 19). Here then is one of these

20—2

exhortations, which is delivered after the 'God of truth' has been first heard in the scriptures[1]; and, this being so, the preacher was doubtless, as Justin describes him, ὁ προεστώς, the leading minister of the Church, i.e. the bishop or one of the presbyters, as the case might be. A different view indeed has been taken by Harnack. He supposes that the homily was delivered by a layman[2], drawing his inference from the mention of the presbyters (in § 17 just quoted) as persons whom the preacher and his hearers alike were bound to listen to. But this language can only be regarded, I think, as an example of a very common rhetorical figure, by which the speaker places himself on a level with his audience, and of which several instances are furnished by the genuine Epistle of Clement, who again and again identifies himself with the factious brethren at Corinth (see the note on § 17). On very rare occasions indeed we read of laymen preaching in the early Church; but such concessions were only made to persons who had an exceptionally brilliant reputation, like Origen[3]. As a rule, this function belonged to the chief ecclesiastical officer in the congregation. A presbyter did not preach when the bishop was present; a deacon was for the most part regarded as incompetent to preach on any occasion[4].

The question therefore respecting the class of writings to which this document belongs is settled beyond dispute. The homiletic character of the work was suggested long ago by Grabe and others; and in my own edition I had regarded the opinion that it was a sermon or treatise

---

[1] Exception has been taken to this expression μετὰ τὸν Θεὸν τῆς ἀληθείας. Zahn (Gött. Gel. Ans. p. 1418) and Donaldson (Theol. Rev. January, 1877, p. 46) propose λόγον for Θεόν, while Gebhardt suggests τόνων or τόνου (ΤΟΝΩΝ or ΤΟΝΟΥ for ΤΟΝΩΝ). But it is difficult to see why our preacher should not have used this phrase, when he elsewhere introduces an evangelical quotation with λέγει ὁ Θεός, § 13; see the note on the passage. We do not even know whether the lesson to which he here refers was taken from the Old or the New Testament.

[2] See p. lxxii, note 11, p. 138 (ed. 2). So also Hilgenfeld, p. 106 (ed. 2).

[3] The objections raised in his case show that the practice was rare. Alexander of Jerusalem and Theoctistus of Caesarea (Euseb. H.E. vi. 19), writing to Demetrius of Alexandria, defend themselves for according this privilege to Origen, as follows; προσέθηκε δὲ τοῖς γράμμασιν, ὅτι τοῦτο οὐδέ ποτε ἡκούσθη οὐδὲ νῦν γεγένηται, τὸ παρόντων ἐπισκόπων λαϊκοὺς ὁμιλεῖν, οὐκ οἶδ' ὅπως προφανῶς οὐκ ἀληθῆ λέγων. ὅπου γοῦν εὑρίσκονται οἱ ἐπιτήδειοι πρὸς τὸ ὠφελεῖν τοὺς ἀδελφούς, καὶ παρακαλοῦνται τῷ λαῷ προσομιλεῖν ὑπὸ τῶν ἁγίων ἐπισκόπων, ὥσπερ ἐν Λαράνδοις Εὐέλπις ὑπὸ Νέωνος καὶ ἐν Ἰκονίῳ Παυλῖνος ὑπὸ Κέλσου καὶ ἐν Συννάδοις Θεόδωρος ὑπὸ Ἀττικοῦ τῶν μακαρίων ἀδελφῶν· εἰκὸς δὲ καὶ ἐν ἄλλοις τόποις τοῦτο γίνεσθαι, ἡμᾶς δὲ μὴ εἰδέναι.

[4] See Bingham Antiq. XIV. 4. 2, 4, Augusti Christl. Archäol. VI. p. 315 sq., Probst Lehre u. Gebet pp. 18 sq., 222.

rather than a letter as *prima facie* probable, though so long as the end was wanting this view could not be regarded as certain[1]. On the other hand the theory propounded by Hilgenfeld, that we had here the letter of Soter bishop of Rome to the Corinthians, mentioned by Dionysius of Corinth about A.D. 170 (see pp. 3, 174, 180), was eagerly accepted by subsequent critics and editors. In a courteous review of my edition which appeared in the *Academy* (July 9, 1870) Lipsius espoused this theory as probable. And still later, on the very eve of the discovery of Bryennios, Harnack in the excellent edition of the *Patres Apostolici* of which he is coeditor had confidently adopted Hilgenfeld's opinion; 'Nullus dubito quin Hilgenfeldius verum invenerit,' 'Mireris... neminem ante Hilgenfeldium verum invenisse' (Prol. pp. xci, xcii, ed. 1). This view was highly plausible and attractive; but it was open to one objection which I pointed out as fatal to it. It did not satisfy the primary conditions of the letter mentioned by Dionysius of Corinth, which was written in the name of the whole Roman Church, whereas our author speaks in the singular throughout (p. 180 sq.).

But while the newly recovered ending decides the character of the document beyond the reach of dispute, it leaves the questions of *place, date,* and *authorship* still undetermined. On all these points we are obliged to fall back on such slight indications as the homily from time to time affords.

(i) As regards the *place,* Corinth seems to me still to have the highest claims to be considered. If the homily were delivered in that city, we have an explanation of two facts which are not so easily explained on any other hypothesis.

First. The allusion to the athletic games, and presumably to the

---

[1] See esp. pp. 177, 178. I call attention to this, because my view has been misrepresented. Thus Lipsius (*Academy,* July 9, 1870) says of me, 'He holds strongly with Hilgenfeld that the document is really a letter, not a homily.' So far from holding this view strongly, I have stated that we find in the document 'nothing which would lead to this inference,' and again that it '*bears no traces* of the epistolary form, though it may *possibly* have been a letter'; but I did not consider that in the existing condition of the work certainty on this point was attainable, and I therefore suspended judgment. When my able reviewer goes on to say of me 'He also agrees with Hilgenfeld in the opinion, that the epistle was composed during the persecution under Marcus Aurelius,' he imputes to me a view directly opposed to that which I have expressed (p. 177).

I think also that the reader would gather from the manner in which I am mentioned by Harnack (p. lxvi, note 2, p. lxxv) as 'refuting' Grabe, that I had maintained the document to be an epistle and not a homily; though probably this was not intended. See the Addenda on p. 179, l. 32 sq.

Isthmian festival, is couched in language which is quite natural if addressed to Corinthians, but not so if spoken elsewhere. When the preacher refers to the crowds that 'land' to take part in the games (εἰς τοὺς φθαρτοὺς ἀγῶνας καταπλέουσιν, § 7) without any mention of the port, we are naturally led to suppose that the homily was delivered in the neighbourhood of the place where these combatants landed. Otherwise we should expect εἰς τὸν Ἰσθμόν, or εἰς Κόρινθον, or some explanatory addition of the kind[1].

Secondly. This hypothesis alone satisfactorily explains the dissemination and reputed authorship of the document. It was early attached to the Epistle of Clement in the MSS (see p. 247) and came ultimately to be attributed to the same author. How did this happen? The First Epistle was read from time to time in the Church of Corinth, as we know. This homily was first preached, if my view be correct, to these same Corinthians; it was not an *extempore* address, but was delivered from a manuscript[2]; it was considered of sufficient value to be carefully preserved; and (as we may venture to suppose) it was read publicly to the Christian congregation at Corinth from time to time, like the genuine Epistle of Clement. The fact that these Corinthians took for public

---

[1] Thus in Plat. *Euthyd.* 297 C νεωστί, μοι δοκεῖν, κατατετλευκότι, where the word is used absolutely, we naturally understand the place in which the speaker is at the time.

[2] § 19 μετὰ τὸν Θεὸν τῆς ἀληθείας ἀναγινώσκω ὑμῖν ἔντευξιν εἰς τὸ προσέχειν τοῖς γεγραμμένοις, ἵνα καὶ ἑαυτοὺς σώσητε καὶ τὸν ἀναγινώσκοντα ἐν ὑμῖν. It is possible however, that the homily was originally delivered *extempore* and taken down by short-hand writers (ταχυγράφοι, notarii), and that the references to the reader were introduced afterwards when it was read in the Church as a homily. The employment of short-hand writers was frequent. We read of discourses of Origen taken down in this way (Euseb. *H.E.* vi. 36): and Origen himself on one occasion (*Comm. in Ioann.* vi. Præf., IV. p. 101) excuses himself for not having gone on with his work by the fact that the 'customary short-hand writers' were not there, καὶ οἱ συνήθεις δὲ ταχυγράφοι μὴ παρόντες τοῦ ἔχεσθαι τῶν ὑπαγορεύσεων

ἐκώλυον; comp. Photius *Bibl.* 121. At a later date this became a common mode of preserving pulpit oratory: see Bingham *Ant.* xiv. 4. 11. It was not uncommon for sermons and lectures to be taken down surreptitiously: see Gaudent. *Praf.* p. 220 (*Patrol. Lat.* XX. p. 831 Migne) 'notariis, ut comperi, latenter appositis' (with the note). On stenography among the ancients see Ducange *Glossarium* IV. p. 642 sq. (ed. Henschel) s. v. *Nota*, together with the references collected in Mayor's *Bibl. Clue to Lat. Lit.* p. 175 sq. See also *Contemporary Review* October 1875, p. 841 note. This alternative is suggested by Harnack *Zeitschr. f. Kirchengesch.* I. p. 268. The hypothesis would at all events have the merit of explaining the incoherence and looseness of expression which we find in this work; but in the absence of evidence it is safer to assume that the sermon was committed to writing by the preacher himself.

reading not only the Epistle of Clement, which might be thought to have acquired a peculiar sanctity by its venerable age, but also the much later letter of the Romans under bishop Soter, shows the practice of this Church in reference to uncanonical documents. In this way it would be bound up with the Epistle of Clement for convenience. In such a volume as is here supposed, the Epistle of Clement would be numbered and entitled thus:

ἀ

ΚΛΗΜΕΝΤΟC ΠΡΟC ΚΟΡΙΝΘΙΟΥC

with or without the addition ΕΠΙCΤΟΛΗ; while the homily which stood next in the volume might have had the heading

Β

ΠΡΟC ΚΟΡΙΝΘΙΟΥC

with or without the addition ΛΟΓΟC or ΟΜΙΛΙΑ, just as Orations of Dion Chrysostom bear the titles ΠΡΟC ΑΛΕΞΑΝΔΡΕΙC, ΠΡΟC ΑΠΑΜΕΙC; the author of the sermon however not being named. In the course of transcription the enumeration ἀ, Β, would easily be displaced, so that the two works would seem to be of the same kind and by the same author[1]. As a matter of fact, indications are not wanting in our existing authorities, that after this homily had been attached to S. Clement's epistle it remained anonymous in the common document which contained both works. In the Alexandrian MS there is no heading at all to the so-called Second Epistle (see pp. 22, 174). This fact however cannot be pressed, for it seems not unlikely that the title has been cut off[2]. But in the case of the Syriac

---

[1] This opinion was arrived at independently of the remarks of Zahn (*Gött. Gel. Anz.* Nov. 8, 1876, p. 1430 sq.), and I am the more glad to find that he accounts for the common heading of this sermon in a similar way.

[2] This possibility was overlooked by me in my edition pp. 22, 174. My attention was directed to it by a remark of Harnack (*Z. f. K.* I. p. 275, note 1), who however incorrectly states that in A the First Epistle has 'page-headings over the columns.' There is only one such page-heading, which stands over the first column as the title to the work. Having omitted to inspect the MS myself with this view, I requested Mr E. M. Thompson

of the British Museum to look at it and to give me his opinion. His report is to this effect:

The title to the First Epistle has small ornamental flourishes beneath. Between the bottom of these and the text there is a space of ⅓ of an inch. Over the first column of the Second Epistle (where the title should be, if there were any) the top of the leaf is cut obliquely so that the space left between the top of the leaf and the text varies from ⅓ to ¾ of an inch. Thus the space is quite consistent with the supposition that the title has been cut away. Moreover there is a single spot at the top of the page, which may have been the end of an

Version the testimony is free from suspicion. Here the genuine letter is called in the heading not 'The First Epistle of Clement' but 'The Catholic Epistle of Clement,' as if it were the only known letter written by this father (see p. 233). In both cases however the scribes themselves have in some other part of their respective MSS designated our work the Second Epistle of Clement; and this fact renders the survival of the older form only the more significant.

For these reasons I adhere to Corinth as the place of writing. On the other hand Harnack has with much ability maintained the Roman origin of this document[1]; and it is due to his arguments to consider them.

The *external evidence* seems to him to point in this direction. He remarks on the fact that this writing appears to have been very little known in the East during the earliest ages. It is first mentioned by Eusebius, and Eusebius himself, as Harnack argues from his language, only knew it from hearsay[2]. It is very far from certain, however, that this is the correct inference from the historian's words, ἰστέον δ' ὡς καὶ δευτέρα τις εἶναι λέγεται τοῦ Κλήμεντος ἐπιστολή· οὐ μὴν ἔθ' ὁμοίως τῇ προτέρᾳ καὶ ταύτην γνώριμον ἐπιστάμεθα, ὅτι μηδὲ τοὺς ἀρχαίους αὐτῇ κεχρημένους ἴσμεν (H. E. iii. 38). The hearsay implied in λέγεται may refer equally well to the authorship as to the contents of the book. In other words, Eusebius does not throw any doubt on the existence of such a work, but on its genuineness; and the language which follows suggests that the historian was himself acquainted with it. If the testimony of Eusebius be set aside, the earliest reference to its contents is found in the *Quæst. et Resp. ad Orthodoxos* § 74, falsely ascribed to Justin Martyr[3]. This work is supposed to have been written at the end of the fourth or beginning of the fifth century, and, as Harnack says, unless all appearances are deceptive, to have emanated from the Syro-Antiochene Church[4]. Our next direct witness in point of date is probably the Alexandrian MS, about the middle of

ornamental flourish under the title, though this is doubtful.

The photograph for the most part represents these facts fairly well.

[1] In two careful and valuable articles in the *Zeitschrift f. Kirchengeschichte* I. p. 264 sq., p. 329 sq., as well as in the prolegomena to the 2nd ed. of the *Patres Apostolici* Pt. i, p. lxiv sq. He stated this view first in a review of the edition of Bryennios in the *Theologische Literatur-zeitung* Feb. 19, 1876.

[2] *Z. f. K.* I. p. 269 sq.; Prol. p. lxiv, note 2.

[3] The passage is quoted above, p. 167 sq. For the reasons which make it highly probable now that the Pseudo-Justin refers to the so-called Second Epistle, and not (as there maintained) to the First Epistle, see the Addenda on p. 167, l. 9 and the notes on ii. § 16.

[4] See the article by Gass in Illgen's

the fifth century. From that time forward the testimonies are neither few nor indistinct (see above, p. 174 sq.)[1].

This evidence is somewhat slight; but it cannot be alleged against the Eastern origin of the work. Such as it is, it *all emanates from the East*. Neither early nor late do we hear a single voice from the West testifying to the existence of this Clementine writing, except such as are mere echoes of some Greek witness. External testimony therefore, though it may not be worth much, is directly opposed to Harnack's theory.

From the *internal character* of the work again Harnack draws the same inference. He remarks on the close resemblances to the Shepherd of Hermas, and thence infers that it must have emanated 'ex eadem communione ac societate[2].' Thus he makes it a product of the Church of Rome.

If these resemblances had referred to any peculiarities of the Roman Church generally, or of the Shepherd of Hermas in particular, the argument would have been strong. But this is not the case. The most striking perhaps is the doctrine of the heavenly Church (§ 14). But the passage which is quoted in my notes from Anastasius (see below, p. 327) shows that this distinction of the celestial and the terrestrial Church, so far from being peculiar, was a common characteristic of the earliest Christian writers. And the statement of Anastasius is borne out by extant remains, as will appear from parallel passages also cited there (pp. 325, 328). Again the pre-incarnate Son is spoken of in both documents as 'Spirit'; but here also, though such language was repugnant to the dogmatic precision of a later age, the writers of the second century and of the earlier part of the third constantly use it without misgiving (see above, p. 202). Again both writings speak of baptism as 'the seal,' and the exhortation to purity of life takes the form of an injunction to 'guard the seal.' But in this case likewise we have an image, which is common in Christian writers of the second century (see above, p. 198 sq.). Nor are other coincidences wanting, though less striking than these.

On the other hand the two writings present marked contrasts on points of special prominence. There is a wide divergence for instance between the rigid, almost Encratite, view of the relations between the sexes which our Clementine author enunciates[3], and the reasonable position

Zeitschr. f. d. hist. Theol. 1842, IV. p. 143 sq., quoted by Harnack *Z. f. K.* I. p. 274.

[1] The references in my notes seem to show that it was known to a very early writer, the author of *Apost. Const.* i—vi.

[2] Prol. p. lxx sq.: comp. *Z. f. K.* I. pp. 340, 344 sq., 363.

[3] § 12 τοῦτο λέγει ἵνα ἀδελφὸς κ.τ.λ.

of Hermas, which led the fierce Tertullian to denounce him as 'pastor mœchorum[1].' And again the difference of language regarding the relations of the two covenants is equally great. I cannot indeed regard the author of the Shepherd as a Judaizer, any more than I could regard our Clementine writer as a Marcionite: but the tendency of the one is to see in the Church a development of the Synagogue, whereas the other delights to set them in sharp contrast. And altogether it may be said that the points of difference in the two documents are more fundamental than the points of coincidence.

(ii) The second question, relating to the *date* of this work, receives some illustration from the newly discovered ending, though not so much as might have been hoped. Generally speaking the notices in this portion confirm the view which was indicated in my edition (p. 177), that it belongs to the first half of the second century, nor do they contain anything that is adverse to this view. Harnack, as the result of a thorough examination of the whole epistle, sets the limits of date as A.D. 130—160; and, if it emanated from Rome (as he supposes to have been the case), he thinks that it must have been written within the first two decades of this period, i.e. within A.D. 130—150[2].

This view is reasonable. If it were necessary to mention any limits of date, where so much uncertainty exists, I should name A.D. 120—140; but, as there is nothing in the work which militates against a still earlier date, so again it is impossible to affirm confidently that it might not have been written a few years later. The two main points

---

On the other hand Hermas (*Mand.* iv. 1) writes Ἐντέλλομαί σοι, φησί, φυλάσσειν τὴν ἁγνείαν· καὶ μὴ ἀναβαινέτω σου ἐπὶ τὴν καρδίαν περὶ γυναικὸς ἀλλοτρίας ἢ περὶ πορνείας τινὸς ἢ περὶ τοιούτων τινῶν ὁμοιωμάτων πονηρῶν· τοῦτο γὰρ ποίων ἁμαρτίαν μεγάλην ἐργάζῃ· τῆς δὲ σῆς μνημονεύων πάντοτε γυναικὸς οὐδέποτε ἁμαρτήσεις. In this same section the husband is enjoined to take back into his society the wife who has been unfaithful, and just below (§ 4) second marriages are permitted to Christians, though the greater honour is assigned to those who remain in widowhood. On the other hand Harnack (*Z. f. K.* I. p. 348) quotes *Vis.* ii. 2 τῇ συμβίῳ σου τῇ μελλούσῃ σου ἀδελφῇ, as showing that Hermas looked upon the single life

as the ideal state, and he concludes that neither writer 'thought of stopping marriage among Christians for the present.' It is not clear what the words in *Vis.* ii. 2 may mean; nor again is it certain that our Clementine preacher intended to enforce an absolute rule or to do more than give counsels of perfection. But the fact remains that the direct language of the one is in favour of latitude, of the other in favour of restraint.

[1] Tertull. *de Pudic.* 10 'scriptura Pastoris quæ sola mœchos amat...adultera et ipsa et inde patrona sociorum,' *ib.* 20 'illo apocrypho Pastore mœchorum.'

[2] *Z. f. K.* I. p. 363; comp. Prol. p. lxxiii sq. (ed. 2), where, supposing it to be of Roman origin, he places it not later than A.D. 135—140 (145).

in which the recently recovered portion strengthens the existing data for determining the age of the document are these.

First. We are furnished with additional information respecting the relations of the author to the Canon of the New Testament. He distinguishes between the Old and New Testament: the former he styles 'the Books,' 'the Bible' (τὰ βιβλία), while the latter (or a part of it) is designated 'the Apostles' (§ 14). This distinction separates him by a broad line from the age of the Muratorian writer (c. A.D. 170 —180), of Irenæus, and of Clement of Alexandria, i.e. from the last quarter of the second century. The fact also that he uses at least one apocryphal Gospel, which we can hardly be wrong in identifying with the Gospel of the Egyptians (see above, pp. 192, 193, 207 sq.), apparently as an authoritative document, points in the same direction. The writers just mentioned are all explicit in the acceptance of our four Canonical Gospels alone, as the traditional inheritance of the Church. This argument would be very strong in favour of an early date, if we could be quite sure that our homily was written by a member of the Catholic Church, and not by some sectarian or half-sectarian writer. On this point there is perhaps room for misgiving, though on the whole it seems the more probable supposition. The general acceptance of this homily and its attribution to Clement certainly point to a Catholic origin; and in its Christology also it is Catholic as opposed to Gnostic or Ebionite (see above, p. 182), but its Encratite tendencies (not to mention other phenomena) might suggest the opposite conclusion.

On the other hand our preacher quotes as 'scripture' (§ 6) a saying which appears in our Canonical Gospels. But this same passage is quoted in the same way in the Epistle of Barnabas, which can hardly have been written many years after A.D. 120 at the very latest, and may have been written much earlier; and even Polycarp (§ 12), if the Latin text may be trusted, cites Ephes. iv. 26 as 'scripture.' Stronger in the same direction is the fact that in the newly recovered portion our anonymous author introduces a saying of our Lord in the Gospels with the words 'God saith' (§ 13), having immediately before referred to 'the Oracles of God' in this same connexion, and that he elsewhere describes the reading of the Scriptures as the voice of 'the God of truth' speaking to the congregation (§ 19). As regards this latter passage however we do not know whether the scriptural lessons which had preceded the delivery of this homily were taken from the Old or from the New Testament.

Secondly. The relations of the preacher to Gnosticism furnish an indication of date though not very precise. He attacks a certain type of this heresy, but it is still in an incipient form. The doctrinal point on which he especially dwells is the denial of the resurrection of the body, or (as he states it) the 'resurrection of this flesh' (§§ 8, 9, 14) [1]. As the practical consequence of this denial, the false teachers (§ 10 κακοδιδασκα-λοῦντες) were led to antinomian inferences. They inculcated an indifference (ἀδιαφορία) with regard to fleshly lusts, and they permitted their disciples to deny their faith in times of persecution. This antinomian teaching is denounced by the preacher [2]. But his polemic against Gnosticism does not go beyond this. There is no attack, direct or indirect, on the peculiar tenets of Valentinus and the Valentinians, of Marcion, or even of Basilides. And not only so, but he even uses language with regard to the heavenly Church which closely resembles the teaching of Valentinus respecting the æon Ecclesia (see below, p. 328), and which he would almost certainly have avoided, if he had written after this heresiarch began to promulgate his doctrine [3]. In like manner the language in which he sets the Church against the Synagogue would probably have been more guarded, if it had been uttered after Marcion had published his Antitheses in which the direct antagonism of the Mosaic and Christian dispensations was maintained. As it is a reasonable inference from the near approaches to Valentinian language in the Ignatian Epistles that they were written in the pre-Valentinian epoch [4], seeing that the writer is a determined opponent of Gnosticism, and would not have compromised himself by such language after it had been abused, so also the same inference may be drawn here.

These considerations seem to point to a date not later than A.D. 140: and altogether the topics in this homily suggest a very primitive, though not apostolic, age of the Church. Whether we regard the exposition of doctrine or the polemic against false teachers or the state of the Christian society or the relation to the Scriptural Canon, we cannot but feel that we are confronted with a state of things separated by a wide interval from the epoch of Irenæus and Clement of Alexandria. At the same time other arguments have been alleged in favour of an early date, which will not bear the stress that has been laid upon them. Thus it is said that the preacher betrays no knowledge of the writings of S. John, or possibly even of S. Paul [5]. As regards S. John, I have called attention

---

[1] See above, p. 201.

[2] See above, pp. 177, 201, and comp. § 16.

[3] This argument drawn from the relation of the writer to Gnosticism is justly insisted upon by Harnack *Prol.* p. lxxii,

Z. f. K. I. pp. 359, 360.

[4] See *Contemporary Review*, February 1875, p. 357 sq.

[5] Harnack *Prol.* p. lxxiii, *Z. f. K.* I. p. 361 sq. He regards it as uncertain, though probable, that our author had

to an indication that our author was not unacquainted with the Fourth Gospel (see p. 336), though the inference is not certain. As regards S. Paul, I cannot see any probable explanation of his appeal to 'the Apostles' as supporting his doctrine respecting the heavenly Church, except that which supposes him to be referring to S. Paul, and more especially to the Epistle to the Ephesians—not to mention echoes of this Apostle's language elsewhere in this homily[1]. But even if it be granted that he shows no knowledge of the writings of either Apostle, does it follow that he had none? What numbers of sermons and tracts, published in the name of authors living in this nineteenth century, must on these grounds be relegated to the first or second! And again, if he says nothing about episcopacy[2], does it follow that he knew nothing about it, and therefore must have written before this institution existed? This argument again would, I imagine, remove to a remote antiquity a large portion, probably not less than half, of the theological literature of our own age.

(iii) But, while criticism suggests probable or approximate results with regard to the locality and the date, it leaves us altogether in the dark as respects the *authorship;* for the opinions maintained by the three editors who have discussed this question since the recent discovery of the lost ending, must, I venture to think, be discarded. All three alike agree in the retention of Clement as the author, but understand different persons bearing this name.

(1) In the first place Bryennios (p. ρνθ´) maintains that the homily is the work of none other than the famous Clement whose name it bears, the bishop of Rome. This view however has nothing to recommend it, and has found no favour with others. Indeed all the arguments which were urged against it, when the work was still a fragment, are considerably strengthened, now that we have it complete. Thus for instance the gulf which separates our preacher from the genuine Clement in their respective relations to the New Testament Scriptures (see above, p. 176 sq.) has been widened by the additional evidence furnished on this point. And again the divergence of style between the two writings has been still further emphasized by the recent discovery. Indeed to those who had studied the two works carefully in their fragmentary state, no proof of the genuineness of the recent discovery could have been more

read S. Paul's Epistles. At the same time he considers it strange that S. Paul's name is not mentioned. As most of our author's quotations (even when taken from the Old Testament) are ano-

nymous, this fact can hardly surprise us.
[1] See the notes pp. 187, 189, 198.
[2] Harnack *Prol.* p. lxxii, *Z. f. K.* I. p. 359.

satisfactory than the finding that each document, as distinguished from the other, retained in the new portions the most subtle peculiarities of thought and diction which had been observed in the old.

(2) On the other hand Hilgenfeld (p. xlix, ed. 2) surmises that the author was not the Roman Clement but the Alexandrian. He argues that our preacher was not a presbyter, but a catechist[1]. He points to the passage (§ 19) in which (as he reads it) the duty of studying 'philosophy' is inculcated[2]. And, as Dodwell had done before him (see above, p. 180), he imagines that he sees resemblances in this sermon to the style and thought of the Alexandrian Clement. He therefore suggests that this was an early production of the Alexandrian father.

The inference however with regard to the preacher's office is highly precarious, as we have seen already (p. 304); nor does it materially affect the question. The mention of 'philosophy' again disappears, when the passage is correctly read. The Syriac Version shows clearly that φιλοπονεῖν is the true reading, and that φιλοσοφεῖν, as a much commoner word, was written down first from mere inadvertence by the scribe of C and afterwards corrected by him[3]. Nor again is it possible to see any closer resemblance to the Alexandrian Clement in the diction and thoughts, than will often appear between one early Christian writer and another; while on the other hand the difference is most marked. The wide learning, the extensive vocabulary, the speculative power, the vigorous and epigrammatic expression, of the Alexandrian Clement are all wanting to this sermon, which is confused in thought and slipshod in expression, and is only redeemed from common-place by its moral earnestness and by some peculiarities of doctrinal exposition. Where there is want of arrangement in the Alexandrian Clement, it is due to his wealth of learning and of thought. In our author on the other hand the confusion is the result of intellectual poverty. Nor again is the difference between the two writers less wide as regards their relation to the Canon of the New Testament. It is true that both alike quote the Gospel of the Egyptians, and (as

---

[1] See pp. xlix, 106. He explains § 17 εἰ γὰρ ἐντολὰς ἔχομεν...ἀπὸ τῶν εἰδώλων ἀποσπᾶν καὶ κατηχεῖν as referring to the official position of the preacher; but compare e.g. 1 Cor. xiv. 19, Gal. vi. 6.

[2] See pp. xlix, 84, 106.

[3] Compare the note on this word φιλοπονεῖν § 19 (p. 338, l. 8) with that on

μεταλήψεται § 14 (p. 328, l. 5). In both cases the scribe has corrected the word which he first wrote down, and in both the correction is supported by the Syriac Version. Hilgenfeld has consistently adopted the scribe's first writing in both cases. On p. 84 he has incorrectly given φιλοποιεῖν as the correction in C. It should be φιλοπονεῖν.

it so happens) the same passage from this Gospel. But this very fact enables us to realize the gulf which separates the two. Our author uses this apocryphal work as authoritative, and apparently as his chief evangelical narrative; Clement on the other hand depreciates its value on the ground that it is not one of the four traditionally received by the Church. Our author interprets the passage in question as favouring ascetic views respecting the relation of the sexes: Clement on the other hand refutes this interpretation, and explains it in a mystical sense[1].

(3) Lastly; Harnack is disposed to assign this homily neither to the Roman bishop nor to the Alexandrian father, but to a third person bearing the name of Clement, intermediate in date between the two.

In the Shepherd of Hermas (*Vis.* ii. 4) the writer relates how he was directed in a vision to send a copy of his book to 'Clement,' and it is added 'Clement shall send it to the cities abroad; for he is charged with this business' (πέμψει οὖν Κλήμης εἰς τὰς ἔξω πόλεις· ἐκείνῳ γὰρ ἐπιτέτραπται). As Hermas is stated to have written this work during the episcopate of his brother Pius (c. A.D. 140—155), it is urged that the Clement here mentioned cannot have been the same with the illustrious bishop of Rome[2]. Thus the notice in the Shepherd gives us another Roman Clement, who flourished about the time when our homily must have been written. Here, argues Harnack, we have an explanation of the phenomena of the so-called Second Epistle of Clement. If we suppose that towards the end of the third century a homily known to have emanated from the early Church of Rome and

---

[1] *Strom.* iii. 13 p. 553 (quoted above, p. 209 sq.). Julius Cassianus, like our preacher, had interpreted the passage as discountenancing marriage; and Clement of Alexandria controverts him, substituting another interpretation. While the passage was still mutilated, the opinion was expressed in my notes (p. 210) that it was doubtful whether our author's explanation was more closely allied to the interpretation of Cassianus or to that of Clement of Alexandria, though I inclined to the latter supposition. The discovery of the conclusion of the passage however decides in favour of the former.

It is in reference to this very passage from the Gospel of the Egyptians, that Clement of Alexandria urges in answer to Cassianus, ἐν τοῖς παραδεδομένοις ἡμῖν τέτταρσιν εὐαγγελίοις οὐκ ἔχομεν τὸ ῥητόν, ἀλλ᾽ ἐν τῷ κατ᾽ Αἰγυπτίους. Thus he is diametrically opposed to our preacher on the one point where we are able to compare their opinions.

[2] Prol. p. lxxiv, *Z. f. K.* I. p. 363 sq. See also his remarks in the *Theolog. Literatur.* Feb. 3, 1877, p. 55 sq. The distinction of this Clement mentioned by Hermas from the famous Roman bishop is maintained also by G. Heyne (*Quo tempore Hermæ Pastor scriptus sit*, 1872, p. 15 sq.) quoted in Harnack, and by Skworzow (*Patrol. Unters.* p. 54 sq.): see also Donaldson *Apostolic Fathers* p. 330, ed. 2.

bearing the name of Clement was carried to the East, it would not unnaturally be attributed to the famous bishop, and thus, being attached to his genuine epistle, might easily before the close of the fourth century be furnished with the incorrect title Κλήμεντος πρὸς Κορινθίους ἐπιστολὴ β'.

This view has much more to recommend it, than the two which have been considered already. But the foundation on which it rests is insecure. Notwithstanding the chronological difficulty, it is not easy to resist the conviction that the famous bishop of Rome himself was intended by the author of the Shepherd. The function assigned to him of communicating with foreign cities is especially appropriate to one who was known as the author and transmitter of the epistle written in the name of the Roman Church to the Corinthians. Nor, if we remember the obscurity which shrouds the authorship and date of the Shepherd, is the chronological difficulty serious. The Shepherd indeed is stated by our earliest authority, the Muratorian Fragmentist, to have been written *during* the episcopate of Pius[1]. But, considering that we only possess this testimony in a very blundering Latin translation, it may reasonably be questioned whether the Greek original stated as much definitely. Again, it is quite possible that, though the book may have been published as late as A.D. 140, yet the epoch of the supposed revelation was placed at a much earlier period in the writer's life, while the Roman bishop was still living. For, though the latest date mentioned by any authority for the death of the Roman bishop is A.D. 100 or 101[2], yet no weight can be attached to any testimony which we possess on this point, and we may without hesitation suppose Clement to have lived several years after the close of the century, if independent facts seem to require it. Even if this explanation of the chronological difficulty should fail, the possibility still remains that Hermas is a *nom de plume* assumed by the brother of Pius for the purposes of dramatic fiction, and that the epoch of

---

[1] The words in the *Muratorian Canon* are 'Pastorem vero nuperrime temporibus nostris in urbe Roma Hermas conscripsit sedente cathedram urbis Romæ ecclesiæ Pio episcopo fratre ejus' (see Westcott *Canon* pp. 519, 530, ed. 4), when some obvious errors of orthography and transcription are corrected. Considering the blunders of which this translation elsewhere is guilty, the probability is that the translator would not carefully distinguish between the absence and presence of the article, e. g. between ἐπικαθημένου and τοῦ ἐπικαθημένου: see *Philippians* p. 166 sq. There is no reason to suppose that the notice in the *Liberian Chronicle* 'Sub huius [Pii] episcopatu frater eius Ermes librum scripsit etc.' is independent of this notice in the *Muratorian Canon*.

[2] Euseb. *H. E.* iii. 34.

this fiction is placed by him half a century or so before he wrote, and while Clement the bishop was still living. In this case he may have had in his mind the Hermas mentioned by S. Paul among the Roman Christians. On the whole however it seems probable that, like Dante's relation to Beatrice in the Commedia, the fiction of the Shepherd is founded on the actual circumstances of the writer's own life.

As all these hypotheses fail us, we must be content to remain still in ignorance of the author; nor is it likely now that the veil will ever be withdrawn. The homily itself, as a literary work, is almost worthless. As the earliest example of its kind however, and as the product of an important age of which we possess only the scantiest remains, it has the highest value. Nor will its intellectual poverty blind us to its true grandeur, as an example of the lofty moral earnestness and the triumphant faith which subdued a reluctant world and laid it prostrate at the foot of the Cross.

THE CONCLVSION OF

AN ANCIENT· HOMILY

COMMONLY CALLED THE

SECOND EPISTLE OF S. CLEMENT.

21—2

καὶ τὸ ἄρϲεν μετὰ τᾶϲ θηλείαϲ οὔτε ἄρϲεν οὔτε
θᾶλυ, τοῦτο λέγει, ἵνα ἀδελφὸς ἰδὼν ἀδελφὴν †οὐδὲν†
φρονῇ περὶ αὐτῆς θηλυκόν, μηδὲ φρονῇ τι περὶ αὐτοῦ
ἀρσενικόν. ταῦτα ὑμῶν ποιούντων, φησίν, ἐλεύσεται
5 ἡ βασιλεία τοῦ πατρός μου.

XIII. 'Αδελφοὶ †οὖν† ἤδη ποτὲ μετανοήσωμεν·

2 οὐδὲν φρονῇ] οὐδὲν φρονεῖ C.   3 μηδὲ] add. *quum soror videbit fratrem* S.
6 'Αδελφοὶ οὖν] 'Αδελφοὶ [μου] S, omitting οὖν. As S commonly renders ἀδελφοί
alone by אחי *fratres mei*, it is uncertain whether the translator had μου in his text.

1. καὶ τὸ ἄρσεν κ.τ.λ.] The lacuna
in the Alexandrian MS commences
after τοῦτο: see p. 209. But the
previous words in the sentence are
here printed again for the sake of
convenience.

2. οὐδέν] The previous editors,
while substituting φρονῇ for φρονεῖ,
have passed over οὐδέν in silence.
But with φρονῇ we should certainly
expect μηδέν. The reading οὐδέν
can only be explained by treating
οὐδὲν θηλυκόν as a separate idea,
'should entertain thoughts which
have no regard to her sex', so as
to isolate οὐδέν from the influence of
ἵνα ; but the order makes this explanation very difficult. The gram-
mars do not give any example of
the use of οὐ (οὐδέν) which is analogous; see Kühner II p. 747 sq.,
Winer § lv. p. 599 sq. The sentence
is elliptical, and words must be
understood in the second clause,
μηδὲ [ἀδελφὴ ἰδοῦσα ἀδελφὸν] φρονῇ
κ.τ.λ. Similar words, it will be seen,
are supplied in the Syriac; but I
attribute this to the exigencies of
translation, rather than to any difference in the Greek text which the
translator had. Gebhardt ingeni-
ously reads μηδ' ἤδε; but ἤδε...αὐτοῦ
does not seem a natural combination
of pronouns here.

4. φησίν] It does not follow that
the preacher is quoting the exact

words of the Gospel according to
the Egyptians; for φησίν may mean
nothing more than 'he says in effect',
'he signifies'. See e.g. Barnab. 7
οὕτω, φησίν, οἱ θέλοντές με ἰδεῖν κ.τ.λ.,
a passage which has been wrongly
understood as preserving a saying
of Christ elsewhere unrecorded, but
in which the writer is really giving
only an *explanation* of what has
gone before. This use of φησίν
occurs many times elsewhere in
Barnab. §§ 6, 10, 11, 12, where the
meaning is indisputable.

XIII. 'Let us therefore repent
and be vigilant: for now we are full
of wickedness. Let us wipe out our
former sins ; and not be men-pleasers.
Yet we must approve ourselves by
our righteousness to the heathen,
lest God's Name be blasphemed, as
the Scriptures warn us. And how
is it blasphemed? When the Oracles of God command one thing,
and we do another: for then they
treat the Scriptures as a lying fable.
When for instance God's Word tells
us to love those that hate us, and
they find that, so far from doing
this, we hate those that love us,
they laugh us to scorn, and they
blaspheme the holy Name'.

6. οὖν] This particle cannot stand
after the vocative, and indeed is
omitted in the Syriac. Perhaps οὖν
is a corruption of μου, as ἀδελφοί

νήψωμεν ἐπὶ τὸ ἀγαθόν· μεστοὶ γάρ ἐσμεν πολλῆς
ἀνοίας καὶ πονηρίας. ἐξαλείψωμεν ἀφ' ἡμῶν τὰ πρό-
τερα ἁμαρτήματα, καὶ μετανοήσαντες ἐκ ψυχῆς σωθῶμεν. καὶ μὴ γινώμεθα ἀνθρωπάρεσκοι· μηδὲ θέλωμεν
μόνον ἑαυτοῖς ἀρέσκειν, ἀλλὰ καὶ τοῖς ἔξω ἀνθρώποις 5
ἐπὶ τῇ δικαιοσύνῃ, ἵνα τὸ ὄνομα δι' ἡμᾶς μὴ βλασφη-
μῆται. Λέγει γὰρ καὶ ὁ Κύριος Διὰ παντὸς τὸ ὄνομά μου
βλασφημεῖται ἐν πᾶσιν τοῖς ἔθνεσιν· καὶ πάλιν Οὐαὶ δι' ὃν
βλασφημεῖται τὸ ὄνομά μου ἐν τίνι βλασφημεῖται;

6 τὸ ὄνομα] add. *Domini* S.   ἡμᾶς] S; ὑμᾶς C.   7 καί] S; om. C.
8 βλασφημεῖται] add. δι' ὑμᾶς S.   πᾶσιν] om. S.   πάλιν Οὐαὶ δι' ὅν] S; Διὸ C.
See the lower note.   9 ἐν τίνι] add. δὲ S: comp. ii. § 3.   10 ὑμᾶς ἃ βούλομαι]
ἡμᾶς ἃ λέγομεν S.   11 ἡμῶν] S; ὑμῶν C.   12 ἔπειτα] add. δὲ S.   15 μῦθόν

μου occurs several times, §§ 9, 10, 11;
or the scribe has here tampered with
the connecting particles, as he has
done elsewhere (§ 7 ὥστε οὖν, ἀδελφοί
μου), and in this case has blundered.

1. νήψωμεν ἐπὶ κ.τ.λ.] 1 Tim. ii. 26
ἀνανήψωσιν...εἰς τὸ ἐκείνου θέλημα,
1 Pet. iv. 7 νήψατε εἰς προσευχάς,
Polyc. *Phil.* 7 νήφοντες πρὸς τὰς εὐχάς.

2. ἐξαλείψωμεν] Harnack quotes
Acts iii. 19 μετανοήσατε οὖν καὶ
ἐπιστρέψατε εἰς τὸ ἐξαλειφθῆναι
ὑμῶν τὰς ἁμαρτίας.

4. ἀνθρωπάρεσκοι] Ephes. vi. 6,
Col. iii. 22. See also the note on
ἀνθρωπαρεσκεῖν Ign. *Rom.* 2.

5. ἑαυτοῖς] 'one another', i. e.
'our fellow-Christians', as rightly
explained here by Harnack; comp.
§ 4 ἐν τῷ ἀγαπᾶν ἑαυτούς, § 12 λαλῶμεν
ἑαυτοῖς ἀλήθειαν, but not § 15.

τοῖς ἔξω ἀνθρώποις] 'the heathen'.
For the expression οἱ ἔξω see the
note *Colossians* iv. 5.

6. τὸ ὄνομα] 'the Name'; so
Tertull. *Idol.* 14 'ne nomen blas-
phemetur'. For other instances of
this absolute use, and for the manner in which (as here) translators
and transcribers supply the imagined
defect, see the note on Ign. *Ephes.* 3.

7. Διὰ παντὸς κ.τ.λ.] From the
LXX Is. lii. 5 τάδε λέγει ὁ Κύριος, Δι'
ὑμᾶς διὰ παντὸς τὸ ὄνομά μου βλασφημεῖται ἐν τοῖς ἔθνεσιν. The Syriac
translator inserts δι' ὑμᾶς, and omits
πᾶσιν; but these are obvious alterations to conform to the familiar LXX
of Isaiah.

8. καὶ πάλιν Οὐαὶ κ.τ.λ.] I have
adopted the reading of the Syriac
here, because the Greek text is
obviously due to the accidental o-
mission of some letters (perhaps
owing to homœoteleuton), a common
phenomenon in our MS. On the
other hand it is hardly conceivable
that any scribe or translator could
have invented the longer reading
of the Syriac out of the shorter
reading of the Greek. The Syriac
reading however is not without its
difficulty. If the first quotation Διὰ
παντὸς κ.τ.λ. is taken from Is. lii.
5, whence comes the second Οὐαὶ
κ.τ.λ.? The explanation seems to
be, that Is. lii. 5 itself was very
frequently quoted in the early ages
Οὐαὶ δι' ὅν (or δι' οὗ) κ.τ.λ. (see
instances collected in the note to
Ign. *Trall.* 8), though there is no
authority for it either in the LXX or

10 ἐν τῷ μὴ ποιεῖν ὑμᾶς ἃ βούλομαι. τὰ ἔθνη γάρ,
ἀκούοντα ἐκ τοῦ στόματος ἡμῶν τὰ λόγια τοῦ Θεοῦ,
ὡς καλὰ καὶ μεγάλα θαυμάζει· ἔπειτα, καταμαθόντα
τὰ ἔργα ἡμῶν ὅτι οὐκ ἔστιν ἄξια τῶν ῥημάτων ὧν
λέγομεν, ἔνθεν εἰς βλασφημίαν τρέπονται, λέγοντες
15 εἶναι μῦθόν τινα καὶ πλάνην. ὅταν γὰρ ἀκούσωσιν
παρ' ἡμῶν ὅτι λέγει ὁ Θεός Οϒ χάρις ϒΜῖΝ εἰ ἀΓαΠᾶτε
τοϒϲ ἀΓαΠῶΝταϲ ϒΜᾶϲ, ἀλλὰ χάρις ϒΜῖΝ εἰ ἀΓαΠᾶτε τοϒϲ
ἐχθροϒϲ καὶ τοϒϲ ΜιϲοϒΝταϲ ϒΜᾶϲ· ταῦτα ὅταν ἀκοϒ-

 Τωα] add. *delirii* S, the word being doubtless added to bring out the force of
μῦθον.   17 ἀλλὰ] add. τότε S.   18 ἐχθρούς] add. ὑμῶν S. The addition of
pronouns is very common in S ; and I have not thought it necessary to record
several instances which occur below.

in the Hebrew. Our preacher therefore seems to have cited the same
passage in two different forms—the
first from the LXX, the second from
the familiar language of quotation—
supposing that he was giving two
distinct passages.

9. ἐν τίνι κ.τ.λ.] This is no longer
any part of the quotation, but belongs
to the preacher's explanation. He has
however put the words into the mouth
of God Himself, after his wont: e. g.
§ 12 ταῦτα ὑμῶν ποιούντων κ.τ.λ., § 14
τηρήσατε τὴν σάρκα κ.τ.λ. The reading of the Syriac, μὴ ποιεῖν ἡμᾶς ἃ
λέγομεν, is obviously a correction
to overcome this difficulty. For other
examples where this preacher begins
his explanations with ἐν τίνι see
§§ 3, 9.

11. τὰ λόγια τοῦ Θεοῦ] A synonyme
for the Scriptures ; comp. Rom. iii.
2, Heb. v. 12 ; Clem. Rom. 19, 53,
62, etc. The point to be observed
is that the expression here refers to
an *evangelical* record: see the next
note below. Thus it may be compared with the language of Papias,
Euseb. *H. E.* iii. 39 Ματθαῖος...συνε-
γράψατο τὰ λόγια, which must have
been nearly contemporaneous. See

Contemporary Review, August 1875,
p. 400 sq. Similarly our author
above § 2 quotes a Gospel as γραφή
(see pp. 177, 190).

12. ἔπειτα κ.τ.λ.] *Apost. Const.* ii. 8
ὁ τοιοῦτος...βλασφημίαν προσέτριψε τῷ
κοινῷ τῆς ἐκκλησίας καὶ τῇ διδασκαλίᾳ,
ὡς μὴ ποιούντων ἐκεῖνα ἃ λέγομεν εἶναι
καλὰ κ.τ.λ.

16. λέγει ὁ Θεός] 'God saith'. The
passage quoted therefore is regarded
as one of τὰ λόγια τοῦ Θεοῦ. As the
words of our Lord follow, it might
perhaps be thought that the expression λέγει ὁ Θεός refers not to the
Divine inspiration of the Gospel,
but to the Divine personality of
Christ, of whom the writer says § 1
οὕτως δεῖ ἡμᾶς φρονεῖν περὶ Ἰησοῦ
Χριστοῦ ὡς περὶ Θεοῦ. But, not to
mention that such a mode of speaking would be without a parallel in
the early ages of Christianity, the
preceding τὰ λόγια τοῦ Θεοῦ determines the sense here.

Οὐ χάρις κ.τ.λ.] A loose quotation
from Luke vi. 32, 35 εἰ ἀγαπᾶτε τοὺς
ἀγαπῶντας ὑμᾶς, ποία ὑμῖν χάρις ἐστίν;
...πλὴν ἀγαπᾶτε τοὺς ἐχθροὺς ὑμῶν...
καὶ ἔσται ὁ μισθὸς ὑμῶν πολύς. For the
use of χάρις comp. 1 Pet. ii. 19, 20.

σωσιν, θαυμάζουσιν τὴν ὑπερβολὴν τῆς ἀγαθότητος·
ὅταν δὲ ἴδωσιν ὅτι οὐ μόνον τοὺς μισοῦντας οὐκ ἀγα-
πῶμεν, ἀλλ᾽ ὅτι οὐδὲ τοὺς ἀγαπῶντας, καταγελῶσιν
ἡμῶν, καὶ βλασφημεῖται τὸ ὄνομα.

XIV. ῞Ωστε, ἀδελφοί, ποιοῦντες τὸ θέλημα τοῦ 5
πατρὸς ἡμῶν Θεοῦ ἐσόμεθα ἐκ τῆς ἐκκλησίας τῆς πρώ-

3 ὅτι] om. S, perhaps owing to the exigencies of translation.　4 καί] om. S.
βλασφημεῖται] add. οὖν S.　τὸ ὄνομα] add. τοῦ Χριστοῦ S.　9 ἐκ τῆς γραφῆς

1. ἀγαθότητος] 'goodness' in the
sense of 'kindness' 'beneficence',
as ἀγαθοποιεῖν in the context of St
Luke (vv. 33, 35). This substantive
does not occur in the N. T., and only
rarely (Wisd. vii. 26, xii. 22, Ecclus.
xlv. 23) in the LXX; the form commonly used being ἀγαθωσύνη.

XIV. 'If we do God's will, we
shall be members of the eternal,
spiritual Church; if not, we shall
belong to that house which is a den
of thieves. The living Church is
Christ's body. God made male and
female, saith the Scripture. The male
is Christ, the female the Church.
The Bible and the Apostles teach
us that the Church existed from
eternity. Just as Jesus was manifested in the flesh, so. also was the
Church. If therefore we desire to
partake of the spiritual archetype,
we must preserve the fleshly copy
in its purity. This flesh is capable
of life and immortality, if it be united
to the Spirit, that is to Christ. And
the blessings which await His elect
are greater than tongue can tell.'

6. τῆς πρώτης κ.τ.λ.] This doctrine of an eternal Church seems to
be a development of the Apostolic
teaching which insists on the fore-
ordained purpose of God as having
elected a body of men to serve Him
from all eternity; see esp. Ephes.

i. 3 sq. ὁ εὐλογήσας ἡμᾶς ἐν πάσῃ
εὐλογίᾳ πνευματικῇ ἐν τοῖς ἐπου-
ρανίοις ἐν Χριστῷ, καθὼς ἐξελέξατο
ἡμᾶς ἐν αὐτῷ πρὸ καταβολῆς κόσμου
...προορίσας ἡμᾶς εἰς υἱοθεσίαν κ.τ.λ.,
a passage aptly quoted by Bryennios.
The language of our preacher stands
midway in point of development,
and perhaps also in point of chronology, between this teaching of S.
Paul and the doctrine of the Valentinians, who believed in an eternal
æon 'Ecclesia', thus carrying the
Platonism of our pseudo-Clement a
step in advance.

7. πρὸ ἡλίου κ.τ.λ.] This expression is probably taken from Ps.
lxxi (lxxii). 5 συμπαραμενεῖ τῷ ἡλίῳ
καὶ πρὸ τῆς σελήνης γενεὰς γενεῶν
and ib. ver. 17 πρὸ τοῦ ἡλίου διαμενεῖ
τὸ ὄνομα αὐτοῦ; for though in these
passages, as the Hebrew shows, πρὸ
has or ought to have a different
meaning (Aquila εἰς πρόσωπον τῆς
σελήνης, Symmachus ἔμπροσθεν τῆς
σελήνης), yet it was commonly so
interpreted, as appears from Justin
Dial. 64 (p. 288) ἀποδείκνυται...ὅτι
οὗτος (i. e. ὁ Χριστός) καὶ πρὸ τοῦ
ἡλίου ἦν, in proof of which statement
he cites the passages just quoted;
comp. ib. 45 (p. 264) ὃς καὶ πρὸ
ἑωσφόρου καὶ σελήνης ἦν, 34 (p. 252),
76 (p. 302); and so Athanasius c.
Arian. i. 41 (I. p. 351) εἰ δὲ καί, ὡς

της, τῆς πνευματικῆς, τῆς πρὸ ἡλίου καὶ σελήνης ἐκτισ-
μένης· ἐὰν δὲ μὴ ποιήσωμεν τὸ θέλημα Κυρίου, ἐσόμεθα
ἐκ τῆς γραφῆς τῆς λεγούσης Ἐγενήθη ὁ οἶκόс μογ
10 cΠΗΛΑΙΟΝ ΛΗсΤῶΝ. ὥστε οὖν αἱρετισώμεθα ἀπὸ τῆς
ἐκκλησίας τῆς ζωῆς εἶναι, ἵνα σωθῶμεν. οὐκ οἴομαι
δὲ ὑμᾶς ἀγνοεῖν ὅτι ἐκκλησία ζῶσα сῶΜΆ ἐсΤΙΝ

τῆς λεγούσης] ex iis de quibus scriptum est S.   10 ὥστε οὖν] ὥστε, ἀδελφοί [μου]
S, omitting οὖν. See p. 321.

ψάλλει Δαυὶδ ἐν τῷ ἑβδομηκοστῷ πρώτῳ
ψαλμῷ, Πρὸ τοῦ ἡλίου διαμένει τὸ
ὄνομα αὐτοῦ, καὶ πρὸ τῆς σελήνης εἰς
γενεὰς γενεῶν, πῶς ἐλάμβανεν ὁ εἶχεν
ἀεί κ.τ.λ. Similarly too in his *Expos.
in Psalm.* lxxi (I. p. 897) he explains
the two expressions, vv. 5, 17, πρὸ
αἰώνων and πρὸ καταβολῆς κόσμου
respectively. Meanwhile Eusebius
Comm. in Psalm. ad loc. (*Op.* v. p.
800 ed. Migne) had mentioned and
rejected this meaning; οὐ γὰρ πρὸ
τῆς σελήνης, τούτεστι πρὶν γενέσθαι
τὴν σελήνην, ἀλλ' ἐνώπιον ὥσπερ καὶ
ἔμπροσθεν ἡγούμενος τῆς σελήνης.
For the idea see esp. Hermas *Vis.*
ii. 4 Τίς οὖν ἐστίν ; φημί. Ἡ Ἐκκλησία,
φησίν. εἶπον οὖν αὐτῷ, Διὰ τί οὖν
πρεσβυτέρα ; Ὅτι, φησίν, πάντων πρώτη
ἐκτίσθη· διὰ τοῦτο πρεσβυτέρα, καὶ διὰ
ταύτην ὁ κόσμος κατηρτίσθη, quoted by
Bryennios. Comp. also Orig. *c. Cels.*
vi. 35, where speaking of the phrase
ἀπορροίας ἐκκλησίας ἐπιγείου which
Celsus had attributed among other
absurdities to the Christians, he
writes, τάχα ἐλήφθη ἀπὸ τοῦ ὑπό τινων
λέγεσθαι ἐκκλησίας τινὸς ἐπουρανίου
καὶ κρείττονος αἰῶνος ἀπόρροιαν εἶναι
τὴν ἐπὶ γῆς ἐκκλησίαν. And see the
passages quoted in the notes on
τὰ βιβλία κ.τ.λ. and ἀντίτυπον. Hilgenfeld quotes Clem. Alex. *Strom.*
iv. 8 (p. 593) εἰκὼν δὲ τῆς οὐρανίου
ἐκκλησίας ἡ ἐπίγειος (this father has

just before cited Ephes. v. 21 sq.,
Col. iii. 18 sq.), *ib.* vi. 13 (p. 793)
αἱ ἐνταῦθα κατὰ τὴν ἐκκλησίαν προκοπαὶ
...μιμήματα, οἶμαι, ἀγγελικῆς δόξης
κἀκείνης τῆς οἰκονομίας τυγχάνουσιν
ἣν ἀναμένειν φασὶν αἱ γραφαὶ τοὺς κατ'
ἴχνος κ.τ.λ.

9. ἐκ τῆς γραφῆς κ.τ.λ.] A loose
expression, meaning 'of those persons
described in the Scripture'. The
Syriac translator has paraphrased
accordingly. The passage is Jer. vii.
11 μὴ σπήλαιον λῃστῶν ὁ οἶκός μου, οὗ
ἐπικέκληται τὸ ὄνομά μου ἐπ' αὐτῷ
κ.τ.λ., to which also our Lord alludes
(Matt. xxi. 13, Mark xi. 17, Luke
xix. 46). For the application here
comp. *Apost. Const.* ii. 17.

10. ὥστε οὖν] A pleonasm which
our author repeats elsewhere; §§ 4, 7.

αἱρετισώμεθα] '*choose*', *prefer*';
a common word in the LXX. In
the N.T. it is found only Matt. xii.
18, in a quotation from Is. xlii. 1,
where however it does not occur in
the LXX. See Sturz *Dial. Mac.* 144.

11. τῆς ζωῆς] Harnack writes 'Iu-
dæorum synagoga est ecclesia mortis'. The contrast however is not
between the Synagogue and the
Church of Christ, but between mere
external membership in the visible
body and spiritual communion in the
celestial counterpart.

12. σῶμά ἐστιν Χριστοῦ] Ephes. i.

Χριστοῦ· λέγει γὰρ ἡ γραφὴ Ἐποίηςεν ὁ Θεός τόν
ἄνθρωπον ἄρcεν καὶ θῆλυ· τὸ ἄρσεν ἐστὶν ὁ Χριστός,
τὸ θῆλυ ἡ ἐκκλησία· καὶ ὅτι τὰ βιβλία καὶ οἱ ἀπόστολοι τὴν ἐκκλησίαν οὐ νῦν εἶναι, ἀλλὰ ἄνωθεν [λέγουσιν,

3 τὸ θῆλυ] καὶ τὸ θῆλυ S.   καὶ ὅτι] atque etiam S.   τὰ βιβλία] add.
prophetarum S.   4 οὐ νῦν] add. dicunt S.   λέγουσιν δῆλον] om. C S; see the

23 τῇ ἐκκλησίᾳ, ἥτις ἐστὶν τὸ σῶμα
αὐτοῦ; comp. ib. iv. 4, 12 sq., 16,
v. 23, 30, Rom. xii. 5, 1 Cor. x. 17,
xii. 12—27, Col. i. 18, 24, ii. 19,
iii. 15.

1. Ἐποίησεν κ.τ.λ.] Gen. i. 27
ἐποίησεν ὁ Θεὸς τὸν ἄνθρωπον, κατ'
εἰκόνα Θεοῦ ἐποίησεν αὐτόν· ἄρσεν καὶ
θῆλυ ἐποίησεν αὐτούς. The application seems to be suggested by S.
Paul's treatment of this portion of
the Mosaic account, Ephes. v. 31 sq.;
where, after representing the Church
as the body and spouse of Christ,
and quoting Gen. ii. 24, he says, τὸ
μυστήριον τοῦτο μέγα ἐστίν· ἐγὼ δὲ
λέγω εἰς Χριστὸν καὶ [εἰς] τὴν ἐκκλησίαν.

3. καὶ ὅτι] Some words have
evidently dropped out in the MS
here: see the introduction, pp. 246 sq.
The lacuna is conveniently supplied
by λέγουσιν δῆλον after ἄνωθεν, as I
have done. This seems to me better
than the more obvious solution of
Bryennios, who would attach this
ὅτι to the preceding ὑμᾶς ἀγνοεῖν, and
understand merely φασί or διδάσκουσι
or the like. The Syriac translator
omits the ὅτι and inserts a λέγουσι
or some similar word. This is
clearly an arbitrary correction.

τὰ βιβλία καὶ οἱ ἀπόστολοι] This is
a rough synonyme for the Old and
New Testaments respectively. Though
the Apostolic and Evangelical writings are elsewhere in this epistle
treated as γραφαί (§ 2) and even as
λόγια τοῦ Θεοῦ (§ 13), being thus co-

ordinated in point of authority with
the Old Testament, yet the term
τὰ βιβλία, 'the Books', is not yet
extended to them. For somewhat
similar expressions for the Old and
New Testaments in early writers, see
the note on Ign. Philad. 5. The
exact mode of expression is however
unique. The Syriac translator's
'books of the prophets' is the obvious gloss of a later age.

But what Books of the Old Testament and what Apostolic writings
had the preacher in view?

(1) As regards the O. T. the answer is partly supplied by his own
context. In the first place the history
of creation in Genesis is contemplated. Such treatment was altogether in accordance with the theological teaching of his age. Anastasius
of Sinai (Routh's Rel. Sacr. I. p. 15;
comp. Anastas. Op. p. 860, Migne)
says, Παπίου τοῦ πάνυ τοῦ Ἱεραπολίτου
τοῦ ἐν τῷ ἐπιστηθίῳ φοιτήσαντος, καὶ
Κλήμεντος Πανταίνου τῆς Ἀλεξαν-
δρέων ἱερέως, καὶ Ἀμμωνίου σοφωτά-
του, τῶν ἀρχαίων καὶ πρώτων συνόδων
ἐξηγητῶν, εἰς Χριστὸν καὶ τὴν
ἐκκλησίαν πᾶσαν τὴν ἐξαήμερον νοη-
σάντων. We might almost suppose
that Anastasius was here alluding
to our pseudo-Clement, if he had
not in a parallel passage (p. 962
Migne), where he is again enume-
rating ancient interpreters who explained the statements respecting
paradise in Genesis as εἰς τὴν Χριστοῦ
ἐκκλησίαν ἀναφερόμενα, specified Κλή-

5 δῆλον]· ἦν γὰρ πνευματική, ὡς καὶ ὁ Ἰησοῦς ἡμῶν, ἐφανερώθη δὲ ἐπ' ἐσχάτων τῶν ἡμερῶν ἵνα ἡμᾶς σώσῃ·
ἡ ἐκκλησία δὲ πνευματικὴ οὖσα ἐφανερώθη ἐν τῇ σαρκὶ

lower note.   5 ὡς καὶ ὁ Ἰησοῦς ἡμῶν, ἐφανερώθη δὲ κ.τ.λ.] et vir eius autem
(δὲ) spiritalis est, is qui est Jesus Christus Dominus noster, manifestatus est autem,
etc. S.   6 ἡμερῶν] temporum S.

μης ὁ Στρωματεύς. He writes again
(p. 964), 'admirabiles quos diximus
interpretes...decreverunt...duos quos-
dam esse paradisos...terrestrem et
cælestem, qui cernitur et qui in-
telligitur, sicut etiam est Christus
cælestis simul et terrestris, congru-
enter typo duarum ecclesiarum, ter-
renæ, inquam, et cælestis civitatis
Domini virtutum etc.' (a passage
which illustrates the language of our
preacher respecting the Church);
and he himself accordingly maintains
that whatever is said of Adam and
Eve applies to Christ and the Church
(e.g. pp. 999, 1007, 1027, 1050). But
besides the Hexaemeron, our preacher
may have been thinking of other
parts of the O.T., such as Ps. xliv (xlv),
in which 'the queen' was already
interpreted of the Church (Justin
Dial. 63, p. 287). So too he would
not improbably have the Song of
Solomon in his mind.

(2) As regards the 'Apostles'
again his context indicates his chief
reference. The Epistle to the E-
phesians seemed to him more especially to inculcate this doctrine.
But he would find it elsewhere.
There are some indications that he
was acquainted with the Epistle to
the Hebrews; and, if so, he would see
a confirmation of his view in πόλει
Θεοῦ ζῶντος Ἰερουσαλὴμ ἐπουρανίῳ...
πανηγύρει καὶ ἐκκλησίᾳ πρωτοτόκων ἀπο-
γεγραμμένων ἐν οὐρανοῖς (xii. 22, 23).
Again such words as Apoc. xxi. 9, 10,
τὴν νύμφην τὴν γυναῖκα τοῦ ἀρνίου...

τὴν ἁγίαν Ἰερουσαλὴμ καταβαίνουσαν
ἐκ τοῦ οὐρανοῦ ἀπὸ τοῦ Θεοῦ, would
suit his purpose admirably.

4. οὐ νῦν κ.τ.λ.] 'not now for the
first time, but from the beginning'.
For this sense of ἄνωθεν see Luke
i. 3, Acts xxvi. 5; comp. Justin Dial.
24 (p. 242) ὥσπερ ἄνωθεν ἐκηρύσσετο,
ib. 63 (p. 286) ὅτι ἄνωθεν ὁ Θεὸς...
γεννᾶσθαι αὐτὸν ἔμελλε, where it is an
explanation of πρὸ ἑωσφόρου ἐγέννησά
σε. Harnack compares Gal. iv. 26,
etc., but the opposition to νῦν here
suggests the temporal rather than
the local meaning of ἄνωθεν.

5. ὁ Ἰησοῦς ἡμῶν] sc. πνευματικὸς
ἦν, so that ὁ Ἰησοῦς, not ἡ ἐκκλησία,
is the nominative of ἐφανερώθη: comp.
§ 9 Χριστὸς ὁ Κύριος, ὁ σώσας ἡμᾶς,
ὢν μὲν τὸ πρῶτον πνεῦμα, ἐγένετο
σὰρξ καὶ οὕτως ἡμᾶς ἐκάλεσεν. For
ἐφανερώθη δὲ κ.τ.λ. comp. 1 Pet. i.
20 Χριστοῦ προεγνωσμένου μὲν πρὸ
καταβολῆς κόσμου, φανερωθέντος δὲ
ἐπ' ἐσχάτου (v.l. ἐσχάτων) τῶν χρό-
νων δι' ὑμᾶς κ.τ.λ.

6. ἐπ' ἐσχάτων τῶν ἡμερῶν] 'when
the days were drawing to a close',
'at the end of all things'; a not
uncommon LXX expression, Gen.
xlix. 1, Deut. iv. 30 (v. l.), Dan. ii.
28, x. 14, Hos. iii. 5, Mic. iv. 1; and
so 2 Pet. iii. 3, but in Heb. i. 2 the
correct reading is ἐπ' ἐσχάτου τῶν
ἡμερῶν.

7. ἐν τῇ σαρκὶ Χριστοῦ] When Christ
took a bodily external form, the
Church did the same. Moreover this
external form might be said to be

Χριστοῦ, δηλοῦσα ἡμῖν ὅτι, ἐάν τις ἡμῶν τηρήσῃ αὐτὴν
ἐν τῇ σαρκὶ καὶ μὴ φθείρῃ, ἀπολήψεται αὐτὴν ἐν τῷ
πνεύματι τῷ ἁγίῳ· ἡ γὰρ σὰρξ αὕτη ἀντίτυπός ἐστιν
τοῦ πνεύματος· οὐδεὶς οὖν τὸ ἀντίτυπον φθείρας τὸ
αὐθεντικὸν μεταλήψεται. ἄρα οὖν τοῦτο λέγει, ἀδελ- 5
φοί, Τηρήσατε τὴν σάρκα ἵνα τοῦ πνεύματος μετα-
λάβητε. εἰ δὲ λέγομεν εἶναι τὴν σάρκα τὴν ἐκκλησίαν
καὶ τὸ πνεῦμα Χριστόν, ἄρα οὖν ὁ ὑβρίσας τὴν σάρκα

3 ἀντίτυποι] *typus* S, and so τὸ ἀντίτυπον just below; but this is probably owing to
the poverty of the language.   5 μεταλήψεται] C S. In C however it was first
written ἀπολήψεται, and μετα is written above by the same hand. See the note on
φιλοπονεῖν below, § 19.   8 ὁ ὑβρίσας...τὴν ἐκκλησίαν] *is qui contumelia affecit car-*

ἐν τῇ σαρκὶ αὐτοῦ, since the Church
exists by union with Him.

1. τηρήσῃ αὐτήν] '*keep her* pure
and undefiled', i.e. so far as con-
cerns his own conduct as one member
of the body. The believer in his own
special department is required to do
that which Christ does throughout
the whole, Ephes. v. 27 παραστῆσαι
ἔνδοξον τὴν ἐκκλησίαν, μὴ ἔχουσαν
σπίλον ἢ ῥυτίδα κ.τ.λ.

2. ἀπολήψεται αὐτήν] i.e. by being
incorporated in the celestial, spiritual
Church.

4. τὸ ἀντίτυπον] '*the counterpart,
or copy*'. The Platonic doctrine of
ideas underlies these expressions.
The αὐθεντικόν is the eternal, spiritual
archetype, the *original document*, as
it were, in God's own handwriting:
comp. Tertull. *de Monog.* 11 'in
Græco authentico', 'the Greek original', before it was corrupted by transcription; *de Praescr.* 36 'ipsae au-
thenticae literae eorum', 'the auto-
graph letters of the Apostles'; Dig.
xxviii. 3. 12 'exemplo quidem aperto
nondum apertum est testamentum;
quod si authenticum patefactum est
totum, apertum', where 'authenticum' is the original, and 'exemplum'

the copy; Julius in Athan. *Apol. c.
Arian.* 28 (I. p. 116) προεκόμισε χεῖρα
ὀλόγραφον αὐθεντικήν, i.e. 'written
from first to last by his own hand'.
The ἀντίτυπον is the material, temporary, manifestation, the imperfect
and blurred *transcript* of the original:
comp. Synes. *Epist.* 68 (p. 217) τοῖς
ταχυγράφοις τὰ ἀντίτυπα δοῦναι τῶν
τότε γραφέντων ἐπέταξα, Epist. in
Athan. *Apol. c. Arian.* 85 (I. p. 158)
τῷ ἀντιτύπῳ τοῦ θείου γράμματος. For
ἀντίτυπον, thus contrasted with the
heavenly and true, comp. Heb. ix. 24
ἀντίτυπα τῶν ἀληθινῶν, where the
ἀντίτυπα are defined in the context
as τὰ ὑποδείγματα τῶν ἐν τοῖς οὐρανοῖς
and the ἀληθινά as αὐτὰ τὰ ἐπουράνια.
See also the anonymous Valentinian
in Epiph. *Hær.* xxxi. 5 (pp. 168, 169)
ἀντίτυπος τοῦ προόντος Ἀγεννήτου, ἀντίτυπον τῆς προούσης τετράδος. And
more especially for the pseudo-Clement's teaching here compare the
Valentinian language, Iren. I. 5. 6
ὃ δὴ καὶ αὐτὸ ἐκκλησίαν εἶναι λέγουσιν,
ἀντίτυπον τῆς ἄνω Ἐκκλησίας.
In such senses ἀντίτυπον depreciates
relatively; and with this meaning
the material elements in the eucha-
rist were commonly called by the

ὕβρισεν τὴν ἐκκλησίαν. ὁ τοιοῦτος οὖν οὐ μεταλή-
10 ψεται τοῦ πνεύματος, ὅ ἐστιν ὁ Χριστός. τοσαύτην
δύναται ἡ σὰρξ αὕτη μεταλαβεῖν ζωὴν καὶ ἀφθαρσίαν,
κολληθέντος αὐτῇ τοῦ πνεύματος τοῦ ἁγίου. οὔτε
ἐξειπεῖν τις δύναται οὔτε λαλῆσαι ἃ ΗΤΟΙΜΑϹΕΝ ὁ
ΚΥΡΙΟϹ τοῖς ἐκλεκτοῖς αὐτοῦ.

15　XV. Οὐκ οἴομαι δὲ ὅτι μικρὰν συμβουλίαν ἐποιη-
σάμην περὶ ἐγκρατείας, ἣν ποιήσας τις οὐ μετανοήσει,

---

nem suam contumelia affecit carnem Christi ecclesiam S. This might possibly represent ὁ ὑβρίσας τὴν σάρκα [τὴν ἰδίαν, τοῦ Χριστοῦ τὴν σάρκα] ὕβρισεν, τὴν ἐκκλησίαν, the
words in brackets having been omitted in C by homœoteleuton; but I am disposed
to regard it as merely a paraphrastic rendering of S.　15 ἐποιησάμην] add. ὑμῖν S.

---

fathers ἀντίτυπα of the body and
blood of Christ, e.g. *Apost.Const.* v. 14,
vi. 30, vii. 25 : see Suicer *Thes.* s.v.
On the other hand ἀντίτυπον is sometimes opposed to τύπος, as the finished work to the rough model,
the realization to the foreshadowing,
in which case it extols relatively ;
comp. 1 Pet. iii. 21.

5. ἄρα οὖν κ.τ.λ.] This apparently
refers not to what has immediately
preceded, but to an application which
the preacher has made of an evangelical text several chapters before, § 8
ἄρα οὖν τοῦτο λέγει Τηρήσατε τὴν σάρκα
ἁγνὴν κ.τ.λ. It is almost impossible
however to trace the connexion of
thought in so loose a writer.

7. τὴν σάρκα] as being the *body*
of Christ. This language does not
occur in S. Paul, for in Ephes. v. 30
ἐκ τῆς σαρκὸς αὐτοῦ is an interpolation.
The relation of Christ to the Church
is represented by S. Paul as that of
the *head* to the body, whereas here it
is that of the *spirit* to the body, so
that 'body' is equivalent to 'flesh'.

Altogether our preacher seems to
be guilty of much confusion in his
metaphor in this context; for here
the relation of flesh to spirit repre-

sents the relation of the Church to
Christ, whereas just above it has represented the relation of the earthly
Church and Christ to the heavenly
Church and Christ. The insertion
in the Syriac does not remove the
difficulty. See the criticism of Photius on the inconsequence of this
writer's sentiments, quoted above on
§ 1, p. 187.

11. μεταλαβεῖν] with an accusative, as e.g. Acts xxiv. 25, and commonly in classical writers. On the
different sense of the two cases with
this verb see Kühner II. p. 294 sq.
The propriety of the change here
will be obvious. Similarly τὸ αὐθεντικὸν μεταλήψεται above.

12. τοῦ πνεύματος τοῦ ἁγίου] See
above pp. 202, 227. The language here
is still more unguarded than in § 9.

13. ἐξειπεῖν] '*express*': Clem. Rom.
48.

ἃ ἡτοίμασεν] A reference to the
same passage of which part has been
already quoted by our preacher at
the end of § 11. See the note on
Clem. Rom. 34, p. 114.

XV. 'He, that obeys this exhortation to chastity, will save both himself and the preacher. It is no small

ἀλλὰ καὶ ἑαυτὸν σώσει κἀμὲ τὸν συμβουλεύσαντα.
μισθὸς γὰρ οὐκ ἔστιν μικρὸς πλανωμένην ψυχὴν καὶ
ἀπολλυμένην ἀποστρέψαι εἰς τὸ σωθῆναι. ταύτην γὰρ
ἔχομεν τὴν ἀντιμισθίαν ἀποδοῦναι τῷ Θεῷ τῷ κτίσαντι
ἡμᾶς, ἐὰν ὁ λέγων καὶ ἀκούων μετὰ πίστεως καὶ ἀγάπης 5
καὶ λέγῃ καὶ ἀκούῃ. ἐμμείνωμεν οὖν ἐφ' οἷς ἐπιστεύ-
σαμεν δίκαιοι καὶ ὅσιοι, ἵνα μετὰ παρρησίας αἰτῶμεν
τὸν Θεὸν τὸν λέγοντα Ἔτι λαλοῦντός coy ἐρῶ Ἰδού πάρ-
ειμι· τοῦτο γὰρ τὸ ῥῆμα μεγάλης ἐστὶν ἐπαγγελίας
σημεῖον· ἑτοιμότερον γὰρ ἑαυτὸν λέγει ὁ Κύριος εἰς 10
τὸ διδόναι τοῦ αἰτοῦντος. τοσαύτης οὖν χρηστότητος
μεταλαμβάνοντες μὴ φθονήσωμεν ἑαυτοῖς τυχεῖν τοσού-

5 ὁ λέγων καὶ ἀκούων] S translates as if it had read ὅ τε λέγων καὶ ὁ ἀκούων.
μετὰ πίστεως καὶ ἀγάπης] *cum caritate et cum fide* S, transposing the words. On the
repetition of the preposition see above, p. 239.   10 εἰς τὸ διδόναι τοῦ αἰτοῦντος] *in
illud ut det petitionem eius qui petit ab ipso* S, thus supplying a substantive to govern

recompense to convert and save a
perishing soul. Faith and love are
the only return that speaker and
hearer alike can make to God their
Creator. So therefore let us be true
to our belief, for God promises an
immediate response, declaring Himself more ready to give than we to
ask. We must not grudge ourselves
these bounties of His goodness; for
as the rewards of submission are
great, so the punishment of disobedience is great also'.

15. οἴομαι] The word has occurred twice already in this writer
§§ 6, 14.

1. καὶ ἑαυτὸν κ.τ.λ.] 1 Tim. iv. 16
καὶ σεαυτὸν σώσεις καὶ τοὺς ἀκούοντάς
σου. See also below, § 19. Harnack
quotes Barnab. 1 μᾶλλον συγχαίρω
ἐμαυτῷ ἐλπίζων σωθῆναι, ὅτι ἀληθῶς
βλέπω ἐν ὑμῖν ἐκκεχυμένον...πνεῦμα.

2. μισθὸς κ.τ.λ.] James v. 20 ὁ ἐπι-
στρέψας ἁμαρτωλὸν ἐκ πλάνης ὁδοῦ

αὐτοῦ σώσει ψυχὴν ἐκ θανάτου κ.τ.λ.

4. ἀντιμισθίαν] A favourite word
with our author, especially in this
connexion ; see the note on § 1.

7. δίκαιοι καὶ ὅσιοι] See on §§ 1, 5.

8. Ἔτι λαλοῦντός κ.τ.λ.] Is. lviii.
9 ὁ Θεὸς εἰσακούσεταί σου, ἔτι λαλοῦντός σου ἐρεῖ Ἰδού πάρειμι. Comp.
Apost. Const. iii. 7, where, as here, it
is quoted ἐρῶ (though with a v.l.),
probably (as Lagarde points out)
from a confusion with Is. lxv. 24 ἔτι
λαλούντων αὐτῶν ἐρῶ, Τί ἐστιν; So too
it is given '*dicam*' in Iren. iv. 17. 3,
but ἐρεῖ in Justin *Dial.* 15 (p. 233).

11. τοῦ αἰτοῦντος] sc. εἰς τὸ αἰτεῖν
'more prompt to give than the asker
is to ask'; as in the Collect 'more
ready to hear than we to pray'. The
Syriac translator has misunderstood
the sense.

XVI.   'Therefore let us repent
and return to God betimes. If we
conquer our appetites and desires,

τῶν ἀγαθῶν. ὅσην γὰρ ἡδονὴν ἔχει τὰ ῥήματα ταῦτα
τοῖς ποιήσασιν αὐτά, τοσαύτην κατάκρισιν ἔχει τοῖς
15 παρακούσασιν.

XVI. "Ὥστε, ἀδελφοί, ἀφορμὴν λαβόντες οὐ
μικρὰν εἰς τὸ μετανοῆσαι, καιρὸν ἔχοντες ἐπιστρέψωμεν
ἐπὶ τὸν καλέσαντα ἡμᾶς Θεόν, ἕως ἔτι ἔχομεν τὸν
παραδεχόμενον ἡμᾶς. ἐὰν γὰρ ταῖς ἡδυπαθείαις ταύ-
20 ταις ἀποταξώμεθα καὶ τὴν ψυχὴν ἡμῶν νικήσωμεν ἐν
τῷ μὴ ποιεῖν τὰς ἐπιθυμίας αὐτῆς τὰς πονηράς, μετα-
ληψόμεθα τοῦ ἐλέους Ἰησοῦ. Γινώσκετε δὲ ὅτι ἔρχεται
ἤδη Η ΗΜέρΑ Τῆς ΚρΙΣεΩΣ ὡς ΚΛΙΒΑΝΟΣ ΚΑΙόΜΕΝΟΣ, ΚΑΙ
ΤΑΚΗΣΟΝΤΑΙ †ΤΙΝΕΣ† Τῶν ΟΥΡΑΝῶΝ, ΚΑΙ πᾶΣΑ ἡ γῆ ὡς

τοῦ αἰτοῦντος and mistaking the sense.   11 τοσαύτης ... μεταλαμβάνοντες] quoniam
igitur hac jucunditate et bonitate Dei jucundamur S.   12 τοσούτων] τοιούτων (?) S.
16 ἀδελφοί] add. ἀγαπητοί S.   18 τὸν παραδεχόμενον] patrem qui accipit S, i.e.
ΠΡΑ for ΠΑΡΑ·   22 Ἰησοῦ] Domini nostri Jesu Christi S.

---

we shall obtain mercy of Jesus. For be assured, the day of judgment is at hand; as a heated furnace shall it be; the heavens shall be fused and the earth shall be as melting lead; and all the deeds of men shall be revealed. Almsgiving is a token of repentance. Fasting is greater than prayer, and almsgiving than both. Love covereth a multitude of sins, and prayer delivereth from death. Blessed is he that aboundeth in these things. For almsgiving removeth the burden of sin[1].

16. ἀφορμὴν λαβόντες] So Rom. vii. 8, 11. Conversely ἀφορμὴν δι-δόναι 2 Cor. v. 12, 1 Tim. v. 14, Ign. Trall. 8.

17. καιρὸν ἔχοντες] So § 8 ἕως ἔχομεν καιρὸν μετανοίας, § 9 ὡς ἔχομεν καιρὸν τοῦ ἰαθῆναι.

19. τὸν παραδεχόμενον] It is yet the καιρὸς εὐπρόσδεκτος (2 Cor. vi. 2).

ἡδυπαθείαις] See again § 17. Not

a Biblical word. On this word, which was highly distasteful to the Stoics, see Wyttenbach on Plut. Mor. 132 c. It occurs at least as early as Xenophon, Cyr. vii. 5. 74.

20. ἀποταξώμεθα] See on § 6.

22. ἔρχεται κ.τ.λ.] Mal. iv. 1 ἰδοὺ ἡμέρα ἔρχεται καιομένη ὡς κλίβανος.

24. τινες] This is obviously cor-rupt, though both our authorities are agreed. I think that for τινες we should probably read [αἱ] δυνάμεις, the expression being taken from Is. xxxiv. 4 καὶ τακήσονται πᾶσαι αἱ δυνά-μεις τῶν οὐρανῶν; comp Apoc. Petr. in Macar. Magn. iv. 7 (p. 165, Blondel) καὶ τακήσεται πᾶσα δύναμις οὐρανοῦ. Where the MS was torn and letters had dropped out, it might easily be read ΤΙΝΕΣ. Comp. 2 Pet. iii. 7, 10, Orac. Sib. iii. 689 sq., Melito Apol. 12, p. 432 (Otto). Though the existing text might be explained with Harnack and Hilgenfeld by the common belief in

μόλιβος ἐπὶ πυρὶ τηκόμενος, καὶ τότε φανήσεται τὰ
κρύφια καὶ φανερὰ ἔργα τῶν ἀνθρώπων. καλὸν οὖν
ἐλεημοσύνη ὡς μετάνοια ἁμαρτίας· κρείσσων νηστεία
προσευχῆς, ἐλεημοσύνη δὲ ἀμφοτέρων· ἀγάπη δὲ κα-

3 κρείσσων νηστεία προσευχῆς] bonum jejunium, oratio, S; but probably ܝܬ has
dropped out. This insertion would bring the Syriac into conformity with the Greek.

several heavens (comp. e.g. Orig. c.
Cels. vi. 23), I can hardly think that
our Clementine writer would have expressed himself in this way, even if
he had believed that some of the
heavens would be spared from the
conflagration. The pseudo-Justin
Quæst. ad Orthod. 74 probably refers
to this passage: see the Addenda on
p. 167, l. 9.

1. μόλιβος] This seems to be the
correct form in the LXX generally,
Exod. xv. 10, Num. xxxi. 22, Job
xix. 24, etc. Both μόλιβος and μόλιβ-
δος are certified by their occurrence
in metre.

2. κρύφια καὶ φανερά] An exhaus-
tive expression: comp. Wisd. vii. 21
ὅσα τέ ἐστι κρυπτὰ καὶ ἐμφανῆ ἔγνων.

καλὸν οὖν κ.τ.λ.] If there is no corruption in the text of this passage, it
offers another illustration of the criticism of Photius on our pseudo-
Clement, Bibl. 126, quoted above,
p. 187. This however may be doubtful. The preacher seems to be
thinking of Tobit xii. 8, 9 ἀγαθὸν
προσευχὴ μετὰ νηστείας καὶ ἐλεημοσύ-
νης καὶ δικαιοσύνης ... καλὸν ποιῆσαι
ἐλεημοσύνην ἢ θησαυρίσαι χρυσίον·
ἐλεημοσύνη γὰρ ἐκ θανάτου ρύεται καὶ
αὕτη ἀποκαθαριεῖ πᾶσαν ἁμαρτίαν, where
the first sentence as read in ℵ is
ἀγαθὸν προσευχὴ μετὰ νηστείας καὶ
ἐλεημοσύνη μετὰ δικαιοσύνης ὑπὲρ ἀμφότερα. Here the very same function
ἐκ θανάτου ρύεσθαι, which our text assigns to prayer, is assigned to almsgiving. Moreover our text having

stated that almsgiving is greater than
prayer immediately afterwards assigns a more important work to
prayer than to almsgiving. These two
facts combined throw doubt on the
integrity of the text. It would seem
as though some words had been transposed and others perhaps omitted.

3. ὡς μετάνοια ἁμαρτίας] 'as repentance from sin is good', if the text be
correct; for the sense will hardly
allow us to translate 'as being repentance from sin'. I suppose that
ἐλεημοσύνη here has its restricted
sense of 'almsgiving', as in every
passage where it occurs in the N.T.

4. ἀμφοτέρων] See Ecclus. xl.
24 ὑπὲρ ἀμφότερα ἐλεημοσύνη ρύσε-
ται, where however the ἀμφότερα
are ἀδελφοὶ καὶ βοήθεια εἰς καιρὸν
θλίψεως.

ἀγάπη δὲ κ.τ.λ.] Taken from 1 Pet.
iv. 8, where it is doubtless a quotation from Prov. x. 12. See the note
on Clem. Rom. 49, where also it is
quoted. There can be no doubt that
in the original context it refers to
passing over without notice, and so
forgiving, the sins of others; nor is
there any reason for interpreting it
otherwise as adopted by S. Peter or
by the genuine Clement. In James
v. 20 the expression καλύψει πλῆθος
ἁμαρτιῶν seems still to be used of the
sins of others, but in the sense of
'burying them from the sight of
God, wiping them out by the con-
version and repentance of the sinner'.
On the other hand our preacher

5 λύπτει πλῆθος ἁμαρτιῶν· προσευχὴ δὲ ἐκ καλῆς συνειδήσεως ἐκ θανάτου ῥύεται.   μακάριος πᾶς ὁ εὑρεθεὶς
ἐν τούτοις πλήρης· ἐλεημοσύνη γὰρ κούφισμα ἁμαρτίας γίνεται.

XVII.   Μετανοήσωμεν οὖν ἐξ ὅλης καρδίας, ἵνα

4 ἐλεημοσύνη δὲ] add. melior (κρείσσων) S.

seems certainly to take it as meaning 'atones for a multitude of one's
own sins', as it is taken by some
modern commentators : and so too
Tertull. *Scorp.* 6. Clement of Alexandria is hardly consistent with himself. In *Strom.* ii. 15 (p. 463) he explains it of God's love in Christ
which forgives the sins of men;
whereas in *Quis div. salv.* 38 (p.
956) he takes it to mean that love,
working in a man, enables him to
repent and put away his own sins;
and so apparently in *Strom.* i. 27 (p.
423). Origen *In Lev. Hom.* ii. § 5 (II.
p. 190) refers it to the man's own
sins; but the turn which he gives to
the passage is shown by his quoting
in juxtaposition Luke vii. 47 ἀφέωνται
αὐτῆς αἱ ἁμαρτίαι αἱ πολλαί, ὅτι ἠγάπη-
σεν πολύ—an explanation which removes the doctrinal objection to this
interpretation, though the exegetical
argument against it from the connexion of the passage in its original context (Prov. x. 12) still remains.

5. καλῆς συνειδήσεως] Heb. xiii.
18. A commoner expression is ἀγαθὴ
συνείδησις; see the note Clem. Rom.
41. For καθαρὰ συνείδησις see Clem.
Rom. 45 with the note.

6. ἐκ θανάτου ῥύεται] This is said
of ἐλεημοσύνη in Tobit iv. 10, xii. 9
(already quoted); and of δικαιοσύνη,
which also signifies 'almsgiving', in
Prov. x. 2, xi. 4; but not of προσευχή.
See the note on καλὸν οὖν κ.τ.λ. above.

7. ἐν] Comp. Ecclus. l. 6 σελήνη
πλήρης ἐν ἡμέραις.

ἐλεημοσύνη γὰρ κ.τ.λ.] Prov. xvi. 6
(xv. 27) ἐλεημοσύναις καὶ πίστεσιν
ἀποκαθαίρονται ἁμαρτίαι, Ecclus. iii. 30
ἐλεημοσύνη ἐξιλάσεται ἁμαρτίας : comp.
Dan. iv. 24 τὰς ἁμαρτίας σου ἐν ἐλεημοσύναις λύτρωσαι (Theod.).

κούφισμα ἁμαρτίας] i.e. 'removes
the load of sin', as with Bunyan's
pilgrims. So 3 Esdr. viii. 83 σύ, Κύριε, ὁ κουφίσας τὰς ἁμαρτίας ἡμῶν;
comp. Ezr. ix. 13 ἐκούφισας ἡμῶν τὰς
ἀνομίας.

XVII. 'Let us therefore repent
lest we perish. For, if we are commanded to convert even the heathen
from their idolatry, how unpardon-
able would it be to allow the ruin
of a soul which has once known the
true God! Therefore let us assist
the weak, that we and they alike
may be saved. And let us not give
heed only while we are listening to
the instructions of our presbyters, but
also when we have departed to our
homes. Let us also meet together
more frequently, and thus endeavour
to make progress in the commandments of the Lord. He has declared
that He will come to gather together
all nations and languages. Then the
unbelievers shall see His glory and
shall bewail their past obstinacy.
Their worm shall not die; and their
sufferings shall be a spectacle to all
men. Meanwhile the righteous, seeing their torments, shall give glory
to God, because there is hope for
His true and zealous servants'.

9. Μετανοήσωμεν κ.τ.λ.] The ex-

μή τις ἡμῶν παραπόληται. εἰ γὰρ ἐντολὰς ἔχομεν,
ἵνα καὶ τοῦτο πράσσωμεν, ἀπὸ τῶν εἰδώλων ἀποσπᾶν
καὶ κατηχεῖν, πόσῳ μᾶλλον ψυχὴν ἤδη γινώσκουσαν
τὸν Θεὸν οὐ δεῖ ἀπόλλυσθαι; συλλάβωμεν οὖν ἑαυτοῖς
καὶ τοὺς ἀσθενοῦντας ἀνάγειν περὶ τὸ ἀγαθόν, ὅπως 5
σωθῶμεν ἅπαντες· καὶ ἐπιστρέψωμεν ἀλλήλους καὶ
νουθετήσωμεν. καὶ μὴ μόνον ἄρτι δοκῶμεν προσέχειν
καὶ πιστεύειν ἐν τῷ νουθετεῖσθαι ἡμᾶς ὑπὸ τῶν πρεσ-
βυτέρων, ἀλλὰ καὶ ὅταν εἰς οἶκον ἀπαλλαγῶμεν, μνη-

2 ἵνα καὶ τοῦτο πράσσωμεν] S; καὶ τοῦτο πράσσομεν (om. ἵνα) C. Similar omissions of ἵνα appear in *AC in § 48 ἐξομολογησώμαι (where S is correct), and in S itself in ii § 11 κομισώμεθα (where AC are correct).   5 περὶ] C; ad (adversus) S, as if πρός: but it perhaps does not represent a different reading.   7 προσέχειν καὶ πιστεύειν] S; πιστεύειν καὶ προσέχειν C.   9 εἰς οἶκον ἀπαλλαγῶμεν] C; domum dimissi fuerimus et cessaverimus ab his omnibus S. The variation might

pression μετανοεῖν ἐξ ὅλης [τῆς] καρδίας has occurred already § 8, and will occur again § 19; comp. also § 9 μετανοῆσαι ἐξ εἰλικρινοῦς καρδίας.

I. παραπόληται] 'perish by the way,' i. e. 'unexpectedly, through carelessness, without sufficient cause'; as e. g. Lucian Gymn. 13 ὁρῶ οὐδενὸς μεγάλου ἕνεκα παραπολλυμένας, Nigr. 13 δέδοικα μὴ παραπόληται μεταξὺ λυνόμενος, Hermot. 21 περιόψει με παραπολόμενον.

ἐντολὰς ἔχομεν] It was our Lord's command, Matt. xxviii. 19 sq.; comp. Mark xvi. 15. If we adopt the reading of the Greek MS, καὶ τοῦτο πράσσομεν must be taken as parenthetical so far as regards the structure, 'and we obey this command'; so that ἀποσπᾶν will then be governed by ἐντολὰς ἔχομεν.

4. συλλάβωμεν κ.τ.λ.] 'Let us therefore assist one another, that we may elevate the weak also as concerning that which is good'. This may be the meaning, if the text is correct; but it would seem as though some verb

had fallen out after καί. For ἑαυτοῖς see the note on § 13; and for ἀνάγειν comp. Clem. Rom. 49.

6. καὶ ἐπιστρέψωμεν] to be connected with συλλάβωμεν, and not made dependent on ὅπως, as it is punctuated by Bryennios.

7. μὴ μόνον ἄρτι κ.τ.λ.] This clearly shows that the work before us is a sermon delivered in church (see p. 304 sq.); comp. § 19 μετὰ τὸν Θεὸν τῆς ἀληθείας ἀναγινώσκω ὑμῖν ἔντευξιν κ.τ.λ.

8. τῶν πρεσβυτέρων] 'the presbyters' who delivered their exhortations after the reading of the Scriptures; see the note on § 19 μετὰ τὸν Θεὸν κ.τ.λ. This sermon itself was obviously such an exhortation; but the preacher, doubtless himself a 'presbyter', puts himself in the position of his hearers and uses the third person, by a common form of speech, to avoid egotism: comp. e. g. Clem. Rom. 63 ἡσυχάσαντες τῆς ματαίας στάσεως...καταντήσωμεν.

10. ἀντιπαρελκώμεθα] 'be dragged

10 μονεύωμεν τῶν τοῦ Κυρίου ἐνταλμάτων, καὶ μὴ ἀντι-
παρελκώμεθα ἀπὸ τῶν κοσμικῶν ἐπιθυμιῶν, ἀλλὰ
πυκνότερον προσερχόμενοι πειρώμεθα προκόπτειν ἐν
ταῖς ἐντολαῖς τοῦ Κυρίου, ἵνα πάντες τὸ αὐτὸ φρο-
νοῦντες συνηγμένοι ὦμεν ἐπὶ τὴν ζωήν. εἶπεν γὰρ ὁ
15 Κύριος Ἔρχομαι cynaraγειν πάντα τὰ ἔθνη, φυλὰc καὶ
γλώccac· τοῦτο δὲ λέγει τὴν ἡμέραν τῆς ἐπιφανείας
αὐτοῦ, ὅτε ἐλθὼν λυτρώσεται ἡμᾶς ἕκαστον κατὰ τὰ
ἔργα αὐτοῦ. καὶ ὄψονται τὴν δόΣαν αὐτοῦ καὶ τὸ

easily be explained by an omission in C owing to homoeoteleuton, but it is more
probably a periphrastic rendering of S to express the full force of ἀπαλλάττεσθαι:
see above p. 239.   12 προσερχόμενοι] προσευχόμενοι S.   16 τὴν ἡμέραν]
super (dé) die S.   18 τὴν δόξαν αὐτοῦ καὶ τὸ κράτος] gloriam ejus in robore et
potestate S. This again might be explained by an omission in C owing to the repetition of similar beginnings of words, τὴν δόξαν αὐτοῦ [κατὰ τὴν δύναμιν (or τὴν

off in the opposite direction'; comp.
Pers. Sat. v. 154 'duplici in diversum
scinderis hamo'. The lexicons do
not give this word.

11. κοσμικῶν ἐπιθυμιῶν] The expression occurs Tit. ii. 12. The word
κοσμικὸς is apparently not found in
the LXX, and only once besides (in
a somewhat different sense) in the
N. T., Heb. ix. 1.

12. πυκνότερον προσερχόμενοι] 'coming more frequently', i.e. 'to this
place of meeting', or perhaps 'to
the presence of God' (comp. Heb.
x. 1, 22, Clem. Rom. 23, 29). On
these injunctions to more frequent
services, see the note on Ign. Eph.
13 σπουδάζετε πυκνότερον συνέρχεσ-
θαι; comp. ib. Polyc. 4 πυκνότερον
συναγωγαὶ γινέσθωσαν. The Syriac
reading however may be correct.

14. ὁ Κύριος] Perhaps meaning
'Christ', as Harnack takes it, referring to § 3, where Is. xxix. 13
seems to be put into the mouth of
our Lord.

15. Ἔρχομαι κ.τ.λ.] From Is. lxvi. 18

ἔρχομαι συναγαγεῖν πάντα τὰ ἔθνη καὶ
τὰς γλώσσας, καὶ ἥξουσι καὶ ὄψονται
τὴν δόξαν μου. There is nothing corresponding to φυλὰς in either the
Hebrew or the LXX; and our preacher must have got it from the familiar
combination of 'nations and tongues'
in Daniel, e.g. iii. 7 πάντα τὰ ἔθνη
φυλαὶ καὶ γλῶσσαι in the LXX.

16. τοῦτο δὲ λέγει] 'but by this he
means': see the note on § 8.

τὴν ἡμέραν κ.τ.λ.] The same expression has occurred § 12, where
see the note on ἐπιφανείας.

17. λυτρώσεται] It is called ἡμέρα
ἀπολυτρώσεως in Ephes. iv. 30. For
other passages, where ἀπολύτρωσις
refers to the final redemption, see
Luke xxi. 28, Rom. viii. 23.

ἕκαστον κ.τ.λ.] As only those who
shall be released are contemplated,
this must imply different grades of
happiness. I do not see sufficient
reason for doubting the genuineness
of λυτρώσεται.

18. καὶ ὄψονται] A continuation
of the quotation from Isaiah, the

22—2

κράτος οἱ ἄπιστοι, καὶ ξενισθήσονται ἰδόντες τὸ βασίλειον τοῦ κόσμου ἐν τῷ Ἰησοῦ λέγοντες, Οὐαὶ ἡμῖν,
ὅτι σὺ ἦς καὶ οὐκ ἤδειμεν καὶ οὐκ ἐπιστεύομεν, καὶ
οὐκ ἐπειθόμεθα τοῖς πρεσβυτέροις τοῖς ἀναγγέλλουσιν
ἡμῖν περὶ τῆς σωτηρίας ἡμῶν· καὶ Ὁ ϲκώληϟ αϒτῶν οϒ 5
τελεϒτήϲει καὶ τὸ πῦρ αϒτῶν οϒ ϲβεϲθήϲεται καὶ ἔϲονται
εἰϲ ὅραϲιν πάϲῃ ϲαρκί. τὴν ἡμέραν ἐκείνην λέγει τῆς
κρίσεως, ὅταν ὄψονται τοὺς ἐν ἡμῖν ἀσεβήσαντας καὶ
παραλογισαμένους τὰς ἐντολὰς Ἰησοῦ Χριστοῦ. οἱ
δὲ δίκαιοι εὐπραγήσαντες καὶ ὑπομείναντες τὰς βασά- 10
νους καὶ μισήσαντες τὰς ἡδυπαθείας τῆς ψυχῆς, ὅταν

ἰσχὺν)] καὶ τὸ κράτος; but such an expression in Greek would be very awkward. It is more probable therefore that *robur et potestas* is a double rendering of τὸ κράτος. The preposition (in place of the conjunction) may then be accounted for in two ways; (1) The translator read κατὰ κράτος for καὶ τὸ κράτος; or (2) A Syriac transcriber inadvertently wrote ܒ for ܘ. The latter explanation seems to be more probable: see above p. 296.   1 ἰδόντες] εἰδότες (from ιδό|τες) S.   2 τοῦ κόσμου]

intervening words being a parenthetical explanation. See also Matt.
xxiv. 30, Rev. i. 7.

1. ξενισθήσονται] '*shall be a-
mazed*', as 1 Pet. iv. 4, 12. The
active ξενίζοντα, 'perplexing', 'amaz-
ing', occurs in Acts xvii. 20. This
sense is found in Polybius and from
his time onward. See also the note
on ξενισμόν, Ign. *Ephes.* 19.
τὸ βασίλειον] '*the kingdom*' or
'*sovereignty*'; see the note on § 6.
We must understand ἐν τῷ Ἰησοῦ
'in the hands, in the power, of Jesus',
as in the common idiom εἶναι ἔν τινι:
see Rost u. Palm *Griech. Wörterb.*
s. v. ἐν i. 2. b.

3. σὺ ἦς] '*Thou wast He*'; see
esp. John viii. 24 ἐὰν μὴ πιστεύσητε
ὅτι ἐγώ εἰμι, ἀποθανεῖσθε ἐν ταῖς
ἁμαρτίαις ὑμῶν, ib. ver. 28 τότε γνώ-
σεσθε ὅτι ἐγώ εἰμι, xiii. 19 ἵνα
πιστεύσητε...ὅτι ἐγώ εἰμι. The

preacher seems to be alluding to
this language of our Lord, as recorded by St John.

5. ὁ σκώληξ κ.τ.λ.] From Is. lxvi.
24, the last verse of the prophet.
Our preacher has already quoted
this passage § 7; see the note there.

8. ὅταν ὄψονται] '*when men
shall see*', the nominative being suggested by the preceding εἰς ὅρασιν
πάσῃ σαρκί. For the future indicative
with ὅταν see Winer xlii. p. 388; but
no dependence can be placed on the
MS in such a case.

9. παραλογισαμένους] '*played false
with*', '*attempted to cheat*'; see
Ign. *Magn.* 3 τὸν ἀόρατον παραλογί-
ζεται (with the note)

10. εὐπραγήσαντες] If the reading
be correct, it must mean 'having
been virtuous' and not (as elsewhere) 'having been prosperous';
comp. δικαιοπραγεῖν.

θεάσωνται τοὺς ἀστοχήσαντας καὶ ἀρνησαμένους διὰ
τῶν λόγων ἢ διὰ τῶν ἔργων τὸν Ἰησοῦν, ὅπως κολάζονται δειναῖς βασάνοις πυρὶ ἀσβέστῳ, ἔσονται δόξαν
15 διδόντες τῷ Θεῷ αὐτῶν, λέγοντες ὅτι Ἔσται ἐλπὶς
τῷ δεδουλευκότι Θεῷ ἐξ ὅλης καρδίας.

XVIII. Καὶ ἡμεῖς οὖν γενώμεθα ἐκ τῶν εὐχαριστούντων, τῶν δεδουλευκότων τῷ Θεῷ, καὶ μὴ ἐκ τῶν
κρινομένων ἀσεβῶν. καὶ γὰρ αὐτὸς πανθαμαρτωλὸς
20 ὢν καὶ μήπω φυγὼν τὸν πειρασμόν, ἀλλ' ἔτι ὢν ἐν
μέσοις τοῖς ὀργάνοις τοῦ διαβόλου, σπουδάζω τὴν
δικαιοσύνην διώκειν, ὅπως ἰσχύσω κἂν ἐγγὺς αὐτῆς
γενέσθαι, φοβούμενος τὴν κρίσιν τὴν μέλλουσαν.

mundi kuius S. See the note on § 19 ἐν τῷ κόσμῳ.   ἐν τῷ Ἰησοῦ] om. S.
λέγοντες] *et tunc dicent* S.   8 ἡμῖν] S: ὑμῖν C.   12 διὰ] ἢ διὰ S.
14 πυρὶ] *et igne* S.   ἔσονται] add. ἐν ἀγαλλιάσει S.   15 διδόντες] S; δόντες C.
17 οὖν] add. ἀδελφοί [μου] S.   20 φυγὼν] φεύγων C; S has כ'פ which perhaps
represents φυγών.

11. ἡδυπαθείας] See the note on § 16.

12. ἀστοχήσαντας] 'missed the mark', 'gone astray'; see 1 Tim. i. 6, vi. 21, 2 Tim. ii. 18 The word is not uncommon in Polybius and later classical authors.

14. πυρὶ ἀσβέστῳ] Matt. iii. 12, Mark ix. 43, Luke iii. 17. For the reference of pseudo-Justin to this statement see the Addenda on p. 167, l. 9.

XVIII. 'Let us take our place with those who, having served God, will join in this thanksgiving. I myself, though I am still surrounded by the temptations of the devil, yet strive to follow after righteousness, that I may escape the judgment to come'.

19. πανθαμαρτωλός] The word is not given in the lexicons. Compare πανθαμαρτητὸς *Apost. Const.* vii. 18, Barnab. 20 (where the MSS agree in writing it without an aspirate), παιτά-

δικος Philo *de Creat. Pr.* 3 (II p. 362).

21. ὀργάνοις] 'the instruments, engines'; comp. Ign. *Rom.* 4. The word does not occur in the N. T.; and in the LXX it seems to be applied only to musical instruments or military engines, or the like. The metaphor here is probably military; comp. 2 Macc. xii. 27 ἐνθάδε ὀργάνων καὶ βελῶν πολλαὶ παραθέσεις, and see Ephes. vi. 16 τὰ βέλη τοῦ πονηροῦ [τὰ] πεπυρωμένα. The preacher finds himself ἐν ἀμφιβόλῳ, the enemy having environed him with his engines of war.

22. δικαιοσύνην διώκειν] A phrase occurring in the Pastoral Epistles, 1 Tim. vi. 11, 2 Tim. ii. 22 (comp. Rom. ix. 30).

κἂν ἐγγύς] 'at all events near', if I cannot actually reach it'. For this use of κἂν comp. Ign. *Ephes.* 10 κἂν ἐκ τῶν ἔργων, with the note.

XIX. Ὥστε, ἀδελφοὶ καὶ ἀδελφαί, μετὰ τὸν Θεὸν τῆς ἀληθείας ἀναγινώσκω ὑμῖν ἔντευξιν εἰς τὸ προσέχειν τοῖς γεγραμμένοις, ἵνα καὶ ἑαυτοὺς σώσητε καὶ τὸν ἀναγινώσκοντα ἐν ὑμῖν· μισθὸν γὰρ αἰτῶ ὑμᾶς τὸ μετανοῆσαι ἐξ ὅλης καρδίας σωτηρίαν ἑαυτοῖς καὶ 5 ζωὴν διδόντας. τοῦτο γὰρ ποιήσαντες σκοπὸν πᾶσιν τοῖς νέοις θήσομεν τοῖς βουλομένοις περὶ τὴν εὐσέβειαν καὶ τὴν χρηστότητα τοῦ Θεοῦ φιλοπονεῖν. καὶ μὴ ἀηδῶς ἔχωμεν καὶ ἀγανακτῶμεν οἱ ἄσοφοι, ὅταν τις

2 ἔντευξιν] C; *supplicationem, id est, admonitionem* S ; clearly a gloss. See above p. 244. S governs τῆς ἀληθείας by ἔντευξιν. 4 τὸν ἀναγινώσκοντα ἐν ὑμῖν] *me qui lego vobis verba* (or *oracula*) *Dei* S. 6 σκοπὸν] S ; κόπον C. This reading of S was anticipated by Bensly, Gebhardt, and Hilgenfeld. 8 φιλοπονεῖν] *manifestent amorem laboris* S : see Michaelis in Castell. *Lex. Syr.* p. 656. The scribe of C has first written φιλοσοφεῖν, but has afterwards corrected it so as to be read φιλοπονεῖν. See p. 314. 9 οἱ ἄσοφοι] *tanquam illi insipientes* S.

XIX. 'Therefore, brothers and sisters, I have exhorted you to give heed to the Scriptures, that ye may save both me and yourselves. Your hearty repentance and earnest pursuit of salvation is the return which I ask for my trouble. Your zeal will thus stimulate all the young who have any regard for godliness. And let us not be annoyed when we are admonished and turned away from sin. Half-heartedness and disbelief obscure our sense of right and wrong; and our understandings are darkened by our lusts. Let us practise righteousness. Blessed are they who obey these precepts. They may suffer in this world, but they will reap the fruit of immortality. Let not the godly man be sorrowful, if he suffer now. An eternal life in heaven awaits him, where he shall live in bliss with the fathers, and where sorrow shall have no place'.

1. ἀδελφοὶ καὶ ἀδελφαί] Comp. § 20. So *Barnab.* 1 υἱοὶ καὶ θυγα-

τέρες, *Rel. Jur. Eccl.* p. 74 (Lagarde). μετὰ τὸν Θεὸν κ.τ.λ.] i. e. 'After you have heard the voice of God in the Scriptures', as it is rightly explained by Bryennios. The sermon or exhortation followed immediately after the reading of the Scriptures in the weekly gatherings of the early Church: Justin *Apol.* i. 67 συνέλευσις γίνεται καὶ τὰ ἀπομνημονεύματα τῶν ἀποστόλων ἢ τὰ συγγράμματα τῶν προφητῶν ἀναγινώσκεται, μέχρις ἐγχωρεῖ· εἶτα, παυσαμένου τοῦ ἀναγινώσκοντος, ὁ προεστὼς διὰ λόγου τὴν νουθεσίαν καὶ πρόκλησιν τῆς τῶν καλῶν τούτων μιμήσεως ποιεῖται; Orig. *c. Cels.* iii. 50 καὶ δι' ἀναγνωσμάτων καὶ διὰ τῶν εἰς αὐτὰ διηγήσεων προτρέποντες μὲν ἐπὶ τὴν εἰς τὸν Θεὸν τῶν ὅλων εὐσέβειαν καὶ τὰς συνθρόνους ταύτῃ ἀρετάς, ἀποτρέποντες δὲ κ.τ.λ.; *Apost. Const.* ii. 54 μετὰ τὴν ἀνάγνωσιν καὶ τὴν ψαλμῳδίαν καὶ τὴν ἐπὶ ταῖς γραφαῖς διδασκαλίαν. See also the notes on § 17 μὴ μόνον ἄρτι κ.τ.λ. and the introduction, p. 303 sq. For the ex-

10 ἡμᾶς νουθετῇ καὶ ἐπιστρέφῃ ἀπὸ τῆς ἀδικίας εἰς τὴν
δικαιοσύνην. ἐνίοτε γὰρ πονηρὰ πράσσοντες οὐ γινώ-
σκομεν διὰ τὴν διψυχίαν καὶ ἀπιστίαν τὴν ἐνοῦσαν ἐν
τοῖς στήθεσιν ἡμῶν, καὶ ἐϲκοτίϲμεθα τὴν Διάνοιαν ὑπὸ
τῶν ἐπιθυμιῶν τῶν ματαίων. πράξωμεν οὖν τὴν δι-
15 καιοσύνην ἵνα εἰς τέλος σωθῶμεν. μακάριοι οἱ τούτοις
ὑπακούοντες τοῖς προστάγμασιν· κἂν ὀλίγον χρόνον
κακοπαθήσωσιν ἐν τῷ κόσμῳ, τὸν ἀθάνατον τῆς ἀνα-
στάσεως καρπὸν τρυγήσουσιν. μὴ οὖν λυπείσθω ὁ εὐ-

11 ἐνίοτε] S; ἔνια C.   17 τῷ κόσμῳ] S; add. τούτῳ C. I have the less hesitation in striking out τούτῳ here because the general tendency of S is to insert the
pronoun, not to omit it, in this connexion: e. g. § 5, 19, 38, 60, ii. 18.   ἀθάνα-
τον] S; δὲ θάνατον C. The correction was obvious, even before the reading of S
was known; and the only question was whether to read τὸν δ' ἀθάνατον or τὸν
ἀθάνατον. For another instance of the same error comp. § 36 θανάτου γνώσεως for
ἀθανάτου γνώσεως in S itself.   18 τρυγήσουσιν] delectabuntur...in S, i.e. τρυ-

pression ὁ Θεὸς τῆς ἀληθείας comp.
§ 3 τὸν πατέρα τῆς ἀληθείας (comp.
§ 20). Its use here as a synonyme
for the Scripture is explained by the
preacher's language above § 13, τὰ
λόγια τοῦ Θεοῦ, λέγει ὁ Θεός.

2. ἔντευξιν] 'appeal' 'entreaty';
as e.g. Justin Apol. i. 1 (p. 53),
Joseph. Ant. xvi. 2. 5, Phil. Vit.
Moys. iii. 32 (I. p. 172), and so most
frequently in classical authors. For
its commoner sense in Christian
writers, 'supplication to God', see
the note on Clem. Rom. 63.

3. ἵνα καὶ κ.τ.λ.] Comp. Ezek.iii.21.

5. μετανοῆσαι κ.τ.λ.] See the
note § 17.

8. φιλοπονεῖν] Ecclus. Prol. τῶν
κατὰ τὴν ἑρμηνείαν πεφιλοπονημένων.
The word occurs in classical writers of the best age.

9. μὴ ἀγανακτῶμεν] Clem. Rom.
56 παιδείαν ἐφ' ᾗ οὐδεὶς ὀφείλει
ἀγανακτεῖν.

οἱ ἄσοφοι] 'fools that we are', for
this is the force of the article; comp.

§ 1 οἱ ἀκούοντες (with the note). For
ἄσοφος comp. Ephes. v. 15. It seems
not to occur again in the Bible
(except Prov. ix. 8 in A, where there
is nothing corresponding in the Hebrew); and is not very common
elsewhere.

12. διψυχίαν] As above § 11 μὴ
διψυχῶμεν. See the notes on Clem.
Rom. 11, 23. To the references there
given add Barnab. 19 οὐ μὴ διψυχήσῃς
πότερον ἔσται ἢ οὔ.

13. ἐσκοτίσμεθα κ.τ.λ.] From Ephes.
iv. 17, 18, ἐν ματαιότητι τοῦ νοὸς αὐτῶν, ἐσκοτωμένοι (v.l. ἐσκοτισμένοι)
τῇ διανοίᾳ; comp. Clem. Rom. 36 ἡ
ἀσύνετος καὶ ἐσκοτωμένη διάνοια ἡμῶν.

16. ὀλίγον χρόνον κ.τ.λ.] Comp.
1 Pet. i. 6 ὀλίγον ἄρτι, εἰ δέον, λυπη-
θέντες, v. 10 ὀλίγον παθόντας. For
κακοπαθεῖν see 2 Tim. ii. 9, iv. 5,
James v. 13; comp. συγκακοπαθεῖν
2 Tim. i. 8, ii. 3.

18. καρπὸν τρυγήσουσιν] Hos. x. 12
σπείρατε ἑαυτοῖς εἰς δικαιοσύνην, τρυ-
γήσατε εἰς καρπὸν ζωῆς.

σεβής, ἐὰν ἐπὶ τοῖς νῦν χρόνοις ταλαιπωρῇ· μακάριος
αὐτὸν ἀναμένει χρόνος· ἐκεῖνος ἄνω μετὰ τῶν πατέρων
ἀναβιώσας εὐφρανθήσεται εἰς τὸν ἀλύπητον αἰῶνα.

XX. Ἀλλὰ μηδὲ ἐκεῖνο τὴν διάνοιαν ὑμῶν ταρασσέτω, ὅτι βλέπομεν τοὺς ἀδίκους πλουτοῦντας, καὶ 5
στενοχωρουμένους τοὺς τοῦ Θεοῦ δούλους. πιστεύωμεν
οὖν, ἀδελφοὶ καὶ ἀδελφαί· Θεοῦ ζῶντος πεῖραν ἀθλοῦμεν,
καὶ γυμναζόμεθα τῷ νῦν βίῳ ἵνα τῷ μέλλοντι στεφανω-
θῶμεν. οὐδεὶς τῶν δικαίων ταχὺν καρπὸν ἔλαβεν, ἀλλ᾽

φήσουσιν; for the same word (ΟΟ⅃) and its derivatives are used to translate τρυφή,
ii § 10, and τρυφή, ἐντρυφᾶν 2 Pet. ii. 13.   4 μηδὲ ἐκεῖνο...ταρασσέτω] CS
(but S has ἡμῶν) μὴ ταρασσέτω τὴν καρδίαν ὑμῶν Rup. 783.   6 πιστεύωμεν]
S; πιστεύομεν C.   7 Θεοῦ] ὅτι Θεοῦ S.   9 ταχὺν] C Rup.; celeriter (ταχὺ) S,
using the same adverb which renders συντόμως just below.   11 συντόμως ἀπεδί-

3. ἀναβιώσας] 2 Macc. vii, 9 ἀπο-
θανόντας ἡμᾶς ὑπὲρ τῶν αὐτοῦ νόμων
εἰς αἰώνιον ἀναβίωσιν ζωῆς ἡμᾶς ἀνα-
στήσει.

ἀλύπητον] 'inaccessible to sorrow',
stronger than ἄλυπον; comp. Clem.
Hom. xi. 17 σὺν ἡμῖν τὸν ἄλυπον
αἰῶνα κληρονομῆσαι.

XX. 'Be not dismayed, if you see
wrong-doers prospering, while the
servants of God are straitened. Believe it, this present life is the arena
of our conflict; the crown will be
awarded in the future. Our reward
is not instantaneous. If it were so,
then the pursuit of it would be a
matter of traffic and not of piety'.

'To the one invisible God of truth,
who sent us a Saviour and through
Him manifested truth and life to us,
be the glory for ever'.

4. Ἀλλὰ μηδὲ ἐκεῖνο κ.τ.λ.] This
passage is quoted loosely and with
some omissions in the Sacr. Parall.
(MS Rupef.), which bear the name
of Joannes Damascenus, Op. II. p.

783 (Le Quien). See above p. 210 sq.
It will be seen that in the quotation
the original words are altered, so as
to conform to well-known scriptural
passages; e.g. μὴ ταρασσέτω τὴν
καρδίαν ὑμῶν is substituted for μηδὲ
ἐκεῖνο τὴν διάνοιαν ὑμῶν ταρασσέτω,
after John xiv. 1, 27; and εὐσέβειαν
is substituted for θεοσέβειαν, after
1 Tim. vi. 5.

7. πεῖραν] For the accusative
after ἀθλεῖν comp. e.g. Plato Leg.
viii. p. 830 A, Plut. Vit. Demetr. 5;
and for such accusatives generally
see Kühner II. p. 264. For an elaborate application of the same metaphor see § 7.

12. θεοσέβειαν] See 1 Tim. ii. 10.
It occurs occasionally in the LXX.

13. διὰ τοῦτο κ.τ.λ.] i.e. 'on account of these sordid motives Divine
judgment overtakes and cripples the
spirit of a man, seeing that it is not upright, and loads it with chains'. The
word βλάπτειν is used especially of Divine vengeance surprising its victim,

10 ἐκδέχεται αὐτόν. εἰ γὰρ τὸν μισθὸν τῶν δικαίων ὁ
Θεὸς συντόμως ἀπεδίδου, εὐθέως ἐμπορίαν ἠσκοῦμεν καὶ
οὐ θεοσέβειαν· ἐδοκοῦμεν γὰρ εἶναι δίκαιοι, οὐ τὸ
εὐσεβὲς ἀλλὰ τὸ κερδαλέον διώκοντες· καὶ διὰ τοῦτο
θεία κρίσις ἔβλαψεν πνεῦμα μὴ ὂν δίκαιον, καὶ ἐβά-
15 ρυνεν δεσμοῖς.

Τῷ μόνῳ Θεῷ ἀοράτῳ, πατρὶ τῆς ἀληθείας, τῷ
ἐξαποστείλαντι ἡμῖν τὸν σωτῆρα καὶ ἀρχηγὸν τῆς
ἀφθαρσίας, δι' οὗ καὶ ἐφανέρωσεν ἡμῖν τὴν ἀλήθειαν

δου, εὐθέως] CS; εὐθέως ἀπεδίδου Rup.　　12 οὐ θεοσέβειαν] CS; οὐκ εὐσέβειαν
Rup.　　οὐ τὸ] CS; οὐ διὰ τὸ Rup.　　13 εὐσεβὲς] C Rup.; θεοσεβὲς S.
15 δεσμοῖς] S; δεσμὸι C.　　16 τῆς ἀληθείας] add. *Domini nostri Jesu Christi* (in
apposition) S.　　17 ἡμῖν τὸν σωτῆρα καὶ ἀρχηγὸν τῆς ἀφθαρσίας] *salvatorem et
principem vitæ et salutis nostræ* S.

checking and maiming him in his mid career; e.g. Hom. *Od.* i. 195 ἀλλά νυ τόν γε θεοὶ βλάπτουσι κελεύθου, *ib.* xiii. 178 τοῦ δέ τις ἀθανάτων βλάψε φρένας, Xen. *Symp.* viii. 43 ἢν μὴ Θεὸς βλάπτῃ, Plut. *Vit. Cæs.* 45 ὑπὸ Θεοῦ μάλιστα βλαπτομένῳ τὴν γνώμην ἐοικὼς κ.τ.λ., Trag. in Lycurg. *c. Leacr.* p. 159 ὅταν γὰρ ὀργὴ δαιμόνων βλάπτῃ τινά, τοῦτ' αὐτὸ πρῶτον, ἐξαφαιρεῖται φρενῶν τὸν νοῦν τὸν ἐσθλὸν κ.τ.λ., and so frequently. Sordid motives bring their own punishment in a judicial blindness (βλάπτει πνεῦμα). The aorist here has its common *gnomic* sense, and is the most appropriate tense: see Kühner II. p. 136 sq. Previous editors seem to have mistaken the sense. Bryennios says μὴ ὂν δίκαιον, τουτέστιν, ἀδίκως, but it is not clear what he means. Hilgenfeld reads δεσμούς, and explains 'Christiani non omni ex parte justi persecutionem gentilium patiebantur'. Harnack, misled by the aorist, says 'auctor *diabolum* respi-

cere videtur, quem tamquam avaritiæ principem et auctorem hic infert (?)... censuit igitur, diabolum jam hoc tempore catenis onustum esse'. He might have quoted Wolsey's warning to Cromwell in *Henry VIII*, 'By that sin fell the angels'.

16. τῷ μόνῳ Θεῷ ἀοράτῳ] Comp. 1 Tim. i. 17 ἀοράτῳ μόνῳ Θεῷ.

πατρὶ τῆς ἀληθείας] As in § 3. So also ὁ Θεὸς τῆς ἀληθείας § 19. The Syriac translator takes 'the Truth' here to denote Christ Himself (John xiv. 6); comp. Orig. *c. Cels.* viii. 63 ὑπὸ τοῦ Θεοῦ καὶ τῆς μονογενοῦς αὐτῷ ἀληθείας. So Papias (Euseb. *H. E.* iii. 39) speaks of Christ's personal disciples as receiving commandments ἀπ' αὐτῆς τῆς ἀληθείας.

17. Τὸν σωτῆρα κ.τ.λ.] Acts v. 31 ἀρχηγὸν καὶ σωτῆρα compared with iii. 15 τὸν ἀρχηγὸν τῆς ζωῆς: see also Heb. ii. 10 τὸν ἀρχηγὸν τῆς σωτηρίας. Comp. *Epist. Vienn.* 17 (in Euseb. *H. E.* v. 1) ἀρχηγὸν τῆς ζωῆς τοῦ Θεοῦ.

καὶ τὴν ἐπουράνιον ζωήν, αὐτῷ ἡ δόξα εἰς τοὺς αἰῶνας τῶν αἰώνων. ἀμήν.

1 ζωήν] *delectationem* (בוסמא) S; which word elsewhere is a rendering of τρυφή (see above ii § 19) or of ἀπόλαυσις (see i § 20).   αὐτῷ ἡ δόξα] *atque etiam Jesu Christo Domino nostro cum Spiritu Sancto gloria et honor et imperium* (i. e. ἡ δόξα καὶ ἡ τιμὴ καὶ τὸ κράτος) S.

TRANSLATIONS.

.

THE EPISTLE OF S. CLEMENT

TO

THE CORINTHIANS.

THE Church of God which sojourneth in Rome to the Church of God which sojourneth in Corinth, to them which are called and sanctified by the will of God through our Lord Jesus Christ. Grace to you and peace from Almighty God through Jesus Christ be multiplied.

1. By reason of the sudden and repeated calamities and reverses which are befalling us, brethren, we consider that we have been somewhat tardy in giving heed to the matters of dispute that have arisen among you, dearly beloved, and to the detestable and unholy sedition, so alien and strange to the elect of God, which a few headstrong and self-willed persons have kindled to such a pitch of madness that your name, once revered and renowned and lovely in the sight of all men, hath been greatly reviled. For who that had sojourned among you did not approve your most virtuous and stedfast faith? Who did not admire your sober and forbearing piety in Christ? Who did not publish abroad your magnificent disposition of hospitality? Who did not congratulate you on your perfect and sound knowledge? For ye did all things without respect of persons, and ye walked after the ordinances of God, submitting yourselves to your rulers and rendering to the older men among you the honour which is their due. On the

young too ye enjoined modest and seemly thoughts : **and** the women ye charged to perform all their duties in a blameless and seemly and pure conscience, cherishing their own husbands, as is meet; and ye taught them to keep in the rule of obedience, and to manage the affairs of their household in seemliness, with all discretion.

2.   And ye were all lowly in mind and free from arrogance, yielding rather than claiming submission, *more glad to give than to receive*, and content with the provisions which God supplieth. And giving heed unto His words, ye laid them up diligently in your hearts, and His sufferings were before your eyes. Thus a profound and rich peace was given to all, and an insatiable desire of doing good.   An abundant outpouring also of the Holy Spirit fell upon all ; and, being full of holy counsel, in excellent zeal and with a pious confidence ye stretched out your hands to Almighty God, supplicating Him to be propitious, if unwillingly ye had committed any sin.   Ye had conflict day and night for all the brotherhood, that the number of His elect might be saved with fearfulness and intentness of mind. Ye were sincere and simple and free from malice one towards another.   Every sedition and every schism was abominable to you.   Ye mourned over the transgressions of your neighbours : ye judged their shortcomings to be your own.   Ye repented not of any well-doing, but were *ready unto every good work*. Being adorned with a most virtuous and honourable life, ye performed all your duties in the fear of Him.   The commandments and the ordinances of the Lord were *written on the tables of your hearts.*

3.   All glory and enlargement was given unto you, and that was fulfilled which is written; *My beloved ate and drank and was enlarged and waxed fat and kicked.*   Hence come jealousy and envy, strife and sedition, persecution and tumult, war and captivity.   So men were stirred up, *the mean against the honourable*, the ill-reputed against the highly-reputed, the foolish against the wise, *the young against the elder.*   For this cause *righteousness* and peace *stand aloof,* while each

man hath forsaken the fear of the Lord and become purblind in the faith of Him, neither walketh in the ordinances of His commandments nor liveth according to that which becometh Christ, but each goeth after the lusts of his evil heart, seeing that they have conceived an unrighteous and ungodly jealousy, through which also *death entered into the world.*

4. For so it is written, *And it came to pass after certain days that Cain brought of the fruits of the earth a sacrifice unto God, and Abel he also brought of the firstlings of the sheep and of their fatness. And God looked upon Abel and upon his gifts, but unto Cain and unto his sacrifices He gave no heed. And Cain sorrowed exceedingly, and his countenance fell. And God said unto Cain, Wherefore art thou very sorrowful? and wherefore did thy countenance fall? If thou hast offered aright and hast not divided aright, didst thou not sin? Hold thy peace. Unto thee shall he turn, and thou shalt rule over him. And Cain said unto Abel his brother, Let us go over unto the plain. And it came to pass, while they were in the plain, that Cain rose up against Abel his brother and slew him.* Ye see, brethren, jealousy and envy wrought a brother's murder. By reason of jealousy our father Jacob ran away from the face of Esau his brother. Jealousy caused Joseph to be persecuted even unto death, and to come even unto bondage. Jealousy compelled Moses to flee from the face of Pharaoh king of Egypt while it was said to him by his own countryman, *Who made thee a judge or a decider over us? Wouldest thou slay me, even as yesterday thou slewest the Egyptian?* By reason of jealousy Aaron and Miriam were lodged outside the camp. Jealousy brought Dathan and Abiram down alive to hades, because they made sedition against Moses the servant of God. By reason of jealousy David was envied not only by aliens, but was persecuted also by Saul king of Israel.

5. But, to pass from the examples of ancient days, let us come to those champions who lived nearest to our time. Let us set before us the noble examples which belong to our generation. By reason of jealousy and envy the greatest and

most righteous pillars of the Church were persecuted, and contended even unto death. Let us set before our eyes the good Apostles. There was Peter who by reason of unrighteous jealousy endured not one nor two but many labours, and thus having borne his testimony went to his appointed place of glory. By reason of jealousy and strife Paul by his example pointed out the prize of patient endurance. After that he had been seven times in bonds, had been driven into exile, had been stoned, had preached in the East and in the West, he won the noble renown which was the reward of his faith, having taught right-eousness unto the whole world and having reached the farthest bounds of the West; and when he had borne his testimony before the rulers, so he departed from the world and went unto the holy place, having been found a notable pattern of patient endurance.

6. Unto these men of holy lives was gathered a vast multi-tude of the elect, who through many indignities and tortures, being the victims of jealousy, set a brave example among ourselves. By reason of jealousy matrons and maidens and slave-girls being persecuted, after that they had suffered cruel and unholy insults, safely reached the goal in the race of faith, and received a noble reward, feeble though they were in body. Jealousy hath estranged wives from their husbands and changed the saying of our father Adam, *This now is bone of my bones and flesh of my flesh.* Jealousy and strife have overthrown great cities and uprooted great nations.

7. These things, dearly beloved, we write, not only as admonishing you, but also as putting ourselves in remembrance. For we are in the same lists, and the same contest awaiteth us. Wherefore let us forsake idle and vain thoughts; and let us conform to the glorious and venerable rule which hath been handed down to us; and let us see what is good and what is pleasant and what is acceptable in the sight of Him that made us. Let us fix our eyes on the blood of Christ and under-stand how precious it is unto His Father, because being shed for our salvation it won for the whole world the grace

of repentance. Let us review all the generations in turn, and learn how from generation to generation the Master hath given a place for repentance unto them that desire to turn to Him. Noah preached repentance, and they that obeyed were saved. Jonah preached destruction unto the men of Nineveh; but they, repenting of their sins, obtained pardon of God by their supplications and received salvation, albeit they were aliens from God.

8. The ministers of the grace of God through the Holy Spirit spake concerning repentance. Yea and the Master of the universe Himself spake concerning repentance with an oath; *For, as I live, saith the Lord, I desire not the death of the sinner, so much as his repentance;* and He added also a merciful judgment: *Repent ye, O house of Israel, of your iniquity; say unto the sons of my people, Though your sins reach from the earth even unto the heaven, and though they be redder than scarlet and blacker than sack-cloth, and ye turn unto me with your whole heart and say Father, I will give ear unto you as unto an holy people.* And in another place He saith on this wise, *Wash, be ye clean. Put away your iniquities from your souls out of my sight. Cease from your iniquities; learn to do good; seek out judgment; defend him that is wronged: give judgment for the orphan, and execute righteousness for the widow; and come and let us reason together, saith He; and though your sins be as crimson, I will make them white as snow; and though they be as scarlet, I will make them white as wool. And if ye be willing and will hearken unto Me, ye shall eat the good things of the earth; but if ye be not willing, neither hearken unto Me, a sword shall devour you; for the mouth of the Lord hath spoken these things.* Seeing then that He desireth all His beloved to be partakers of repentance, He confirmed it by an act of His almighty will.

9. Wherefore let us be obedient unto His excellent and glorious will; and presenting ourselves as suppliants of His mercy and goodness, let us fall down before Him and betake ourselves unto His compassions, forsaking the vain toil and the strife and the jealousy which leadeth unto death. Let us fix

our eyes on them that ministered perfectly unto His excellent glory. Let us set before us Enoch, who being found righteous in obedience was translated, and his death was not found. Noah, being found faithful, by his ministration preached regeneration unto the world, and through him the Master saved the living creatures that entered into the ark in concord.

10. Abraham, who was called the 'friend,' was found faithful in that he rendered obedience unto the words of God. He through obedience went forth from his land and from his kindred and from his father's house, that leaving a scanty land and a feeble kindred and a mean house he might inherit the promises of God. For He saith unto him; *Go forth from thy land and from thy kindred and from thy father's house unto the land which I shall show thee, and I will make thee into a great nation, and I will bless thee and will magnify thy name, and thou shalt be blessed. And I will bless them that bless thee, and I will curse them that curse thee; and in thee shall all the tribes of the earth be blessed.* And again, when he was parted from Lot, God said unto him; *Look up with thine eyes, and behold from the place where thou now art, unto the north and the south and the sunrise and the sea; for all the land which thou seest, I will give it unto thee and to thy seed for ever; and I will make thy seed as the dust of the earth. If any man can count the dust of the earth, then shall thy seed also be counted.* And again He saith; *And God led Abraham forth and said unto him, Look up unto the heaven and count the stars, and see whether thou canst count them. So shall thy seed be. And Abraham believed God, and it was reckoned unto him for righteousness.* For his faith and hospitality a son was given unto him in old age, and by obedience he offered him a sacrifice unto God on one of the mountains which He showed him.

11. For his hospitality and godliness Lot was saved from Sodom, when all the country round about was judged by fire and brimstone; the Master having thus foreshown that He forsaketh not them which set their hope on Him, but appointeth unto punishment and torment them which swerve aside. For

when his wife had gone forth with him, being otherwise-minded and not in accord, she was appointed for a sign hereunto, so that she became a pillar of salt unto this day, that it might be known unto all men that they which are double-minded and they which doubt concerning the power of God are set for a judgment and for a token unto all the generations.

12. For her faith and hospitality Rahab the harlot was saved. For when the spies were sent forth unto Jericho by Joshua the son of Nun, the king of the land perceived that they were come to spy out his country, and sent forth men to seize them, that being seized they might be put to death. So the hospitable Rahab received them and hid them in the upper chamber under the flax-stalks. And when the messengers of the king came near and said, *The spies of our land entered in unto thee: bring them forth, for the king so ordereth:* then she answered, *The men truly, whom ye seek, entered in unto me, but they departed forthwith and are journeying on the way;* and she pointed out to them the opposite road. And she said unto the men, *Of a surety I perceive that the Lord your God delivereth this city unto you; for the fear and the dread of you is fallen upon the inhabitants thereof. When therefore it shall come to pass that ye take it, save me and the house of my father.* And they said unto her, *It shall be even so as thou hast spoken unto us. Whensoever therefore thou perceivest that we are coming, thou shalt gather all thy folk beneath thy roof, and they shall be saved; for as many as shall be found without the house shall perish.* And moreover they gave her a sign, that she should hang out from her house a scarlet thread, thereby showing beforehand that through the blood of the Lord there shall be redemption unto all them that believe and hope on God. Ye see, dearly beloved, not only faith, but prophecy, is found in the woman.

13. Let us therefore be lowly-minded, brethren, laying aside all arrogance and conceit and folly and anger, and let us do that which is written. For the Holy Ghost saith, *Let not the wise man boast in his wisdom, nor the strong in his strength, neither the rich in his riches; but he that boasteth let*

23—2

him boast in the Lord, that he may seek Him out, and do judg-
ment and righteousness; most of all remembering the words of
the Lord Jesus which He spake, teaching forbearance and long-
suffering: for thus He spake; *Have mercy, that ye may receive*
mercy: forgive that it may be forgiven to you. As ye do, so
shall it be done to you. As ye give, so shall it be given unto you.
As ye judge, so shall ye be judged. As ye show kindness, so shall
kindness be showed unto you. With what measure ye mete, it
shall be measured withal to you. With this commandment and
these precepts let us confirm ourselves, that we may walk in
obedience to His hallowed words, with lowliness of mind. For
the holy word saith, *Upon whom shall I look, save upon him*
that is gentle and quiet and feareth mine oracles?

14. Therefore it is right and proper, brethren, that we
should be obedient unto God, rather than follow those who
in arrogance and unruliness have set themselves up as leaders
in abominable jealousy. For we shall bring upon us no common harm, but rather great peril, if we surrender ourselves
recklessly to the purposes of men who launch out into strife
and seditions, so as to estrange us from that which is right.
Let us be good one towards another according to the compassion and sweetness of Him that made us. For it is written:
The good shall be dwellers in the land, and the innocent shall be
left on it; but they that transgress shall be destroyed utterly from
it. And again He saith; *I saw the ungodly lifted up on high*
and exalted as the cedars of Lebanon. And I passed by, and
behold he was not; and I sought out his place, and I found it
not. Keep innocence and behold uprightness; for there is a
remnant for the peaceful man.

15. Therefore let us cleave unto them that practise peace
with godliness, and not unto them that desire peace with dissimulation. For He saith in a certain place; *This people honoureth*
me with their lips, but their heart is far from me; and again,
They blessed with their mouth, but they cursed with their heart.
And again He saith, *They loved Him with their mouth, and*
with their tongue they lied unto Him; and their heart was not

upright with Him, neither were they stedfast in His covenant. For this cause *Let the deceitful lips be made dumb which speak iniquity against the righteous.*   And again ; *May the Lord utterly destroy all the deceitful lips, the tongue that speaketh proud things, even them that say, Let us magnify our tongue ; our lips are our own ; who is Lord over us?   For the misery of the needy and for the groaning of the poor I will now arise, saith the Lord. I will set him in safety ; I will deal boldly by him.*

16.   For Christ is with them that are lowly of mind, not with them that exalt themselves over the flock.   The sceptre of the majesty of God, even our Lord Jesus Christ, came not in the pomp of arrogance or of pride, though He might have done so, but in lowliness of mind, according as the Holy Spirit spake concerning Him.   For He saith ; *Lord, who believed our report? and to whom was the arm of the Lord revealed?   We announced Him in His presence.   As a child was He, as a root in a thirsty ground.   There is no form in Him, neither glory.   And we beheld Him, and He had no form nor comeliness, but His form was mean, lacking more than the form of men.   He was a man of stripes and of toil, and knowing how to bear infirmity: for His face is turned away.   He was dishonoured and held of no account. He beareth our sins and suffereth pain for our sakes : and we accounted Him to be in toil and in stripes and in affliction.   And He was wounded for our sins and hath been afflicted for our iniquities.   The chastisement of our peace is upon Him.   With His bruises we were healed.   We all went astray like sheep, each man went astray in his own path : and the Lord delivered Him over for our sins.   And He openeth not his mouth, because He is afflicted.   As a sheep He was led to slaughter ; and as a lamb before his shearer is dumb, so openeth He not His mouth. In His humiliation His judgment was taken away.   His generation who shall declare?   For His life is taken away from the earth.   For the iniquities of my people He is come to death. And I will give the wicked for His burial, and the rich for His death ; for He wrought no iniquity, neither was guile found in His mouth.   And the Lord desireth to cleanse Him from*

His stripes. If ye offer for sin, your soul shall see a long-lived seed. And the Lord desireth to take away from the toil of His soul, to show Him light and to mould Him with understanding, to justify a Just One that is a good servant unto many. And He shall bear their sins. Therefore He shall inherit many, and shall divide the spoils of the strong; because His soul was delivered unto death, and He was reckoned unto the transgressors; and He bare the sins of many, and for their sins was He delivered up. And again He Himself saith; *But I am a worm and no man, a reproach of men and an outcast of the people. All they that beheld me mocked at me; they spake with their lips; they wagged their heads, saying, He hoped on the Lord; let Him deliver him, or let Him save him, for He desireth him.* Ye see, dearly beloved, what is the pattern that hath been given unto us; for, if the Lord was thus lowly of mind, what should we do, who through Him have been brought under the yoke of His grace?

17. Let us be imitators also of them which went about in goatskins and sheepskins, preaching the coming of Christ. We mean Elijah and Elisha and likewise Ezekiel, the prophets, and besides them those men also that obtained a good report. Abraham obtained an exceeding good report and was called the friend of God; and looking stedfastly on the glory of God, he saith in lowliness of mind, *But I am dust and ashes.* Moreover concerning Job also it is thus written; *And Job was righteous and unblameable, one that was true and honoured God and abstained from all evil.* Yet he himself accuseth himself saying, *No man is clean from filth; no, not though his life be but for a day.* Moses was called *faithful in all His house,* and through his ministration God judged Egypt with the plagues and the torments which befel them. Howbeit he also, though greatly glorified, yet spake no proud words, but said, when an oracle was given to him at the bush, *Who am I, that Thou sendest me? Nay, I am feeble of speech and slow of tongue.* And again he saith, *But I am smoke from the pot.*

18. But what must we say of David that obtained a good

report? of whom God said, *I have found a man after my heart, David the son of Jesse: with eternal mercy have I anointed him.* Yet he too saith unto God ; *Have mercy upon me, O God, according to thy great mercy ; and according to the multitude of thy compassions, blot out mine iniquity. Wash me yet more from mine iniquity, aud cleanse me from my sin. For I acknowledge mine iniquity, and my sin is ever before me. Against Thee only did I sin, and I wrought evil in Thy sight; that Thou mayest be justified in Thy words, and mayest conquer in Thy pleading. For behold, in iniquities was I conceived, and in sins did my mother bear me. For behold Thou hast loved truth : the dark and hidden things of Thy wisdom hast Thou showed unto me. Thou shalt sprinkle me with hyssop, and I shall be made clean. Thou shalt wash me, and I shall become whiter than snow. Thou shalt make me to hear of joy and gladness. The bones which have been humbled shall rejoice. Turn away Thy face from my sins, and blot out all mine iniquities. Make a clean heart within me, O God, and renew a right spirit in mine inmost parts. Cast me not away from Thy presence, and take not Thy Holy Spirit from me. Restore unto me the joy of Thy salvation, and strengthen me with a princely spirit. I will teach sinners Thy ways, and godless men shall be converted unto Thee. Deliver me from bloodguilti-ness, O God, the God of my salvation. My tongue shall rejoice in Thy righteousness. Lord, Thou shalt open my mouth, and my lips shall declare Thy praise. For, if Thou hadst desired sacrifice, I would have given it: in whole burnt-offerings Thou wilt have no pleasure. A sacrifice unto God is a contrite spirit; a contrite and humbled heart God will not despise.*

19. The humility therefore and the submissiveness of so many and so great men, who have thus obtained a good report, hath through obedience made better not only us but also the generations which were before us, even them that received His oracles in fear and truth. Seeing then that we have been par-takers of many great and glorious doings, let us hasten to re-turn unto the goal of peace which hath been handed down to

us from the beginning, and let us look stedfastly unto the
Father and Maker of the whole world, and cleave unto His
splendid and excellent gifts of peace and benefits. Let us
behold Him in our mind, and let us look with the eyes of
our soul unto His long-suffering will. Let us note how free
from anger He is towards all His creatures.

20.   The heavens are moved by His direction and obey Him
in peace. Day and night accomplish the course assigned to them
by Him, without hindrance one to another. The sun and the
moon and the dancing stars according to His appointment circle
in harmony within the bounds assigned to them, without any
swerving aside. The earth, bearing fruit in fulfilment of His will
at her proper seasons, putteth forth the food that supplieth
abundantly both men and beasts and all living things which
are thereupon, making no dissension, neither altering anything
which He hath decreed. Moreover, the inscrutable depths of the
abysses and the unutterable †statutes† of the nether regions are
constrained by the same ordinances. The basin of the boundless
sea, gathered together by His workmanship into its reservoirs,
passeth not the barriers wherewith it is surrounded; but even
as He ordered it, so it doeth. For He said, *So far shalt thou
come, and thy waves shall be broken within thee*. The ocean which
is impassable for men, and the worlds beyond it, are directed
by the same ordinances of the Master. The seasons of spring
and summer and autumn and winter give way in succession
one to another in peace. The winds in their several quarters
at their proper season fulfil their ministry without disturbance ;
and the everflowing fountains, created for enjoyment and health,
without fail give their breasts which sustain the life of men.
Yea, the smallest of living things come together in concord and
peace. All these things the great Creator and Master of the
universe ordered to be in peace and concord, doing good unto
all things, but far beyond the rest unto us who have taken
refuge in His compassionate mercies through our Lord Jesus
Christ, to whom be the glory and the majesty for ever and ever.
Amen.

21. Look ye, brethren, lest His benefits, which are many, turn unto judgment to all of us, if we walk not worthily of Him, and do those things which are good and well-pleasing in His sight with concord. For He saith in a certain place, *The Spirit of the Lord is a lamp searching the closets of the belly.* Let us see how near He is, and how that nothing escapeth Him of our thoughts or our devices which we make. It is right therefore that we should not be deserters from His will. Let us rather give offence to foolish and senseless men who exalt themselves and boast in the arrogance of their words, than to God. Let us fear the Lord Jesus, whose blood was given for us. Let us reverence our rulers; let us honour our elders; let us instruct our young men in the lesson of the fear of God. Let us guide our women toward that which is good: let them show forth their lovely disposition of purity; let them prove their sincere affection of gentleness; let them make manifest the moderation of their tongue through their silence; let them show their love, not in factious preferences but without partiality towards all them that fear God, in holiness. Let our children be partakers of the instruction which is in Christ: let them learn how lowliness of mind prevaileth with God, what power chaste love hath with God, how the fear of Him is good and great and saveth all them that walk therein in a pure mind with holiness. For He is the searcher out of the intents and desires; whose breath is in us, and when He listeth, He shall take it away.

22. Now all these things the faith which is in Christ confirmeth: for He Himself through the Holy Spirit thus inviteth us: *Come, my children, hearken unto me, I will teach you the fear of the Lord. What man is he that desireth life and loveth to see good days? Make thy tongue to cease from evil, and thy lips that they speak no guile. Turn aside from evil and do good. Seek peace and ensue it. The eyes of the Lord are over the righteous, and His ears are turned to their prayers. But the face of the Lord is upon them that do evil, to destroy their memorial from the earth. The righteous cried out, and the Lord heard him, and delivered him from all his troubles.*

Many are the troubles of the righteous, and the Lord shall de-liver them from them all. And again; *Many are the stripes of the sinner, but them that set their hope on the Lord mercy shall compass about.*

23. The Father, who is pitiful in all things, and ready to do good, hath compassion on them that fear Him, and kindly and lovingly bestoweth His favours on them that draw nigh unto Him with a single mind. Wherefore let us not be double-minded, neither let our soul indulge in idle humours respecting His exceeding and glorious gifts. Let this scripture be far from us where He saith; *Wretched are the double-minded, which doubt in their soul and say, These things we did hear in the days of our fathers also, and behold we have grown old, and none of these things hath befallen us. Ye fools, compare your-selves unto a tree; take a vine. First it sheddeth its leaves, then a shoot cometh, then a leaf, then a flower, and after these a sour berry, then a full ripe grape.* Ye see that in a little time the fruit of the tree attaineth unto mellowness. Of a truth quickly and suddenly shall His will be accomplished, the scripture also bearing witness to it, saying; *He shall come quickly and shall not tarry; and the Lord shall come suddenly into His temple, even the Holy One, whom ye expect.*

24. Let us understand, dearly beloved, how the Master continually showeth unto us the resurrection that shall be here-after; whereof He made the Lord Jesus Christ the firstfruit, when He raised Him from the dead. Let us behold, dearly beloved, the resurrection which happeneth at its proper season. Day and night show unto us the resurrection. The night falleth asleep, and day ariseth; the day departeth, and night cometh on. Let us mark the fruits, how and in what manner the sowing taketh place. *The sower goeth forth* and casteth into the earth each of the seeds; and these falling into the earth dry and bare decay: then out of their decay the mightiness of the Master's providence raiseth them up, and from being one they increase manifold and bear fruit.

25. Let us consider the marvellous sign which is seen in

the regions of the east, that is, in the parts about Arabia.
There is a bird, which is named the phœnix. This, being
the only one of its kind, liveth for five hundred years; and
when it hath now reached the time of its dissolution that it
should die, it maketh for itself a coffin of frankincense and myrrh
and the other spices, into the which in the fulness of time
it entereth, and so it dieth. But, as the flesh rotteth, a certain
worm is engendered, which is nurtured from the moisture of
the dead creature and putteth forth wings. Then, when it is
grown lusty, it taketh up that coffin where are the bones of its
parent, and carrying them journeyeth from the country of
Arabia even unto Egypt, to the place called the City of the
Sun; and in the day time in the sight of all, flying to the
altar of the Sun, it layeth them thereupon; and this done, it
setteth forth to return. So the priests examine the registers
of the times, and they find that it hath come when the five
hundredth year is completed.

26. Do we then think it to be a great and marvellous thing,
if the Creator of the universe shall bring about the resurrection
of them that have served Him with holiness in the assurance
of a good faith, seeing that He showeth to us even by a bird
the magnificence of His promise? For He saith in a certain
place; *And thou shalt raise me up, and I will praise Thee; and
I went to rest and slept, I was awaked, for Thou art with me.*
And again Job saith; *And Thou shalt raise this my flesh which
hath endured all these things.*

27. With this hope therefore let our souls be bound unto
Him that is faithful in His promises and that is righteous in
His judgments. He that commanded not to lie, much more
shall He Himself not lie: for nothing is impossible with God
save to lie. Therefore let our faith in Him be kindled within
us, and let us understand that all things are nigh unto Him.
By a word of His majesty He compacted the universe; and by
a word He can destroy it. *Who shall say unto Him, What
hast thou done? or who shall resist the might of His strength?*
When He listeth, and as He listeth, He will do all things; and

nothing shall pass away of those things that He hath decreed. All things are in His sight, and nothing escapeth His counsel, seeing that *The heavens declare the glory of God, and the firmament proclaimeth His handiwork. Day uttereth word unto day, and night proclaimeth knowledge unto night; and there are neither words nor speeches, whose voices are not heard.*

28. .Since therefore all things are seen and heard, let us fear Him and forsake the abominable lusts of evil works, that we may be shielded by His mercy from the coming judgments. For where can any of us escape from His strong hand? And what world will receive any of them that desert from His service? For the holy writing saith in a certain place; *Where shall I go, and where shall I be hidden from Thy face? If I ascend into the heaven, Thou art there; if I depart into the farthest parts of the earth, there is Thy right hand; if I make my bed in the depths, there is Thy Spirit.* Whither then shall one depart, or where shall one flee, from Him that embraceth the universe?

29. Let us therefore approach Him in holiness of soul, lifting up pure and undefiled hands unto Him, with love towards our gentle and compassionate Father who made us an elect portion unto Himself. For thus it is written: *When the Most High divided the nations, when He dispersed the sons of Adam, He fixed the boundaries of the nations according to the number of the angels of God. His people Jacob became the portion of the Lord, and Israel the measurement of His inheritance.* And in another place He saith; *Behold, the Lord taketh for Himself a nation out of the midst of the nations, as a man taketh the firstfruits of his threshing floor; and the holy of holies shall come forth from that nation.*

30. Seeing then that we are the special portion of a Holy God, let us do all things that pertain unto holiness, forsaking evil-speakings, abominable and impure embraces, drunkennesses and tumults and hateful lusts, abominable adultery, hateful pride; *For God,* He saith, *resisteth the proud, but giveth grace to the lowly.* Let us therefore cleave unto those to whom

grace is given from God. Let us clothe ourselves in con-cord, being lowly-minded and temperate, holding ourselves aloof from all backbiting and evil speaking, being justified by works and not by words. For He saith; *He that saith much shall hear also again. Doth the ready talker think to be righteous? Blessed is the offspring of a woman that liveth but a short time. Be not thou abundant in words.* Let our praise be with God, and not of ourselves: for God hateth them that praise them-selves. Let the testimony to our well-doing be given by others, as it was given unto our fathers who were righteous. Boldness and arrogance and daring are for them that are ac-cursed of God; but forbearance and humility and gentleness are with them that are blessed of God.

31. Let us therefore cleave unto His blessing, and let us see what are the ways of blessing. Let us study the records of the things that have happened from the beginning. Wherefore was our father Abraham blessed? Was it not because he wrought righteousness and truth through faith? Isaac with confidence, as knowing the future, was led a willing sacrifice. Jacob with humility departed from his land because of his brother, and went unto Laban and served; and the twelve tribes of Israel were given unto him.

32. If any man will consider them one by one in sin-cerity, he shall understand the magnificence of the gifts that are given by Him. For of Jacob are all the priests and levites who minister unto the altar of God; of him is the Lord Jesus as concerning the flesh; of him are kings and rulers and governors in the line of Judah; yea and the rest of his tribes are held in no small honour, seeing that God promised saying, *Thy seed shall be as the stars of heaven.* They all therefore were glorified and magnified, not through themselves or their own works or the righteous doing which they wrought, but through His will. And so we, having been called through His will in Christ Jesus, are not justified through ourselves or through our own wisdom or understanding or piety or works which we wrought in holi-ness of heart, but through faith, whereby the Almighty God

justified all men that have been from the beginning; to whom be the glory for ever and ever. Amen.

33. What then must we do, brethren? Must we idly abstain from doing good, and forsake love? May the Master never allow this to befal us at least; but let us hasten with instancy and zeal to accomplish every good work. For the Creator and Master of the universe Himself rejoiceth in His works. For by His exceeding great might He established the heavens, and in His incomprehensible wisdom He set them in order. And the earth He separated from the water that surroundeth it, and He set it firm on the sure foundation of His own will; and the living creatures which walk upon it He commanded to exist by His ordinance. Having before created the sea and the living creatures therein, He enclosed it by His own power. Above all, as the most excellent and exceeding great work of His intelligence, with His sacred and faultless hands He formed man in the impress of His own image. For thus saith God; *Let us make man after our image and after our likeness. And God made man; male and female made He them.* So having finished all these things, He praised them and blessed them and said, *Increase and multiply.* We have seen that all the righteous were adorned in good works. Yea, and the Lord Himself having adorned Himself with works rejoiced. Seeing then that we have this pattern, let us conform ourselves with all diligence to His will; let us with all our strength work the work of righteousness.

34. The good workman receiveth the bread of his work with boldness, but the slothful and careless dareth not look his employer in the face. It is therefore needful that we should be zealous unto well-doing, for of Him are all things: since He forewarneth us saying, *Behold, the Lord, and His reward is before His face, to recompense each man according to his work.* He exhorteth us therefore to believe on Him with our whole heart, and to be not idle nor careless unto every good work. Let our boast and our confidence be in Him: let us submit ourselves to His will; let us mark the whole host of His angels, how they

stand by and minister unto His will. For the scripture saith *Ten thousands of ten thousands stood by Him, and thousands of thousands ministered unto Him: and they cried aloud, Holy, holy, holy is the Lord of Sabaoth; all creation is full of His glory.* Yea, and let us ourselves then, being gathered together in concord with intentness of heart, cry unto Him as from one mouth earnestly that we may be made partakers of His great and glorious promises. For He saith, *Eye hath not seen and ear hath not heard, and it hath not entered into the heart of man what great things He hath prepared for them that patiently await Him.*

35. How blessed and marvellous are the gifts of God, dearly beloved! Life in immortality, splendour in righteousness, truth in boldness, faith in confidence, temperance in sanctification! And all these things fall under our apprehension. What then, think ye, are the things preparing for them that patiently await Him? The Creator and Father of the ages, the All-holy One Himself knoweth their number and their beauty. Let us therefore contend, that we may be found in the number of those that patiently await Him, to the end that we may be partakers of His promised gifts. But how shall this be, dearly beloved? If our mind be fixed through faith towards God; if we seek out those things which are well pleasing and acceptable unto Him; if we accomplish such things as beseem His faultless will, and follow the way of truth, casting off from ourselves all unrighteousness and iniquity, covetousness, strifes, malignities and deceits, whisperings and back-bitings, hatred of God, pride and arrogance, vainglory and inhospitality. For they that do these things are hateful to God; and not only they that do them, but they also that consent unto them. For the scripture saith; *But unto the sinner said God, Wherefore dost thou declare mine ordinances, and takest my covenant upon thy lips? Yet thou didst hate instruction and didst cast away my words behind thee. If thou sawest a thief, thou didst keep company with him, and with the adulterers thou didst set thy portion. Thy mouth multiplied wickedness, and thy tongue wove deceit. Thou sattest and spakest against thy brother, and against the son of thy mother thou didst lay a stumbling-block.*

These things thou hast done, and I kept silence. Thou thoughtest, unrighteous man, that I should be like unto thee. I will convict thee and will set thee face to face with thyself. Now understand ye these things, ye that forget God, lest at any time He seize you as a lion, and there be none to deliver. The sacrifice of praise shall glorify Me, and there is the way wherein I will show him the salvation of God.

36. This is the way, dearly-beloved, wherein we found our salvation, even Jesus Christ the High-priest of our offerings, the Guardian and Helper of our weakness. Through Him let us look stedfastly unto the heights of the heavens; through Him we behold as in a mirror His faultless and most excellent visage; through Him the eyes of our hearts were opened; through Him our foolish and darkened mind springeth up unto the light; through Him the Master willed that we should taste of the immortal knowledge; *Who being the brightness of His majesty is so much greater than angels, as He hath inherited a more excellent name.* For so it is written; *Who maketh His angels spirits and His ministers a flame of fire;* but of His Son the Master said thus; *Thou art My Son, I this day have begotten Thee. Ask of Me, and I will give Thee the Gentiles for Thine inheritance, and the ends of the earth for Thy possession.* And again He saith unto Him; *Sit thou on My right hand, until I make Thine enemies a footstool for Thy feet.* Who then are these enemies? They that are wicked and resist His will.

37. Let us therefore enlist ourselves, brethren, with all earnestness in His faultless ordinances. Let us mark the soldiers that are enlisted under our rulers, how exactly, how readily, how submissively, they execute the orders given them. All are not prefects, nor rulers of thousands, nor rulers of hundreds, nor rulers of fifties, and so forth; but each man in his own rank executeth the orders given by the king and the governors. *The great without the small* cannot exist, neither *the small without the great.* There is a certain mixture in all things, and therein is utility. Let us take our body as an example. The head

without the feet is nothing; so likewise the feet without the head are nothing: even the smallest limbs of our body are necessary and useful for the whole body: but all the members conspire and unite in subjection, that the whole body may be saved.

38. So in our case let the whole body be saved in Christ Jesus, and let each man be subject unto his neighbour, according as also he was appointed with his special grace. Let not the strong neglect the weak; and let the weak respect the strong. Let the rich minister aid to the poor; and let the poor give thanks to God, because He hath given him one through whom his wants may be supplied. Let the wise display his wisdom, not in good words, but in good works. He that is lowly in mind, let him not bear testimony to himself, but leave testimony to be borne to him by his neighbour. He that is pure in the flesh, let him be so, and not boast, knowing that it is Another who bestoweth his continence upon him. Let us consider, brethren, of what matter we were made; who and what manner of beings we were, when we came into the world; from what a sepulchre and what darkness He that moulded and created us brought us into His world, having prepared His benefits aforehand ere ever we were born. Seeing therefore that we have all these things from Him, we ought in all things to give thanks to Him, to whom be the glory for ever and ever. Amen.

39. Senseless and stupid and foolish and ignorant men jeer and mock at us, desiring that they themselves should be exalted in their imaginations. For what power hath a mortal? or what strength hath a child of earth? For it is written; *There was no form before mine eyes; only I heard a breath and a voice. What then? Shall a mortal be clean in the sight of the Lord; or shall a man be unblameable for his works? seeing that He is distrustful against His servants and noteth some perversity against His angels. Nay, the heaven is not clean in His sight. Away then, ye that dwell in houses of clay, whereof, even of the same clay, we ourselves are made. He smote them like a moth, and from morn to even they are no more. Because*

they could not succour themselves, they perished. He breathed upon them and they died, because they had no wisdom. But call thou, if perchance one shall obey thee, or if thou shalt see one of the holy angels. For wrath killeth the foolish man, and envy slayeth him that is gone astray. And I have seen fools throwing out roots, but forthwith their habitation was eaten up. Far be their sons from safety. May they be mocked at the gates of inferiors, and there shall be none to deliver them. For the things which are prepared for them, the righteous shall eat; but they themselves shall not be delivered from evils.

40. Forasmuch then as these things are manifest beforehand, and we have searched into the depths of the Divine knowledge, we ought to do all things in order, as many as the Master hath commanded us to perform at their appointed seasons. Now the offerings and ministrations He commanded to be performed with care, and not to be done rashly or in disorder, but at fixed times and seasons. And where and by whom He would have them performed, He Himself fixed by His supreme will: that all things being done with piety according to His good pleasure might be acceptable to His will. They therefore that make their offerings at the appointed seasons are acceptable and blessed: for while they follow the institutions of the Master they cannot go wrong. For unto the high-priest his proper services have been assigned, and to the priests their proper office is appointed, and upon the levites their proper ministrations are laid. The layman is bound by the layman's ordinances.

41. Let each of you, brethren, in his own order give thanks unto God, maintaining a good conscience and not transgressing the appointed rule of his service, but acting with all seemliness. Not in every place, brethren, are the continual daily sacrifices offered, or the freewill offerings, or the sin offerings and the trespass offerings, but in Jerusalem alone. And even there the offering is not made in every place, but before the sanctuary in the court of the altar; and this too through the high-priest and the aforesaid ministers, after that the victim to be offered hath

been inspected for blemishes. They therefore who do any thing contrary to the seemly ordinance of His will receive death as the penalty. Ye see, brethren, in proportion as greater knowledge hath been vouchsafed unto us, so much the more are we exposed to danger.

42. The Apostles received the Gospel for us from the Lord Jesus Christ; Jesus Christ was sent forth from God. So then Christ is from God, and the Apostles are from Christ. Both therefore came of the will of God in the appointed order. Having therefore received a charge, and having been fully assured through the resurrection of our Lord Jesus Christ and confirmed in the word of God with full assurance of the Holy Ghost, they went forth with the glad tidings that the kingdom of God should come. So preaching everywhere in country and town, they appointed their first-fruits, when they had proved them by the Spirit, to be bishops and deacons unto them that should believe. And this they did in no new fashion; for indeed it had been written concerning bishops and deacons from very ancient times; for thus saith the scripture in a certain place, *I will appoint their bishops in righteousness and their deacons in faith.*

43. And what marvel, if they which were entrusted in Christ with such a work by God appointed the aforesaid persons? seeing that even the blessed Moses who was *a faithful servant in all His house* recorded for a sign in the sacred books all things that were enjoined upon him. And him also the rest of the prophets followed, bearing witness with him unto the laws that were ordained by him. For he, when jealousy arose concerning the priesthood, and there was dissension among the tribes which of them was adorned with the glorious name, commanded the twelve chiefs of the tribes to bring to him rods inscribed with the name of each tribe. And he took them and tied them and sealed them with the signet rings of the chiefs of the tribes, and put them away in the tabernacle of the testimony on the table of God. And having shut the tabernacle he sealed the keys and likewise also the doors. And he said unto them, *Brethren, the tribe whose rod shall bud, this hath God chosen to be*

priests and ministers unto Him. Now when morning came, he
called together all Israel, even the six hundred thousand men,
and showed the seals to the chiefs of the tribes and opened the
tabernacle of the testimony and drew forth the rods. And the
rod of Aaron was found not only with buds, but also bearing
fruit. What think ye, dearly beloved? Did not Moses know
beforehand that this would come to pass? Assuredly he
knew it. But that disorder might not arise in Israel, he did
thus, to the end that the Name of the true and only God
might be glorified: to whom be the glory for ever and ever.
Amen.

44. And our Apostles knew through our Lord Jesus Christ
that there would be strife over the name of the bishop's office.
For this cause therefore, having received complete foreknowledge,
they appointed the aforesaid persons, and afterwards they pro-
vided a continuance, that if these should fall asleep, other approved men should succeed to their ministration. Those therefore who were appointed by them, or afterward by other men of
repute with the consent of the whole Church, and have ministered
unblameably to the flock of Christ in lowliness of mind, peace-
fully and with all modesty, and for long time have borne a good
report with all—these men we consider to be unjustly thrust out
from their ministration. For it will be no light sin for us, if we
thrust out those who have offered the gifts of the bishop's office
unblameably and holily. Blessed are those presbyters who
have gone before, seeing that their departure was fruitful and
ripe : for they have no fear lest any one should remove them
from their appointed place. For we see that ye have displaced
certain persons, though they were living honourably, from the
ministration which they had kept blamelessly.

45. Be ye contentious, brethren, and jealous about the
things that pertain unto salvation. Ye have searched the
scriptures, which are true, which were given through the Holy
Ghost ; and ye know that nothing unrighteous or counterfeit is
written in them. Ye will not find that righteous persons have
been thrust out by holy men. Righteous men were persecuted,

but it was by the lawless; they were imprisoned, but it was by the unholy. They were stoned by transgressors: they were slain by those who had conceived a detestable and unrighteous jealousy. Suffering these things, they endured nobly. For what must we say, brethren? Was Daniel cast into the lions' den by them that feared God? Or were Ananias and Azarias and Misael shut up in the furnace of fire by them that professed the excellent and glorious worship of the Most High? Far be this from our thoughts. Who then were they that did these things? Abominable men and full of all wickedness were stirred up to such a pitch of wrath, as to bring cruel suffering upon them that served God in a holy and blameless purpose, not knowing that the Most High is the champion and protector of them that in a pure conscience serve His excellent Name: unto whom be the glory for ever and ever. Amen. But they that endured patiently in confidence inherited glory and honour; they were exalted, and had their names recorded by God in their memorial for ever and ever. Amen.

46. To such examples as these therefore, brethren, we also ought to cleave. For it is written; *Cleave unto the saints, for they that cleave unto them shall be sanctified.* And again He saith in another place; *With the guiltless man thou shalt be guiltless, and with the elect thou shalt be elect, and with the crooked thou shalt deal crookedly.* Let us therefore cleave to the guiltless and righteous: and these are the elect of God. Wherefore are there strifes and wraths and factions and divisions and war among you? Have we not one God and one Christ and one Spirit of grace that was shed upon us? And is there not one calling in Christ? Wherefore do we tear and rend asunder the members of Christ, and stir up factions against our own body, and reach such a pitch of folly, as to forget that we are members one of another? Remember the words of Jesus our Lord: for He said, *Woe unto that man, It were good for him if he had not been born, rather than that he should offend one of Mine elect. It were better for him that a mill-stone were hanged about him, and he cast into the sea, than that he should*

pervert one of Mine elect. Your division hath perverted many; it hath brought many to despair, many to doubting, and all of us to sorrow. And your sedition still continueth.

47. Take up the epistle of the blessed Paul the Apostle. What wrote he first unto you in the beginning of the Gospel? Of a truth he charged you in the Spirit concerning himself and Cephas and Apollos, because that even then ye had made parties. Yet that making of parties brought less sin upon you; for ye were partisans of Apostles that were highly reputed, and of a man approved in their sight. But now mark ye, who they are that have perverted you and diminished the glory of your renowned love for the brotherhood. It is shameful, dearly beloved, yes, utterly shameful and unworthy of your conduct in Christ, that it should be reported that the very stedfast and ancient Church of the Corinthians, for the sake of one or two persons, maketh sedition against its presbyters. And this report hath reached not only us, but them also which differ from us, so that ye even heap blasphemies on the Name of the Lord by reason of your folly, and moreover create peril for yourselves.

48. Let us therefore root this out quickly, and let us fall down before the Master and intreat Him with tears, that He may show Himself propitious and be reconciled unto us, and may restore us to the seemly and pure conduct which belongeth to our love of the brethren. For this is a gate of righteousness opened unto life, as it is written; *Open me the gates of righteousness, that I may enter in thereby and praise the Lord. This is the gate of the Lord; the righteous shall enter in thereby.* Seeing then that many gates are opened, this is that gate which is in righteousness, even that which is in Christ, whereby all are blessed that have entered in and direct their path in holiness and righteousness, performing all things without confusion. Let a man be faithful, let him be able to expound a deep saying, let him be wise in the discernment of words, let him be strenuous in deeds, let him be pure; for so much the more ought he to be lowly in mind, in proportion as he

seemeth to be the greater; and he ought to seek the common advantage of all, and not his own.

49. Let him that hath love in Christ fulfil the commandments of Christ. Who can declare the bond of the love of God? Who is sufficient to tell the majesty of its beauty? The height, whereunto love exalteth, is unspeakable. Love joineth us unto God; love covereth a multitude of sins; love endureth all things, is long-suffering in all things. There is nothing coarse, nothing arrogant in love. Love hath no divisions, love maketh no seditions, love doeth all things in concord. In love were all the elect of God made perfect; without love nothing is well-pleasing to God: in love the Master took us unto Himself; for the love which He had toward us, Jesus Christ our Lord hath given His blood for us by the will of God, and His flesh for our flesh and His life for our lives.

50. Ye see, dearly beloved, how great and marvellous a thing is love, and there is no declaring its perfection. Who is sufficient to be found therein, save those to whom God shall vouchsafe it? Let us therefore entreat and ask of His mercy, that we may be found blameless in love, standing apart from the factiousness of men. All the generations from Adam unto this day have passed away: but they that by God's grace were perfected in love dwell in the abode of the pious; and they shall be made manifest in the visitation of the Kingdom of God. For it is written: *Enter into the closet for a very little while, until Mine anger and My wrath shall pass away, and I will remember a good day and will raise you from your tombs.* Blessed were we, dearly beloved, if we should be doing the commandments of God in concord of love, to the end that our sins may through love be forgiven us. For it is written; *Blessed are they whose iniquities are forgiven, and whose sins are covered. Blessed is the man to whom the Lord shall impute no sin, neither is guile in his mouth.* This declaration of blessedness was pronounced upon them that have been elected by God through Jesus Christ our Lord, to whom be the glory for ever and ever. Amen.

51. For all our transgressions which we have committed

through any of the wiles of the adversary, let us entreat that we may obtain forgiveness. Yea and they also, who set themselves up as leaders of faction and division, ought to look to the common ground of hope. For such as walk in fear and love desire that they themselves should fall into suffering rather than their neighbours; and they pronounce condemnation against themselves rather than against the harmony which hath been handed down to us nobly and righteously. For it is good for a man to make confession of his trespasses rather than to harden his heart, as the heart of those was hardened who made sedition against Moses the servant of God; whose condemnation was clearly manifest, for they went down to hades alive, and *Death shall be their shepherd.* Pharaoh and his host and all the rulers of Egypt, *their chariots and their horsemen,* were overwhelmed in the depths of the Red Sea, and perished for none other reason but because their foolish hearts were hardened after that the signs and the wonders had been wrought in the land of Egypt by the hand of Moses the servant of God.

52. The Master, brethren, hath need of nothing at all. He desireth not anything of any man, save to confess unto Him. For the elect David saith; *I will confess unto the Lord, and it shall please Him more than a young calf that groweth horns and hoofs. Let the poor see it, and rejoice.* And again He saith; *Sacrifice to God a sacrifice of praise, and pay thy vows to the Most High: and call upon Me in the day of thine affliction, and I will deliver thee, and thou shalt glorify Me. For a sacrifice unto God is a broken spirit.*

53. For ye know, and know well, the sacred scriptures, dearly beloved, and ye have searched into the oracles of God. We write these things therefore to put you in remembrance. When Moses went up into the mountain and had spent forty days and forty nights in fasting and humiliation, God said unto him; *Moses, Moses, come down quickly hence, for My people whom thou leddest forth from the land of Egypt have wrought iniquity: they have transgressed quickly out of the way which thou didst command unto them: they have made for themselves molten*

images. And the Lord said unto him; *I have spoken unto thee once and twice, saying, I have seen this people, and behold it is stiff-necked. Let Me destroy them utterly, and I will blot out their name from under heaven, and I will make of thee a nation great and wonderful and numerous more than this.* And Moses said; *Nay, not so, Lord. Forgive this people their sin, or blot me also out of the book of the living.* O mighty love! O unsurpassable perfection! The servant is bold with his Master; he asketh forgiveness for the multitude, or he demandeth that himself also be blotted out with them.

54. Who therefore is noble among you? Who is compassionate? Who is fulfilled with love? Let him say; If by reason of me there be faction and strife and divisions, I retire, I depart, whither ye will, and I do that which is ordered by the people: only let the flock of Christ be at peace with its duly appointed presbyters. He that shall have done this, shall win for himself great renown in Christ, and every place will receive him: for *the earth is the Lord's and the fulness thereof.* Thus have they done and will do, that live as citizens of that kingdom of God which bringeth no regrets.

55. But, to bring forward examples of Gentiles also; many kings and rulers, when some season of pestilence pressed upon them, being taught by oracles have delivered themselves over to death, that they might rescue their fellow citizens through their own blood. Many have retired from their own cities, that they might have no more seditions. We know that many among ourselves have delivered themselves to bondage, that they might ransom others. Many have sold themselves to slavery, and receiving the price paid for themselves have fed others. Many women being strengthened through the grace of God have performed many manly deeds. The blessed Judith, when the city was beleaguered, asked of the elders that she might be suffered to go forth into the camp of the aliens. So she exposed herself to peril and went forth for love of her country and of her people which were beleaguered; and the Lord delivered Holophernes into the hand of a woman. To no less

peril did Esther also, who was perfect in faith, expose herself, that she might deliver the twelve tribes of Israel, when they were on the point to perish. For through her fasting and her humiliation she entreated the all-seeing Master, the God of the ages ; and He, seeing the humility of her soul, delivered the people for whose sake she encountered the peril.

56.   Therefore let us also make intercession for them that are in any transgression, that forbearance and humility may be given them, to the end that they may yield not unto us, but unto the will of God.   For so shall the compassionate remembrance of them with God and the saints be fruitful unto them, and perfect.   Let us accept chastisement, whereat no man ought to be vexed, dearly beloved.   The admonition which we give one to another is good and exceeding useful ; for it joineth us unto the will of God.   For thus saith the holy word; *The Lord hath indeed chastened me, and hath not delivered me over unto death. For whom the Lord loveth He chasteneth, and scourgeth every son whom He receiveth.   For the righteous*, it is said, *shall chasten me in mercy and shall reprove me, but let not the mercy of sinners anoint my head.*   And again He saith; *Blessed is the man whom the Lord hath reproved, and refuse not thou the admonition of the Almighty.   For He causeth pain, and He restoreth again: He hath smitten, and His hands have healed.   Six times shall He rescue thee from afflictions: and at the seventh no evil shall touch thee.   In famine He shall deliver thee from death, and in war He shall release thee from the arm of the sword. And from the scourge of the tongue shall He hide thee, and thou shalt not be afraid when evils approach.   Thou shalt laugh at the unrighteous and wicked, and of the wild beasts thou shalt not be afraid.   For wild beasts shall be at peace with thee.   Then shalt thou know that thy house shall be at peace : and the abode of thy tabernacle shall not go wrong, and thou shalt know that thy seed is many, and thy children as the plenteous herbage of the field.   And thou shalt come to the grave as ripe corn reaped in due season, or as the heap of the threshing floor gathered together at the right time.*   Ye see, dearly beloved, how great

protection there is for them that are chastened by the Master: for being a kind father He chasteneth us to the end that we may obtain mercy through His holy chastisement.

57. Ye therefore that laid the foundation of the sedition, submit yourselves unto the presbyters and receive chastisement unto repentance, bending the knees of your heart. Learn to submit yourselves, laying aside the arrogant and proud stubbornness of your tongue. For it is better for you to be found little in the flock of Christ and to have your name on God's roll, than to be had in exceeding honour and yet be cast out from the hope of Him. For thus saith the All-virtuous Wisdom; *Behold I will pour out for you a saying of My breath, and I will teach you My word. Because I called and ye obeyed not, and I held out words and ye heeded not, but made My counsels of none effect, and were disobedient unto My reproofs; therefore I also will laugh at your destruction, and will rejoice over you when ruin cometh upon you, and when confusion overtaketh you suddenly, and your overthrow is at hand like a whirlwind, or when anguish and beleaguerment come upon you. For it shall be, when ye call upon Me, yet will I not hear you. Evil men shall seek Me and shall not find Me: for they hated wisdom, and chose not the fear of the Lord, neither would they give heed unto My counsels, but mocked at My reproofs. Therefore they shall eat the fruits of their own way, and shall be filled with their own ungodliness. For because they wronged babes, they shall be slain, and inquisition shall destroy the ungodly. But he that heareth Me shall dwell safely trusting in hope, and shall be quiet from fear of all evil.*

58. Let us therefore be obedient unto His most holy and glorious Name, thereby escaping the threatenings which were spoken of old by the mouth of Wisdom against them which disobey, that we may dwell safely, trusting in the most holy Name of His majesty. Receive our counsel, and ye shall have no occasion of regret. For as God liveth, and the Lord Jesus Christ liveth, and the Holy Spirit, who are the faith and the hope of the elect, so surely shall he, who with

lowliness of mind and instant in gentleness hath without regret-
fulness performed the ordinances and commandments that
are given by God, be enrolled and have a name among the
number of them that are saved through Jesus Christ, through
whom is the glory unto Him for ever and ever.   Amen.

59. But if certain persons should be disobedient unto the
words spoken by Him through us, let them understand that
they will entangle themselves in no slight transgression and
danger; but we shall be guiltless of this sin.   And we will
ask, with instancy of prayer and supplication, that the Creator
of the universe may guard intact unto the end the number
that hath been numbered of His elect throughout the whole
world, through His beloved Son Jesus Christ, through whom
He called us from darkness to light, from ignorance to the full
knowledge of the glory of His Name.

Grant unto us, Lord, that we may set our hope on Thy
Name which is the primal source of all creation, and open the
eyes of our hearts, that we may know Thee, who alone *abidest
Highest in the highest, Holy in the holy;* who *layest low the inso-
lence of the proud,* who *scatterest the imaginings of nations;* who
settest the lowly on high, and *bringest the lofty low;* who
makest rich and makest poor; who *killest and makest alive;* who
alone art the Benefactor of spirits and the God of all flesh;
who *lookest into the abysses,* who scannest the works of man; the
Succour of them that are in peril, the *Saviour of them that are
in despair;* the Creator and Overseer of every spirit; who multipliest the nations upon earth, and hast chosen out from all
men those that love Thee through Jesus Christ, Thy beloved
Son, through whom Thou didst instruct us, didst sanctify
us, didst honour us.   We beseech Thee, Lord and Master, to
be our help and succour.   Save those among us who are in
tribulation; have mercy on the lowly; lift up the fallen;
show Thyself unto the needy; heal the ungodly; convert the
wanderers of Thy people; feed the hungry; release our
prisoners; raise up the weak; comfort the faint-hearted.   Let
all the Gentiles know that *Thou art God alone,* and Jesus

Christ is Thy Son, and *we are Thy people and the sheep of Thy pasture.*

60. Thou through Thine operations didst make manifest the everlasting fabric of the world. Thou, Lord, didst create the earth. Thou that art faithful throughout all generations, righteous in Thy judgments, marvellous in strength and excellence, Thou that art wise in creating and prudent in establishing that which Thou hast made, that art good in the things which are seen and faithful with them that trust on Thee, pitiful and compassionate, forgive us our iniquities and our unrighteousnesses and our transgressions and shortcomings. Lay not to our account every sin of Thy servants and Thine handmaids, but cleanse us with the cleansing of Thy truth, and guide our steps to walk in holiness and righteousness and singleness of heart and to do such things as are good and well-pleasing in Thy sight and in the sight of our rulers. Yea, Lord, make Thy face to shine upon us in peace for our good, that we may be sheltered by Thy mighty hand and delivered from every sin by Thine uplifted arm. And deliver us from them that hate us wrongfully. Give concord and peace to us and to all that dwell on the earth, as Thou gavest to our fathers, when they called on Thee in faith and truth with holiness, that we may be saved, while we render obedience to Thine almighty and most excellent Name, and to our rulers and governors upon the earth.

61. Thou, Lord and Master, hast given them the power of sovereignty through Thine excellent and unspeakable might, that we knowing the glory and honour which Thou hast given them may submit ourselves unto them, in nothing resisting Thy will. Grant unto them therefore, O Lord, health, peace, concord, stability, that they may administer the government which Thou hast given them without failure. For Thou, O heavenly Master, King of the ages, givest to the sons of men glory and honour and power over all things that are upon the earth. Do Thou, Lord, direct their counsel according to that which is good and well-pleasing in Thy sight,

that, administering in peace and gentleness with godliness the power which Thou hast given them, they may obtain Thy favour. O Thou, who alone art able to do these things and things far more exceeding good than these for us, we praise Thee through the High-priest and Guardian of our souls, Jesus Christ, through whom be the glory and the majesty unto Thee both now and for all generations and for ever and ever. Amen.

62. As touching those things which befit our religion and are most useful for a virtuous life to such as would guide their steps in holiness and righteousness, we have written fully unto you, brethren. For concerning faith and repentance and genuine love and temperance and sobriety and patience we have handled every argument, putting you in remembrance, that ye ought to please Almighty God in righteousness and truth and long-suffering with holiness, laying aside malice and pursuing concord in love and peace, being instant in gentleness; even as our fathers, of whom we spake before, pleased Him, being lowly-minded towards their Father and God and Creator and towards all men. And we have put you in mind of these things the more gladly, since we knew well that we were writing to men who are faithful and highly accounted and have diligently searched into the oracles of the teaching of God.

63. Therefore it is right for us to give heed to so great and so many examples and to submit the neck and occupying the place of obedience to take our side with them that are the leaders of our souls, that ceasing from this foolish dissension we may attain unto the goal which lieth before us in truthfulness, keeping aloof from every fault. For ye will give us great joy and gladness, if ye render obedience unto the things written by us through the Holy Spirit, and root out the unrighteous anger of your jealousy, according to the entreaty which we have made for peace and concord in this letter. And we have also sent faithful and prudent men that have walked among us from youth unto old age unblameably, who shall also be witnesses between you and us. And this we have done that ye might

know that we have had, and still have, every solicitude that ye should be speedily at peace.

64. Finally may the All-seeing God and Master of spirits and Lord of all flesh, who chose the Lord Jesus Christ, and us through Him for a peculiar people, grant unto every soul that is called after His excellent and holy Name faith, fear, peace, patience, long-suffering, temperance, chastity and soberness, that they may be well-pleasing unto His Name through our High-priest and Guardian Jesus Christ, through whom unto Him be glory and majesty, might and honour, both now and for ever and ever. Amen.

65. Now send ye back speedily unto us our messengers Claudius Ephebus and Valerius Bito, together with Fortunatus also, in peace and with joy, to the end that they may the more quickly report the peace and concord which is prayed for and earnestly desired by us, that we also may the more speedily rejoice over your good order.

The grace of our Lord Jesus Christ be with you and with all men in all places who have been called by God and through Him, through whom is glory and honour, power and greatness and eternal dominion, unto Him, from the ages past and for ever and ever. Amen.

AN ANCIENT HOMILY.

BRETHREN, we ought so to think of Jesus Christ, as of God, as of the Judge of quick and dead. And we ought not to think mean things of our Salvation: for when we think mean things of Him, we expect also to receive mean things. And they that listen as concerning mean things do wrong; and we ourselves do wrong, not knowing whence and by whom and unto what place we were called, and how many things Jesus Christ endured to suffer for our sakes. What recompense then shall we give unto Him? or what fruit worthy of His own gift to us? And how many mercies do we owe to Him! For He bestowed the light upon us; He spake to us, as a father to his sons; He saved us, when we were perishing. What praise then shall we give to Him? or what payment of recompense for those things which we received? we who were maimed in our understanding, and worshipped stocks and stones, gold and silver and bronze, the works of men; and our whole life was nothing else but death. While then we were thus wrapped in darkness, and oppressed with this thick mist in our vision, we recovered our sight, putting off by His will the cloud wherein we were wrapped. For He had mercy on us, and in His compassion saved us, having beheld in us much error and perdition, even when we had no hope of salvation, save that which came from Him. For He called us, when we were not, and from not being He willed us to be.

2. *Rejoice, thou barren that bearest not. Break out and cry, thou that travailest not; for more are the children of the desolate than of her that hath the husband.* In that He said *Rejoice, thou barren that bearest not,* He spake of us: for our Church was barren, before that children were given unto her. And in that He said, *Cry aloud, thou that travailest not,* He meaneth this; Let us not, like women in travail, grow weary of offering up our prayers with simplicity to God. Again, in that He said, *For the children of the desolate are more than of her that hath the husband,* He so spake, because our people seemed desolate and forsaken of God, whereas now, having believed, we have become more than those who seemed to have God. Again another scripture saith, *I came not to call the righteous, but sinners.* He meaneth this; that it is right to save them that are perishing. For this indeed is a great and marvellous work, to establish, not those things which stand, but those which are falling. So also Christ willed to save the things which were perishing. And He saved many, coming and calling us when we were even now perishing.

3. Seeing then that He bestowed so great mercy on us; first of all, that we, who are living, do not sacrifice to these dead gods, neither worship them, but through Him have known the Father of truth. What else is this knowledge to Himward, but not to deny Him through whom we have known Him? Yea, He Himself saith, *Whoso confesseth Me, Him will I confess before the Father.* This then is our reward, if verily we shall confess Him through whom we were saved. But wherein do we confess Him? When we do that which He saith and are not disobedient unto His commandments, and not only *honour Him with our lips,* but *with our whole heart and with our whole mind.* Now He saith also in Isaiah, *This people honoureth Me with their lips, but their heart is far from Me.*

4. Let us therefore not only call Him Lord, for this will not save us: for He saith, *Not every one that saith unto Me, Lord, Lord, shall be saved, but he that doeth righteousness.* So then, brethren, let us confess Him in our works, by loving one another, by not committing adultery nor speaking evil one against another nor envying, but being temperate, merciful, kindly. And we ought to have fellow-feeling one with another and not to be covetous. By these works let us confess Him, and not by the contrary. And we ought not rather to fear men but God. For this cause, if ye do these things, the Lord said, *Though ye be gathered together with Me in My bosom, and do not My commandments, I will cast you away and will say unto you, Depart from Me, I know you not whence ye are, ye workers of iniquity.*

5. Wherefore, brethren, let us forsake our sojourn in this world and do the will of Him that called us, and let us not be afraid to depart out of this world. For the Lord saith, *Ye shall be as lambs in the midst of wolves.* But Peter answered and said unto Him, *What then, if the wolves should tear the lambs?* Jesus said unto Peter, *Let not the lambs fear the wolves after they are dead; and ye also, fear ye not them that kill you and are not able to do anything to you; but fear him that after ye are dead hath power over soul and body, to cast them into the gehenna of fire.* And ye know, brethren, that the sojourn of this flesh in this world is mean and for a short time, but the promise of Christ is great and marvellous, even the rest of the kingdom that shall be and of life eternal. What then can we do to obtain them, but walk in holiness and righteousness, and consider these worldly things as alien to us, and not desire them? For when we desire to obtain these things we fall away from the righteous path.

6. But the Lord saith, *No servant can serve two masters.* If we desire to serve both God and mammon, it is unprofitable for us: *For what advantage is it, if a man gain the whole world and forfeit his soul?* Now this age and the future are two enemies. The one speaketh of adultery and defilement and avarice and deceit, but the other biddeth farewell to these. We cannot

therefore be friends of the two, but must bid farewell to the one and hold companionship with the other. Let us consider that it is better to hate the things which are here, because they are mean and for a short time and perishable, and to love the things which are there, for they are good and imperishable. For, if we do the will of Christ, we shall find rest; but if otherwise, then nothing shall deliver us from eternal punishment, if we should disobey His commandments. And the scripture also saith in Ezekiel, *Though Noah and Job and Daniel should rise up, they shall not deliver their children* in the captivity. But if even such righteous men as these cannot by their righteous deeds deliver their children, with what confidence shall we, if we keep not our baptism pure and undefiled, enter into the kingdom of God? Or who shall be our advocate, unless we be found having holy and righteous works?

7. So then, my brethren, let us contend, knowing that the contest is nigh at hand, and that, while many resort to the corruptible contests, yet not all are crowned, but only they that have toiled hard and contended bravely. Let us then contend that we all may be crowned. Wherefore let us run in the straight course, the incorruptible contest. And let us resort to it in throngs and contend, that we may also be crowned. And if we cannot all be crowned, let us at least come near to the crown. We ought to know that he which contendeth in the corruptible contest, if he be found dealing corruptly with it, is first flogged, and then removed and driven out of the race-course. What think ye? What shall be done to him that hath dealt corruptly with the contest of incorruption? For as concerning them that have not kept the seal, He saith, *Their worm shall not die, and their fire shall not be quenched, and they shall be for a spectacle unto all flesh.*

8. While we are on earth then, let us repent: for we are clay under the craftsman's hand. For in like manner as the potter, if he be making a vessel, and it get twisted or crushed in his hands, reshapeth it again; but if he have once put it into the fiery oven, he shall no longer mend it: so also let us, while we are in

25—2

this world, repent with our whole heart of the evil things which we have done in the flesh, that we may be saved by the Lord, while we have yet time for repentance. For after that we have departed out of the world, we can no more make confession there, or repent any more. Wherefore, brethren, if we shall have done the will of the Father and kept the flesh pure and guarded the commandments of the Lord, we shall receive life eternal. For the Lord saith in the Gospel, *If ye kept not that which is little, who shall give unto you that which is great? For I say unto you that he which is faithful in the least, is faithful also in much.* So then He meaneth this, Keep the flesh pure and the seal unstained, to the end that we may receive life.

9. And let not any one of you say that this flesh is not judged neither riseth again. Understand ye. In what were ye saved? In what did ye recover your sight? if ye were not in this flesh. We ought therefore to guard the flesh as a temple of God: for in like manner as ye were called in the flesh, ye shall come also in the flesh. If Christ the Lord who saved us, being first spirit, then became flesh, and so called us, in like manner also shall we in this flesh receive our reward. Let us therefore love one another, that we all may come unto the kingdom of God. While we have time to be healed, let us place ourselves in the hands of God the physician, giving Him a recompense. What recompense? Repentance from a sincere heart. For He discerneth all things beforehand and knoweth what is in our heart. Let us therefore give unto Him eternal praise, not from our lips only, but also from our heart, that He may receive us as sons. For the Lord also said, *These are My brethren, which do the will of My Father.*

10. Wherefore, my brethren, let us do the will of the Father which called us, that we may live; and let us the rather pursue virtue, but forsake vice as the forerunner of our sins, and let us flee from ungodliness, lest evils overtake us. For if we be diligent in doing good, peace will pursue us. For for this cause is a man unable to attain happiness, seeing

that they call in the fears of men, preferring rather the enjoyment which is here than the promise which is to come. For they know not how great torment the enjoyment which is here bringeth, and what delight the promise which is to come bringeth. And if verily they were doing these things by themselves alone, it had been tolerable: but now they continue teaching evil to innocent souls, not knowing that they shall have their condemnation doubled, both themselves and their hearers.

11. Let us therefore serve God in a pure heart, and we shall be righteous; but if we serve Him not, because we believe not the promise of God, we shall be wretched. For the word of prophecy also saith: *Wretched are the double-minded, that doubt in their heart and say, These things we heard of old in the days of our fathers also, yet we have waited day after day and have seen none of them. Ye fools! compare yourselves unto a tree; take a vine. First it sheddeth its leaves, then a shoot cometh, after this a sour berry, then a full ripe grape. So likewise My people had tumults and afflictions: but afterward they shall receive good things.* Wherefore, my brethren, let us not be double-minded but endure patiently in hope, that we may also obtain our reward. *For faithful is He that promised* to pay to each man the recompense of his works. If therefore we shall have wrought righteousness in the sight of God, we shall enter into His kingdom and shall receive the promises which *ear hath not heard nor eye seen, neither hath it entered into the heart of man.*

12. Let us therefore await the kingdom of God betimes in love and righteousness, since we know not the day of God's appearing. For the Lord Himself, being asked by a certain person when His kingdom would come, said, *When the two shall be one, and the outside as the inside, and the male with the female, neither male nor female.* Now *the two are one,* when we speak truth among ourselves, and in two bodies there shall be one soul without dissimulation. And by *the outside as the inside* He meaneth this: by the inside He meaneth the soul

and by the outside the body. Therefore in like manner as thy body appeareth, so also let thy soul be manifest in its good works. And by *the male with the female, neither male nor female*, He meaneth this; that a brother seeing a sister should have no thought of her as of a female, and that a sister seeing a brother should not have any thought of him as of a male. These things if ye do, saith He, the kingdom of my Father shall come.

13. Therefore, brethren, let us repent forthwith. Let us be sober unto that which is good: for we are full of much folly and wickedness. Let us wipe away from us our former sins, and let us repent with our whole soul and be saved. And let us not be found men-pleasers. Neither let us desire to please one another only, but also those men that are without, by our righteousness, that the Name be not blasphemed by reason of us. For the Lord saith, *Every way My Name is blasphemed among all the Gentiles;* and again, *Woe unto him by reason of whom My Name is blasphemed.* Wherein is it blasphemed? In that ye do not the things which I desire. For the Gentiles, when they hear from our mouth the oracles of God, marvel at them for their beauty and greatness; then, when they discover that our works are not worthy of the words which we speak, forth-with they betake themselves to blasphemy, saying that it is an idle story and a delusion. For when they hear from us that God saith, *It is no thank unto you, if ye love them that love you, but this is thank unto you, if ye love your enemies and them that hate you;* when they hear these things, I say, they marvel at their exceeding goodness; but when they see that we not only do not love them that hate us, but not even them that love us, they laugh us to scorn, and the Name is blasphemed.

14. Wherefore, brethren, if we do the will of God our Father, we shall be of the first Church, which is spiritual, which was created before the sun and moon; but if we do not the will of the Lord, we shall be of the scripture that saith, *My house was made a den of robbers.* So therefore let us choose rather to be of the Church of life, that we may be saved. And I do not suppose ye are ignorant that the living Church is the

body of Christ: for the scripture saith, *God made man, male and female.* The male is Christ and the female is the Church. And the Books and the Apostles plainly declare that the Church existeth not now for the first time, but hath been from the beginning: for she was spiritual, as our Jesus also was spiritual, but was manifested in the last days that He might save us. Now the Church, being spiritual, was manifested in the flesh of Christ, thereby showing us that, if any of us guard her in the flesh and defile her not, he shall receive her again in the Holy Spirit: for this flesh is the counterpart and copy of the spirit. No man therefore, when he hath defiled the copy, . shall receive the original for his portion. This therefore is what He meaneth, brethren ; Guard ye the flesh, that ye may partake of the spirit. But if we say that the flesh is the Church and the spirit is Christ, then he that hath dealt wantonly with the flesh hath dealt wantonly with the Church. Such an one therefore shall not partake of the spirit, which is Christ. So excellent is the life and immortality which this flesh can receive as its portion, if the Holy Spirit be joined to it. No man can declare or tell those things which the Lord hath prepared for His elect.

15. Now I do not think that I have given any mean counsel respecting continence, and whosoever performeth it shall not repent thereof, but shall save both himself and me his counsellor. For it is no mean reward to convert a wandering and perishing soul, that it may be saved. For this is the recompense which we are able to pay to God who created us, if he that speaketh and heareth both speak and hear with faith and love. Let us therefore abide in the things which we believed, in righteousness and holiness, that we may with boldness ask of God who saith, *Whiles thou art still speaking I will say, Behold, I am here.* For this word is the token of a great promise: for the Lord saith of Himself that He is more ready to give than he that asketh to ask. Seeing then that we are partakers of so great kindness, let us not grudge ourselves the obtaining of so many good things. For in proportion as the pleasure is great which

these words bring to them that have performed them, so also is the condemnation great which they bring to them that have been disobedient.

16.   Therefore, brethren, since we have found no small opportunity for repentance, seeing that we have time, let us turn again unto God that called us, while we have still One that receiveth us.   For if we bid farewell to these enjoyments and conquer our soul in refusing to fulfil its evil lusts, we shall be partakers of the mercy of Jesus.   But ye know that the day of judgment cometh even now *as a burning oven*, and *the powers of the heavens shall melt*, and all the earth as lead melting on the fire, and then shall appear the secret and open works of men. Almsgiving therefore is a good thing, even as repentance from sin.   Fasting is better than prayer, but almsgiving than both. And *love covereth a multitude of sins*, but prayer out of a good conscience delivereth from death.   Blessed is every man that is found full of these.   For almsgiving lifteth off the burden of sin.

17.   Let us therefore repent with our whole heart, lest any of us perish by the way.   For if we have received commands, that we should make this also our business, to tear men away from idols and to instruct them, how much more is it wrong that a soul which knoweth God already should perish!   Therefore let us assist one another, that we may also lead the weak upward as touching that which is good, to the end that we all may be saved: and let us convert and admonish one another. And let us not think to give heed and believe now only, while we are admonished by the presbyters; but likewise when we have departed home, let us remember the commandments of the Lord, and not suffer ourselves to be dragged off the other way by our worldly lusts; but coming hither more frequently, let us strive to go forward in the commands of the Lord, that we all having the same mind may be gathered together unto life.   For the Lord said, *I come to gather together all the nations, tribes, and languages*.   Herein He speaketh of the day of His appearing, when He shall come and redeem us, each man according to his works.   *And* the unbelievers *shall see His glory* and His might:

and they shall be amazed when they see the kingdom of the world given to Jesus, saying, Woe unto us, for Thou wast, and we knew it not, and believed not; and we obeyed not the presbyters when they told us of our salvation. And *Their worm shall not die, and their fire shall not be quenched, and they shall be for a spectacle unto all flesh.* He speaketh of that day of judgment, when men shall see those among us that lived ungodly lives and dealt falsely with the commandments of Jesus Christ. But the righteous, having done good and endured torments and hated the pleasures of the soul, when they shall behold them that have done amiss and denied Jesus by their words or by their deeds, how that they are punished with grievous torments in unquenchable fire, shall give glory to God, saying, There will be hope for him that hath served God with his whole heart.

18.   Therefore let us also be found among those that give thanks, among those that have served God, and not among the ungodly that are judged. For I myself too, being an utter sinner and not yet escaped from temptation, but being still amidst the engines of the devil, do my diligence to follow after righteousness, that I may prevail so far at least as to come near unto it, while I fear the judgment to come.

19.   Therefore, brothers and sisters, after the God of truth hath been heard, I read to you an exhortation to the end that ye may give heed to the things which are written, so that ye may save both yourselves and him that readeth in the midst of you. For I ask of you as a reward that ye repent with your whole heart, and give salvation and life to yourselves. For doing this we shall set a goal for all the young who desire to toil in the study of piety and of the goodness of God. And let us not be displeased and vexed, fools that we are, whensoever any one admonisheth us and turneth us aside from unrighteousness unto righteousness. For sometimes while we do evil things, we perceive it not by reason of the double-mindedness and unbelief which is in our breasts, and *we are darkened in our understanding* by our vain lusts. Let us therefore practise righteousness that we may be saved unto the end. Blessed are they that obey these ordi-

nances. Though they may endure affliction for a short time in the world, they will gather the immortal fruit of the resurrection. Therefore let not the godly be grieved, if he be miserable in the times that now are: a blessed time awaiteth him. He shall live again in heaven with the fathers, and shall have rejoicing throughout a sorrowless eternity.

20. Neither suffer ye this again to trouble your mind, that we see the unrighteous possessing wealth, and the servants of God straitened. Let us then have faith, brothers and sisters. We are contending in the lists of a living God; and we are trained by the present life, that we may be crowned with the future. No righteous man hath reaped fruit quickly, but waiteth for it. For if God had paid the recompense of the righteous speedily, then straightway we should have been training ourselves in merchandise, and not in godliness; for we should seem to be righteous, though we were pursuing not that which is godly, but that which is gainful. And for this cause Divine judgment overtaketh a spirit that is not just, and loadeth it with chains.

To the only God invisible, the Father of truth, who sent forth unto us the Saviour and Prince of immortality, through whom also He made manifest unto us the truth and the heavenly life, to Him be the glory for ever and ever. Amen.

ADDENDA.

ADDENDA.

THE following editions succeeded in the interval between the appearance of my own in 1869 and the publication of the discovery of Bryennios at the end of 1875.

1. *Clementis Romani ad Corinthios Epistula. Insunt et altera quam ferunt Clementis Epistula et Fragmenta.* Ed. J. C. M. LAURENT, 8vo. Lipsiæ 1870.

The editor had already distinguished himself in this field by one or two admirable conjectures, § 38 ἴστω, § 45 ἔγγραφοι. This edition is furnished with prolegomena and notes, but the text is perhaps the most important part. The editor has made use of Tischendorf's earlier text and of the photograph (see above, p. 24); but he was not acquainted with my edition which had then but recently appeared.

2. *Clementis Romani Epistulæ. Ad ipsius Codicis Alexandrini fidem ac modum repetitis curis, edidit* CONST. DE TISCHENDORF, 4to. Lipsiæ 1873.

In his Prolegomena and Commentarius the editor discusses the points of difference between himself and me with regard to the reading of the Alexandrian MS. At his request our common friend Dr W. Wright, the distinguished Oriental Scholar, consulted the MS in the more important and doubtful passages; and in some points decided in favour of Tischendorf, while in others he confirmed my reading (see p. viii sq.). Over and above these passages there still remained a few differences. In some of these cases I was undoubtedly wrong; in others the newly discovered MS has proved me to be unquestionably right. These points will be mentioned in the following Addenda. I congratulate myself in having criticisms on my work from a writer so eminently competent in this department as Tischendorf; and probably the Alexandrian MS has now by successive labours been almost as fully and correctly deciphered, as it ever will be. It is a happy incident that this result was mainly achieved before the discovery of the second Greek MS and the Syriac Version, which have furnished new data for the construction of the text. While preparing for this present volume, I have again consulted the Alexandrian MS, where doubtful points still remained, and the result of this inspection will be given in the following pages.

3. *Barnabæ Epistula Græce et Latine, Clementis Romani Epistulæ. Recensuerunt atque illustraverunt, etc.* OSCAR DE GEBHARDT *Estonus*, ADOLFUS HARNACK *Livonus.* Lipsiæ 1875. This forms the first fasciculus of the new *Patrum Apostolicorum Opera*, which is called *Editio post Dresselianam alteram tertia*, but is in fact a new work from beginning to end.

The joint editors of this valuable edition have divided their work so that the text and apparatus criticus with those portions of the prolegomena which refer to this department are assigned to Gebhardt, while Harnack takes the exegetical notes and the parts of the prolegomena which refer to date, authorship, reception, etc. The text is constructed with sobriety and judgment; and in other respects the work is a useful and important contribution to early patristic literature.

Besides these editions, the following reviews (among others which appeared) of my own volume may be mentioned.

Göttingen Gelehrte Anzeigen, March 23, 1870. H. E. [EWALD].

Academy, July 9, 1870, R. A. LIPSIUS.

Zeitschrift für Wissenschaftliche Theologie, 1870, p. 394 sq. (containing a review of Laurent's edition also). A. HILGENFELD.

A full catalogue of the literature of the subject which appeared during this interval is given by Harnack in his second edition.

The discovery of BRYENNIOS, and his edition founded upon it, have been already described (p. 224 sq). This was the beginning of a new epoch in the criticism of the Epistles of the Clement.

It will be remembered that the learned editor had not seen any of the editions published in Western Europe, later than Hilgenfeld's (1866). He was therefore unacquainted with the most recent and accurate collations of the Alexandrian MS, and not unfrequently misstates its readings accordingly; but he seems to have given the readings of the new MS with accuracy. His edition is furnished with elaborate and learned prolegomena and with a continuous commentary. In the newly recovered portion of the genuine epistle more especially he has collected the Biblical references, which are very numerous here, with great care; and in this respect his diligence has left only gleanings for subsequent editors. Altogether the execution of this work is highly creditable to the editor, allowance being made for the difficulties which attend an editio princeps.

This work has been followed by two other editions, the one by HILGENFELD, the other by GEBHARDT AND HARNACK, which appeared almost simultaneously in the autumn of last year (1876). These editors have largely altered their respective first editions, making such changes as the new discovery suggested. They may thus be regarded as (to no inconsiderable extent) new works.

Besides these editions, the discovery and publication of Bryennios has occasioned a flood of periodical literature. Among the reviews and articles which have appeared since the edition of Bryennios, the following may be mentioned.

Theologische Literaturzeitung, February 19, 1876. A. HARNACK (A review of Bryennios).

Jahrbücher f. Deutsche Theologie, i. p. 161 sq., 1876. WAGENMANN (A review of Bryennios).

Academy, May 6 and 13, 1876. C. W. RUSSELL (*The New MS of Clement of Rome*).

Church Quarterly Review, April 1876 (p. 255 sq.), October 1876 (p. 239 sq.). ANONYMOUS (Notices of the edition of Bryennios).

Academy, July 29, 1876. J. B. LIGHTFOOT (A review of Gebhardt and Harnack, ed. 1).

Zeitschrift f. Kirchengeschichte, 1876, p. 264 sq., p. 329 sq. A. HARNACK (*Ueber den sogenannten Zweiten Brief des Clemens an die Korinther*, two papers).

Zeitschrift f. Kirchengeschichte, 1876, p. 305 sq. O VON GEBHARDT (*Zur Textkritik der Neuen Clemensstücke*).

Studien u. Kritiken, 1876, iv. p. 707 sq., JACOBI (*Die beiden Briefe des Clemens v. Rom*).

Theologische Literaturzeitung, June 24, 1876. F. OVERBECK (A review of Gebhardt and Harnack, ed. 1).

Göttingen Gelehrte Anzeigen, November 8, 1876, p. 1409 sq. TH. ZAHN (A review of Gebhardt and Harnack, ed. 2).

Theologische Quartalschrift, 1876, p. 252 sq. BRÜLL (*Ursprung u. Verfasser des Briefes Clemens von Rom an die Korinther*).

Theologische Quartalschrift, 1876, p. 286 sq. FUNK (*Ein Patristicher Fund*).

Zeitschrift f. Protestantismus u. Kirche, 1876, p. 194 sq. TH. ZAHN (*Das älteste Kirchengebet u. die älteste Christliche Predigt*).

Theologische Quartalschrift, 1876, p. 434 sq. BRÜLL (*Ursprung des Episkopats nach dem Briefe des Clemens*, etc.).

Theologische Quartalschrift, 1876, p. 717 sq. FUNK (A review of recent editions).

Zeitschrift f. Wissenschaftliche Theologie, 1877, p. 138 sq. A. HILGENFELD (A notice of recent editions).

Theological Review, January 1877, p. 35 sq. J. DONALDSON (*The new MS of Clement of Rome*).

Jenaer Literaturzeitung, January 13, 1877. R. A. LIPSIUS (A review of recent editions).

The First Epistle.

p. 9 l. 9. The parallels in Polycarp's epistle are carefully collected by Harnack, Prol. p. xxiv sq. (ed. 2).

p. 11 l. 1. On the objection which Harnack has made to this statement that the epistle is quoted by Leontius and John see below, Addenda on p. 109 note.

p. 11 l. 15. The question of the ecclesiastical use and canonical authority of this epistle is discussed again in the light of the newly discovered Syriac Version, p. 272 sq.

p. 12 l. 36. On this catalogue in the Apostolical Canons see again p. 274 sq.

p. 17 l. 23.. The wrong Timotheus of Alexandria is named here and elsewhere (pp. 21, 175, 185). The person who wrote against the Council of Chalcedon and whose work contains these extracts was Timotheus Ælurus, who became bishop of Alexandria A.D. 457 (Cave *Script. Eccl.* I. p. 444 sq.); see Wright's *Catalogue of Syriac Manuscripts in the British Museum* no. DCCXXIX. pp. 639 sq., 644. The Syriac MS itself which contains these extracts (*Add.* 12, 156) was written before A.D. 562.

p. 19 note 1. For all that relates to this forgery see *Decretales Pseudo-Isidorianæ*, ed. Hinschius, Lips. 1863. The Clementine Epistles will be found on p. 30 sq. For the treatment of the First and Second Epistles in this forged collection see Præf. p. lxxxi.

p. 19 l. 32. In his review of my edition (*Academy*, July 9, 1870) R. A. Lipsius writes on this passage:

'The conjecture...that the *Liber Pontificalis*, which mentions (in the *Vita Clementis*) two epistles written by Clement, meant the two epistles to James, and not those to the Corinthians, will scarcely bear examination. The earliest text, written 530 A.D., reads only 'et fecit duas epistolas'; the words 'quæ catholicæ nominantur', like the mention of the (earlier) 'Epistola ad Iacobum', do not occur earlier than the recension of 687. The statement, 'hic scripsit duas epistolas Iacobo Hierosolymorum episcopo quæ catholicæ nominantur', is not found in any document older than *Vitæ Romanorum Pontificum* ascribed to Liutprand. The statement in the original edition of the *Liber Pontificalis* was probably borrowed from a more ancient source, which I have succeeded in discovering in the *Catalogus Leoninus* of the year 440. At that time it would seem that the second epistle to James was not yet extant. The only question for us is therefore whether those two epistles of Clement spoken of are the two to the Corinthians, or the first to the Corinthians and the earlier epistle to James.'

The reference in this criticism of Lipsius is to his valuable book, *Chronologie der römischen Bischöfe*, Kiel 1869.

He has repeated this objection again recently (*Jenaer Literaturz.* Jan. 13, 1877, p. 19).

In answer to it, I prefer quoting a review of Lipsius written without any reference to the question at issue between us by one who has paid much more attention to these catalogues of Roman bishops than I can pretend to have done. Dr Hort writes in the *Academy* (Sept. 15, 1871):

'By a brilliant combination Lipsius succeeds in reaching an earlier date [than the Felician list A.D. 530]. He supposes a lost catalogue written under Leo, say about 440...So far well. When Lipsius goes on to maintain that his Leonine catalogue contained biographies... he passes into conjecture beyond the reach of verification,' with more to the same effect.

Thus, though Lipsius has shown reasons for postulating a Leonine list giving names and dates, he has no ground for assuming that it would contain such notices as 'et fecit duas epistolas'. Even if such a notice had existed in the Leonine Catalogue, it would still be just possible that the two Epistles to James might be meant. But we should hardly expect the second of these epistles to have been written, or at least generally received, at so early a date (see p. 19); and in this case the notice would probably be a parrot-like repetition of the statement in Jerome (*Vir. Ill.* 15) by a Latin writer who himself had no acquaintance with the epistles in question. When however we

descend as low as the date of the Felician list A.D. 530, all probability leads to the belief that the compiler of this list, even if he copied
an earlier statement (of which there is no evidence), would himself
understand by 'duas epistolas' the two Epistles to James; and this
identification becomes more precise with the addition 'quæ canonicæ
(or catholicæ) nominantur', whichever reading be adopted.

p. 22 l. 1. The newly recovered ending of the Second Epistle does
not contain the passage; and, as there is no reason for supposing with
Hilgenfeld (p. 77, ed. 2) that a great lacuna still exists in this epistle,
the account of this quotation which I have suggested must be abandoned: see these Addenda below on pp. 210, 211.

In the following account of the readings in our new documents
it may be assumed that the conjectural modes of filling up the lacunæ
in the Alexandrian MS (A), and the readings generally which are
adopted in my text, have been confirmed by the Constantinopolitan
MS (C) and by the Syriac Version (S), unless it is otherwise stated.

I have not thought it necessary to mention variations of punctuation or of accent in C, except in cases where they have some real
interest or importance. Nor again have I recorded the omission of
the so-called ν ἐφελκυστικόν before consonants (see above, p. 226).
Its omission seems to be habitual in C, as its insertion is habitual
in A.

The extent to which it has appeared advisable to record the
renderings of S has been indicated above, p. 240. No variation is
omitted (except by inadvertence), where any reasonable probability
existed that the translation might represent a different reading in the
original.

προc κορινθιογc α] For the titles of the epistle in CS see pp. 225,
233.

p. 31 l. 1 παροικοῦσα] A good illustration of this sense of παροικεῖν
is Orig. c. Cels. iii. 29 αἱ δὲ τοῦ Χριστοῦ ἐκκλησίαι, συνεξεταζόμεναι ταῖς
ὧν παροικοῦσι δήμων ἐκκλησίαις, ὡς φωστῆρές εἰσιν ἐν κόσμῳ, ib. 30
ἐκκλησίας τοῦ Θεοῦ παροικούσας ἐκκλησίαις τῶν καθ' ἑκάστην πόλιν
δήμων.

p. 32 l. 2 παντοκράτοροc] τοῦ παντοκράτορος C. Clement's form of
salutation is copied in Apost. Const. i. 1.

I.

p. 32 l. 4 ἐπαλλήλους] Comp. Philo in Flacc. 14 (II. p. 534 M) τὰς

συνεχεῖς καὶ ἐπαλλήλους κακώσεις.   *ib.* γενομένας] C; but S has a
present tense and seems to have read γινομένας. On the historical
bearing of this fact see above, p. 267.

p. 33 l. 5 ἡμῖν] S; καθ' ἡμῶν C.   *ib.* περιπτώσεις] περιστάσεις C.
S evidently had περιπτώσεις, but translates, as frequently (see above,
p. 238 sq.), by two words *lapsus et damna*.   *ib.* ἀδελφοί] ἀγαπητοί S;
om. C.

p. 33 l. 6 πεποιηκέναι] πεποιῆσθαι C, as the common Greek idiom
requires. This ought not to have been overlooked by all the editors,
myself included.

p. 33 l. 7 παρ' ὑμῖν πραγμάτων] πραγμάτων παρ' ὑμῖν C. S is
uncertain. The reader must be cautioned against the rendering adopted
in some English translations; 'those things which you enquired of us'
(Wake); 'the points respecting which you consulted us' (Antenicene
Fathers). This rendering involves a historical mis-statement. The
expression contains no allusion to any letter or other application from
the Corinthians to the Romans. Clement does not write παρ' ὑμῶν,
but παρ' ὑμῖν: and τὰ ἐπιζητούμενα means simply 'the matters of dispute'.   *ib.* ἀγαπητοί] C; om. S. See the note on ἀδελφοί just above,
l. 5.   *ib.* τῆς τε ἀλλοτρίας κ.τ.λ.] The passage which follows is para-
phrastically and badly rendered in S, but the rendering does not
seem to imply any different reading.

p. 34 l. 4 βλασφημηθῆναι] βλασφημεῖσθαι C.

p. 34 l. 8 οὐκ] C; om. S.

p. 35 l. 1 ἀπροσωπολήμπτως] ἀπροσωπολήπτως C.

p. 35 l. 11 νομίμοις] νόμοις C with A; *in lege* (אסומנב) S. But this
last shows nothing as regards the reading: for (1) the preposition would
be required in any case; (2) the singular is explained by the accidental
omission of *ribui;* and (3) νόμιμον is commonly translated by נמוסא
(νόμος) in this version (comp. §§ 3, 40). The word νόμος, it should be
added, does not occur elsewhere in Clement.

p. 35 l. 12 ὑμῶν] S; om. C.

p. 35 l. 13 παρ' ὑμῖν] S; παρ' ἡμῖν C. It may be questioned whether
πρεσβυτέροις here indicates age or office. The former view is taken
by Laurent, the latter by Harnack. The former sense is suggested by
c. 3 οἱ νέοι ἐπὶ τοὺς πρεσβυτέρους. The 'presbyters', properly so called,
would be intended by οἱ ἡγούμενοι. But these were not the only
'elders' or 'seniors' to whom reverence was due; and Clement
may have desired in the words καὶ τοῖς παρ' ὑμῖν πρεσβυτέροις to extend
the statement to all, thus preparing the way for the mention of 'the
young' as a class. The ideas of age and office are sometimes so

closely connected in this word, that it is difficult to separate the two. Compare 1 Pet. v. 1 sq., Polyc. *Phil.* 5, 6, in both which passages the use of πρεσβύτεροι, in connexion with νεώτεροι, presents the same difficulty as here.

p. 35 l. 14 ἀμώμῳ καὶ σεμνῇ καὶ ἀγνῇ] C; ἀγνῇ καὶ ἀμώμῳ S (certainly omitting καὶ σεμνῇ, but the transposition of ἀγνῇ and ἀμώμῳ may be due merely to the convenience of translation: see above, p. 239).

p. 35 l. 18 οἰκουρεῖν] Here C reads οἰκουργεῖν; and so too apparently S. There can be no doubt that the correct Greek forms were οἰκουρός, οἰκουρεῖν (comp. *e.g.* Philo *de Spec. Leg.* 31, II p. 327, θηλείαις δὲ οἰκουρία καὶ ἔνδον μονή); but the coincidence of the best authorities here, and Tit. ii. 5, in favour of οἰκουργός, οἰκουργεῖν, suggests that these latter forms may have taken their place in the common language (at least in some countries), and have acquired something of their meaning.

II.

p. 36 l. 2 ὑποτασσόμενοι κ.τ.λ.] *Apost. Const.* ii. 6 βλαπτόμενος μᾶλλον ἢ βλάπτων.

p. 36 l. 3 τοῦ Θεοῦ] τοῦ Χριστοῦ CS. On this important variation see above, pp. 227, 272.

The reading τοῦ Χριστοῦ is accepted by Bryennios and Hilgenfeld (ed. 2) on the authority of C. On the other hand Harnack retains τοῦ Θεοῦ with A; while Donaldson hesitates between the two readings, but would still read μαθήματα for παθήματα. This last had also been advocated, though with some hesitation, by Dr Ezra Abbot in a learned paper on Acts xx. 28 (*Bibliotheca Sacra*, April 1876, p. 313 sq.), before the reading of C was known to him. Notwithstanding the reasons to my mind are still as strong as ever against it, and the authority of A for παθήματα is now reinforced by CS. On the other hand the alternative of τοῦ Χριστοῦ for τοῦ Θεοῦ deserves serious consideration.

As regards external evidence, I think that the balance is fairly even. If the view maintained above (p. 227 sq., 241, 245) of the relative value of our authorities be correct, A is entitled to as much weight as CS together. Moreover the obvious doctrinal motive which in C has led to the deliberate substitution of λόγος for πνεῦμα in another place (ii. § 9) must deprive it of much weight in the present case. On the other hand it seems probable that Photius (*Bibl.* 126 quoted above, p. 37), when he wrote that Clement speaking of our

Lord does not use τὰς θεοπρεπεῖς καὶ ὑψηλοτέρας φωνάς of Him, had
τοῦ Χριστοῦ in his text. But this would not go far, even if the inference were more certain, for Photius is a late writer. If therefore a
decision on the reading here is possible, it must be founded upon
internal evidence.

And here the considerations which present themselves are numerous.

(1) As a question of accidental error in transcription, the probability is evenly balanced; for χ͞γ instead of θ͞γ, and θ͞γ instead of χ͞γ,
are equally common with scribes.

(2) On the other hand, if we have here a deliberate alteration,
the chances that χ͞γ would be substituted for θ͞γ are, I think, greater
than the chances of the converse change. Such language as αἷμα Θεοῦ,
παθήματα Θεοῦ, and the like, though common in the second and third
centuries, became highly distasteful in later ages; and this from various
motives. The great Athanasius himself protests against such phrases,
c. Apollin. ii. 13, 14 (I. p. 758) πῶς οὖν γεγράφατε ὅτι Θεὸς ὁ διὰ σαρκὸς
παθὼν καὶ ἀναστάς;... οὐδαμοῦ δὲ αἷμα Θεοῦ δίχα σαρκὸς παραδεδώκασιν
αἱ γραφαὶ ἢ Θεὸν διὰ σαρκὸς παθόντα καὶ ἀναστάντα. And how liable
to correction such expressions would be, we may infer from the long
recension of the Ignatian Epistles, where the original language of the
writer is deliberately altered by the interpolator, who appears to have
lived in the latter half of the fourth century (Ephes. 1 ἐν αἵματι Θεοῦ,
where Χριστοῦ is substituted for Θεοῦ; Rom. 6 τοῦ πάθους τοῦ Θεοῦ μου,
where this interpolator softens down the language by inserting Χριστοῦ
before τοῦ Θεοῦ μου, while others substitute τοῦ Κυρίου μου or τοῦ Χριστοῦ).
At this time the heresy to which such expressions seemed to give
countenance was Apollinarianism. At a later date, when the Monophysite controversy arose, there would be a still greater temptation
on the part of an orthodox scribe to substitute τοῦ Χριστοῦ for τοῦ
Θεοῦ. The language of Anastasius of Sinai (Hodeg. 12, 13, p. 97 sq.)
shows that these passages of earlier writers (he mentions among others
Ign. Rom. 6) were constantly alleged in favour of Monophysite
doctrine, and he himself has some trouble in explaining them away.
Writing against these same heretics Isidore of Pelusium (Ep. i. 124)
says Θεοῦ πάθος οὐ λέγεται, Χριστοῦ γὰρ τὸ πάθος γέγονε κ.τ.λ. On
the other hand, it might be said that the Monophysites themselves
would be under a temptation to alter χ͞γ into θ͞γ; and accordingly
Bryennios supposes that in this passage the reading of A is due to the
Monophysites (or, as he adds, perhaps to the Alexandrian divines).

This does not seem very likely. (*a*) In the first place, it would be a roundabout and precarious way of getting a testimony in favour of their doctrine. If τοῦ Χριστοῦ (thus assumed to be the original reading) had been in direct connexion with τὰ παθήματα, a change in this direction would not be improbable : but it would never have occurred to any one to alter τοῖς ἐφοδίοις τοῦ Χριστοῦ into τοῖς ἐφοδίοις τοῦ Θεοῦ, because there happened to be an expression τὰ παθήματα αὐτοῦ in the next sentence so that αὐτοῦ would naturally be referred to the genitive after τοῖς ἐφοδίοις. It would have been much simpler to change αὐτοῦ into τοῦ Θεοῦ at once. (*b*) Secondly, the dates are not favourable to this supposition. The MS which has Θεοῦ is assigned by the most competent authorities to the fifth century, and by some of them to the earlier half of the century ('not later than A.D. 450', Scrivener *Introduction* p. 93 (ed. 2) ; 'the middle of the fifth century or a little later', Tregelles *Horne's Introduction* p. 155; 'saeculi v ejusque fere exeuntis', Tischendorf, p. ix, ed. 8); and, though not impossible, it is not probable that the Monophysite controversy would have influenced the transcription of the MS at this date. On the other hand our earliest authority for τοῦ Χριστοῦ, Photius (supposing that his evidence be accepted), wrote four centuries later, when there had been ample time for such manipulation of the text. But, besides the *doctrinal* motive which might have suggested the change from Θεοῦ to Χριστοῦ, there may also have been an *exegetical* reason. The word ἐφόδιον, *viaticum*, was used especially of the eucharistic elements (e.g. *Lit. D. Marc.* p. 29, *Lit. D. Iacob.* p. 75, Neale), and there would be a natural desire to fix this sense on S. Clement here.

(3) The probability that such language as τὰ παθήματα τοῦ Θεοῦ should have been used by an early Christian writer can hardly be questioned. In addition to the passages quoted in my note (p. 37) see *Test. Duod. Patr.* Levi 4 ἐπὶ τῷ πάθει τοῦ ὑψίστου (a very ancient writing; see *Galatians* p. 307 sq.), Tatian *ad Græc.* 13 τοῦ πεπονθότος Θεοῦ, Tertull. *de Carn. Chr.* 5 'passiones Dei', *ad Uxor.* ii. 3 'sanguine Dei' (and so elsewhere Tertullian speaks of 'God crucified', 'God dead', 'the flesh of God', 'the murderers of God'); see *de Carn. Chr.* 5 *adv. Marc.* ii. 16, 27, v. 5), *Anc. Syr. Doc.* p. 8 (ed. Cureton) 'God was crucified for all men', etc. And similar passages from writers of these and the succeeding generations might be multiplied. See Abbot l. c. p. 340 sq., Otto *Corp. Apol. Christ.* ix. p. 445.

(4) It is more to the purpose to urge that, though such language

is not uncommon in other writers, it has no parallel in Clement;
that he elsewhere speaks of the blood 'of Christ' (§§ 7, 21, 49) and
describes it as 'precious to God His Father' (§ 7); and that throughout
this epistle he applies the term Θεός to the Father as distinguished
from Christ. This argument has considerable weight: but must not
be overstrained. The Catholic doctrine of the Person of Christ
admits both ways of speaking. Writers like Tertullian, who use the
most extravagant and unguarded language on the other side, are
commonly and even in the same context found speaking of Christ
as distinct from God; and the exact proportions which the one
mode of speaking will bear to the other in any individual writer must
be a matter of evidence. It is clear from the newly discovered ending
(§ 58 ζῇ γὰρ ὁ Θεὸς κ.τ.λ.) that he could have had no sympathy with
Ebionite views of the Person of Christ. Moreover, in the passage
especially quoted (§ 7) one authority, which probably preserves the
right reading, omits Θεῷ (see below, p. 411). And after all the
alternative remains, which Dr Abbot is disposed to favour (p. 343),
that Clement wrote αὐτοῦ negligently, not remembering that τοῦ
Θεοῦ had immediately preceded and referring it in his own mind to
Christ.

(5) It remains to enquire whether the connexion is more favourable to τοῦ Θεοῦ or τοῦ Χριστοῦ. This will depend much on the connexion of the sentences. The punctuation given in my text is adopted
also by Gebhardt and Harnack and acquiesced in by Dr Abbot.
The reasons which influenced me are stated in my note, and seem
to me as strong as ever. If this punctuation be retained, τοῦ Θεοῦ
is almost necessary; for τὰ ἐφόδια then refers to the ordinary means
of subsistence. Hilgenfeld reads and punctuates τοῖς ἐφοδίοις τοῦ
Χριστοῦ ἀρκούμενοι καὶ προσέχοντες (so too S), understanding by the term
'spiritual sustenance'. This seems to me to give an awkward sense
(for the mention of 'contentment' is then somewhat out of place) and
an unnatural punctuation (for καὶ προσέχοντες then becomes a clumsy
addition).

p. 37 l. 5 ἐνεστερνισμένοι] So it is read in C. S attaches καὶ
προσέχοντες to the preceding sentence, and then translates as if it
had read τούς τε λόγους...ἐνεστερνισμένοι (om. ἦτε).

p. 37 l. 6] Comp. 4 Macc. iii. 20 ἐπειδὴ γὰρ βαθεῖαν εἰρήνην διὰ τὴν
εὐνομίαν ἡμῶν εἶχον, Heges. in Euseb. H. E. iii. 32 γενομένης εἰρήνης
βαθείας ἐν πάσῃ ἐκκλησίᾳ, Liturg. S. Basil. p. 165 (Neale) βαθεῖαν καὶ
ἀναφαίρετον εἰρήνην.

p. 38 l. 3 πλήρης ἔκχυσις...ἐγίνετο] C; plenæ effusiones...erant S, as if πλήρεις ἐκχύσεις...ἐγίνοντο, for the plural cannot be accounted for here by *ribui*.

ib. ὁσίας] S; θείας C: see above, p. 231. And for instances of the same confusion § 14 (p. 414), § 21 (p. 420). For ὁσίας see § 45 ἐν ὁσίᾳ καὶ ἀμώμῳ προθέσει, § 56 διὰ τῆς ὁσίας παιδείας αὐτοῦ; for θείας, § 40 τὰ βάθη τῆς θείας γνώσεως. There might possibly be a question which of the two words should be read here : but (1) We have a combination of two authorities (including the best) against one ; and (2) The other instances show that the tendency is to change ὅσιος into θεῖος, and not conversely.

p. 38 l. 4 ἐξετείνατε] ἐξετείνετε CS.

p. 38 l. 6 ἵλεως] ἵλεων C. *ib.* ἄκοντες] C ; ἀκόντες S. *ib.* ἡμάρτετε] C ; *peccabatis* (ἡμαρτάνετε) S.

p. 39 l. 8 μετ' ἐλέους καὶ συνειδήσεως] So too S, translating συνειδήσεως *bona conscientia.* The difficulty of referring συνειδήσεως to God has led to several emendations, of which some are mentioned in my note. Others have been added since my edition appeared; συνείξεως by Laurent (ad loc.), συνδεήσεως by Lipsius (*Academy*, July 9, 1870). Harnack (ed. 1) suggested overcoming the difficulty by a different exegesis, 'vobis miserantibus piamque recolentibus fratrum memoriam'. The Constantinople MS however comes to the rescue with a reading which could not have been foreseen, but which commends itself, μετὰ δέους καὶ συνειδήσεως (ΜΕΤΑΔΕΟΥϹ for ΜΕΤΕΛΕΟΥϹ). Thus the whole clause is transferred from God to the believer, and συνειδήσεως becomes intelligible. With the whole expression comp. *Liturg. D. Jacob.* p. 55 (Neale) δὸς ἡμῖν, Κύριε, μετὰ παντὸς φόβου καὶ συνειδήσεως καθαρᾶς προσκομίσαι κ.τ.λ. For the idea of fear as an agent in the work of salvation see Phil. ii. 12; and for the expression μετὰ δέους Heb. xii. 28 λατρεύωμεν εὐαρέστως τῷ Θεῷ μετὰ εὐλαβείας καὶ δέους (the correct reading), an epistle which has largely influenced Clement's language elsewhere. For the use of συνείδησις here comp. § 34 συναχθέντες τῇ συνειδήσει. It denotes inward concentration and assent. Zahn (*Gött. Gel. Anz.* Nov. 8, 1876) still retains the reading μετ' ἐλέους, explaining it of brotherly kindness shown towards offenders, and proposes συναθλήσεως for συνειδήσεως. He might have quoted *Apost. Const.* ii. 13 ἔπειτα μετὰ ἐλέους καὶ οἰκτιρμοῦ καὶ προσλήψεως οἰκείου ὑπισχνούμενος αὐτῷ σωτηρίαν for this sense. Lipsius (*Jenaer Literaturz.* Jan. 13, 1877) accepts μετὰ δέους, but holds by his conjecture συνδεήσεως, though it is now rendered unnecessary. Donaldson (*Theol. Rev.* Jan. 1877) suggests μετὰ τελείας συνελεύσεως.

p. 39 l. 11 βδελυκτὸν] add. ἦν C ; and so probably S.

p. 39 l. 12 τοῖς πλησίον] τῶν πλησίον C; vicinorum S.

p. 39 l. 13 ἴδια] C ; ἰδίᾳ S.

p. 40 l. 1 σεβασμίῳ] and so apparently S ; σεβασμιωτάτῃ C. See above, p. 228.

III.

p. 40 l. 7 καὶ ἔρις] ἔρις (om. καί) CS.

p. 40 l. 8 ἀκαταστασία] Comp. *Apost. Const.* ii. 43 ἀκαταστασίας καὶ ἔριδος καὶ διχοστασίας.

p. 41 l. 11 ἄπεστιν] S; ἀπέστη C. This brings it nearer to the LXX of Is. lix. 14 which has ἀφέστηκεν : see above, p. 227.

p. 41 l. 12 ἀπολείπειν] ἀπολιπεῖν C, and so probably S.

p. 41 l. 16 ἀλλὰ] ἀλλ' C.

ib. τὰς ἐπιθυμίας αὐτοῦ τὰς πονηράς] τὰς πονηρὰς being substituted for τησ πονηρασ of A. The reading of CS is τὰς ἐπιθυμίας τῆς καρδίας αὐτοῦ τῆς πονηρᾶς, thus showing that τῆς καρδίας has accidentally dropped out of A and that all the editors have been on the wrong tack in substituting τας for της.

p. 42 l. 2 καὶ] C ; om. S.

IV.

p. 42 l. 3 οὕτως] S ; om. C.

p. 42 l. 4 τῷ Θεῷ] S ; τῷ Κυρίῳ C, as in the LXX : see p. 227.

p. 43 l. 9 τῷ προσώπῳ] τὸ πρόσωπον CS, in conformity with the words which follow.

p. 43 l. 11 ἐὰν] ἂν C.

p. 43 l. 13 ἄρξεις αὐτοῦ] αὐτοῦ ἄρξεις C. S has the same order as A, but this would be more natural in the Syriac.

p. 43 l. 14 διέλθωμεν] C ; add. *igitur* (= δή) S. This reading is found in some MSS of the LXX.

p. 43 l. 16 ἀδελφοί] C ; ἀγαπητοί S.

p. 44 l. 1 κατειργάσατο] S ; κατειργάσαντο C.

ib. ζῆλος] ζῆλον C.

p. 44 l. 4 εἰσελθεῖν] ἐλθεῖν C, and so probably S.

p. 44 l. 7 κριτὴν ἢ δικαστήν] ἄρχοντα καὶ δικαστήν CS, in accordance with the LXX; see pp. 227, 241. Comp. *Apost. Const.* vi. 2.

p. 44 l. 8 ἐχθὲς] χθές C.

p. 44 l. 9 διὰ ζῆλος] διὰ ζῆλον C.   *ib.* Μαριὰμ κ.τ.λ.] See *Apost. Const.* vi. 1.

p. 44 l. 10 ζῆλος] S ; διὰ ζῆλον C, falling into the same error as A (in inserting the preposition from the previous sentence), but substituting the masculine for the neuter form.

p. 45 l. 12 διὰ ζῆλος] διὰ ζῆλον C.

ib. Δαυείδ] If Bryennios gives the reading of C correctly, this MS has here and elsewhere Δαβίδ; but probably he has written out in full in the later spelling the contraction δαδ.

p. 45 l. 13 ὑπό] ἀπό C.

p. 45 l. 14 ὑπὸ Σαούλ] ἀπὸ τοῦ Σαούλ C.

ib. βασιλέως Ἰσραήλ] S; om. C.

V.

p. 45 l. 18 φθόνον] S; ἔριν C.

ib. κάλλιστοι] Tisch. writes, 'Spatii ratione κρατιστοι et κάλλιστοι magis quam αριστοι et μεγιστοι commendantur. Equidem haud scio an και οι pro οι proponam'; and Gebh. (ed. 1) read κράτιστοι. This however is one among several instances where the calculation of space (at the end of a line) has failed. The word is μέγιστοι in CS.

p. 45 l. 19 ἦλθον] ἔπαθον Laur. Here again the calculation of space has misled. CS have ἠθλησαν.

p. 45 l. 20 ἀγαθούς] This is also the reading of CS. Harnack appositely quotes Clem. Hom. i. 16 ὁ δ᾽ ἀγαθὸς Πέτρος προσπηδήσας κ.τ.λ.

p. 46 l. 1 ὁ Πέτρος] Petrus S; Πέτρον ὅς C. This reading could not have been foreseen, but it is consistent with the space in A, more especially as Πετρον coming at the end of the line might have been written πετρο. The reading of C moreover obviates a difficulty in the common mode of filling in the lacuna of A, which is stated by Tisch., who accepts ὁ Πέτρος on the ground that 'Vix aliud nomen substitui posse videtur', but adds 'Tamen non ita scribi solet ut πετρ exeunte versu, οσ ineunte ponatur'. Nor is the awkwardness of construction difficult to explain. Clement seems to have commenced this sentence intending to follow it up with καὶ Παῦλον ὃς διὰ τὴν αὐτὴν αἰτίαν, or words to this effect. But his account of S. Peter occupies so much space, that for the sake of clearness he is obliged to start with an independent sentence when he comes to S. Paul. The rendering of S is a translator's simplification.

p. 47 l. 1 μαρτυρήσας] To the references in the note add Tertull. Prax. 1 'de jactatione martyrii inflatus ob solum et simplex et breve carceris tædium'. The passage, Ign. Ephes. 1, should be omitted, as μαρτυρίου probably has no place in the correct text. On this passage generally see Hilgenfeld Zeitschr. f. Wissensch. Theol. xv. p. 353 sq. (1872), XIX p. 59 sq. (1876).

p. 47 l. 2 ὑπήνεγκεν] So it is read in C; and so doubtless S, סבל *tulit*, *portavit* (see § 14).

p. 48 l. 2 καὶ ὁ] καὶ ἔριν CS. Though this is much longer than the lacuna in A had led previous editors to supply, still, as the lines are uneven at the end and as this immediate neighbourhood furnishes several instances where the final letters of a line are crowded and small, there is no reason for questioning it as the reading of A also.

ib. ὑπέδειξεν] This same conjecture which I offered (in place of the ὑπεσχεν of previous editors) occurred independently to Laurent, who had not seen my edition, and it was accepted by Gebhardt (ed. 1); C however has the simple verb ἔδειξεν. But if Mill and Jacobson are right, this cannot have been the reading of A, as the initial Υ was once visible. I gave reasons however for doubting whether this was possible, at least in the later condition of the MS (p. 48); and, if so, ἔδειξεν might perhaps be accepted. On the other hand ὑπέδειξεν is supported by a passage in the newly discovered work of Macarius Magnes *Apocr.* iv. 14 (p. 181, Blondel), where speaking of S. Peter and S. Paul he says, ἔγνωσαν ὑποδεῖξαι τούτοις [i.e. τοῖς πιστεύουσιν], ποίοις ἀγῶσιν ὁ τῆς πίστεως συγκεκρότηται στέφανος. In the context, which describes the labours and martyrdom of these same two Apostles, the language of Macarius appears to give many echoes of this passage in Clement; ὑπέμειναν εὐσεβῶς διδάσκοντες, τῶν ἀδικουμένων ὑπέρμαχοι, πολλά...τῷ κόσμῳ μηνύσαντες, τοῦ βίου τὸ τέλος ἀπήντησεν, μέχρι θανάτου ...προκινδυνεύσωσι, τῆς εὐκλείας τὸν ἔπαινον, οἱ γεννάδαι, ἀνὰ τὴν οἰκουμένην, βραβεῖον...κτώμενοι, τύποι ἀνδρείας...γενόμενοι, πολλὰ τῶν καλῶν ἀγωνισμάτων, τῆς διδαχῆς καὶ τοῦ κηρύγματος, μαρτυρίου δόξαν, πικραῖς...βασάνοις, ὑπομονῇ πολλῇ, γενναίως φέρειν. It seems highly probable therefore that the use of ὑποδεικνύναι in this somewhat strange connexion was derived by him from the same source. Comp. also *Ep. Vienn.* § 23 in Euseb. *H. E.* v. 1 εἰς τὴν τῶν λοιπῶν ὑποτύπωσιν ὑποδεικνύων ὅτι μηδὲν φοβερὸν ὅπου πατρὸς ἀγάπη, μηδὲ ἀλγεινὸν ὅπου Χριστοῦ δόξα. S. Paul himself says (Acts xx. 35) ὑπέδειξα ὑμῖν ὅτι κ.τ.λ. C is found in other cases to substitute the simple verb, where A has the compound (see p. 229), and would naturally do so here, where the meaning of the compound was not obvious. S has *tulit* (*portavit*) סיבר (translating βραβεῖον by *certamen*), which corresponds fairly with ὑπεσχεν suggested by some editors; but this was certainly not the reading of A. I have inspected the MS again, and see no traces of a deliberate erasure of ξ, though the letter is worn. So far as it goes, S favours ὑπέδειξεν as against ἔδειξεν.

p. 48 l. 3 φυγαδευθείς] So it stands in CS.

p. 49 l. 1 τε] C ; om. S.

p. 49 l. 5 δικαιοσύνην] connected with ἔλαβε by punctuation in C and apparently also by S. The Syriac translator seems also to have read δικαιοσύνης.

p. 50 l. 2 τοῦ κόσμου] C ; *ab hoc mundo* S. See above, p. 339.

ib. ἐπορεύθη] C ; *susceptus est* S.

VI.

p. 51 l. 5, 6 πολλαῖς κ.τ.λ.] The dative is read in CS.

p. 51 l. 6 ζῆλος] ζῆλον C ; and so again in l. 7.

νεάνιδες, παιδίσκαι] It was stated in my note that the first word is written in A δαηαιδεσ not δαναιδεσ, as commonly read. Dr Wright however inspected the MS afterwards at the request of Tisch., and pronounced the letter to be N, not H. It is often impossible to distinguish these two letters, where the MS is blurred or crumpled; our new authorities however must be taken to rule the reading. Tisch. also pointed out an error into which (by an accident which I need not explain) I had fallen in stating that the second Δ begins a new line. The actual division of the lines is Δλ | ΝΛΙΔΕCΚΛΙΚΛΙΔΙΡΚΛΙ as the photograph shows. On the other hand Tisch. · is himself mistaken in making Bp Wordsworth also responsible for my reading or misreading of the MS. I said nothing which could imply this. The reading of A is confirmed in the main by C, which has Δαναῖδες καὶ Δεὶρ καί, and by S which has *Danaides et Dircae et,* where the *et* may be a duplication of the last syllable of Δίρκαι or may be due to the exigencies of translation. If therefore Δαναῖδες καὶ Δίρκαι be incorrect, as I still believe, the error must have existed already in that archetypal MS from which all our three extant authorities were ultimately derived. This supposition however presents no difficulty, as this common ancestor of ACS was certainly at fault in other places (see above, p. 247).

Since my edition appeared, the reading Δαναῖδες καὶ Δίρκαι has been emphasized and illustrated by M. Renan (*L'Antechrist,* p. 167, 169 sq., 173, 182, 187 sq.), whose frequent reiteration of the words has given them a prominence not unlikely to mislead the reader on the merits of the question. Of his speculations on this passage I need say nothing, for they are merely speculations : and it would have been well if in his imaginary reconstruction of Nero's history he had remembered the sound maxim which directs ʻflagitia abscondi'.

The common reading, if correct, must refer to those refinements of cruelty, patronized by Nero and Domitian but not confined to them, which combined theatrical representations with judicial punishments, so that the offender suffered in the character of some hero of ancient legend or history. On reading over my former note, I see that I have not assigned sufficient weight to the frequency of such exhibitions. For illustrations see Friedländer *Sittengeschichte Roms* II. p. 234 sq. Thus one offender would represent Hercules burnt in the flames on Œta (Tertull. *Apol.* 15 'qui vivus ardebat Herculem induerat'); another, Ixion tortured on the wheel (*de Pudic.* 22 'puta in axe jam incendio adstructo'). We read also of criminals who, having been exhibited in the character of Orpheus (Martial *de Spect.* 21) or of Dædalus (*ib.* 8) or of Atys (Tertull. *Apol.* 15), were finally torn to pieces by wild beasts. The story of Dirce, tied by the hair and dragged along by the bull, would be very appropriate for this treatment; but M. Renan's attempts to make anything of the legend of the Danaids entirely fail. And the difficulty still remains, that the mode of expression in Clement is altogether awkward and unnatural on this hypothesis. Harnack, who however expresses himself doubtfully on the reading, quotes Heb. x. 32 πολλὴν ἄθλησιν ὑπεμείνατε παθημάτων, τοῦτο μὲν ὀνειδισμοῖς τε καὶ θλίψεσιν θεατριζόμενοι; but here θεατριζόμενοι is best explained by 1 Cor. iv. 9 θέατρον ἐγενήθημεν τῷ κόσμῳ κ.τ.λ., where no literal scenic representation is intended. Laurent explains the words by saying that the punishment of the Danaids and of Dirce 'in proverbium abiisse videtur'. But he can only quote for the former ἐς τὸν τῶν Δαναΐδων πίθον ὑδροφορεῖν Lucian *Tim.* 18, which is hardly to the point, as it merely denotes labour spent in vain.

I am therefore obliged still to abide by Bp Wordsworth's conjectural emendation γυναῖκες, νεάνιδες, παιδίσκαι. Tischendorf calls it 'liberrima conjectura'. So it is, but there is a freedom which justifies itself; and the corruption is just such as might have occurred at an early date, when the epistle was written on papyrus. I am informed by Mr Basil H. Cooper, through a common friend, that he proposed this very same emendation in the *Monthly Christian Spectator*, January 1853, p. 16 note *. He assures me that it had occurred to him independently; and that, till quite recently, he believed the credit which had been assigned to another to be due to himself, and wrote to this effect to the *Western Times* as lately as 1871, not knowing that Bp Wordsworth's emendation was published in 1844. The fact of its having occurred independently to two minds is a strong testimony in its favour. Bunsen (*Hippolytus* I. p. xviii, ed. 2, 1854) enthusiastically welcomes this emendation as relieving him 'from two monsters which disfigured a beautiful passage in the epistle of the Roman Clement'. Lipsius also in a review of my edition (*Academy* July 9, 1870) speaks favourably of it; and Donaldson (*Apostolical Fathers* p. 122, ed. 2) calls it admirable, though elsewhere (*Theol. Rev.* January 1877, p. 45) he himself offers another conjecture, γενναῖαί τε καὶ δοῦλαι. To the illustrations given in my note add Minuc. Fel. 37 'viros cum Mucio vel cum Aquilio aut Regulo comparo? pueri et mulierculae nostrae cruces et tormenta, feras et omnes suppliciorum terriculas, inspirata patientia doloris inludunt'.

p. 52 l. 5 ὀστέων] ὀστῶν C.

p. 52 l. 6 κατέστρεψεν] S; κατέσκαψε C. Jacobson refers to Jortin, who supposes that Clement had in his mind Horace *Carm.* i. 16. 17 sq. 'Irae Thyesten exitio gravi stravere, et altis urbibus ultimae stetere causae cur perirent funditus'.

p. 52 l. 7 ἐξερίζωσεν] ἐξερρίζωσε C.

VII.

p. 53 l. 9 ὑπομνήσκοντες] ὑπομιμνήσκοντες C. There is the same divergence of form in the MSS of the Pseudo-Ignat. *Tars.* 9.

p. 53 l. 10 ἐν γάρ] S; καὶ γὰρ ἐν C. *ib.* σκάμματι] For πηδᾶν ὑπὲρ τὰ ἐσκαμμένα see Clem. Alex. *Strom.* v. 13 (p. 696).

p. 53 l. 10, 11 ἡμῖν ἀγών] ἀγὼν ἡμῖν C. S is doubtful. For ὁ αὐτὸς ἀγὼν comp. Phil. i. 30.

p. 53 l. 11 ἀπολείπωμεν] ἀπολίπωμεν C.

p. 54 l. 1 τῆς τελειώσεως] τῆς παραδόσεως CS. This reading of the lacuna could hardly have been anticipated; but it adds to the closeness of the parallel in Polycarp *Phil.* 7 διὸ ἀπολιπόντες τὴν ματαιότητα τῶν πολλῶν καὶ τὰς ψευδοδιδασκαλίας ἐπὶ τὸν ἐξ ἀρχῆς ἡμῖν παραδοθέντα λόγον ἐπιστρέψωμεν, a passage already quoted by the editors. By τὸν τῆς παραδόσεως ἡμῶν κανόνα Clement apparently means 'the rule (i.e. measure of the leap or race), which we have received by tradition', referring to the examples of former athletes quoted in the context: comp. § 19 ἐπὶ τὸν ἐξ ἀρχῆς παραδεδομένον ἡμῖν τῆς εἰρήνης σκοπόν (to which passage again Polycarp is indebted), § 51 τῆς παραδεδομένης ἡμῖν καλῶς καὶ δικαίως ὁμοφωνίας. Clement's phrase is borrowed by his younger namesake, *Strom.* i. 1 (p. 324) προβήσεται ἡμῖν κατὰ τὸν εὐκλεῆ καὶ σεμνὸν τῆς παραδόσεως κανόνα. For examples of the use of κανών see Lagarde *Rel. Jur. Eccl. Ant.* Praef. p. vi sq.

ib. γινώσκωμεν] καὶ ἴδωμεν CS.

p. 54 l. 2 καὶ εὐπροσδεκτόν] καὶ τί προσδεκτὸν CS, as proposed by Tisch.

p. 54 l. 4 ἴδωμεν] γνῶμεν CS. · *ib.* τῷ Θεῷ καὶ πατρὶ αὐτοῦ] This reading of the lacuna, which I suggested, is approved by Tisch. and was adopted by Gebhardt (ed. 1). C has τῷ πατρὶ αὐτοῦ τῷ Θεῷ; but this was not the reading of A, as the remaining letters show. S has simply τῷ πατρὶ αὐτοῦ, which, as being the briefest, is probably the original reading. The varying positions of τῷ Θεῷ in A and C also show that it was a later addition.

p. 55 l. 4 μετανοίας τόπον] *Apost. Const.* ii. 38 τόπον μετανοίας ὥρισεν, v. 19 λαβεῖν αὐτὸν τόπον μετανοίας.

p. 55 l. 5 ὅτι] S translates as if ὅ τι *id quod.*

p. 55 l. 6 μετανοίας χάριν] C ; μετανοίαν S. Mr Bensly points out to me that the omission in S is easily explained by the homœoteleuton in the Syriac ܬܝܒܘܬܐ ܕܚܝܒܘܬܐ. *ib.* ὑπήνεγκεν] *sustulit* ܣܝܒܪ S ; ἐπήνεγκε C. *ib.* ἀνέλθωμεν εἰς] διέλθωμεν (om. εἰς) C; *transeamus super* S, apparently reading διέλθωμεν εἰς, which probably stood in A also. Comp. Rom. v. 12 εἰς πάντας ἀνθρώπους ὁ θάνατος διῆλθεν, where however both Peshito and Harclean have ܥܒܪ ܒ and not ܥܒܪ ܥܠ, as the Syriac has here. In § 4 διελθεῖν εἰς is rendered by ܠܥܒܪ. Strictly ܥܒܪ ܥܠ should represent διελθεῖν ἐπί, but this is no sufficient reason for supposing a various reading in the preposition here. Διελθεῖν is a very favourite word in the LXX.

p. 55 l. 7 καί] C ; om. S : see below on p. 167 l. 9.

p. 55 l. 8 ὁ δεσπότης] C ; om. S. This passage is copied in *Apost. Const.* ii. 55 ὁ γὰρ Θεός, Θεὸς ὢν ἐλέους, ἀπ' ἀρχῆς ἑκάστην γενεάν ἐπὶ μετάνοιαν καλεῖ διὰ τῶν δικαίων...τοὺς δὲ ἐν τῷ κατακλυσμῷ διὰ τοῦ Νῶε, τοὺς ἐν Σοδόμοις διὰ τοῦ φιλοξένου Λώτ (see below § 11) κ.τ.λ.

p. 56 l. 2 οἱ δέ] C ; οἶδε S.

p. 56 l. 3 ἱκετεύσαντες] ἱκετεύοντες C, and so apparently S.

VIII.

p. 57 l. 9 γάρ] S ; om. C.

p. 57 l. 11 ὑμῶν] S ; τοῦ λαοῦ μου C.

p. 57 l. 12 εἶπον] C ; *dum dicis tu* (εἰπών) S. *ib.* ἐάν] C ; κἄν (?) S.

p. 58 l. 3 καρδίας] ψυχῆς CS.

p. 58 l. 5 λέγει οὕτως] οὕτω λέγει CS. *ib.* καί] om. CS. *ib.* ἀφέλεσθε] ἀφέλετε C.

p. 58 l. 9 καὶ δικαιώσατε] C ; δικαιώσατε (om. καί) S. *ib.* χήρᾳ] χήραν C, with the LXX. S is doubtful.   *ib.* καὶ διελεγχθῶμεν] καὶ διαλεχθῶμεν C, *loquamur cum alterutro* (om. καὶ) S.

p. 58 l. 10 λέγει] add. κύριος CS.

p. 59 l. 14 γὰρ] C; om. S.

IX.

p. 59 l. 19 γενόμενοι] C; but S seems to have read γινόμενοι.

p. 59 l. 21 ἀπολιπόντες] C; but S apparently ἀπολείποντες. *ib.* ματαιοπονίαν] So too CS.

p. 60 l. 1 τελείως] C; τελείους S.

p. 60 l. 2 sq. Ἐνὼχ κ.τ.λ.] With this enumeration of the ancient worthies which follows comp. *Clem. Hom.* xviii. 13 οὐδὲ Ἐνὼχ ὁ εὐαρεστήσας...οὔτε Νῶε ὁ δίκαιος...οὔτε Ἀβραὰμ ὁ φίλος. This designation of Abraham, 'the friend of God', is the subject of a paper by Rönsch *Zeitschr. f. Wissensch. Theol.* xvi. p. 583 sq. (1873).

p. 60 l. 3 θάνατος] ὁ θάνατος C.

p. 60 l. 4 διὰ τῆς λειτουργίας] S; ἐν τῇ λειτουργίᾳ C.

X.

p. 62 l. 3 καταράσομαι] καταράσσομαι C.

p. 62 l. 8 ἦν] S; om. C.

p. 62 l. 9 αἰῶνος] τοῦ αἰῶνος C.

p. 62 l. 12 Ἐξήγαγεν] Ἐξήγαγε δὲ CS.

p. 62 l. 14 τοὺς ἀστέρας] C; add. τοῦ οὐρανοῦ S.

p. 63 l. 17 γήρᾳ] γήρει C. On this form see the note on § 63, p. 300; and to the examples there given add. *Apost. Const.* iv. 3.

p. 63 l. 18 τῷ Θεῷ] S; om. C. See a similar omission in some texts of Ign. *Rom.* 4.   *ib.* πρὸς] εἰς C; *super* S.

XI.

p. 63 l. 21 κριθείσης] Dr Wright agrees with Tisch. in taking κριθησησ as the reading of A; and Tisch. appeals also to the photograph. The word in the photograph still seems to me to be more like κριθεισησ, and another inspection of the MS itself confirms me in this reading. I see no traces of the left-hand stroke of an H.

p. 63 l. 22 ποιήσας] C. S translates as if ἐποίησεν.

p. 63 l. 23 ἐπ' αὐτὸν] So too apparently S; εἰς αὐτὸν C.

p. 63 l. 24 κόλασιν] C; but S translates as if κρίσιν.

p. 63 l. 25 ἑτερογνώμονος] So C. Of the reading of A Tisch. writes 'ετερογνωμοσ (pro -γνωμονοσ) est, ut jam Iacobsonus legerat. VanSittart legit ετερογνωμου, falsus aversa pagina, unde teste Wright υ in ευρεθη translucet'. A fresh examination of the MS leads me to acquiesce in Wright's explanation.

p. 63 l. 26 τοῦτο] S ; om. C.

p. 64 l. 1 κρίμα] κρῖμα C.

XII.

p. 64 l. 3 φιλοξενίαν] C ; but S repeats the preposition διὰ φιλοξενίαν. It is not however to be entirely depended upon in such cases ; see p. 239 sq.

ib. ἡ πόρνη] ἡ ἐπιλεγομένη πόρνη CS ; see above, pp. 228, 241. The object of the interpolation is to suggest a figurative sense of the word : comp. Orig. in Ies. Nave Hom. iii. § 3 (II. p. 403) 'Raab interpretatur latitudo. Quæ est ergo latitudo nisi ecclesia hæc Christi, quæ ex peccatoribus velut ex meretricatione collecta est?...Talis ergo et hæc meretrix esse dicitur, quæ exploratores suscepit Iesu'; comp. ib. vi. § 3 (p. 411). From a like motive the Targum interprets the word in Josh. ii. 1 by פונדקיתא = πανδοκευτρία 'an innkeeper', and so Joseph. Ant. v. 1. 2 ὑποχωροῦσιν εἴς τι καταγώγιον...ὄντες ἐν τῷ τῆς Ῥαχάβης καταγωγίῳ, etc. This explanation has been adopted by several Jewish and some Christian interpreters ; see Gesenius Thes. s. v. זנה, p. 422. Others again have interpreted the word as meaning 'Gentile'. The earliest Christian fathers took a truer view, when they regarded this incident as an anticipation of the announcement in Matt. xxi. 31 ; e.g. Justin Dial. 111, Iren. iv. 20. 12.

p. 64 l. 4 τοῦ τοῦ] τοῦ C (omitting the second τοῦ).

p. 64 l. 5 τὴν] om. C.

p. 64 l. 7, 8 συλλημψομένους...συλλημφθέντες] συλληψομένους...συλληφθέντες C. They are translated by two different words in S.

p. 64 l. 11 λεγόντων] C ; add. illi S.

ib. ἰδού, εἰσῆλθον] πρὸς σὲ εἰσῆλθον CS, as proposed by Tisch.

p. 65 l. 12 γῆς· σὺ οὖν] γῆς ἡμῶν CS, thus confirming the reading of the editors generally.

p. 65 l. 13 οἱ δύο ἄνδρες] μὲν οἱ ἄνδρες CS, confirming the conjecture of Gebhardt.

p. 65 l. 14 ἀλλὰ ταχέως ἀπῆλθον] ἀλλ᾽ εὐθέως ἐξῆλθον CS.

p. 65 l. 15 ὁδὸν] τῇ ὁδῷ C ; in via ipsorum S.

ib. ἐναντίαν] ἐναλλάξ CS. This use of the word, which commonly means 'interchangeably', is somewhat strange, though the meaning is clear, 'crosswise', i.e. 'in an opposite direction'.

p. 65 l. 16 ἐγώ] S ; om. C.

p. 65 l. 17 ὑμῶν] om. CS.   ib. πόλιν] γῆν CS.

p. 65 l. 18 φόβος...τρόμος] C. The two words are transposed in S.

p. 65 l. 19 ἐὰν] ἂν C.   ib. αὐτὴν] C ; τὴν γῆν S.

p. 65 l. 21 ἐλάλησας] λελάληκας C.   ib. ὡς] C ; not translated in S.   ib. ἐὰν] ἂν C.   ib. παραγινομένους] S (by the pointing); παραγενομένους C.

p. 65 l. 22 sq. τέγος σου] στέγος (om. σου) C ; tectum domus tuæ S.

p. 66 l. 1 ἐὰν] ἂν C.   ib. ὅσοι γὰρ] C ; et omnes illi qui (καὶ ὅσοι) S.

p. 66 l. 3 κρεμάσῃ] ἐκκρεμάσῃ CS.

p. 66 l. 5 καὶ ἐλπίζουσιν] C ; om. S.

p. 66 l. 6 οὗ] ὅτι οὐ CS. See above, pp. 228, 241.   ib. ἀλλὰ] add. καὶ CS.

p. 66 l. 7 γέγονεν] ἐγενήθη C ; see above, p. 228. In such a case the reading of S is indeterminable. Here γέγονεν, ' is found', must unquestionably be the right reading; comp. 1 Tim. ii. 14 ἡ δὲ γυνὴ ἐξαπατηθεῖσα ἐν παραβάσει γέγονεν, where, as here, the perfect denotes the permanence of the record and the example. See also Gal. iii. 18 τῷ δὲ Ἀβραὰμ δι' ἐπαγγελίας κεχάρισται ὁ Θεός, iv. 23 ὁ ἐκ τῆς παιδίσκης κατὰ σάρκα γεγέννηται, where the explanation of the perfect is the same. So too frequently in the Epistle to the Hebrews, e.g. vii. 6 δεδεκάτωκεν, xi. 28 πεποίηκεν.

XIII.

p. 66 l. 9 τύφος] τύφον C.

p. 67 l. 13 ἀλλ' ἢ ὁ] ἀλλ' ὁ C, and so perhaps S.

p. 67 l. 16 οὕτως γὰρ εἶπεν κ.τ.λ.] See Apost. Const. ii. 21, where the words of Christ are quoted, Ἄφετε καὶ ἀφεθήσεται ὑμῖν· δίδοτε καὶ δοθήσεται ὑμῖν.

p. 67 l. 17 ἐλεᾶτε] ἐλεεῖτε C.   ib. ἀφίετε] ἄφετε C.

p. 67 l. 18 οὕτως] οὕτω C, and similarly p. 68 l. 1, 2.

p. 68 l. 1 κριθήσεται ὑμῖν] κριθήσεσθε CS.

p. 68 l. 2 ᾧ μέτρῳ...μετρηθήσεται ὑμῖν] here, S; before ὡς κρίνετε κ.τ.λ., C.   ib. ἐν αὐτῷ] S ; οὕτω C.

p. 68 l. 4 στηρίξωμεν] στηρίζωμεν C.   ib. πορεύεσθαι] πορεύεσθε C.

p. 68 l. 5 ἡμᾶς] ὄντας CS, thus confirming the conjecture of Laur.

p. 68 l. 7 πραΰν| πρᾷον C.

p. 68 l. 8 τὰ λόγια] τοὺς λόγους C. The reading of S is uncertain.

XIV.

p. 68 l. 9 ὅσιον] C ; θεῖον S. See for other instances of the same confusion § 2 (p. 404), § 21 (p. 420).

p. 68 l. 10 ἡμᾶς] S ; ὑμᾶς C.   *ib.* γενέσθαι τῷ Θεῷ] τῷ Θεῷ γενέσθαι CS.

p. 69 l. 11 ζήλους] ζήλου C. For the form μυσεροῦ comp. μιεράν in Boeckh *Corp. Inscr.* no. 3588. See also the play on ἱερεύς, μιερεύς; *Apost. Const.* ii. 28. C apparently writes μυσαράν (for μυσεράν) in § 30, but not so here.

p. 69 l. 15 ἔριν] αἱρέσεις C, with Nicon ; ἔρεις S, but the plural merely depends on the presence of *ribui.* See above, p. 228.

p. 69 l. 16 αὐτοῖς] ἑαυτοῖς CS.

p. 69 l. 19 sq. οἱ δὲ παρανομοῦντες...ἀπ᾽ αὐτῆς] C ; om. S (by homœoteleuton).

p. 69 l. 19 ἐξολεθρευθήσονται] ἐξολοθρευθήσονται C. The form varies in the most ancient mss of the LXX.

p. 69 l. 20 ἀσεβῆ] τὸν ἀσεβῆ C, with the LXX.

p. 70 l. 2 sq. τὸν τόπον...εὗρον] C ; αὐτὸν καὶ οὐχ εὑρέθη ὁ τόπος αὐτοῦ S, as in the LXX.

p. 70 l. 4 ἐνκατάλειμμα] ἐγκατάλλειμμα C.

XV.

p. 70 l. 7 οὗτος ὁ λαός] S (apparently) ; ὁ λαὸς οὗτος C.

ib. τοῖς χείλεσιν] S ; τῷ στόματι C.

p. 70 l. 8 ἄπεστιν] ἀπέχει C ; dub. S.

p. 70 l. 9 εὐλογοῦσαν] εὐλόγουν C ; see above, p. 229.

ib. τῇ δὲ] C ; καὶ τῇ S, with the LXX.   *ib.* κατηρῶντο] So also Dr Wright reads A, against Tisch.'s κατηρουντο. I myself have looked at the ms again and cannot feel certain.

p. 71 l. 11 ἐψεύσαντο] S ; ἔψεξαν C.

p. 71 l. 13 ῎Αλαλα] διὰ τοῦτο῎Αλαλα CS.   *ib.* γενηθήτω] γενηθείη C.

p. 71 l. 13 sq. τὰ χείλη τὰ δόλια...τὰ δόλια, γλῶσσαν μεγαλορήμονα, τοὺς εἰπόντας κ.τ.λ.] The words omitted by homœoteleuton are supplied otherwise by S, which reads, τὰ χείλη τὰ δόλια τὰ λαλοῦντα κατὰ τοῦ δικαίου ἀνομίαν· καὶ πάλιν· Ἐξολεθρεύσαι Κύριος πάντα τὰ χείλη τὰ δόλια, γλῶσσαν μεγαλορήμονα, τοὺς εἰπόντας κ.τ.λ. This is doubtless the correct text. On the other hand C reads quite differently ; τὰ χείλη τὰ δόλια, γλῶσσα μεγαλορήμων· καὶ πάλιν· Τοὺς εἰπόντας κ.τ.λ. The transcriber clearly had a text before him in which the words were omitted, as they are in A: and he patched it up by insertion and alteration, so as to run grammatically and to make sense. See above, p. 245.

p. 71 l. 15 μεγαλύνωμεν] μεγαλυνοῦμεν C. The reading of S is indeterminable.

p. 71 l. 16 παρ᾽ ἡμῖν] παρ᾽ ἡμῶν CS.

p. 71 l. 17 ἀπό] om. CS.

p. 71 l. 18 ἐν σωτηρίᾳ] S (or ἐν σωτηρίῳ); om. C, at least if we interpret the note of Bryennios strictly, in which case he must have supplied ἐν σωτηρίῳ in his text from the LXX after Hilgenfeld. Gebhardt however supposes that he has accidentally omitted ἐν σωτηρίῳ in his note, when giving the reading of C.

XVI.

p. 72 l. 2 τῆς μεγαλωσύνης] C; om. S with Jerome.

p. 72 l. 3 ἡμῶν] om. C, Hieron. The reading of S is doubtful, for it uses מרא equally for ὁ Κύριος and ὁ Κύριος ἡμῶν.

ib. Χριστὸς Ἰησοῦς] Ἰησοῦς Χριστὸς CS, Hieron.

p. 72 l. 5 ταπεινοφρονῶν] C; add. ἦλθεν S.

p. 72 l. 8 παιδίον] S; πεδίον C.

p. 72 l. 9 εἶδος αὐτῷ] αὐτῷ εἶδος C. The order of S agrees with C, but the fact cannot be pressed.

p. 73 l. 10 κάλλος] C; δόξα S.

p. 73 l. 11 τὸ εἶδος τῶν ἀνθρώπων] C; πάντας ἀνθρώπους S, in accordance with one reading of the LXX.

p. 73 l. 16 ἐτραυματίσθη] C; occisus est S.

p. 73 l. 17 ἁμαρτίας, ἀνομίας] transposed in CS.

p. 74 l. 7 τὴν γενεὰν] C; καὶ τὴν γενεὰν S.

p. 74 l. 8 ἥκει] C; ἤχθη S, as it is commonly read in the LXX.

p. 75 l. 14 τῆς ψυχῆς] C; ἀπὸ τῆς ψυχῆς S. The מן which represents ἀπὸ before τοῦ πόνου is pointed as if = μέν.

p. 75 l. 18 τοῖς] ἐν τοῖς C, and so probably S, which has ב, not ל.

p. 76 l. 3 δὲ] S; om. C.

p. 76 l. 6 ὅτι] C; εἰ S.

p. 76 l. 9 ποιήσωμεν] ποιήσομεν C.

p. 76 l. 10 ἐλθόντες] S; ἀπελθόντες C.

XVII.

p. 77 l. 14 Ἐλισαιὲ] Ἐλισσαιὲ C.   ib. ἔτι δὲ] S; om. C. ib. καὶ] C; om. S.   ib. πρὸς τούτοις] C; add. δὲ S.

p. 77 l. 15 ἐμαρτυρήθη] S; add. δὲ C.

p. 77 l. 17 ἀτενίζων] ἀτενίσας C. S apparently read Ἀτενίσω, for it translates 'et dicit cogitans humiliter, videbo gloriam Dei'.

p. 77 l. 19 Ἰὼβ] add. δὲ CS, with Clem. Alex.   ib. καὶ] C; om. S with LXX.

p. 77 l. 20 κακοῦ] C; πονηροῦ πράγματος S, with the LXX.

p. 77 l. 21 κατηγορεῖ λέγων] My reading of the lacuna was followed by Gebhardt, and is now confirmed by C. S however translates as if it had read κατηγορῶν λέγει.

ib. οὐδ' εἰ] οὐδ' ἂν C. S may have read either one or the other, but not ἐὰν καί. The same text is quoted with οὐδ' ἂν in *Apost. Const.* ii. 18.

p. 78 l. 2 αὐτοῦ] S; om. C.

p. 78 l. 3 ἔκρινεν] C; κρίνει (apparently) S.

p. 78 l. 5 ἐκ τῆς βάτου] ἐπὶ τοῦ τῆς βάτου C; but A cannot have so read, unless this line was very much longer than the preceding or following one. Moreover ἐπὶ τοῦ τῆς βάτου χρηματισμοῦ αὐτῷ διδομένου is in itself a very awkward and unlikely expression. Probably A read ἐπὶ τῆς βάτου or ἐπὶ τοῦ βάτου, this being a common mode of referring to the incident; Luke xx. 37 (comp. Mark xii. 26), Justin *Dial.* 128 (p. 357), *Clem. Hom.* xvi. 14, *Apost. Const.* v. 20. The reading of C must be attributed to the indecision of a scribe hesitating between the masculine and feminine genders; the word being sometimes masculine, ὁ βάτος (e.g. Exod. iii. 2, 3, 4, *Apost. Const.* vii. 33), sometimes feminine (Deut. xxxiii. 16, Acts vii. 35, Justin *Dial.* 127, 128, *Clem. Hom.* xvi. 14, *Apost. Const.* v. 20). So we have ἐπὶ τοῦ βάτου Mark xii. 26 (though with an illsupported v. l.), but ἐπὶ τῆς βάτου Luke xx. 37. In Justin *Dial.* 60 (p. 283) we meet with ἀπὸ τῆς βάτου, ὁ βάτος, ὁ βάτος, ὁ βάτος, ἐκ τῆς βάτου, in the same chapter. See on this double gender of the word Fritzsche on Mark l. c. [The above note was written before S was discovered. S reads either ἐπὶ τοῦ βάτου or ἐπὶ τῆς βάτου.]

XVIII.

p. 79 l. 9 εἴπωμεν] εἴποιμεν C.

p. 79 l. 10 ὁ Θεός] S; om. C.

p. 79 l. 11 ἐν ἐλέει] This is also the reading of C; but S has ἐν ἐλαίῳ.

p. 80 l. 2 ἐπὶ πλεῖον κ.τ.λ.] The rest of the quotation to ἐξουθενώσει at the end of the chapter is omitted in C. See above p. 230.

p. 80 l. 10 σου] om. S.

p. 81 l. 23 sq. τὸ στόμα...τὰ χείλη] C; transposed in S in accordance with the LXX and Hebrew.

XIX.

p. 81 l. 28 τοσούτων, τοιούτων] transposed in CS.   *ib.* οὕτως] om. C; καὶ οὕτως S.

p. 81 l. 29 ταπεινοφρονοῦν] ταπεινόφρον C. Though A has ταπεινοφρόνον, there can be little doubt about the reading, since Clement uses ταπεινοφρονεῖν ten times elsewhere, but ταπεινόφρων never. See the note p. 17. Moreover, C elsewhere (§ 38) alters ταπεινοφρονῶν into ταπεινοφρών.

ib. τὸ ὑποδεὲς] '*submissiveness*', '*subordination*'. This seems to be the meaning of the word, which is very rare in the positive, though common in the comparative ὑποδεέστερος; see Epiphan. *Hær.* lxxvii. 14 τὸ ὑποδεὲς καὶ ἠλαττωμένον, a passage pointed out to me by Bensly. Accordingly in the Syriac it is rendered *diminutio et demissio*. Laurent says 'Colomesius male substantivo *subjectio* vertit. Collaudatur enim h. l. voluntaria sanctorum hominum egestas. Vid. Luk. x. 4'; and Harnack accepts this rendering 'egestas'. But this sense is not well suited to the context, besides being unsupported; nor indeed is it easy to see how ὑποδεής could have this meaning, which belongs rather to ἐνδεής. It might possibly mean 'fearfulness', a sense assigned to it by Photius, Suidas, and Hesychius, who explain it ὑπόφοβος. But usage suggests its connexion with δέομαι '*indigeo*', like ἀποδεής, ἐνδεής, καταδεής, rather than with δέος *timor*, like ἀδεής, περιδεής.

p. 81 l. 30 sq. τὰς πρὸ ἡμῶν γενεάς] S; τοὺς πρὸ ἡμῶν C, omitting γενεάς.

p. 82 l. 1 τε] C; om. S.

p. 82 l. 2 αὐτοῦ] C; τοῦ Θεοῦ S.

p. 82 l. 3 πράξεων] C; add. τούτων, ἀδελφοὶ ἀγαπητοί S.

p. 82 l. 6 κόσμου] C; *hujus mundi* S. See above p. 339.

p. 82 l. 8 κολληθῶμεν] C; *consideremus* (= νοήσωμεν) *et adhæreamus* S, but this is probably only one of the periphrases in which the translator abounds.

XX.

p. 83 l. 12 διοικήσει] C; δικαιώσει S.

p. 83 l. 15 ἥλιός τε καὶ] S; ἥλιος καὶ C.

ib. ἀστέρων τε χόροι] C; but S translates as if ἀστερές τε καὶ χόροι.

p. 83 l. 16 παρεκβάσεως] παραβάσεως C, which destroys the sense. S translates *in omni egressu cursus ipsorum*, which probably represents παρεκβάσεως, and where it seems to have read διὰ for δίχα. For the whole passage comp. *Apost. Const.* vii. 34 φωστῆρες...ἀπαράβατον σώζοντες τὸν δολιχὸν καὶ κατ᾽ οὐδὲν παραλλάσσοντες τῆς σῆς προσταγῆς. In the immediate neighbourhood is the same quotation from Job xxxviii. 11 as here in Clement.

p. 83 l. 19 πανπλήθη] παμπλήθη C.

p. 83 l. 20 ἐπ᾽ αὐτήν] ἐπ᾽ αὐτῆς C; *in illa* S.

p. 83 l. 23 κρίματα] This is also the reading of CS. It must have been read moreover by the writer of the later books of the *Apostolic Constitutions*, vii. 35 ἀνεξιχνίαστος κρίμασιν. Dr Hort calls my attention to the connexion of words in Ps. xxxvi (xxxv). 5 τὰ κρίματά σου [ὡσεὶ] ἄβυσσος πολλή.

p. 84 l. 1 τὸ κύτος κ.τ.λ.] See *Apost. Const.* viii. 12 ὁ συστησάμενος ἄβυσσον καὶ μέγα κύτος αὐτῇ περιθείς...πηγαῖς ἀενάοις μεθύσας... ἐνιαυτῶν κύκλοις...νεφῶν ὀμβροτόκων διαδρομαῖς εἰς καρπῶν γονὰς καὶ ζῴων σύστασιν, στάθμον ἀνέμων διαπνεόντων κ.τ.λ., where again the resemblances cannot be accidental.

p. 84 l. 4 οὕτως] οὕτω C.

p. 84 l. 5 συντριβήσεται] συντριβήσονται C.

p. 85 l. 6 ἀνθρώποις ἀπέρατος] ἀπέραντος ἀνθρώποις C. S translates *intransmeabilis* (= ἀπέρατος). The proper meaning of ἀπέραντος, 'boundless', appears from *Clem. Hom.* xvi. 17, xvii. 9, 10, where it is found in close alliance with ἄπειρος. See also Clem. Alex. *Fragm.* p. 1020. On the other hand for ἀπέρατος comp. e.g. Macar. Magn. *Apocr.* iv. 13 (p. 179) ῥεῖ τῷ θέρει καὶ τῷ χειμῶνι πολὺς καὶ ἀπέρατος. The lines in A are divided ΑΠΕΡΑΝ|ΤΟΣ; and this division would assist the insertion of the Ν. An earlier scribe would write ΑΠΕΡΑ|ΤΟΣ for ΑΠΕΡΑ|ΤΟΣ. See Didymus *Expos. Psal.* 138 (p. 1596 ed. Migne) εἰ γὰρ καὶ ὠκεανὸς ἀπέραντος, ἀλλ᾽ οὖν καὶ οἱ μετ᾽ αὐτὸν κόσμοι ταῖς τοῦ δεσπότου διαταγαῖς διϊθύνονται· πάντα γὰρ τὰ πρὸς αὐτοῦ γεγενημένα ὅποι [ὅποια ?] ποτ᾽ ἐστὶν ταγαῖς τῆς ἑαυτοῦ προνοίας διοικούμενα ἰθύνεται, quoted in the *Church Quarterly* III. p. 240. This language may have been derived from Origen, and not directly from Clement. Anyhow the recognition of both the various readings, ταγαῖς, διαταγαῖς, is worthy of notice.

p. 85 l. 8 μεταπαραδιδόασιν] So apparently S; but μεταδιδόασιν C, an apparent simplification, but a real injury to the sense.

ib. ἀνέμων] add. τε CS. S translates *ventique locorum*, as if it had read ἄνεμοί τε σταθμῶν.

p. 86 l. 1 τὴν] S; καὶ τὴν C.

p. 86 l. 2 ἀέναοι] ἀένναοι C.   *ib.* ἀπόλαυσιν] C; add. τε S.

ib. ὑγείαν] ὑγίειαν C.

p. 86 l. 3 πρὸς ζωῆς] πρὸς ζωὴν C. S translates *ea quæ ad vitam*, omitting μαζούς altogether.

p. 86 l. 5 συνελεύσεις] C; but S translates *auxilia*, as if it had read συλλήψεις.

p. 86 l. 8 προσπεφευγότας] S; προσφεύγοντας C.

p. 87 l. 10 καὶ ἡ μεγαλωσύνη] C; om. S.

XXI.

p. 87 l. 13 εἰς κρίμα πᾶσιν ἡμῖν] εἰς κρίματα σὺν ἡμῖν C; while S translates *in judicium nobis*. The reading of C is explained by a confusion of κριμαπαcιν and κριματαcγν; and S is a correction of the reading so corrupted. The singular might be accounted for here by the absence of *ribui*, but in § 28 (see below on p. 101 l. 22) the translator deliberately substitutes the singular for the plural in this same word. The σὺν seems to have been dropped purposely; see above p. 245.

p. 87 l. 14 αὐτοῦ] C; om. S.

p. 87 l. 17 ἐστιν] C; add. *nobis* S.   *ib.* ὅτι] C; om. (?) S.

p. 88 l. 1 λιποτακτεῖν] λειποτακτεῖν C. There is poetical authority for the simple vowel in λιποτάξιον: see Meineke *Fragm. Com.* II. p. 1214, III. p. 71, with the notes. So too in analogous words, wherever they occur in verse, the form in ι is found: e. g. λιπαυγής, λιπόναυς, λιπο-ναύτης, λιπόπνοος, λιποσαρκής, λιποψυχεῖν. The grammarians differed on this point: see Chæroboscus in Cramer's *Anecd.* II. p. 239 λέγει ὁ Ὧρος ὅτι πάντα τὰ παρὰ τὸ λείπω διὰ τῆς ει διφθόγγου γράφεται, οἷον λειπόνεως, λειποταξίᾳ, λειποτάξιον, λειποστράτιον· ὁ δὲ Ὠριγένης διὰ τοῦ ι λέγει γρά-φεσθαι. There seems to be no poetical and therefore indisputable authority for the ει.

p. 88 l. 2 μᾶλλον] C; add. δὲ S.

p. 88 l. 5 Χριστόν] om. CS.

p. 88 l. 7 ἡμῶν] om. CS.

p. 88 l. 8 τοῦ φόβου] C; om. S.

p. 88 l. 10 ἐνδειξάσθωσαν] Bryennios is wrong in giving ἐνδειξάτωσαν as the reading of A and Clem. Alex.; for both have ἐνδειξάσθωσαν. Yet he quotes the passage of Clem. Alex. again in his preface (p. ρκδ') with ἐνδειξάτωσαν.

p. 88 l. 11 βούλημα] C. S translates as if καὶ βούλημα.

p. 88 l. 12 σιγῆς] This reading, which the sense requires and which with Hilgenfeld I had inserted in the text from Clem. Alex., is now confirmed by CS.

p. 88 l. 13 προσκλίσεις] S; προσκλήσεις C. This same itacism occurs several times in C, § 47, 50.

p. 89 l. 15 ἡμῶν] S; ὑμῶν C.

p. 89 l. 17 τῷ Θεῷ] Θεῷ (om. τῷ) C.

p. 89 l. 18 ὁσίως] C; θείως S. For other instances of this same confusion see above (p. 404) the note on p. 38 l. 3.

p. 89 l. 21 ἀνελεῖ] ἀναιρεῖ CS.

XXII.

p. 89 l. 22 δὲ] C ; om. S.

p. 89 l. 23 οὕτως] οὕτω C.

p. 89 l. 25 τίς ἐστιν...p. 90 l. 7 ἐρύσατο αὐτόν] om. C, the words running on διδάξω ὑμᾶς· εἶτα πολλαὶ αἱ μάστιγες κ.τ.λ., where εἶτα is introduced to link the parts together. See above p. 230.

p. 90 l. 1 καὶ] om. S. *ib.* χείλη] add. σου S with the LXX.

p. 90 l. 3 ὀφθαλμοὶ] C ; ὅτι ὀφθαλμοὶ S.

p. 90 l. 7 αὐτὸν] S here adds Πολλαὶ αἱ θλίψεις τοῦ δικαίου καὶ ἐκ πασῶν αὐτῶν ῥύσεται αὐτὸν ὁ Κύριος· καὶ πάλιν. This is from Ps. xxxiv (xxxiii). 20, the verse but one following the preceding quotation. The LXX however has the plural τῶν δικαίων, αὐτούς. The words have obviously been omitted in AC owing to the recurrence of Πολλαὶ αἱ, and should be restored accordingly.

p. 91 l. 8 τοὺς δὲ ἐλπίζοντας] τὸν δὲ ἐλπίζοντα CS, with the LXX.

XXIII.

p. 91 l. 11 φοβουμένους] τοὺς φοβουμένους C.

p. 91 l. 15 πόρρω γενέσθω] S ; πόρρω γε γενέσθω C. See below on p. 110 l. 1.

p. 91 l. 16 αὕτη] S ; αὐτοῦ C. By an inadvertence αὐτὴ is printed for αὕτη in my edition.

p. 92 l. 1 τὴν ψυχήν] τῇ ψυχῇ C. S is doubtful.

p. 92 l. 3 συνβέβηκεν] συμβέβηκεν C.

p. 92 l. 4 πρῶτον μὲν φυλλοροεῖ] S ; om. C.

p. 92 l. 5 sq. καὶ μετὰ ταῦτα] C ; translated in S as if εἶτα, the καὶ being omitted.

XXIV.

p. 93 l. 13 ἐπιδείκνυται διηνεκῶς ἡμῖν] διηνεκῶς ἡμῖν ἐπιδείκνυσι C ; *monstrat nobis perpetuo* S.

p. 93 l. 14 τὴν ἀπαρχήν] C ; add. ἤδη S.

p. 93 l. 15 Χριστὸν] S ; om. C.

p. 93 l. 16 καιροὺς] This reading, which I ventured for reasons given in the note to substitute for the καιρὸν of previous editors, was adopted by Gebhardt (ed. 1). C however has καιρόν. S translates *in omni tempore.* *ib.* γινομένην] C ; add. ἡμῖν S.

p. 93 l. 17 κοιμᾶται...ἡμέρα] C ; S translates as if it had read κοιμᾶταί [τις] νυκτός, ἀνίσταται ἡμέρας, 'a man sleeps in the night, he arises in the day'.

p. 93 l. 18 ἡμέρα] So too Gebh. ; but C has ἡ ἡμέρα. I still think that ἡμέρα is correct on account of the parallelism. The omission or reduplication of a letter in such cases in the MSS is very common. Having inspected A again, I abide by the statement in my note.

ib. βλέπωμεν] λάβωμεν CS.

p. 93 l. 19 ὁ σπόρος τῆς γῆς] This mode of filling the lacuna is approved by Tisch. and was adopted by Gebh. (ed. 1). The grammatical objection which I urged against ὁ σπόρος κόκκου of previous editors is sustained by CS, which however read ὁ σπόρος πῶς καὶ.

p. 93 l. 20 sq. ἔβαλεν εἰς τὴν γῆν· καὶ βληθέντων σπερμάτων, ἅτινα πέπτωκεν κ.τ.λ.] None of the editors have here supplied the lacuna aright. The words in C stand thus; ἔβαλεν εἰς τὴν γῆν ἕκαστον τῶν σπερμάτων, ἅτινα πεσόντα κ.τ.λ. ; and the text of S was the same so far, but the remainder of the sentence is translated as if for ξηρὰ καὶ γυμνά it had read ξηράν.

XXV.

p. 95 note. The passage of Job xxix. 18, in relation to the phœnix, is the subject of a paper by Merx in his *Archiv f. Wiss. Forsch. d. Alt. Test.* II. p. 104 sq. (1871). On the Talmudical references see also Lewysohn *Zoologie des Talmuds* p. 352 sq. The passage in the *Assumption of Moses* is discussed by Rönsch in Hilgenfeld's *Zeitschr. f. Wissensch. Theol.* XVII. p. 553 sq., 1874. Rönsch takes the reading *profectio Phœnices*, and explains it of the 'migration from Phœnicia', i. e. Canaan, into Egypt under Jacob. And others also take *fynicis* to mean Phœnicia, explaining it however in different ways. See Hilgenfeld's note to *Mos. Assumpt.* p. 130. In this way the phœnix entirely disappears from the passage. The phœnix is the subject of an elaborate paper by Larcher in the *Mém. de l'Acad. des Inscriptions etc.* I. p. 166 sq. (1815).

p. 96 l. 1 μονογενές] See also *Paradise Lost* v. 272 'A phœnix gaz'd by all, as that *sole* bird, When to enshrine his reliques in the Sun's Bright temple to Ægyptian Thebes he flies'. Why does Milton despatch his bird to Thebes rather than Heliopolis? The statement about the phœnix in *Apost. Const.* v. 7 φασὶ γὰρ ὄρνεόν τι μονογενὲς ὑπάρχειν κ.τ.λ. is evidently founded on this passage of Clement; comp. e. g. εἰ τοίνυν... δι' ἀλόγου ὀρνέου δείκνυται ἡ ἀνάστασις κ.τ.λ. with Clement's language in § 26.

p. 97 l. 2 γενόμενόν τε] γενόμενον δὲ CS.

p. 98 l. 2 τοῦ χρόνου] C; add. *vitæ suæ* S.

p. 98 l. 3 τελευτᾷ] C; add. *in illo* S.

ib. σηπομένης δὲ] S; σηπομένης τε C.

p. 98 l. 4 γεννᾶται] ἐγγεννᾶται CS. The latter translates *nascitur in ea illic.* *ib.* ὅς] C; ὅστις apparently S. *ib.* τετελευτηκότος] τελευτήσαντος C.

p. 98 l. 6 σηκὸν ἐκεῖνον] C; S adds חדריה מן (= κυκλόθεν αὐτοῦ).

p. 98 l. 8 διανύει] So C, in place of the corrupt form διανεύει of A. S translates *migrat volans.*

p. 98 l. 10 πάντων] ἀπάντων C. *ib.* ἐπιπτὰς] S; om. C, obviously owing to the following ἐπί.

p. 98 l. 11 ἱερεῖς] C; add. οἱ τῆς Αἰγύπτου S.

p. 99 l. 13 πεπληρωμένου] S; πληρουμένου C.

XXVI.

p. 99 l. 21 ἐξηγέρθην] καὶ ἐξηγέρθην CS.

p. 99 l. 23 ἀναντλήσασαν] ἀντλήσασαν C. S has *tulit* (*portavit*).

XXVII.

p. 100 l. 1 προσδεδέσθωσαν] S; προσδεχέσθωσαν C.

p. 100 l. 2 ἐν] om. C. *ib.* τῷ δικαίῳ] δικαίῳ (om. τῷ) C, and so apparently S.

p. 100 l. 5 τῷ] om. C. *ib.* τὸ] So apparently S; om. C.

p. 100 l. 8 τὰ πάντα] So probably S; πάντα C.

p. 100 l. 11 ποιήσει] S; ποιῆσαι C.

p. 101 l. 13 οἱ] om. C.

p. 101 l. 14 χειρῶν] S; om. C.

p. 101 l. 15 sq. ἡ ἡμέρα...γνῶσιν] S; om. C.

p. 101 l. 16 ἀναγγέλλει] C; ἀναγγελεῖ S.

p. 101 l. 16 sq. οὐκ εἰσὶν...οὐχὶ] om. C. S transposes λόγοι and λαλιαί, as in the LXX.

p. 101 l. 17 αὐτῶν] S; om. C. The text of S is perhaps corrupted; but, as it stands, it appears as if it had translated ταῖς φωναῖς, בקלא instead of קלא.

XXVIII.

p. 101 l. 18 οὖν] τε (כיח) S; om. C.

p. 101 l. 19 ἀπολείπωμεν] ἀπολίπωμεν C.

p. 101 l. 20 μιαρὰς] S; βλαβερᾶς C. It is accented in this way by Bryennios.

p. 101 l. 22 τῶν μελλόντων κριμάτων] C; τοῦ μέλλοντος κρίματος (דינא דעתיד) S. As *ribui* will not make the difference here, the singular must have been deliberately substituted. See also § 21 (on p. 87 l. 13).

p. 101 l. 24 ποῦ ἀφήξω] C; ποῖ ἀφήξω (apparently) S.

p. 102 l. 2 εἰ ἐκεῖ] ἐκεῖ εἰ CS.   *ib.* ἐκεῖ ἡ δεξιά σου] S ; σὺ ἐκεῖ εἰ C.

p. 102 L 4 ποῖ οὖν] ποῦ οὖν C ; ποῖ (om. οὖν) S.   *ib.* ποῦ ἀποδράσῃ] ποῖ ἀποδράσῃ (or -σει) S apparently ; ποῦ τις ἀποδράσει C.

p. 102 l. 5 τὰ] om. C ; and so S apparently.

XXIX.

p. 103 L 6 οὖν] C ; om. S.

p. 103 l. 9 μέρος] add. ἡμᾶς CS.

p. 103 l. 10 On this passage, Deut. xxxii. 8, see also Bleek *Hebräerbrief* II. p. 229 sq.

p. 104 l. 1 ἐγενήθη] C ; καὶ ἐγενήθη S.

p. 104 l. 5 ἄγια] C ; S has a singular (קדוש), but it may not represent a different reading.

XXX.

p. 104 l. 6 Ἁγίου οὖν μερὶς] Ἅγια οὖν μέρη C, but this destroys the point of the passage. S reads Ἁγία οὖν μερὶς, an intermediate reading : see the introduction p. 245.

p. 105 L 8 τε] S ; om. C.   *ib.* λάγνους] ἀνάγνους CS.
ib. συμπλοκάς] C ; καὶ συμπλοκάς S, which renders συμπλοκάς by *contentiones* (*jurgia*).

p. 105 L 9 μυσεράν μοιχείαν, βδελυκτὴν κ.τ.λ.] μυσεράν (μυσαράν C) τε μοιχείαν καὶ βδελυκτὴν κ.τ.λ. CS.

p. 105 l. 10 Θεός] ὁ Θεὸς C.

p. 105 L 12 ἀπό] S ; om. C.

p. 105 l. 14 καταλαλιᾶς...ἑαυτούς] C ; S translates as if καταλαλιᾶς... ἑαυτῶν, connecting ἀπὸ παντὸς ψιθυρισμοῦ with ἐγκρατευόμενοι.

p. 105 l. 15 καὶ] S ; om. C.

p. 106 L 1 ἢ] εἰ C ; ᾖ (apparently) S, which translates the whole sentence, *Ille qui multum dicit et audit in hac (hoc) quod qui bene loquitur* etc.

p. 106 l. 2 εὐλογημένος] om. C ; while S substitutes γεννητός, thus repeating the word twice, ילי ארי ילי.

p. 106 L 3 ἡμῶν] S ; ὑμῶν C.

p. 106 l. 4 Θεῷ] τῷ Θεῷ C.   *ib.* γάρ] C ; om. S.
p. 106 L 5 ἀγαθῆς] S ; om. C.   *ib.* ἡμῶν] ὑμῶν CS.
p. 106 L 8 ὑπὸ τοῦ Θεοῦ] S ; om. C ; see above p. 228.

p. 106 l. 9 πραΰτης] πραότης C. S transposes ταπεινοφροσύνη and πραΰτης, but this is probably only for the convenience of translation; see above p. 239.

XXXI.

p. 107 l. 14 διὰ πίστεως] S; om. C.

p. 107 l. 16 ἡδέως] C; καὶ ἡδέως S, if indeed it be not an accidental error of some Syriac transcriber. *ib.* ἐγένετο] προσήγετο CS.

XXXII.

p. 107 l. 20 Ἐάν] This was accepted by Tisch. and Gebh. (ed. 1) in place of εἰ read by previous editors, and is confirmed by C, which reads *Ὁ ἄν. This appears to be a corruption, though accepted by Bryennios and subsequent editors. S has *quæ si* as if ἃ ἐάν.

In my lower note 'conjunctive' should be read for 'conjunction'.

p. 107 l. 21 τά] om. C.

p. 107 l. 22 αὐτοῦ] S; αὐτῶν C, with A. *ib.* ἱερεῖς] οἱ ἱερεῖς C. *ib.* τε] om. CS.

p. 108 l. 3 κατά] C; οἱ κατά S, a repetition of the last syllable of ἡγούμενοι. In Iren. *Fragm.* 17 (Stieren, p. 836) a double descent is ascribed to our Lord, ἐκ δὲ τοῦ Λευὶ καὶ τοῦ Ἰούδα τὸ κατὰ σάρκα, ὡς βασιλεὺς καὶ ἱερεύς, ἐγεννήθη.

p. 108 l. 4 δέ] τε CS. *ib.* αὐτοῦ] S; om. C.

p. 108 l. 5 δόξῃ] S; τάξει C. *ib.* τοῦ] om. C.

p. 108 l. 9 αὐτοῦ] C; τοῦ Θεοῦ S. *ib.* καὶ ἡμεῖς...θελήματος αὐτοῦ] S; om. C, obviously owing to the homœoteleuton.

p. 109 l. 14 πάντας] ἅπαντας C.

p. 109 l. 15 τῶν αἰώνων] S; om. C. See also below on p. 141 l. 20.

XXXIII.

p. 109 l. 16 Τί οὖν ποιήσωμεν, ἀδελφοί] S; Τί οὖν ἐροῦμεν, ἀγαπητοί C. This variation is obviously suggested by S. Paul's language in Rom. vi. 1, where the argument is the same: see above p. 227.

ib. ἀργήσωμεν] ἀργήσομεν C.

p. 109 l. 17 καί] S; om. C. *ib.* ἐγκαταλείπωμεν] καταλίπομεν C. The reading of S is doubtful.

p. 109 note. For 'S. Paul and S. John' read 'S. Paul and S. James'. Mai (*Script. Vet. Nov. Coll.* vii. p. 84) in his extracts from Leontii et Johannis *Rer. Sacr. Lib.* ii, after giving an extract ascribed to Clement of Rome (printed p. 213 of my edition), says in a note 'Et quidem in codice exstat locus ex 1 ad Cor. cap. 33, quem exscribere supersedeo' etc. This language led me (pp. 10, 109) without hesitation to ascribe the quotation from § 33 also to this work of Leontius and John, as Hilgenfeld had done before me. To this Harnack takes exception (p. lxxiii), stating that the extract in question occurs 'in libro quodam *incerti auctoris* (sine jure conjecerunt Hilgf. et Lightf. in *Leontii et Ioannis* Sacr. Rer. lib.)'. He seems to have interpreted Mai's ' in codice' not, as it naturally would be interpreted, 'in *the* manuscript', but 'in *a* manuscript'. Accordingly elsewhere (p. 117) he quotes Dressel's words 'Melius profecto fuisset, si ipsum locum exscripsisset [Maius] aut Msti numerum indicasset. Codicem adhuc quaero', and adds 'Virum summe reverendum Vercellone(†), qui rogatu Dresselii schedulas Angeli Maii summa cum diligentia perquisivit, nihil de hoc capite invenisse, Dresselius mecum Romae mens. April. ann. 1874 communicavit'. Not satisfied with this, I wrote to my very kind friend Signor Ignazio Guidi in Rome, asking him to look at the MS of Leontius and John and see if the extract were not there. There was some difficulty in finding the MS, as it was brought to the Vatican from Grotta Ferrata after the alphabetical catalogue was far advanced, and is not included therein; but through the intervention of Prof. Cozza it was at length found. As I expected, the extract is there. Signor Guidi, whom I sincerely thank for all the trouble which he has taken on my behalf in this as in other matters, sends me the following transcript.

Cod. Grœc. Vat. 1553. f. 22

τοῦ ἁγίου κλήμεντος ῥώμης ἐκ τῆς πρὸς κορινθίους ἐπιστολῆς.

αὐτὸς γὰρ ὁ δημιουργὸς καὶ δεσπότης τῶν ἀπάντων ἐπὶ τοῖς ἔργοις αὐτοῦ ἀγάλλεται τῷ γὰρ παμμεγεστάτῳ (*sic*) αὐτοῦ κράτει οὐρανοὺς ἐστήριξεν καὶ τῇ ἀκαταλήπτῳ αὐτοῦ συνέσει διεκόσμησεν αὐτούς· γῆν δὲ διεχώρισεν ἀπὸ τοῦ περιέχοντος αὐτὴν ὕδατος καὶ ἔδρασεν (*sic*) ἐπὶ τὸν ἀσφαλῆ τοῦ ἰδίου θελήματος θεμέλιον· ἐπὶ τούτοις τὸν ἐξοτατον (*sic*) καὶ παμμεγέθη ἄνθρωπον ταῖς ἰδίαις αὐτοῦ καὶ ἀμώμοις χερσὶν ἔπλασεν τῆς ἑαυτοῦ εἰκόνος χαρακτῆρα· οὕτως γάρ φησιν ὁ θεὸς ποιήσωμεν ἄνθρωπον κατ᾽ εἰκόνα καὶ καθ᾽ ὁμοίωσιν ἡμετέραν· καὶ ἐποίησεν ὁ θεὸς τὸν ἄνθρωπον ἄρσεν καὶ θῆλυ ἐποίησεν αὐτούς· ταῦτα οὖν πάντα τελειώσας ἐπαίνεσεν (*sic*) αὐτὰ καὶ εὐλόγησεν καὶ εἶπεν αὐξάνεσθε καὶ πληθύνεσθε.

τοῦ αὐτοῦ ἐκ τῆς θ̄ ἐπιστολῆς

ἵνα καὶ γενώμεθα κ.τ.λ. (as printed above p. 213).

It will be seen by a comparison of this quotation in Leontius and John from § 33 with the same passage as quoted by John of Damascus, that the latter cannot have taken it directly from Clement but must have derived it from these earlier collectors of extracts.

p. 110 l. 1 ἐφ᾽ ἡμῖν γε γενηθῆναι] ἐφ᾽ ἡμῖν γενηθῆναι CS. In a former passage (see above on p. 91 l. 15) we have seen the same phenomenon, though the relations of A and C are there reversed, A omitting and C inserting γε. The γε is required here.

p. 110 l. 4 δημιουργὸς κ.τ.λ.] So *Clem. Hom.* xvii. 8 πάντων δημιουργὸν καὶ δεσπότην ὄντα. This is not the only passage where the author of the Clementine Homilies betrays the influence of the genuine Clement: see pp. 10, 61.

p. 110 l. 5 ἀγαλλιᾶται] ἀγάλλεται C, and so Leont., Damasc.

p. 110 l. 6 τῇ] Leont., Damasc.; ἐν τῇ C. S is doubtful.

p. 110 l. 10 ἑαυτοῦ] S ; ἑαυτῶν C.   *ib.* διατάξει] I ventured to substitute this for the προστάξει of previous editors. It was accepted by Gebhardt, and is found in C. S has *mandato*, which doubtless represents διατάξει.

p. 111 l. 11 θάλασσάν τε καὶ] θάλασσαν καὶ CS.   *ib.* προδημιουργήσας] προετοιμάσας CS.

p. 111 l. 12 τὸ ἐξοχώτατον...ἄνθρωπον] So also C, except that it has παμμεγεθέστατον for παμμέγεθες (see above p. 228). On the other hand Leont., Damasc., S read τὸν ἐξοχώτατον (ἐξότατον Leont. MS) καὶ παμμεγέθη ἄνθρωπον, omitting κατὰ διάνοιαν. Evidently these two words were a stumbling-block.

p. 111 l. 15 οὕτως] Leont., Damasc.; οὕτω C.

p. 111 l. 19 εἴδομεν] ἴδωμεν CS.   *ib.* †τοτ] In my note I suggested the omission of this word, and Gebhardt accordingly omitted it. It is wanting in CS.

p. 111 l. 20 ἐκοσμήθησαν] C ; ἐκοιμήθησαν S.

p. 112 l. 1 οὖν] δὲ CS.   *ib.* ἔργοις] add. ἀγαθοῖς CS.

p. 112 l. 3 ἐξ] καὶ ἐξ CS.   *ib.* ἰσχύος] τῆς ἰσχύος C.

XXXIV.

p. 112 l. 6 ὁ νωθρὸς] C ; ὁ δὲ νωθρὸς S.

p. 112 l. 7 ἀντοφθαλμεῖν] Comp. ἀντομματεῖν *Apost. Const.* vi. 2.

p. 112 l. 8 ἡμᾶς] C ; ὑμᾶς S.

p. 112 l. 9 ἐξ αὐτοῦ] C. S translates as if it referred to προθύμους ὑμᾶς εἶναι εἰς ἀγαθοποιίαν.

p. 112 l. 10 ὁ Κύριος] Κύριος (om. ὁ) C.

p. 113 l. 12 ἐξ ὅλης] CS insert πιστεύοντας before these words. The insertion simplifies the construction and is doubtless correct; see above p. 226.   *ib.* †μήτετ] μηδὲ C, and so probably S; as it is pointed out in my note that usage requires.

p. 113 l. 18 παρειστήκεισαν...ἐλειτούργουν] C ; but S translates them as presents.

p. 113 l. 20 κτίσις] S ; γῆ C.

p. 113 l. 21 τῇ συνειδήσει] translated in S *in una conscientia*. On the meaning of συνείδησις here, see above, p. 404.

p. 114 l. 2 ὀφθαλμὸς] ἃ ὀφθαλμὸς CS, as in 1 Cor. ii. 9.

p. 114 l. 3 ὅσα] C; om. S. *ib.* ἡτοίμασεν] add. Κύριος CS. In 1 Cor. ii. 9 it is ὁ Θεὸς. *ib.* τοῖς ὑπομένουσιν] τοῖς ἀγαπῶσιν CS; obviously from 1 Cor. ii. 9. It is clear on the other hand, that Clement read τοῖς ὑπομένουσιν from the words which follow at the beginning of the next chapter, τίνα οὖν ἄρα ἐστὶν τὰ ἑτοιμαζόμενα τοῖς ὑπομένουσιν; see below on p. 144 l. 3. For the expedient of S to reestablish the connexion which has thus been severed by the substitution of a different word, see below on p. 116 l. 5.

XXXV.

p. 115 l. 8 ὑπέπιπτεν πάντα] ὑποπίπτει πάντα C; ὑποπίπτοντα S, some letters having dropped out, ΥΠΟΠΙΠΤΕ[ΙΠΑ]ΝΤΑ.

p. 116 l. 2 sq. καὶ πατὴρ τῶν αἰώνων ὁ πανάγιος] S; τῶν αἰώνων καὶ πατὴρ πανάγιος C.

p. 116 l. 3 πανάγιος] Mr Bensly has pointed out to me that the word occurs in 4 Macc. vii. 4, xiv. 7, a work which is supposed to be earlier by a few years than Clement's epistle.

p. 116 l. 5 ὑπομενόντων] C; add. καὶ ἀγαπώντων S, obviously in order to bring the statement into connexion with the altered form of quotation adopted at the end of the preceding chapter, τοῖς ἀγαπῶσιν αὐτὸν for τοῖς ὑπομένουσιν αὐτόν. *ib.* αὐτόν] om. CS.

p. 116 l. 6 τῶν ἐπηγγελμένων δωρεῶν] τῶν δωρεῶν τῶν ἐπηγγελμένων C, and so probably S.

p. 116 l. 7 ἀγαπητοί] C; om. S. *ib.* ᾖ ᾖ] ἦ (om. ᾖ) C. *ib.* διὰ πίστεως] διὰ being absent from A and supplied by the editors generally after Young. This is confirmed by S, which has *per fidem*. On the other hand C reads simply πιστῶς, which was Hilgenfeld's emendation; but it must be regarded merely as a scribe's correction of πίστεως after the διὰ had disappeared; see above, p. 245.

p. 116 l. 8 ἐκζητῶμεν] ἐκζητήσωμεν C. *ib.* τὰ εὐάρεστα καὶ εὐπρόσδεκτα αὐτῷ] S; τὰ ἀγαθὰ καὶ εὐάρεστα αὐτῷ καὶ εὐπρόσδεκτα C.

p. 117 l. 12 ἀνομίαν] πονηρίαν CS. *ib.* πλεονεξίαν] S; om. C.

p. 117 l. 13 ὑπερηφανίαν τε] C; καὶ ὑπερηφανίαν S.

p. 117 l. 14 ἀφιλοξενίαν] the reading of CS. The duty of φιλοξενία was the subject of a special treatise by Melito, Euseb. *H. E.* iv. 26.

p. 117 l. 18 διηγῇ] ἐκδιηγῇ C. This is a various reading in the LXX also. S is doubtful.

p. 117 l. 19 ἐπὶ] διὰ CS.

p. 117 l. 20 σὺ δὲ...p. 118 l. 2 ὁ ῥυόμενος] om. C. After the omission comes καὶ ἐν τῷ τέλει θυσία αἰνέσεως κ.τ.λ.

p. 117 l. 22 ἐπλεόνασεν] ἐπλεόναζεν S.

p. 117 l. 26 ἄνομε] ἀνομίαν S, a various reading in the LXX.

p. 118 l. 1 παραστήσω σε κατὰ πρόσωπόν σου] παραστήσω κατὰ πρόσωπόν σου τὰς ἁμαρτίας σου S, a various reading in the LXX; see p. 244.

p. 118 l. 4 ᾗ] ἦν CS, and so some MSS of the LXX. *ib.* αὐτῷ] C; αὐτοῖς S. *ib.* τοῦ Θεοῦ] S; μου C.

p. 118 l. 8 τούτου] C; τοῦτο S, and so ll. 9, 10, but not ll. 11, 13. *ib.* ἀτενίσωμεν] ἀτενίζομεν C; *contemplemur* (or *contemplabimur*) S.

p. 118 l. 9 ἐνοπτριζόμεθα] C; *videamus* (or *videbimus*) *tanquam in speculo* S.

XXXVI.

p. 119 l. 10 ἠνεώχθησαν] ἀνεώχθησαν C.

p. 119 l. 12 θαυμαστὸν] C; om. S, with Clem. Alex. See the note on § 59, p. 286 above. Comp. also Clem. Alex. *Pæd.* i. 6 (p. 117) πρὸς τὸ ἀΐδιον ἀνατρέχομεν φῶς. *ib.* αὐτοῦ] om. CS, with Clem. Alex.

p. 119 l. 13 τῆς ἀθανάτου γνώσεως] C; but S translates *mortis scientiæ*, i.e. θανάτου γνώσεως, where τῆς has been absorbed in the final syllable of the preceding δεσπότης and θανάτου is written for ἀθανάτου. For an instance of θάνατος for ἀθάνατος see [Clem. Rom.] ii. § 19 (p. 339), and conversely of ἀθάνατος for θάνατος, Ign. *Eph.* 7.

p. 119 l. 15 ὅσῳ] The reading of A is οσω, not οσῶ (= οσων), as I have incorrectly stated.

p. 119 l. 16 ὄνομα κεκληρονόμηκεν] κεκληρονόμηκεν ὄνομα C, as in Heb. i. 4.

p. 119 l. 18 πυρὸς φλόγα] φλόγα πυρὸς C, as e.g. Rev. ii. 18; for here C departs from the text of Heb. i. 7, which has πυρὸς φλόγα.

XXXVII.

p. 121 l. 11 εὐεικτικῶς] ἑκτικῶς C; *leniter* (*placide*) רביבאית S. The word ἑκτικῶς means 'habitually', and so 'familiarly', 'easily', 'readily' (i.e. 'as a matter of habit'); comp. Epict. *Diss.* iii. 24. 78 συλλογισμοὺς ἵν' ἀναλύσῃς ἑκτικώτερον, Plut. *Mor.* 802 F ἑκτικῶς ἢ τεχνικῶς ἢ διαιρετικῶς, Porph. *de Abst.* iv. 20 τὸ αἴτιον τοῦ συμμένειν εἴποις ἂν καὶ τοῦ ἑκτικῶς διαμένειν, Diod. Sic. iii. 4 μελέτῃ πολυχρονίῳ καὶ μνήμῃ γυμνάζοντες τὰς ψυχάς ἑκτικῶς ἕκαστα τῶν γεγραμμένων ἀναγινώσκουσι, i.e. 'fluently' (where he is speaking of reading the hieroglyphics). So here, if the reading be correct, it will mean 'as a matter of course', 'promptly', 'readily'. The adjective is used in the same sense, e.g. Epict. *Diss.* ii. 18. 4 εἴ τι ποιεῖν ἐθέλεις ἑκτικόν.

The reading of C confirms my account of A as against Tischendorf's, though he still adhered to his first opinion after my remarks. There can be little doubt now, I think, that it has εγέκτικ[ως] as described in my note, and not εγέκτω[c] as read by Tisch.; for the latter has no relation to the ἐκτικῶς of C. The εγ (altered from ει, as it was first written) must be explained by the preceding εγ of εὐτάκτως catching the scribe's eye as he was forming the initial letters of either εκτικως or ει+τικως. He had written as far as ει, and at this point he was misled by the same conjunction of letters πωσεγ just before. Whether this ει was the beginning of εικτικως, or an incomplete εκ as the beginning of εκτικως, may be doubtful. In the latter case we must suppose that the second ι, written above the line, was a deliberate (and perhaps later) emendation to get a word with an adequate sense; but on the whole it seems more probable that he had εικτικως in his copy, and not εκτικως as read in C. If so, ἐικτικῶς has the higher claim to be regarded as the word used by Clement. It is difficult to say whether the rendering in S represents εἰκτικῶς or ἐκτικῶς. In the Peshito Luke vii. 25 רביכא stands for μαλακός, and in the Harclean Mark xiii. 28 for ἁπαλός. Thus it seems slightly nearer to εἰκτικῶς than to ἐκτικῶς. The word εἰκτικός occurs Orig. de Princ. iii. 15 (I. p. 124), and occasionally elsewhere. On these adjectives in -ικός see Lobeck Phryn. p. 228.

p. 121 l. 12 ἐπιτελοῦσιν] τελοῦσι C. The reading of S is doubtful.

ib. οὐ πάντες κ.τ.λ.] Comp. Senec. De Tranq. An. 4 'Quid si militare nolis nisi imperator aut tribunus? etiamsi alii primam frontem tenebunt, te sors inter triarios posuerit, inde voce, adhortatione, exemplo, animo milita'.

p. 121 l. 13 ἔπαρχοι] C; S adopts the Greek word ὕπαρχοι, but it perhaps does not imply any variation in the Greek text.

p. 121 l. 15 ἐπιτασσόμενα] ὑποτασσόμενα C. The converse error appears in the MS of Ign. Ephes. 2 ἐπιτασσόμενοι for ὑποτασσόμενοι.

p. 122 l. 3 οὐδέν ἐστιν] So probably S; ἐστιν οὐδέν C.

p. 122 l. 5 συνπνεῖ] συμπνεῖ C.

p. 122 l. 6 χρῆται] χρᾶται C; see the note on p. 195 l. 21 in these Addenda (below, p. 452).

XXXVIII.

p. 122 l. 9 Ἰησοῦ] om. CS.

p. 122 l. 10 καὶ] om. CS.

p. 122 l. 11 μὴ ἀτημελείτω] where A has ΜΗΤΜΜΕΛΕΙΤΩ. CS read τημελείτω, omitting the μή. Obviously the a of ἀτημελείτω had already disappeared in their mss, as it has in A, and they are obliged to strike out the counterbalancing negative μή in order to restore the sense; see above, p. 245.

p. 122 l. 11 sq. ἐντρεπέτω] ἐντρεπέσθω C. This is demanded by the sense. The active ἐντρεπέτω, as read in A, cannot have the meaning 'reverence', which is required here. I cannot explain how I over-looked this very necessary correction. It is no excuse that all the editors before and after me, apparently without exception, were equally guilty with myself. Yet Gebhardt (ed. 2) still retains the solœcistic ἐντρεπέτω.

p. 123 l. 15 sq. ἐν ἔργοις] ἔργοις C, thus omitting the preposition in the second clause, while conversely Clem. Alex. omits it in the first and retains it in the second. S has it in both; but no stress can be laid on the fact, since the translator frequently repeats the preposition when it does not recur in the Greek: see above, p. 239 sq.

p. 123 l. 16 ταπεινοφρονῶν] and so probably S; ταπεινόφρων C, as also Clem. Alex. See above, on p. 81 l. 29.

p. 123 l. 17 ὑφ' ἑτέρου ἑαυτόν] ἑαυτὸν ὑφ' ἑτέρου C. S translates the sentence sed ab aliis testimonium detur (μαρτυρείσθω) super ipso.

p. 123 l. 18 ἔστω καί] Laurent in his edition substitutes ἤτω καί which is an improvement on his first suggestion, since ἤτω is better adapted to the space, besides being the form of the imperative found elsewhere in Clement, § 48. CS omit the words altogether reading ὁ ἁγνὸς ἐν τῇ σαρκὶ μὴ ἀλαζονευέσθω, as does Clem. Alex.: see above, p. 245. Here again the corrector's hand is manifest; see my note, p. 123. Dr Hort would read στήτω καί, comparing 1 Cor. vii. 37.

p. 123 l. 21 καὶ τίνες] C; om. S.   ib. εἰσήλθαμεν] εἰσήλθομεν C.

p. 123 l. 22 ὡς ἐκ τοῦ τάφου] ἐκ ποίου τάφου CS; a great improvement.   ib. ὁ ποιήσας] ὁ πλάσας CS.

p. 124 l. 1 τὸν κόσμον] C; hunc mundum S, but it probably does not represent a various reading; see above, p. 339.

p. 124 l. 3 κατὰ πάντα] C; om. S.

XXXIX.

p. 124 l. 6 Ἄφρονες...ἀπαίδευτοι] S; Ἄφρονες καὶ ἀπαίδευτοι καὶ μωροὶ C.

p. 124 l. 11 καθαρὸς] C; חבלא corruptor S; see above p. 243. The translator may perhaps have had φθόρος in his text.   ib. ἔσται] C; ἔστιν S.   ib. ἔναντι] ἐναντίον C.

p. 124 L 12 εἰ] C; ἢ S.

p. 125 L 13 αὐτοῦ] ἑαυτοῦ C.   ib. οὗ] C; om. S.
ib. πιστεύει] C; πιστεύσει S.

p. 125 L 16 ἔπαισεν αὐτούς] C; ἔπεσον αὐτοῦ S; see above, p. 245.
ib. σητὸς τρόπον] Tisch. now accepts my reading of A.

p. 125 L 17 ἔτι] C; om. S.

p. 125 L 20 εἰ] C; ἢ S.   ib. σοι] so probably S; σου C.
ib. ὄψῃ] ὄψει C.

p. 125 L 22 δὲ] C; om. S.   ib. βαλόντας] βάλλοντας C; and
S also has a present.   ib. εὐθέως] εὐθὺς C.

p. 126 L 1 ἐκείνοις ἡτοίμασται] C; ἐκεῖνοι ἡτοίμασαν S. The LXX.
has ἐκεῖνοι συνήγαγον.

XL.

p. 126 L 3 τούτων] C; add. ἀδελφοί S.

p. 127 L 5 ὅσα] C; sicut (ὡς?) S.

p. 128 L 1 ἐπιμελῶς] Of this conjectural insertion of mine Gebh.
says 'fort. recte'. It is wanting however in C, as well as in A. This
is not the only instance where the recurrence of the same letters has
led to an omission in both MSS. The awkwardness created by the
omission of ἐπιμελῶς is remedied in S by omitting also ἐπιτελεῖσθαι
καί; see above, p. 245.

p. 128 L 2 †ἐκέλευσεν†] The obeli and the critical note are wrongly
assigned to this ἐκέλευσεν through inadvertence. They belong to the
previous ἐκέλευσεν (p. 127 L 5), as indeed the tenour of the note
shows. This error is pointed out by Tisch. (*Præf.* p. viii), and
Gebhardt has tacitly transferred my remarks to the proper ἐκέλευσεν.
C has ἐκέλευσε in p. 127 L 5, and this was also the reading of S.
ib. ἀλλ'] ἀλλὰ C.

p. 128 L 3 ὥραις ποῦ τε] C; S translates as if it had read ὥραις τί
που.

p. 128 l. 4 ὑπερτάτῳ] ὑπερτάτη C.   ib. πάντα] This emendation
is accepted by Gebh. C reads πάντα τὰ with A. The omission of τὰ is
confirmed by S.

p. 128 l. 5 ἐν εὐδοκήσει] C; S seems to have taken ἐνευδοκήσει (one
word) as a verb, also reading εἶναι for εἴη, or translating as if it had so
read. The sentence is rendered, *ita ut, quum omnia pie fiant, velit ut
acceptabilia sint voluntati suæ.*   ib. εἴη] add. πάντα C, notwithstanding
the previous πάντα.

p. 128 L 6 προστεταγμένοις] προσταγεῖσι C.

p. 129 L 9 ἀρχιερεῖ] C; ἀρχιερεῦσι S. This alteration is probably due to a misapprehension of a scribe or of the translator, who supposed that the Christian high-priests (bishops) were alluded to.

p. 129 L 10 ὁ τόπος] τόπος [om. ὁ] C. S translates as if it had read ἰδίοις τόποις.

p. 129 L 11 λευΐταις...ἐπίκεινται] C; levitæ in ministeriis propriis ponuntur S.

p. 129 L 12 δέδεται] δέδοται CS.

XLI.

p. 129 L 13 ὑμῶν] ἡμῶν CS.

p. 129 L 14 εὐχαριστείτω] εὐαρεστείτω CS. Though this seems simpler, εὐχαριστείτω is doubtless the right reading; see my note here and comp. § 38, together with Rom. xiv. 6, 1 Cor. xiv. 17. For another instance of the confusion between εὐαρεστεῖν and εὐχαριστεῖν in our authorities see § 62 (p. 297, above).

p. 130 l. 1 μὴ παρεκβαίνων] C; et perficiens S.

p. 130 l. 2 προσφέρονται] C; om. S.

p. 130 l. 3 εὐχῶν] προσευχῶν C. The same v. l. appears in James v. 15, 16, Ign. Ephes. 10, Rom. 9. The tendency is to substitute προσευχή for εὐχή, as being the commoner word.

p. 130 l. 4 πλημμελείας] πλημμελημάτων C. S has a singular. I have omitted to record in my notes the reading of A, πλημμελιασ. ib. μόνῃ] S; om. C, as a pleonasm after ἀλλ' ἤ. For the language here comp. Apost. Const. ii. 25 ἀπὸ τῶν θυσιῶν καὶ ἀπὸ πάσης πλημμελείας καὶ περὶ ἁμαρτιῶν.

p. 131 l. 5 προσφέρεται] C; offeruntur sacrificia S.

p. 131 l. 7 τῶν] C; cæterorum S.

p. 131 l. 8 βουλήσεως] βουλῆς C. The reading of S is uncertain.

p. 132 L 1 πρόστιμον] It should be added that this is a very common word in inscriptions for 'a fine'.

p. 132 L 2 ὅσῳ] C; add. γὰρ S.

XLII.

p. 132 L 4 εὐηγγελίσθησαν] rendered as a transitive evangelizaverunt in S.

p. 132 l. 5 ὁ Χριστός] Χριστός (om. ὁ) C.

p. 132 L 6 ἐξεπέμφθη...ἀπὸ τοῦ Θεοῦ] om. C, owing to the homœo-teleuton. My punctuation of this passage is accepted by Gebhardt and Harnack and by Hilgenfeld (ed. 2), and is confirmed by S. For other instances of the omission of the verb in similar antithetical clauses see Rom. v. 18, 1 Cor. vi. 13, Gal. ii. 9.

p. 132 l. 8 λαβόντες] C; add. οἱ ἀπόστολοι S.

p. 132 l. 10 ἡμῶν] om. C. The reading of S is uncertain: see above, p. 323.

p. 133 l. 13 καθίστανον] καθιστᾶν C.

p. 133 l. 14 τῷ πνεύματι] C; *spiritu sancto* (or rather *sanctos*, for the word has *ribui*) S.

p. 133 l. 16 καινῶς] C; κενῶς S.

p. 133 l. 18 οὕτως] οὕτω C.

XLIII.

p. 134 l. 6 ἐπηκολούθησαν] ἠκολούθησαν C.

p. 134 l. 9 φυλῶν] C; add. πασῶν [τοῦ] Ἰσραὴλ S.

p. 134 l. 12 αὐτὰς] S; αὐτὸς C.   *ib.* τοῖς] ἐν τοῖς C, a repetition of the last syllable of ἐσφράγισεν.

p. 134 l. 15 ὡσαύτως καὶ] So ὁμοίως καὶ Ign. *Ephes.* 16, 19.

p. 135 l. 16 ῥάβδους] C; θύρας S. This must, I think, be the right reading, for it removes a great difficulty: see above, p. 242.

p. 135 l. 19 τὸν] om. C.

p. 135 l. 20 ἐπεδείξατο] ἐπέδειξε C.

p. 135 l. 21 τὰς σφραγῖδας] C; om. S.

p. 135 l. 22 προέφερεν] Tisch. allows that the reading of A may as well be προε... as προς... and accepts my correction προέφερεν. So too did Gebhardt (ed. 1). C has προεῖλε, which with the ν paragogic (προεῖλεν) must be substituted on the ground of evidence, though προαιρεῖν *promere* is not the most natural word. S has *sustulit.*

p. 135 l. 23 τοῦ Ἀαρὼν] approved by Tisch. and accepted by Gebh. (ed. 1). C however reads Ἀαρὼν without the article.

p. 135 l. 25 προέγνω] προῄδει C.

p. 135 l. 27 εἰς τὸ] ὥστε C, and so apparently S. The variation is to be explained by the uncial letters ειϲτο, ωϲτε.

p. 135 l. 28 Θεοῦ] S; Κυρίου C. S translates as if it had read τοῦ μόνου ἀληθινοῦ Θεοῦ.

XLIV.

p. 136 l. 1 ἔσται] C; but S seems to have read ἐστιν.

ib. ἐπὶ] περὶ C, and so apparently S.

p. 136 l. 2 οὖν] C; om. S.

p. 136 l. 4 ἐπιμονὴν] C has ἐπιδομὴν, a reading which, so far as I am aware, has never been suggested before. It can hardly be correct and is probably an attempt to emend ἐπινομήν. S has ובמעעתא על ביקיא יהבו אף הדא איבנא ראן אנשין מנהון *et in medio* (*interim*) *super probatione* (ἐπὶ δοκιμὴν or ἐπὶ δοκιμῇ) *dederunt etiam hoc ita ut si homines ex iis* etc. Hilgenfeld (ed. 2), not knowing the reading of S, conjectured ἐπὶ δοκιμῇ, which he explains καὶ μεταξύ ('jam conditis ecclesiis') ἐπὶ δοκιμῇ ἔδωκαν (τὸ ὄνομα τῆς ἐπισκοπῆς) ὅπως ('hac ratione inducta') κ.τ.λ., adding 'jam ecclesiarum ai ἀπαρχαὶ spiritu probati episcoporum et diaconorum munera susceperunt, post eos sola probationis ratione episcopi constituti sunt'. But notwithstanding the coincidence of this conjecture with S, I do not think that a reading so harsh can possibly stand. I ought to have said that the original author of the emendation ἐπιμονήν, to which I still adhere, is mentioned by Ussher (Ignat. *Epist.* Proleg. p. cxxxvii) who quoting the passage adds this note in his margin; 'ἐπιμονὴν D. Petrus Turnerus[1] hic legit, ut *continuatio* episcopatus ab Apostolis stabilita significetur; quod Athanasiano illi, καὶ βέβαια μένει, bene respondet'. The word ἐπινομὴν is retained by Laurent, who explains it 'adsignatio muneris episcopalis' (a meaning of ἐπινομή which though possible is unsupported, and which even if allowable in itself would be very awkward here); and (in their first edition) by Gebhardt and Harnack, where it is interpreted 'dispositio, præceptum' (a meaning which would be adequate indeed, but which the word could not, I think, possibly have). In ed. 2 however Harnack expresses a belief that the word is corrupt and suggests ἐπιβολήν. Hagemann (*Römische Kirche* p. 684) conjectures ἐπινομίν, 'd. h. wenn diese Form des Accusativs von ἐπινομία nachgewiesen werden könnte'; and Dr Hort quite independently suggests to me 'ἐπινομίδα, or conceivably but improbably ἐπίνομιν, as we have both χάριτα and χάριν, νήστιδα and νῆστιν, κλεῖδα and κλεῖν', and refers to Philo *de Creat. Princ.* 4 (II. p. 363 M) where Deuteronomy is so called [comp. *Quis rer. div.* 33, 51, I. pp. 495, 509]. Donaldson conjectures ἐπίδομα 'an addition' (*Theol. Rev.* Jan. 1877, p. 45), and Lipsius ἐπιτάγην (*Jen. Lit.* 13 Jan. 1877).

ib. δεδώκασιν] ἔδωκαν C.

p. 136 l. 5 κοιμηθῶσιν] τινες κοιμηθῶσιν C, and similarly *homines ex iis* S.   *ib.* ἄνδρες] S; om. C.   These two last are obviously emendations to make the sense smoother.

p. 137 l. 7 ἀνδρῶν] C; add. ἐκλελεγμένους S.

p. 137 l. 10 ἀβαναύσως] ἀβανάσως C.   *ib.* τι] C; om. S.

p. 138 l. 1 τούτους] C; add. οὖν S.

---

[1] Fellow of Merton and Savilian Professor at Oxford († 1651), a man of great and varied learning. He was a friend of Laud's and was ejected from his fellowship and professorship by the Parliamentarians: see Wood's *Athenæ Oxonienses* II. p. 152 (ed. 2).

p. 138 l. 2 ἀποβαλέσθαι] ἀποβάλλεσθαι C: see my note. It is rendered by an active verb in S.

p. 138 l. 3 ἔσται] S; ἐστίν C.

p. 138 l. 5 μακάριοι] C; add. γὰρ S.

p. 139 l. 9 πολιτευομένους] S; πολιτευσαμένους C. ib. ἀμέμπτως] C; om. S, probably from a feeling that it was inappropriate with τετιμημένης.

p. 139 l. 10 τετιμημένης] So too CS. My emendation τετηρημένης was accepted by Gebh. (ed. 1), and indeed it seems to be required notwithstanding the coincidence of our existing authorities. In their 2nd edition however Gebhardt and Harnack return to τετιμημένης, explaining it 'officio quo inculpabiliter ac legitime honorati erant', and supposing that τιμᾶν τινί τι can mean 'aliquid alicui tamquam honorem tribuere'. But the passages quoted by them, which seem to favour this meaning, Pind. Ol. [l. Pyth.] iv. 270 Παιάν τί σοι τιμᾷ φάος, Soph. Ant. 514 ἐκείνῳ δυσσεβῆ τιμᾷς χάριν [comp. also Aj. 675], are highly poetical. Moreover even in these the expression must be referred to the original meaning of τιμᾶν, 'to respect (and so 'to scrupulously observe') a thing for a person' (comp. e.g. Eur. Orest. 828 πατρῴαν τιμῶν χάριν with Soph. Ant. l.c.); and thus they afford no countenance for a passive use τιμᾶσθαί τινι 'to be bestowed as an honour on a person'. The instances of the passive, which are quoted in their note, all make against this interpretation; e.g. Euseb. H. E. x. 4 γεραρᾷ φρονήσει παρὰ Θεοῦ τετιμημένε, Const. Ap. ii. 26 ὁ ἐπίσκοπος...Θεοῦ ἀξίᾳ τετιμημένος. If τετιμημένης can stand at all here, it must mean 'respected', i.e. 'duly discharged'. Hilgenfeld (ed. 2) speaks favourably of τετηρημένης.

XLV.

p. 140 l. 1 περὶ τῶν ἀνηκόντων] My conjecture was approved by Tisch. and accepted by Gebh., and is now confirmed by C. S translates ἔστε as an indicative, and is obliged in consequence to insert a negative with ἀνηκόντων, thus falling into the same trap as the editors. Omit the reference to Ign. Polyc. 7 in the lower note. ib. ἐνκύπτετε] ἐγκεκύφατε C; εἰ [ἐγ]κεκύφατε S. ib. τὰς γραφάς] C; τὰς ἱερὰς γραφὰς S. This is probably taken from § 53 ἐπίστασθε τὰς ἱερὰς γραφάς, ἀγαπητοί, καὶ ἐγκεκύφατε εἰς τὰ λόγια τοῦ Θεοῦ.

p. 140 l. 2 τὰς τοῦ πνεύματος] This emendation, which I proposed somewhat hesitatingly, was adopted by Gebhardt in place of the ῥήσεις πνεύματος of previous editors. It is confirmed to a greater extent than I could have hoped by CS, which have τὰς διὰ τοῦ πνεύματος. It is difficult however to see how there was room for so many letters in the lacuna of A; for the space left for τασδιατου is at most half a letter more than is taken up in the next line by στιουδ, i. e. six letters. Since the lacunæ here are at the beginnings, not (as commonly) at the ends of the lines, there can be no uncertainty about the spaces.

p. 140 l. 4 γέγραπται] γέγραπτο C. ib. πότε εὑρήσετε] approved by Tisch. and adopted by Gebh. (ed. 1). C however has οὐχ εὑρήσετε, which was anticipated by Laurent, and similarly S *non invenitis* (a present tense).

p. 140 l. 7 ὑπὸ παρανόμων] C; ἀλλ' ὑπὸ παρανόμων S. ib. ὑπὸ τῶν] ἀπὸ τῶν C; ἀλλ' ὑπὸ (or ἀπὸ) τῶν S; see above, p. 244.

p. 140 l. 8 μιαρὸν] This emendation was accepted by Gebh., and is confirmed by C. S has μιαρῶν. ib. ἄδικον] C; ἀδίκων S; see above, p. 245. ib. ταῦτα] C; καὶ ταῦτα S.

p. 140 l. 9 εἴπωμεν] εἴποιμεν C; *dicam* (εἴπω) S.

p. 141 l. 13 τοῦ ὑψίστου] C. The present text of S has ܕܡܪܝܐ, τοῦ Κυρίου, but this is doubtless a corruption of ܕܡܪܝܡܐ, τοῦ ὑψίστου.

ib. κατείρχθησαν] καθείρχθησαν C.

p. 141 l. 15 εἰς] S; om. C.

p. 141 l. 17 περιβαλεῖν] So also C. S has simply *jaciant*.

p. 141 l. 20 τῶν αἰώνων] S; om. C. So also above, p. 109 l. 15.

p. 141 l. 22 ἔγγραφοι] This excellent emendation of Laurent is confirmed by C, as might have been predicted. S has *scripti sunt* for ἔγγραφοι ἐγένοντο.

p. 141 l. 23 αὐτῶν] αὐτοῦ CS.

p. 141 l. 24 ἀμήν] C; om. S.

XLVI.

p. 143 l. 8 πόλεμός τε] C; S has the plural (as determined by *ribui*) πόλεμοί τε and adds *et contentiones* ܘܢܨܝܢܐ, which probably represents καὶ μάχαι, since the same word elsewhere stands for μάχαι (e. g. James iv. 1, Pesh., Hcl.; 2 Tim. ii. 23, Tit. iii. 9, Hcl.). The connecting particles in the Greek are favourable to such an addition; but it is suspicious, as being perhaps borrowed from James iv. 1.

p. 143 l. 9 καὶ ἐν πνεῦμα...ἐν Χριστῷ] The construction and punctuation which I have adopted appear in S.

p. 143 l. 10 διέλκομεν] S; διέλκωμεν C.

p. 143 l. 14 Ἰησοῦ τοῦ Κυρίου ἡμῶν] τοῦ Κυρίου ἡμῶν Ἰησοῦ Χριστοῦ CS.

p. 144 l. 1 οὐκ] μὴ C.

p. 144 l. 3 τῶν μικρῶν μου σκανδαλίσαι] C; τῶν ἐκλεκτῶν μου διαστρέψαι S. I have no doubt that S has preserved the right reading; and this for three reasons. (1) This reading is farther from the language of the Canonical Gospels and therefore more likely to have been changed; (2) Clement of Alexandria, *Strom.* iii. 18 (p. 561), so read the passage in the Roman Clement (see my notes p. 144); (3) The word διαστρέψαι explains the sequel τὸ σχίσμα ὑμῶν πολλοὺς διέστρεψεν ('perverted not one, but many'), it being after Clement's manner to take up and comment on a leading word in his quotations; e.g. § 14 ἀνθρώπῳ εἰρηνικῷ followed by § 15 κολληθῶμεν τοῖς μετ' εὐσεβείας εἰρηνευουσιν, § 27 ὧν οὐχὶ ἀκούονται followed by § 28 πάντων οὖν βλεπομένων καὶ ἀκουομένων, § 29 ἐγενήθη μερὶς Κυρίου...ἅγια ἁγίων followed by § 30 Ἁγίου οὖν μερίς, § 30 Θεός...δίδωσιν χάριν followed by οἷς ἡ χάρις ἀπὸ τοῦ Θεοῦ δέδοται, § 34 ὅσα ἡτοίμασεν τοῖς ὑπομένουσιν αὐτόν followed by § 35 τίνα οὖν ἄρα ἐστὶν τὰ ἑτοιμαζόμενα τοῖς ὑπομένουσιν; § 35 ὁδὸς ᾗ δείξω αὐτῷ τὸ σωτήριον τοῦ Θεοῦ followed by § 36 αὕτη ἡ ὁδός...ἐν ᾗ εὕρομεν τὸ σωτήριον ἡμῶν, § 36 ἕως ἂν θῶ τοὺς ἐχθρούς κ.τ.λ. followed by τίνες οὖν οἱ ἐχθροί, § 46 (just above) μετὰ ἀνδρὸς ἀθῴου ἀθῷος ἔσῃ καὶ μετὰ ἐκλεκτοῦ ἐκλεκτὸς ἔσῃ followed by κολληθῶμεν οὖν τοῖς ἀθῴοις... εἰσὶν δὲ οὗτοι ἐκλεκτοὶ τοῦ Θεοῦ, § 48 ἀνοίξατέ μοι πύλας δικαιοσύνης κ.τ.λ. followed by πολλῶν οὖν πυλῶν ἀνεῳγυιῶν ἡ ἐν δικαιοσύνῃ αὕτη ἐστίν, § 50 ὧν ἀφέθησαν αἱ ἀνομίαι κ.τ.λ. followed by § 51 ὅσα οὖν παρεπέσαμεν...ἀξιώσωμεν ἀφεθῆναι ἡμῖν, § 57 κατασκηνώσει ἐπ' ἐλπίδι πεποιθώς followed by § 58 ἵνα κατασκηνώσωμεν πεποιθότες κ.τ.λ. I have collected these examples, because this characteristic determines the readings in three passages of interest (here and §§ 35, 57; comp. also § 51), where there are variations; see above, pp. 283, 428, and below, p. 442.

p. 144 l. 5 ἡμᾶς] S; ὑμᾶς C.

XLVII.

p. 144 l. 7 τὴν ἐπιστολήν] To the instances given in my note add Iren. i. 8. 2 ἐν τῇ πρὸς Κορινθίους (where the Latin specifies 'in prima ad Corinthios epistola'), *ib.* iv. 27. 3 'in epistola quæ est ad Corinthios', Orig. *c. Cels.* i. 63 ἐν τῇ πρὸς Τιμόθεόν φησι, iii. 20 τῇ πρὸς Θεσσαλονικεῖς, Method. *Symp.* iii. 14 (p. 22 Jahn) λαβέτω δὲ μετὰ χειρὸς ὁ βουλόμενος τὴν πρὸς Κορινθίους ἐπιστολήν, Macarius Magnes *Apocr.* iii. 36 (p. 131 Blondel) καὶ ἐν τῇ πρὸς Κορινθίους δὲ ἐπιστολῇ λέγει Περὶ δὲ τῶν παρθένων ἐπιταγὴν Κυρίου οὐκ ἔχω κ.τ.λ., Hieron. *Epist.* lii, 9 (I. p.

264) 'Lége Pauli epistolam ad Corinthios, quomodo diversa membra unum corpus efficiunt', Anast. Sin. *Hodeg*. 12 (p. 97) *ἐκ τῆς πρὸς Κοριν-θίους*.

p. 145 l. 10 αὐτοῦ τε...'Ἀπολλῶ] ἑαυτοῦ καὶ 'Ἀπολλῶ καὶ Κηφᾶ C, thus conforming the order to 1 Cor. i. 12 (comp. iv. 6). S has the same order as A but omits τε in both places. It also repeats the preposition before each word, but no stress can be laid on this : see above, p. 239.

p. 145 l. 11 προσκλίσεις] *divisiones* S ; προσκλήσεις C, and so l. 12 πρόσκλησις, l. 13 προσεκλήθητε. For this itacism see above § 21. The intermediate note in my edition (p. 144) refers to l. 12, not to l. 11, as incorrectly printed.

ib. ἧττον] ἥττονα C, and so apparently S.   *ib.* προσήνεγκεν] ἐπήνεγκε C, and so apparently S.

p. 145 l. 13 μεμαρτυρημένοις] δεδοκιμασμένοις C ; and conversely μεμαρτυρημένῳ for δεδοκιμασμένῳ in l. 14. S agrees with A.

p. 145 l. 14 παρ' αὐτοῖς] S ; παρ' αὐτῶν C.

p. 145 l. 15 περιβαήτου] C ; om. S.

p. 145 l. 16 αἰσχρά, ἀγαπητοί] C ; om. S.

p. 145 l. 17 Χριστῷ] C ; add. Ἰησοῦ S.   *ib.* ἀγωγῆς] S ; ἀγάπης C.

p. 145 l. 18 καὶ] C ; om. S, translating βεβαιοτάτην, as if βεβαιότητα.

p. 146 l. 4 ἡμῶν] S ; ὑμῶν C.

p. 146 l. 5 ἑαυτοῖς δὲ] ἑαυτοῖς τε C ; *et vobis ipsis* S.

XLVIII.

p. 146 l. 9 ἵλεως γενόμενος] γενόμενος ἵλεως C.

ib. ἡμῖν] S ; ὑμῖν C.   *ib.* ἐπὶ τὴν κ.τ.λ.] S translates loosely *restituat nos ad priorem illam modestiam nostram amoris fraternitatis et ad puram illam conversationem*, but this probably does not represent a various reading.

p. 147 l. 10 ἡμῶν] S ; ὑμῶν C.

p. 147 l. 11 ἡμᾶς] S ; ὑμᾶς C.   *ib.* ἀνεῳγυῖα εἰς ζωὴν] εἰς ζωὴν ἀνεῳγυῖα CS.

p. 147 l. 12 αὕτη] ἐστιν αὕτη C, and so apparently S.

ib. ἀνοίξατε] C ; *aperi* S.

p. 147 l. 13 ἐξομολογήσωμαι] ἐξομολογήσομαι C ; S has ἵνα...ἐξομολογήσωμαι with Clem. Alex. See above, p. 245.

p. 147 l. 16 ἤ] C ; but apparently om. S.

p. 148 l. 1 ἤτω...ἀγνός] This passage is read in C in the same way as in A. S has *sit homo (quispiam) fidelis, sit validus, scientiam possideat (possidebit), laboret (laborabit) sapiens in interpretatione verborum, sit purus in operibus.* This represents substantially the same Greek with AC, except that (as Mr Bensly has pointed out to me) ἤτω δύνατος γνῶσιν ἐξειπᾶν, ἤτω σόφος κ.τ.λ. must have been corrupted into ἤτω δύνατος, γνῶσιν ἔξει, πονείτω σόφος. Notwithstanding this combination of authorities, I am disposed to think still that Clem. Alex. has preserved the original reading, for ἐν ἔργοις is much better adapted to γοργός than to ἀγνός.

p. 148 l. 2 γὰρ] S; om. C. *ib.* ὀφείλει] I have omitted to record that A has οφιλει.

p. 148 l. 3 μᾶλλον] connected with δοκεῖ in S. *ib.* τὸ κοινωφελὲς] See *Apost. Const.* vi. 12 συζητοῦντες πρὸς τὸ κοινωφελές.

XLIX.

p. 148 l. 5 ποιησάτω] So it is read in CS. There is a various reading ποιῶμεν, τηρῶμεν (both well supported), in 1. Joh. v. 2.

p. 149 l. 8 ἀρκετὸς] S; om. C. At least so Bryennios gives the reading of C in his note; but, inasmuch as he puts ἀρκετὸς in his text, it is not easy to see where else he got it from, since he supposes that A read ἀρκεῖ ὡς ἔδει.

p. 149 l. 9 ἐστιν. ἀγάπη] ἐστιν ἡ ἀγάπη C. The whole of the preceding passage is disturbed in CS by false punctuation.

p. 149 l. 10 πλῆθος] C; but S translates שׁוּר 'murum'.

p. 150 l. 4 οὐδὲν εὐάρεστόν ἐστιν τῷ Θεῷ] C; *Deo placere nemo potest* S; i. e., as Mr Bensly suggests, οὐδενὶ εὐαρεστεῖν ἐστιν τῷ Θεῷ. Clem. Alex. however reads with AC, except that he omits ἐστιν. *ib.* οὐκ ἔστιν κ.τ.λ.] C; S translates *non est sermo ullus sufficiens ut inveniatur,* thus reading ἐξήγησίς τις and making ἱκανὸς feminine.

p. 150 l. 5 ἡμᾶς] S; ὑμᾶς C.

p. 150 l. 6 ἔδωκεν] δέδωκεν C.

p. 150 l. 7 ὑπὲρ ἡμῶν Ἰησοῦς Χριστὸς] S; Ἰησοῦς Χριστὸς ὑπὲρ ἡμῶν C.

p. 150 l. 9 τῶν ψυχῶν] S; τῆς ψυχῆς C.

L.

p. 151 l. 11 ἡ ἀγάπη] ἀγάπη C. *ib.* αὐτῆς] αὐτοῦ C. S translates *ejusdem (ipsius) perfectionis.* It seems to have had αὐτῆς, and to have made it agree with τελειότητος.

p. 151 l. 12 εἰ μὴ] C; S apparently adds here ἐν ἀγάπῃ καὶ, but the translation of the whole context is confused owing to a false punctuation.

p. 151 l. 13 καταξιώσῃ] S; καταδιώξῃ C. *ib.* δεώμεθα] My reading was approved by Tisch. and adopted by Gebh. It is now

confirmed by CS; the former having δεόμεθα and the latter *supplicemus.*
ib. οὖν] C; add. ἀγαπητοί S.   *ib.* αἰτώμεθα] S; αἰτούμεθα C.

p. 151 l. 14 αὐτοῦ] C τοῦ Θεοῦ S.   *ib.* ζῶμεν] εὑρεθῶμεν CS.

ib. προσκλίσεως] *adhærentia* S; προσκλήσεως C. On this itacism see above, p. 439.

p. 151 l. 15 πᾶσαι] add. ἀπὸ 'Αδάμ CS, with Clem. Alex.

p. 151 l. 16 τῆσδε ἡμέρας] τῆς ἡμέρας τῆσδε C; while Clem. Alex. has τῆσδε τῆς ἡμέρας. The reading of S is indeterminable.

p. 151 l. 17 χῶρον εὐσεβῶν] Lebas and Waddington *Asie Mineure* Inscr. 168 εὐσεβέων χῶρον δέξατο πᾶσι φίλον, *Apost. Const.* viii. 41 χῶρος εὐσεβῶν ἀνειμένος κ.τ.λ.

p. 151 l. 18 οἵ] S; οἱ δὲ C.   *ib.* φανεροὶ ἔσονται] φανερωθήσονται CS, with Clem. Alex.

p. 151 l. 19 τοῦ Χριστοῦ] τοῦ Θεοῦ CS. I have looked again at A, and still think it impossible to decide whether the reading is θ̄ῡ or χ̄ῡ. *ib.* εἰσέλθε] εἰσέλθετε CS.   *ib.* ταμεῖα] ταμεῖα C. I have omitted to record in its proper place the reading of A, ταμια.

p. 152 l. 1 θυμός] ὁ θυμός C.

p. 152 l. 3 μακάριοι] The critical note giving the v. l. of A μακακαριοι should be transferred to the later μακάριοι l. 6. Hilgenfeld erroneously states the v. l. there to be μαμακαριοι, pp. xviii, 56.   *ib.* ἐσμεν] ἦμεν CS, which should probably be adopted.

p. 152 l. 5 ἡμῖν] S; ὑμῖν C.

p. 152 l. 7 οὗ] ᾧ CS. There is the same v. l. in the LXX.

p. 152 l. 10 τοῦ Θεοῦ] Θεοῦ C.

LI.

p. 153 l. 12 παρέβημεν] παρεπέσαμεν καὶ ἐποιήσαμεν CS. The last word indeed, as now read in the MS of S, is ܚܓܒܢ *transgressi sumus;* but the diacritic point has been altered and it was originally ܚܓܒܢ *fecimus.*

But what was the reading of A? The editors have hitherto given παρέβημεν; but the older collators Young and Wotton professed only to see παρε...μεν, and after C was discovered, Gebhardt (ed. 2), observing that nothing was said either by Tischendorf or by myself 'de litera β adhuc conspicua', suggested that the reading of A was not παρέβημεν but παρεπέσαμεν and that the following words καὶ ἐποιήσαμεν were omitted owing to homœoteleuton, for there certainly is not room for them. I believe he is right. Having my attention thus directed to the matter, I looked at the MS again. I could not discern a β but saw traces of a square letter which looked like π followed by a curved letter which might be ε. Not satisfied with my own inspection, I wrote afterwards to Mr E. M. Thompson of the British Museum to obtain his opinion. He read the letters independently exactly as I had done, and says confidently that the reading was παρεπέσαμεν. This reading is favoured by the words which follow καλὸν γὰρ ἀνθρώπῳ ἐξομολογεῖσθαι περὶ τῶν παραπτωμάτων, as also by the loose paraphrase of the younger Clement *Strom.* iv. 18 (p. 614) ἦν δὲ καὶ περιπέσῃ ἄκων τοιαύτῃ τινὶ περιστάσει διὰ τὰς παρεμπτώσεις τοῦ ἀντικειμένου, where περιπέσῃ seems to have been suggested by the association of sounds.

ib. τινος τῶν τοῦ ἀντικειμένου] So also CS. My misgivings therefore as to the reading of A were not justified. Yet notwithstanding the agreement of our authorities I can hardly think the text correct. Gebhardt (ed. 1) read πειρασμῶν for τινος τῶν, an emendation of Davis; but afterwards (ed. 2) he abandoned it for the reading of the MSS.

p. 153 l. 13 †συγγνώμην†] ἀφεθῆναι ἡμῖν CS. Among other suggestions I had proposed ἀφεθῆναι in my notes; comp. § 50 εἰς τὸ ἀφεθῆναι ἡμῖν...γέγραπται γάρ· Μακάριοι ὧν ἀφέθησαν κ.τ.λ. It is entirely after Clement's manner to take up the key word of a quotation and dwell upon it; see the instances collected above, p. 438. There can be no doubt therefore that Tischendorf misread A. Nevertheless he reiterated the statement to which I took exception and said 'Emendatione veteris scripturæ vix opus est [cΥΓ]ΓΝωΜ[ΗΝ]: literarum ΓΝωΜ pars superior in codice superest, quapropter de vera lectione vix dubito. Dubitat vero Lightf. et dicit etc.' He took no notice of my grammatical objection to this construction of ἀξιοῦν. I might have added a further lexical objection; for neither in the LXX nor in the N.T. nor in the Apostolic Fathers are συγγινώσκειν, συγγνώμη, ever said of God. The fact is that the MS is eaten into holes here and nothing can be *read*. The letters can only be conjectured from the indentations left. Mr E. M. Thompson, whom I consulted here again and whose practised eye I should trust much more than my own, gives it as his opinion that cΥΓΓΝωΜΗΝ would not fit into these indentations but that ΑΦΕΘΗΝΑΙΗΜ[ΙΝ] might.

p. 153 l. 14 τῆς στάσεως] στάσεως C.

p. 153 l. 15 τῆς ἐλπίδος] C; *spei nostra* S; but it perhaps does not represent a different Greek text.

p. 153 l. 16 φόβου] C; add. *Dei* S.

p. 153 l. 17 θέλουσιν] C; *cogunt (coarctant)* S.   *ib.* τοὺς πλησίον] C: τοῖς πλησίον S, which also omits δὲ ἑαυτῶν, thus throwing the syntax of the sentence into confusion.

p. 153 l. 22 στασιαζόντων] στασιασάντων C.   *ib.* θεράποντα] S ; ἄνθρωπον C. Moses is called ἄνθρωπος τοῦ Θεοῦ, Deut. xxxiii. 1, Josh. xiv. 6, 1 Chron. xxiii. 14, 2 Chron. xxx. 16, Ezra iii. 2. Familiarity with the phrase (which is especially prominent in Deut. xxxiii. 1 where it prefaces the Song of Moses) would lead to its introduction here. Elsewhere (§ 53) C alters the designation θεράπων τοῦ Θεοῦ in another way. On the other hand θεράπων τοῦ Θεοῦ is itself a common desig-nation of Moses (see the note on § 4, p. 44 sq.); and might well have been substituted for the other expression here. But the combination AS, as against C, must be considered decisive as to the reading.

p. 154 l. 1 κατέβησαν κ.τ.λ.] *Apost. Const.* ii. 27 Δαθὰν καὶ Ἀβειρὼν ζῶντες κατέβησαν εἰς ᾅδου, καὶ ῥάβδος βλαστήσασα κ.τ.λ. (comp. § 43). See also *ib.* vi. 3.

p. 154 l. 2 κατέπιεν] ποιμανεῖ CS. This reading could not have been foreseen. Clement is quoting from Ps. xlviii (xlix). 14 ὡς πρόβατα ἐν ᾅδῃ ἔθεντο, θάνατος ποιμανεῖ αὐτούς.

p. 154 l. 4 Αἰγύπτου] S ; αὐτοῦ C. Perhaps the archetype of C was partially erased here and ran a..υ.του.

p. 154 l. 7 αὐτῶν] after καρδίας C.

p. 154 l. 8 γῇ Αἰγύπτου] Αἰγύπτῳ CS.

p. 154 l. 9 Μωϋσέως] Μωσέως C.

LII.

p. 154 l. 11 οὐδὲν] om. CS.   *ib.* τὸ] τοῦ C. The οὐδὲν has obviously been omitted by carelessness before οὐδενός, and this has necessitated the further change of τὸ into τοῦ ; see above, p. 245.

p. 154 l. 12 αὐτῷ] C ; add. μόνον S.

p. 155 l. 14 sq. κέρατα...εὐφρανθήτωσαν] S ; om. C.

p. 155 l. 16—18 καὶ ἐπικάλεσαι...δοξάσεις με] S ; om. C.

p. 155 l. 17 σου] om. S.

LIII.

p. 155 l. 19 γὰρ] C ; add. ἀδελφοὶ S, omitting ἀγαπητοὶ l. 20; see above, p. 399.   *ib.* καὶ] S ; om. C.

p. 155 l. 21 εἰς] πρὸς C ; ὡς πρὸς (or ὡς εἰς) S.

ib. δέχεσθε] γράφομεν CS. Dr Wright confirms my statement, as against Tisch., that a final ι is visible in A. It is doubtless the last stroke of the ν in ΓΡΑΦΟΜΕΝ.

p. 155 l. 22 ἀναβαίνοντος] ἀναβάντος C. But the reading in A must certainly have been ἀναβαίνοντος. S has a past tense, but on such a point its authority cannot be urged. As usual, C alters the tenses, where they do not seem appropriate: see above, p. 228.

p. 155 l. 23 τεσσεράκοντα] τεσσαράκοντα C, in both places.

p. 156 l. 1 Μωϋσῆ, Μωϋσῆ] Μωσῆ, Μωσῆ C; om. S.

p. 156 l. 2 ἐκ γῆς Αἰγύπτου] C; ἐξ Αἰγύπτου S with the Hebrew.

p. 156 l. 3 ἐποίησαν] C; καὶ ἐποίησαν S. The καὶ appears in B of the LXX. *ib.* χωνεύματα] C; χώνευμα (owing to the absence of *ribui*) S. In the LXX A has χωνευτά, and B χώνευμα.

p. 156 l. 6 λαὸς] ἐστι CS; as in Clem. Alex. *Strom.* iv. 19 (p. 617), where Potter writes 'Clementis Romani editor lacunam inter ἰδοὺ et σκληροτράχηλος supplevit voce λαὸς ex recensione τῶν ὁ [The LXX is ἰδοὺ λαὸς σκληροτράχηλός ἐστιν]. Erat autem Romanus ex Alexandrino potius supplendus: qui, ut superius, ita proculdubio hic etiam Romanum secutus est'. His warning was overlooked by later editors of the Roman Clement. *ib.* ἔασον] C; καὶ ἔασον S. In the LXX A has simply ἔασον and B καὶ νῦν ἔασον.

ib. ἐξολεθρεῦσαι] ἐξολοθρεῦσαι C; ἐξολεθρεύσω (or -λοθρεύσω) apparently S.

p. 157 l. 9 εἶπεν δὲ] καὶ εἶπε CS. *ib.* Μωϋσῆς] If the silence of Bryennios may be trusted, C here adopts this spelling of the name, contrary to its usual practice.

p. 157 l. 10 τὴν ἁμαρτίαν] C; *peccatum hoc* S.

p. 157 l. 11 ὦ μεγάλης] S; μεγάλης (om. ὦ) C. According to the rule of the grammarians the interjections should have been accentuated ὦ...ὦ, not ὦ...ὦ; see Chandler *Greek Accentuation* § 904, p. 246 sq. The editors here vary.

p. 157 l. 12 θεράπων] S; δεσπότης C, i.e. 'as a master', but this does not represent the fact and cannot be right. The reading of C is adopted by Bryennios, but rejected by Gebhardt and Hilgenfeld.

LIV.

p. 157 l. 15 ὑμῖν] S; ἡμῖν C.

p. 157 l. 16 πεπληροφορημένος] So read also in C; S has *plenus* (*impletus*). *ib.* εἰ δι' ἐμὲ κ.τ.λ.] Mr Bensly has pointed out to me that there are several echoes of this passage in John of Ephesus (iv. 13, 48, 60). Perhaps they were got from some such ὑπομνηματισμοὶ as Epiphanius used (see above, p. 157), rather than directly from Clement himself.

p. 158 l. 1 ἐκχωρῶ] C; ἐγὼ ἐκχωρῶ (apparently) S.

p. 158 l. 8 πολιτείαν τοῦ Θεοῦ] τοῦ Θεοῦ πολιτείαν C. Comp. *Mart. Polyc.* 17 τὴν ἀνεπίληπτον αὐτοῦ πολιτείαν.

LV.

p. 158 l. 9 ὑποδείγματα] S (ribui however being omitted); ὑπομνήματα C. It might almost seem as though Origen had this reading, for in the passage quoted in my note (in Ioann. vi. § 36) he speaks of Clement as οὐκ ἀλόγως πιστεύσας ταῖς ἱστορίαις. ib. ἐνέγκωμεν] C; add. vobis S.

p. 158 l. 10 πολλοί...καιροῦ] C; multi reges et magnates e principibus populorum, qui quum tempus afflictionis vel famis alicujus instaret populo S. This is unusually paraphrastic, but perhaps does not represent a various reading. There is however a confusion of λοιμός and λιμός.

p. 159 l. 15 λυτρώσονται] So also C.

p. 159 l. 16 παρέδωκαν] S (apparently); ἐξέδωκαν C.

p. 160 l. 1 τῆς πόλεως] C; urbe sua S.

p. 160 l. 4 δι' ἀγάπην...λαοῦ] C; propter amorem civitatis patrum suorum et propter populum S.

p. 160 l. 5 συγκλεισμῷ] It is to this συγκλεισμῷ and not to the previous occurrence of the word in l. 1 that my critical note should refer.

p. 160 l. 6 ἥττονι] ἥττον CS.

p. 160 l. 7 τὸ δωδεκάφυλον] C; tribum S.

p. 161 l. 9 τῆς ταπεινώσεως] ταπεινώσεως C.

p. 161 l. 10 δεσπότην] om. C, obviously by homœoteleuton. S has spectatorem universi et dominum sæculorum Deum, as if the order had been δεσπότην τῶν αἰώνων Θεόν.

p. 161 l. 11 ἐρύσατο] ἐρρύσατο C. ib. ὦν χάριν ἐκινδύνευσεν] C; ex iis propter quæ erat in periculo S, probably only a mistranslation.

LVI.

p. 161 l. 16 οὕτως] οὕτω C.

p. 161 l. 17 ἢ πρὸς...ἁγίους] C; sive in Deum sive in sanctos S, as if it had read ἢ...ἢ for ἢ...καὶ. ib. τὸν] om. C.

p. 162 l. 4 οὕτως] οὕτω C.

p. 162 l. 8 δίκαιος] S; Κύριος C. ib. ἔλεος] ἔλεον (i.e. ἔλαιον) C; and so also S. This is doubtless the original reading in the LXX, but may have been a scribe's correction in the text of Clement.

p. 162 l. 9 ἁμαρτωλῶν] ἁμαρτωλοῦ C; and so S, but the singular here depends on the absence of ribui.

p. 162 l. 10 ὂν] ὂν ἂν C. There is nothing to represent ἂν in S.

p. 162 l. 11 ἀπαναίνου] C; rejiciat (or rejiciamus) S.

p. 163 l. 14 οὐχ ἅψεται] οὐ μὴ ἅψηται C; non attrectabit S. Both readings are found in different MSS of the LXX.   *ib. ἐν λιμῷ*] C; add. δὲ S.

p. 163 l. 18 οὐ μὴ φοβηθῇς] οὐ μὴ φοβηθήσῃ C. Both these readings again appear in different MSS of the LXX.   *ib. γὰρ*] C; δὲ S.

p. 163 l. 19 εἰρηνεύσει] C: εἰρηνεύει S.   *ib. ἡ δὲ δίαιτα...ἁμάρτῃ*] C; om. S.

p. 163 l. 20 σου] om. C.

p. 163 l. 21 παμβόταvον] παμβήτανον C.

p. 163 l. 22 ἐλεύσῃ] ἐλεύσει C.

p. 163 l. 24 συνκομισθεῖσα] συγκομισθεῖσα C.   *ib. ὅτι*] πόσος CS.

p. 164 l. 1 καὶ γὰρ...νουθετηθῆναι] πατὴρ γὰρ ἀγαθὸς ὢν παιδεύει εἰς τὸ ἐλεηθῆναι CS (the transposition in S, by which διὰ τῆς ὁσίας παιδείας αὐτοῦ is placed before εἰς τὸ ἐλεηθῆναι ἡμᾶς so as to connect it with παιδεύει Θεός, does not probably represent a different reading). Thus Tischendorf is justified in his remark on the common restoration νουθετηθῆναι; 'id vix recte, quum syllabae non ita dirimi solent [i.e. νουθετ|ηθῆναι]. Requiritur potius simile verbum ac στο|ηθῆναι'.

LVII.

p. 164 l. 5 τὰ γόνατα τῆς καρδίας] So Sir C. Hatton to Q. Elizabeth (Froude XI. p. 166) 'I can use no other means of thankfulness than by bowing the knees of my own heart with all humility' etc.

p. 164 l. 7 ἀλάζονα] C; ἀλαζονείαν S.   *ib. γλώσσης*] γλώττης C.

p. 165 l. 9 ἐλλογίμους] add. ὑμᾶς C. S is doubtful.

p. 165 l. 11 ἰδοὺ] C; add. γὰρ S.

p. 165 l. 12 διδάξω] S; διδάξαι C.

p. 165 l. 13 ὑπηκούσατε] C; ὑπηκούετε S.

p. 165 l. 14 ἐμὰς] τὰς ἐμὰς C.

p. 165 l. 16 ἥνίκα] C; si (ἣν) S.

p. 165 l. 17 ὑμῖν ὄλεθρος] C; ὑμῶν ὄλεθρος S.

p. 166 l. 1 παρῇ] C; om. S.

p. 166 l. 2 θλίψις] add. καὶ στενοχωρία C, a familiar combination in S. Paul, Rom. ii. 9, viii. 35. S has *afflictio* (עוצבא) *et angustia* (וצבא) *qua a prælio* (קרבא רמח); where *afflictio* represents θλίψις and *angustia qua a prælio* is probably a paraphrase of πολιορκία. The possible alternative that *angustia qua a prælio* represents στενοχωρία καὶ πολιορκία, treated as a ἓν διὰ δυοῖν, is not so likely, since the usual practice of S is to expand. The space in A will not admit καὶ στενοχωρία, and these words are wanting also in the LXX.

p. 166 l. 4 ζητήσουσιν] C; ζητοῦσιν (?) S.

p. 166 l. 5 τοῦ] om. C.   *ib.* προσίλαντο] Tischendorf accepts my reading of A (for προσιλαντο); and it is confirmed by C which has προσίλοντο (see above p. 229), and by S which translates *elegerunt.*

p. 167 l. 9

(i) The critical grounds on which I gave a place to this quotation of the Pseudo-Justin in the lacuna of the genuine epistle seemed quite sufficient to justify its insertion there. Harnack indeed objected (ed. 1, pp. 155, 177) that the use of γραφαί, applied to prophets and apostles alike, would be an anachronism in the genuine Clement. I did not mean however that the Pseudo-Justin was giving the exact words of the author quoted, but, as Harnack himself says (*Zeitschr. f. Kirchengesch.* i. p. 273), a free paraphrase. The objection therefore was not, I think, valid.

Still constructive criticism has failed here, and Harnack's opinion has proved correct. We have every reason to believe now that we possess the genuine epistle complete, and the passage to which Pseudo-Justin refers is not found there. When the edition of Bryennios appeared, the solution became evident. The newly recovered ending of the so-called Second Epistle presents references to the destruction of the world by fire and to the punishment of the wicked (§ 16 ἔρχεται ἤδη ἡ ἡμέρα τῆς κρίσεως ὡς κλίβανος καιόμενος κ.τ.λ., § 17 τὴν ἡμέραν ἐκείνην λέγει τῆς κρίσεως ὅταν ὄψονται τοὺς ἐν ἡμῖν ἀσεβήσαντας...ὅπως κολάζονται δειναῖς βασάνοις πυρὶ ἀσβέστῳ) which satisfy the allusion of the Pseudo-Justin, as I pointed out in the *Academy* (May 20, 1876). Harnack also (*Zeitschr.* l. c.) takes the same view. But there is no mention of the Sibyl in these passages. How is this difficulty to be met? Harnack would treat the clause containing this mention as parenthetical in accordance with a suggestion of Hilgenfeld (*Nov. Test. ext. Can. Rec.* i. p. xviii, note 1), and would read accordingly; εἰ τῆς παρούσης καταστάσεως τὸ τέλος ἐστὶν ἡ διὰ τοῦ πυρὸς κρίσις τῶν ἀσεβῶν (καθά φασιν αἱ γραφαὶ προφητῶν τε καὶ ἀποστόλων, ἔτι δὲ καὶ τῆς Σιβύλλης), καθώς φησιν ὁ μακάριος Κλήμης ἐν τῇ πρὸς Κορινθίους ἐπιστολῇ κ.τ.λ. But to this solution it appears to me that there are two grave objections. (1) The mode of expression is rendered very awkward, by the suspension of the last clause, when καθὰ and καθὼς are no longer coordinated. (2) As the writer quotes not the exact words, but only the general sense, of the supposed Clement, he must quote him not for his language, but for his *authority.* But the form of the sentence so interpreted makes Clement's authority paramount and subordinates the prophets and apostles to it; 'If Clement is right in saying that the world will be judged by fire as we are told in the writings of the prophets and apostles'. This sense seems to me to be intolerable; and I must therefore fall back upon a suggestion which is given in my notes (p. 166) that for καθώς we should read καὶ καθώς. The omission of καὶ (which was frequently contracted into a single letter χ) before καθώς would be an easy accident, and probably not a few instances could be produced; comp. e.g. Rom. iii. 8, 1 Joh. ii. 18, 27. The testimony of Clement then falls into its proper place, as subordinate to the scriptures of the Old and New Testament, and even to the writings of the SibyL For other instances of the insertion or omission of καὶ before words beginning with κα in our epistle see § 7 [καὶ] καταμάθωμεν, § 8 [καὶ] κάθαροι, § 53 [καὶ] καλῶς; comp. also Gal. iii. 29 [καὶ] κατ' ἐπαγγελίαν, Ign. *Ephes.* 1 [καὶ] κατὰ πίστιν. Hilgenfeld now offers another solution. He postulates a lacuna in the Second Epistle § 10 (see below, p. 458 sq.), where he supposes the language (including the mention of the Sibyl), to which the Pseudo-Justin refers, to have occurred.

p. 168 l. 13

(ii) This quotation in Basil is found in the newly recovered portion of the epistle : see above p. 284, with the remarks in the introduction p. 271 sq. Gebhardt and Harnack (ed. 1, p. 155) did not venture to insert it in this lacuna 'cum multa spuria sub Clementis nomine a patribus allegata esse constet', though in a later place (p. 177) the opinion was expressed 'Nihil impedit quominus hoc fragm. e priore Clementis epistula depromtum esse censeamus'.

The other quotations, which previous editors (including Hilgenfeld ed. 1, p. 61) had assigned to the genuine epistle and which I have assigned to other sources, are not in the newly recovered portion.

LXIV (LVIII).

p. 169 l. 5 Λοιπὸν] This conjecture was accepted by Gebhardt, and is confirmed by CS. S however reads Λοιπὸν δὲ.

p. 169 l. 7 ἡμᾶς] S; ἡμεῖς C.

p. 169 l. 9 μεγαλοπρεπὲς καὶ ἅγιον] C; *sanctum et decens (in) magnitudine et gloriosum* S; see above p. 239.

p. 169 l. 10 φόβον, εἰρήνην, ὑπομονήν] C; καὶ φόβον καὶ εἰρήνην καὶ ὁμόνοιαν καὶ ἀγάπην καὶ ὑπομονήν S. *ib.* μακροθυμίαν] καὶ μακροθυμίαν CS. *ib.* ἐγκρατείαν, ἀγνείαν] C; καὶ ἐγκρατείαν καὶ ἀγνείαν S.

p. 169 l. 11 καὶ σωφροσύνην] S; σωφροσύνην (om. καὶ) C.

p. 169 l. 12 ὀνόματι] C; add. *sancto* S.

p. 170 l. 1 δόξα] C; πᾶσα δόξα S, which omits the following words καὶ μεγαλωσύνη, κράτος, τιμή, καὶ νῦν καὶ. 　　　　ib. καὶ] om. C.

p. 170 l. 2 τιμή] καὶ τιμή C. 　　　　ib. πάντας] C; om. S.

LXV (LIX).

p. 170 l. 5 καὶ Οὐάλεριον] Valerium (om. καὶ) or et Alerium S; but this is doubtless owing to the accidental omission of a ן before ואלריום by a Syrian scribe. 　　　　ib. Βίτωνα] C; om. S. The punctuation of both C and S is faulty here, in separating names which belong to the same person.

In speaking of the rareness of the name Bito, I ought to have restricted the remark to Latin sources, to which my attention was confined. As a Greek name, it is not uncommon, as Harnack has pointed out. Indeed the familiar story of Cleobis and Bito would have occurred to my mind, if I had thought of Greek writers, and prevented the unguarded statement. I find the cognomen Bitus (?) with the same nomen in an inscription at Bostra, Corp. Insc. Lat. III. no. 104, D.M. L. VALERIO. BITO. NATIONE. BESSVS, etc.

p. 170 l. 5 σὺν καὶ] C; σὺν (om. καὶ) S. 　　　　ib. Φορτουνάτῳ] Φουρτουνάτω C; Frutunato S.

p. 170 l. 7 ἐπιποθήτην] ἐπιπόθητον C. 　　　　ib. εἰρήνην καὶ ὁμόνοιαν] C; ὁμόνοιαν καὶ εἰρήνην S.

p. 171 l. 8 ἀπαγγέλλωσιν] ἀπαγγελλωσιν C.

p. 171 l. 12 καὶ δι' αὐτοῦ] S; δι' αὐτοῦ (om. καὶ) C.

ib. τιμή...ἀπὸ τῶν αἰώνων] C; om. S. As the general tendency of S is rather to add than to omit, the omissions in this neighbourhood (more especially in the proper names) suggest that the translator's copy of the Greek was blurred or mutilated in this part. It must be observed however that the omissions of S, here and above § 64 (58), reduce the doxology to Clement's normal type; comp. e.g. §§ 32, 38, 43, 45, 50.

p. 171 l. 13 εἰς] S; καὶ εἰς C.

The Second Epistle.

p. 173 l. 3 sq. On the possibility that the title to the Second Epistle has been cut off see p. 307, note 2.

p. 179 l. 13 sq. Hagemann's opinion is not correctly stated here. He supposes this so-called Second Epistle to be the letter alluded to in Vis. ii. 4, and to have been attached to the Shepherd of Hermas: but he supposes also that both Hermas and Clement were names assumed by the common writer of both documents for the purposes of his fiction.

p. 179 l. 32 sq. The homiletic character of the document is now proved beyond a doubt, see p. 303 sq.; but the points in Grabe's theory which are here controverted receive no countenance from the newly recovered ending of the document. See p. 305, note 1.

p. 185, προc κορινθιογc β. For the title of this work in CS see above pp. 225, 234.

I.

p. 185 l. 1 note. For these Syriac extracts see Wright's *Catal. of Syr. MSS in the Brit. Mus.* pp. 551, 916, 966, 974, 1004, 1013.

p. 185 l. 1 ἡμᾶς] S; ὑμᾶς C.

p. 186 l. 2 ἡμᾶς] S; ὑμᾶς C.

p. 186 l. 4 λαβεῖν] ἀπολαβεῖν C. The reading of S is uncertain, for ܢܣܒ (the word used here) occurs elsewhere indifferently as a rendering of both λαμβάνειν and ἀπολαμβάνειν, e.g. below §§ 8, 9, 11.

p. 186 l. 4 sq. ὡς περὶ] confirmed by CS, as might have been anticipated.

p. 186 l. 5 μικρῶν] C; add. ἁμαρτάνουσιν, καὶ ἡμεῖς S. The difficulty of the article, οἱ ἀκούοντες, is not perhaps sufficient in itself to condemn the text of AC (see § 19 μὴ ἀγανακτῶμεν οἱ ἄσοφοι, which however is not an exact parallel); but S comes to the rescue, showing that some words have been omitted owing to the repetition of the same beginnings, ἁμαρτάνουσιν, ἁμαρτάνομεν.

p. 187 l. 8 καρπὸν] C; add. *offeremus illi* S. This however does not perhaps imply any additional words in the Greek text.

p. 187 l. 9 δὲ] γάρ S; om. C.

p. 188 l. 1 ποῖον οὖν] C; ποῖον S. Thus the reading of A, ποιουν, is intermediate; see above, p. 246.

p. 188 l. 2 αὐτῷ δώσωμεν] δώσομεν αὐτῷ C. This reading disposes of the grammatical difficulty presented by a future conjunctive, δώσωμεν; see Winer *Gramm.* § xiii. p. 89 (ed. Moulton). Of all such future conjunctives however δώσω is perhaps the best supported; see *ib.* § xiv. p. 95.

p. 188 l. 2 πηροί] *caeci* S; πονηροί C.

p. 188 l. 3 καὶ χρυσὸν] χρυσὸν (om. καὶ) CS.

p. 188 l. 5 ἄλλο οὐδὲν] οὐδὲν ἄλλο C; and so apparently S.

ib. ἀμαυρώσιν] C; *tantam obscuritatem* S.

p. 188 l. 8 τῇ αὐτοῦ θελήσει] τῇ θελήσει αὐτοῦ C; *voluntate nostra* S, as if αὐτῶν.

p. 188 L 9 πολλὴν πλάνην] C; *hunc omnem* (=*tantum*=τοσαύτην) *errorem multum* S.

p. 188 l. 10 μηδεμίαν κ.τ.λ.] So also C; and this was evidently the reading of S, though it translates by a finite verb, *et quod ne una quidem spes salutis sit nobis.*

p. 188 L 11 γὰρ] C; δὲ S.

p. 189 L 12 ἐκ μὴ] ἐκ τοῦ μὴ C.

II.

p. 189 L 13 εὐφράνθητι] C; add. γὰρ, λέγει, S. *ib.* ῥῆξον] C; καὶ ῥῆξον S.

p. 189 l. 17 ἡμῶν] C; om. S.

p. 189 l. 18 τὰς προσευχὰς] C; τὰ πρὸς τὰς προσευχὰς (or τὰ πρὸς εὐχὰς, as suggested by Bensly) S. See above, p. 243.

p. 189 l. 19 αἱ ὠδίνουσαι] C; ἡ ὠδίνουσα S.

p. 189 l. 20 ἐγκακῶμεν] ἐκκακῶμεν C.

p. 189 L 22 τοῦ] om. C.

p. 190 l. 1 δὲ] S; om. C.

p. 190 l. 5 οὕτως] οὕτω C. *ib.* Χριστὸς] S; Κύριος C.

III.

p. 190 L 10 καὶ οὐ προσκυνοῦμεν αὐτοῖς] S; om. C. *ib.* ἀλλὰ] C; S translates as if it had read ἔπειτα δὲ ὅτι; see above, p. 244.

p. 190 l. 11 τίς] C; τίς δὲ S.

p. 190 L 12 ἡ πρὸς αὐτὸν] S; τῆς ἀληθείας C: see above p. 229. *ib.* ἡ] C; om. S. *ib.* ἀρνεῖσθαι] add. αὐτὸν C. The testimony of S cannot be alleged in such a case.

p. 190 L 13 ἐνώπιον τῶν ἀνθρώπων] C; om. S. The reading of S is probably correct, the words having been inserted by scribes from a well-known evangelical passage, Luke xii. 9. For a similar instance, where S preserves the true reading, see Clem. Rom. 46 (p. 437 sq., above). Our preacher is in the habit of dropping out words in his quotations, and presenting them in skeleton.

p. 191 L 14 αὐτὸν] S; om. C.

p. 191 l. 15 μου] C; om. S, which adds *etiam ego* (κἀγώ). *ib.* ὁ μισθὸς ἡμῶν] C; *merces magna* S. *ib.* οὖν] om. CS.

p. 191 L 18 αὐτὸν τιμᾶν] C; *debemus invocare* (*vocare*) *eum* S, as if ὀφείλομεν αὐτὸν ἐπικαλεῖσθαι (καλεῖν).

p. 191 L 19 τῆς] om. C. *ib.* διανοίας] C; δυνάμεως S. *ib.* δὲ] γὰρ S; om. C.

p. 191 L 21 αὐτῶν] S; αὐτοῦ C. *ib.* ἔπεστιν] S; ἀπέστην C.

IV.

p. 191 l. 22 οὖν] S; om. C.

p. 191 l. 23 σώσει] C; σώζει S.

p. 191 l. 25 ὁμολογῶμεν] ὁμολογήσωμεν C.

p. 191 l. 26 ἀγαπᾶν] C; add. τοὺς πλησίον ὡς S: see above p. 244.

p. 192 l. 3 τοιούτοις] τούτοις τοῖς C; *his* S.

p. 192 l. 6 ὑμῶν] ἡμῶν CS.

p. 192 l. 7 Κύριος] C; Ἰησοῦς S. *ib.* ἐν τῷ κόλπῳ μου] C; *in uno sinu* S.

V.

p. 193 l. 11 παροικίαν] C; παροιμίαν S.

p. 193 l. 18 ἀποκτέννοντας] ἀποκτένοντας C.

p. 194 l. 3 πυρὸς] C; om. S.

p. 194 l. 6 Χριστοῦ] C; Κυρίου S. *ib.* ἐστιν] C; om. (apparently) S.

p. 194 l. 7 ἀνάπαυσις] ἡ ἀνάπαυσις C.

p. 194 l. 8 τί ... ἐπιτυχεῖν] C; *quid igitur est id quod facit ut attingatis* S. The translator seems to have had ποιῆσαν for ποιήσαντας in his text, and to have wrested the grammar to make sense of it.

p. 194 l. 11 γὰρ τῷ] τῷ γὰρ C. *ib.* ταῦτα] S; αὐτά C.

VI.

p. 194 l. 13 λέγει δὲ] C: λέγει γὰρ καὶ S.

p. 195 l. 14 ἐὰν] C; add. οὖν S.

p. 195 l. 16 τὸν κόσμον ὅλον] τὸν κόσμον (om. ὅλον) C; *omnem hunc mundum* S, but the insertion of *hunc* probably does not imply any different reading from A: see above p. 339.

p. 195 l. 18 καὶ φθοράν] C; om. S.

p. 195 l. 19 τούτοις] C; τοῖς τοιούτοις S. See conversely below on p. 196 l. 2.

p. 195 l. 21 χρᾶσθαι] χρῆσθαι C. For the form in a comp. συγχρᾶσθαι Ignat. *Magn.* 3, παραχρᾶσθαι *Apost. Const.* vi. 10. *ib.* οἰώμεθα] οἰώμεθα CS. S also adds δὲ ἀδελφοί.

p. 195 l. 23 ἀγαθὰ καὶ] ἀγαθὰ τὰ C; om. S. Here probably the reading of C is to be preferred: for (1) It is more forcible in itself: (2) It explains the omission in S.

p. 195 l. 24 γὰρ] S; om. C.

p. 195 l. 25 ἀνάπαυσιν] C; add. *quæ illic* S, as if it had read τὴν ἐκεῖ, but this may be only a translator's gloss. *ib.* ἡμᾶς] C; om. S.

p. 195 l. 27 δὲ] C; γὰρ S.   *ib. ἐν τῷ*] C; τοῦ S.

p. 196 l. 1 Νῶε κ.τ.λ.] The same order of the names appears in *Apost. Const.* ii. 14.

p. 196 l. 2 οἱ τοιοῦτοι] C; οὗτοι S : see conversely above on p. 195 l. 19.   *ib. δίκαιοι*] C; om. S.   *ib. οὐ δύνανται*] after δικαιοσύναις in C; but S has apparently the same order as A.

p. 196 l. 3 αὐτῶν] ἑαυτῶν C. This is also the reading of A, as it is correctly given by Tischendorf.   *ib. ῥύσασθαι τὰ τέκνα*] τὰ τέκνα ῥύσασθαι C.

p. 196 l. 4 αὐτῶν] om. CS.   *ib. βάπτισμα*] C; add. *quod accepimus* S.

p. 196 l. 5 εἰσελευσόμεθα κ.τ.λ.] The more usual meaning of βασίλειον would have a parallel in S. Anselm *Cur Deus homo* ii. 16 'Ut nullus palatium ejus ingrediatur.'

VII.

p. 197 l. 2 οὖν] om. CS.   *ib. μου*] om. C. As S always adds the possessive pronoun where the vocative ἀδελφοί stands alone in the Greek, its testimony is of no value here: see above p. 321.

p. 197 l. 10 καταπλέουσιν] C; *certant* (= ἀγωνίζονται) S, but it probably does not represent a different reading in the Greek. Lower down S translates καταπλεύσωμεν *descendamus in certamen.*

p. 197 l. 11 εἰ μή] C; add. *solum* S.

θέωμεν] So S distinctly, *curramus*, while C follows A in the corrupt reading θῶμεν. Gebhardt, having read θέωμεν in first edition, has returned to θῶμεν in his second, being apparently persuaded by Bryennios. But the argument of Bryennios appears to me to be based on a misconception. He urges that we cannot read θέωμεν on account of the words immediately following, καὶ πολλοὶ εἰς αὐτὸν καταπλεύσωμεν, and he argues ὁ δὲ ἄρτι ἀγωνιζόμενος χρείαν οὐκ ἔχει εἰς τὸν ἀγῶνα κατελθεῖν, as if the reading θέωμεν involved a hysteron-proteron. But in fact this clause introduces an entirely new proposition, of which the stress lies on πολλοί; 'let us not only take part in this race (θέωμεν τὴν ὁδόν), but let us go there *in great numbers* and contend (πολλοὶ καταπλεύσωμεν καὶ ἀγωνισώμεθα).' On the other hand it has not been shown that θεῖναι τὴν ὁδὸν or τὸν ἀγῶνα can be said of the combatants themselves. Bryennios indeed explains it θῶμεν ἑαυτοῖς ἢ προθώμεθα, but this explanation stands self-condemned by the necessity of using either the reflexive pronoun (ἑαυτοῖς) or the middle voice (προθώμεθα) to bring out the sense. The construction which we have here occurs from time to time with θέειν, but is more common with τρέχειν, because the verb itself is more common; e.g. Heb. xii. 1 τρέχωμεν τὸν προκείμενον ἡμῖν ἀγῶνα (see Bleek's note). Polybius (i. 87. 1, xviii. 35. 6) has the proverb τρέχειν τὴν ἐσχάτην.

p. 198 l. 2 καὶ ἀγωνισώμεθα] C; ἀγωνισώμεθα (om. καὶ) S.

p. 198 l. 3 κἂν ἐγγὺς κ.τ.λ.] See Joseph. *B. I.* i. 21. 8 ἆθλα μέγιστα προθεὶς ἐν οἷς οὐ μόνον οἱ νικῶντες ἀλλὰ καὶ οἱ μετ᾽ αὐτοὺς καὶ οἱ τρίτοι τοῦ βασιλικοῦ πλούτου μετελάμβανον. Comp. *Apost. Const.* ii. 14.

p. 198 l. 4 εἰδέναι] add. δὲ CS.   *ib.* ὁ] transposed so as to stand before ἀγωνιζόμενος in C.

p. 198 l. 6 μαστιγωθείς] See Schweighæuser's note on Epictet. *Diss.* iii. 15. 4 (p. 689).

p. 198 l. 7 φθείρας] φθείρων C; so apparently S.

p. 198 l. 8 παθεῖται] πείσεται C.

p. 199 l. 1 τὸ πῦρ αὐτῶν] S; τὸ πῦρ (om. αὐτῶν) C.

VIII.

p. 199 l. 13 ποιῇ] ποιήσῃ C, but the present tense is wanted here. *ib.* καὶ] omitted by CS here and placed before διαστραφῇ, thus altering the sense. There can be no doubt that the more graphic reading of A is correct. The very point of the comparison is that the breakage happens *in the making* (ποιῇ), happens *under the hands* of the potter (ἐν ταῖς χερσὶν αὐτοῦ διαστραφῇ), and not afterwards, as ποιήσῃ...ταῖς χερσὶν αὐτοῦ καὶ διαστραφῇ would imply.   *ib.* ἐν] om. C; S is doubtful.

p. 199 l. 14 ἤ] S; om. C.

p. 199 l. 15 ἀναπλάσσει] ἀναπλάσει C.   *ib.* τοῦ πυρὸς] C; om. S, but see the next note.

p. 199 l. 16 βαλεῖν] C; add. *et comburat id et pereat* (*perdatur*) S. It is not probable however that any corresponding words stood in the Greek text.   *ib.* βοηθήσει] βοηθεῖ CS.   *ib.* οὕτως] οὕτω C.

p. 200 l. 2 ἅ] C; *si quid* S.   *ib.* τῆς] om. C.

p. 200 l. 3 ἕως] *dum* S; ὡς ἔτι C.   *ib.* ἔχομεν καιρὸν] καιρὸν ἔχομεν C.

p. 200 l. 4 μετανοίας] S; om. C.   *ib.* τοῦ κόσμον] C; τῆς σαρκός S.

p. 200 l. 5 ἐξομολογήσασθαι] C; add. *super peccatis* S.

p. 200 l. 6 ποιήσαντες] C; add. οὖν S.

p. 200 l. 7 σάρκα] C; add. ἡμῶν S.

p. 201 l. 14 αἰώνιον] C; om. S, which is probably correct; comp. § 14 τοσαύτην δύναται ἡ σὰρξ αὕτη μεταλαβεῖν ζωὴν κ.τ.λ., § 17 συνηγμένοι ὦμεν ἐπὶ τὴν ζωήν. The epithet may have been inserted from the expression just above, ληψόμεθα ζωὴν αἰώνιον. Similarly in John xx. 31

αἰώνιον is added after ζωὴν by א CD etc., and in 1 Tim. vi. 19 τῆς αἰωνίου ζωῆς (from ver. 12) is substituted for the less usual τῆς ὄντως ζωῆς by several authorities. In Luke x. 25 Marcion read ζωὴν without αἰώνιον (see Tertull. c. Marc. iv. 25), and so one Latin copy.

ib. ἀπολάβωμεν] ἀπολάβητε CS. The licence in the change of persons (τηρήσατε, ἀπολάβωμεν) has offended the transcribers here, though occasionally indulged in even by the best writers in all languages, e. g. Jeremy Taylor *Works* VI. p. 364 'If *they* were all zealous for the doctrines of righteousness, and impatient of sin, in *yourselves* and in the people, it is not to be imagined what a happy nation *we* should be.' See also e.g. Rom. vii. 4 ἐθανατώθητε, καρποφορήσωμεν, viii. 15 ἐλάβετε, κράζομεν, and frequently in S. Paul.

IX.

p. 201 l. 15 τις] C; S translates, as if it had read μηδείς.

ὅτι αὕτη ἡ σάρξ] Comp. Pseudo-Ign. *Tars.* 2 ἕτεροι δὲ [λέγουσιν] ὅτι ἡ σάρξ αὕτη οὐκ ἐγείρεται, καὶ δεῖ ἀπολαυστικὸν βίον ζῆν καὶ μετιέναι. See also Orig. c. Cels. v. 22.

p. 201 l. 16 οὐδὲ] οὔτε C.

p. 202 l. 3 καὶ ἐν τῇ σαρκὶ...ὁ σώσας] *et in carne venit Christus Dominus (noster), unus existens, is qui salvavit* S. This may be explained by the obliteration of some letters, so that ἐλεύσεσθε was read ἐλ...θε, and translated as if ἦλθε.

p. 202 l. 4 εἰ] εἰς CS. The corruption therefore was very early.

p. 202 l. 5 πνεῦμα] S; λόγος C. See above p. 227 for the motive of this change. ib. ἐγένετο] C; add. δὲ S. ib. σάρξ] C; *in carne* S.

p. 202 l. 6 ἐκάλεσεν] C; add. *existens in carne* (ὢν ἐν τῇ σαρκὶ) S, but this may be only a gloss of οὕτως and probably does not represent any additional words in the Greek text. ib. οὕτως] S; καὶ οὕτω C. The transcriber has felt that with the reading εἰς some connecting particle was needed, and has supplied it.

p. 202 l. 7 οὖν] S; om. C.

p. 203 l. 10 τῷ θεραπεύοντι] C; add. *nos* S.

p. 203 l. 13 τὰ ἐν καρδίᾳ] τὰ ἐγκάρδια C; *ea quæ in corde nostrum* S.

p. 203 l. 13 αἰώνιον] om. CS. Comp. *Apost. Const.* iii. 1 τὸν αἰώνιον ἔπαινον.

p. 203 l. 14 ἡμᾶς] C; καὶ ἡμᾶς S.

X.

p. 204 l. 1 ἀδελφοί μου] ἀδελφοί (om. μου) C; ἀδελφοὶ καὶ ἀδελφαί [μου] S. On the uncertainty respecting the pronoun in S in such cases see above, p. 321.

p. 204 l. 4 προδοίπορον] C; *proditorem* (as if προδότην) S. This rendering again may be due to the obliteration of some letters in the word. *ib.* ἀμαρτιῶν] ἀμαρτημάτων C.

p. 204 l. 7 γὰρ] S; δὲ C. *ib.* οὐκ ἔστιν εὑρεῖν ἄνθρωπον] So too C; and this must also have been the reading of S, which translates '*Non est homini (cuiquam) invenire homines illos qui faciunt timorem humanum,*' as if the construction were οὐκ ἔστιν ἄνθρωπον εὑρεῖν (ἐκείνους) οἵτινες κ.τ.λ. But for the Syriac ܡܣܥܪܝܢ '*qui faciunt,*' ought we not to read ܡܥܒܪܝܢ '*qui transeunt,*' thus more closely representing παράγουσι, which however it mistranslates? Lipsius (*Academy* July 9, 1870 : comp. *Jen. Lit.*, 13 Jan. 1877) would read οὐκ ἔστιν εἰρήνη ἀνθρώποις οἵτινες κ.τ.λ. On the theory of Hilgenfeld, who postulates a great lacuna in the MS at this point, see below p. 458.

p. 204 l. 8 προῃρημένοι] προαιρούμεθα C. S translates, as if it had read προαιρούμενοι, which was also conjectured by Bryennios.

p. 204 l. 9 ἀπόλαυσιν] S; ἀνάπαυσιν C.

p. 205 l. 11 ἀπόλαυσις] S; ἀνάπαυσις C.

p. 205 l. 13 ἀνεκτὸν ἦν] C; S translates *erat iis fortasse respiratio*, but this probably does not represent any different Greek.

p. 205 l. 14 δισσὴν κ.τ.λ.] *Apost. Const.* v. 6 καὶ ἑτέροις αἴτιοι ἀπωλείας γενησόμεθα καὶ διπλοτέραν ὑποίσομεν τὴν τίσιν.

XI.

p. 205 l. 17 sq. δουλεύσωμεν διὰ τοῦ μὴ πιστεύειν κ.τ.λ.] δουλεύσωμεν διὰ τὸ μὴ πιστεύειν κ.τ.λ. C; πιστεύσωμεν, διὰ τὸ δεῖν πιστεύειν κ.τ.λ. S.

p. 205 l. 19 ταλαίπωροι] C; *vere* (ἀληθῶς or ὄντως) *miseri* S.

p. 206 l. 2 πάντα] πάλαι CS. *ib.* ἠκούσαμεν] ἠκούομεν CS.

p. 206 l. 3 καὶ] C; om. S. *ib.* ἐπὶ] C; ἀπὸ S.

p. 206 l. 6 μὲν] C; om. S. *ib.* φυλλοροεῖ] φυλλορροεῖ C.

p. 206 l. 7 μετὰ ταῦτα] S; εἶτα C. *ib.* σταφυλῇ] S; βλαστὸς C. *ib.* οὕτως] οὕτω C.

p. 206 l. 8 ὁ λαός μου] C; add. πρῶτον S.

p. 206 l. 10 ἀλλὰ] ἀλλ' C. *ib.* ἵνα] C; om. S; see above, p. 334.

p. 207 l. 15 οὓς οὐκ ἤκουσεν οὐδὲ ὀφθαλμὸς εἶδεν] C; *oculus non vidit et auris non audivit* (transposing the clauses) S. This latter is the order in 1 Cor. iii. 9, and in Clem. Rom. 34.

p. 207 l. 16 εἶδεν] I have omitted to record that A reads ιδεν.

XII.

p. 207 l. 18 ἐπειδή] ἐπεὶ C.

p. 207 l. 19 τοῦ Θεοῦ] C; αὐτοῦ S.   ib. ἐπερωτηθείς] ἐρωτηθεὶς C.

p. 207 l. 20 ὑπό τινος] C; add. τῶν ἀποστόλων S. The addition is unfortunate, for the questioner was Salome; see the note p. 207. ib. ἥξει] C; venit (a present) S.

p. 208 l. 1 sq. τὸ ἔξω ὡς τὸ ἔσω] S; τὰ ἔξω ὡς τὰ ἔσω C.

p. 208 l. 3 δύο δὲ] δὲ δύο C.

p. 208 l. 4 ἑαυτοῖς] C; nobis S, which represents ἑαυτοῖς. ib. δυσί] δύο C.

p. 209 l. 5 τὸ ἔξω ὡς τὸ ἔσω] C; τὸ ἔσω ὡς τὸ ἔξω S.

p. 209 l. 6 τὸ ἔσω, τὸ δὲ ἔξω] S; τὸ ἔξω τὸ δὲ ἔσω C.

p. 209 l. 7 οὕτως] οὕτω C.

p. 209 l. 8 δῆλος] δήλη C.

p. 209 l. 9 θηλείας] I have omitted to record the reading of A, θηλίας.

p. 210, note. The conjecture in this note as to the probable interpretation which our author put on the words τὸ ἄρσεν κ.τ.λ. is not confirmed by the newly recovered ending: see above p. 315.

p. 211, note. Harnack (p. 176, ed. 1) took exception to this calculation of the length of the lost portion, urging rightly that in the *Stichometria* of Nicephorus the verses cannot have been of the same length in the different books. He considered that the Epistle of Barnabas would afford a safer standard of comparison; and arguing on this basis (since 1360 verses are assigned to that epistle) he arrived at the result that the lost portion of the Second Clementine Epistle must have occupied 'unum folium nec quidem completum.' His estimate is now found to be somewhat under the truth, as mine was considerably above it. The lost portion would have taken up about a leaf and a half in the Alexandrian MS.

In the colophon at the end of the Second Epistle in C we have the enumeration στίχοι χ´· ῥητὰ κε´. Since Nicephorus gives the number of στίχοι in the two Clementine Epistles as ͵βχ´, Bryennios supposes that χ´ here is an error for ͵βχ´, the ͵β having dropped out. Hilgenfeld however points to the fact that the ῥητά, or scriptural quotations, are given as 25 in number, and that this must refer to the Second Epistle alone. The quotations in the Second Epistle, when counted up, amount to 25 (one or two more or less, for in a few cases it is difficult

to say whether the quotations would be reckoned separately or not);
but this number is impossible for the two epistles combined. It
follows therefore that the enumeration of 600 verses must refer to the
Second Epistle alone.

I may add that this accords with the reckoning in Nicephorus.
If we subtract the 600 verses from the 2600 which Nicephorus gives
for the two Epistles, 2000 verses are left for the First. Thus the proportion of the First Epistle to the Second will be approximately as
2000 : 600, or as 10 : 3 ; and this is the case, as may be seen from the
relative spaces occupied by the two epistles in my translation, where
they take up 34¼ pages and 10¼ pages respectively, these numbers
being almost exactly in the ratio of 10 : 3.

This statement therefore in the colophon to C seems to have been
taken from some earlier copy which had an enumeration identical with
that of Nicephorus. In the actual text of C however the distribution
of verses is quite different. Here, as Bryennios states (p. 142), the
number reckoned up is 1120, consisting of 853 for the First Epistle
and 267 for the Second.

Of the fragments (i) (ii), which are here assigned to the Second Epistle,
the first (p. 210), occurring in the *Rochefoucauld Extracts* which bear the
name of John of Damascus, is found in § 20 (see above p. 340), though
it proves not to have been quoted very exactly by the Pseudo-Damascene.
The second however, though quoted in the same work explicitly as
τοῦ ἁγίου Κλήμεντος ἐπισκόπου Ῥώμης ἐκ τῆς β΄ πρὸς Κορινθίους ἐπιστολῆς, has no place in the newly recovered ending. What account
can we give of this fact?

Hilgenfeld (ed. 2, pp. xlviii, 77) supposes that there is still a great
lacuna in this work in § 10 οὐκ ἔστιν εὑρεῖν ἄνθρωπον | οἵτινες παράγουσιν
φόβους ἀνθρωπίνους κ.τ.λ. In this lacuna he finds a place not only for
this quotation in the so-called John of Damascus, but also for the
reference to the Sibyl in Pseudo-Justin which I have discussed already
(pp. 308, 447, sq.). This solution however seems highly improbable for
the following reasons.

(1) Though there is good reason for assuming that the existing text
is faulty at this point in § 10 (see pp. 204, 247), the external facts are
altogether adverse to the supposition that a great lacuna exists here,
such for instance as would be produced by the disappearance of one
or more leaves in an archetypal MS. Such an archetypal MS must
have been of very ancient date, for all our three extant authorities
(see above p. 247) have the same text here. It is not indeed impos-

sible that this archetypal MS should have been defective, seeing that
the common progenitor of ACS certainly had minor corruptions.
But though *possible* in itself, this supposition is hardly consistent with
other facts. It is highly improbable that a long passage which had
disappeared thus early, should have been preserved in any MS acces-
sible to the Pseudo-Damascene, or even to the Pseudo-Justin. Moreover the enumeration of verses in the *Stichometria* of Nicephorus, as
will appear from the calculation just given (p. 458), seems to have
been made when the epistle was of its present size, and is not adapted
to a more lengthy document.

(2) Again; though the two fragments which Hilgenfeld would
assign to this lacuna are not incongruous in subject, yet the sentiments
in the extant context on either side of the supposed lacuna are
singularly appropriate to one another, and in this juxtaposition seem to
have been suggested by the language of Ps. xxxiv. 9 sq. quoted in my
note.

(3) I seem to see now that the style of the fragment quoted by
the Pseudo-Damascene betrays a different hand from our author's.
Its vocabulary is more philosophical (καθόλου, τὰ φευκτά, ὑπόθεσις καὶ
ὕλη, τὰ ἄσπαστα, κατ' εὐχήν), and altogether it shows more literary skill.

We must suppose therefore, that the Pseudo-Damascene got his
quotations from some earlier collection of extracts, e.g. the *Res Sacræ*
of Leontius and John (for the titles of the subjects in their works were
much the same as his, and they had the particular title under which
these words are quoted, περὶ τῶν προσκαίρων καὶ αἰωνίων, in common
with him; see Mai *Script. Vet. Nov. Coll.* VII. p. 80: moreover the
true John of Damascus appears to have owed some of his extracts
to this same source; see above p. 426), and that in transferring these
extracts to his own volume he has displaced the reference to Clement,
which belonged to some other extract in the neighbourhood.

Fragments.

p. 213 l. 14. See above, p. 425 sq. This first fragment is not found
in the newly recovered ending of the Second Epistle. For the manner
in which it is quoted by Leontius and John, see above p. 426. It
will there be seen that the heading is not, as Mai (*Script. Vet. Nov.
Coll.* VII. p. 84) gives it, τοῦ ἁγίου Κλήμεντος 'Ρώμης ἐκ τῆς θ' ἐπιστολῆς,

but τοῦ αὐτοῦ ἐκ τῆς θ ἐπιστολῆς. It is true that this follows immediately after a quotation from the genuine epistle headed 'Of Saint Clement of Rome from the Epistle to the Corinthians.' But this indirectness makes all the difference in the value of the attribution. These extracts for instance may have been taken from an earlier collection containing an intermediate passage from some other author, to whom, and not to Clement, τοῦ αὐτοῦ refers. It is probably therefore in some collection of letters written by a later father that this quotation should be sought.

p. 215 l. 1 sq. In giving the passages from the *Clementine Homilies* which correspond to these fragments I have omitted one which has been pointed out to me by a friend, and which is necessary to complete the parallel; iii. 10 εὐγνωμοσύνη δέ ἐστιν τὸ τὴν πρὸς τὸν τοῦ εἶναι ἡμᾶς αἴτιον ἀποσώζειν στοργήν.

p. 218 l 3. In ascribing to Nolte the first discovery of the source of this fragment, I had overlooked Lagarde *Rel. Jur. Eccl. Ant.* p. xli, note. Lagarde however only refers to *Clem. Hom.* iv. 18, omitting any reference to iv. 11, which covers the larger part of the quotation.

p. 218 l. 13. For δεινὴν σύνοικον comp. *Clem. Hom.* i. 2 σύνοικον καλὴν ἔχων ὄνοιαν.

Appendix.

p. 230, note. Lipsius also (*Jen. Lit.*, 13 Jan. 1877) considers A to be superior to C. On the other hand Donaldson agrees with Hilgenfeld's estimate of their relative value so far as regards the First Epistle, but thinks C inferior in the Second (*Theol. Rev.* p. 41).

p. 235 l. 11. Since the earlier sheets of this Appendix were struck off, I have noticed the following account of a Paris MS in the *Catalogues des Manuscrits Syriaques et Sabéens de la Bibliothèque Nationale* (Paris, 1874) p. 19, no. 52.

1. Les quatre Evangiles, dans la version de THOMAS D'HÉRACLÉE ...La note finale, relative à la rédaction de la version héracléenne... est suivie d'une note du copiste, qui dit avoir exécuté ce ms en l'année 1476 des Grecs (1165 de J. C.) dans le monastère de Mar-Salibo de Bêth-Yehidoyê, sur la montagne sainte d'Édesse, au temps de Mar-Jean, metropolitain de cette ville.

2. (Fol. 204 v°.)...'Leçons de la Passion redemptrice prises dans les quatre évangelistes' etc.

Thus it was written only five years before our MS and at the same monastery. These two MSS therefore may be expected to resemble each other closely. Unfortunately the Paris MS does not contain the Acts and Epistles.

p. 255 l. 5. The person who in the vision gives this direction to Hermas is not the Shepherd himself, but the Church.

p. 267, note 3. To these authorities should be added Georgius Syncellus, who seems to have derived his information from some authority not now extant. He says distinctly of Stephanus (p. 650) τῇ πρὸς τὸν δεσπότην εὐνοίᾳ Κλήμεντα ἐνεδρεύσας κ.τ.λ.

p. 270, note 2. Among the prayers which are acknowledged to be the most ancient is the form called either absolutely *Tephillah* 'The Prayer' (תפלה) or (from the number of the benedictions) *Shemoneh Esreh* 'The Eighteen' (שמונה עשרה). They are traditionally ascribed by the Jews to the Great Synagogue; but this tradition is of course valueless, except as implying a relative antiquity. They are mentioned in the Mishna *Berachoth* iv. 3, where certain precepts respecting them are ascribed to Rabban Gamaliel, Rabbi Joshua, and Rabbi Akiba; while from another passage, *Rosh-ha-Shanah* iv. 5, it appears that they then existed in substantially the same form as at present. Thus their high antiquity seems certain; so that the older parts (for they have grown by accretion) were probably in existence in the age of our Lord and the Apostles, and indeed some competent critics have assigned to them a much earlier date than this. Of these eighteen benedictions the first three and the last three are by common consent allowed to be the oldest. On the date of the *Shemoneh Esreh*, see Zunz *Gottesdienstliche Vorträge* p. 366 sq., Herzfeld *Geschichte des Volkes Jisrael* II. p. 200 sq., Ginsburg in Kitto's *Cyclop. of Bibl. Lit.* (ed. Alexander) s. v. *Synagogue.*

I have selected for comparison the first two and the last two; and they are here written out in full with the parallel passages from Clement opposite to them, so as to convey an adequate idea of the amount of resemblance. The third is too short to afford any material for comparison; while the sixteenth, referring to the temple-service, is too purely Jewish, and indeed appears to have been interpolated after the destruction of the second temple.

[The parallels which belong to the other parts of S. Clement's Epistle are in brackets.]

1. Blessed art Thou, O Lord our God, and the God of our fathers, the God of Abraham, the God of Isaac, and the God of Jacob, the God great and powerful and terrible, God Most High, who bestowest Thy benefits graciously, the Possessor of the Universe, who rememberest the good deeds of the fathers and sendest a redeemer unto their sons' sons for Thy Name's Sake in love. Our King, our Helper and Saviour and Shield, blessed art Thou, O Lord, the Shield of Abraham.

[ὁ πατὴρ ἡμῶν Ἀβραὰμ § 31.]
θαυμαστὸς ἐν ἰσχύϊ καὶ μεγαλοπρεπείᾳ § 60. τὸν μόνον ὕψιστον § 59.

μόνον εὐεργέτην κ.τ.λ. ib. [ὁ οἰκτίρμων κατὰ πάντα καὶ εὐεργετικὸς πατὴρ § 23].

σύ, Κύριε, τὴν οἰκουμένην ἔκτισας § 60. [δεσπότης τῶν ἀπάντων §§ 8, 20, 33, 52].

καθὼς ἔδωκας τοῖς πατράσιν ἡμῶν, ἐπικαλουμένων σε αὐτῶν ὁσίως κ.τ.λ. § 60. [καθὼς καὶ οἱ προδεδηλωμένοι πατέρες ἡμῶν εὐηρέστησαν § 62].

βασιλεῦ τῶν αἰώνων § 61.

ἀξιοῦμέν σε, δέσποτα, βοηθὸν γενέσθαι καὶ ἀντιλήπτορα[1] ἡμῶν § 59.

2. Thou art mighty for ever, O Lord; Thou bringest the dead to life, Thou art mighty to save. Thou sustainest the living by Thy mercy, Thou bringest the dead to life by Thy great compassion, Thou supportest them that fall, and healest the sick, and loosest them that are in bonds, and makest good Thy faithfulness to them that sleep in the dust. Who is like unto Thee, O Lord of might? and who can be compared unto Thee, O King, who killest and makest alive, and causest salvation to shoot forth? And Thou art

ὁ μόνος δυνατὸς ποιῆσαι ταῦτα § 61.

τὸν τῶν ἀπηλπισμένων σωτῆρα § 59.

ὁ ἀγαθός...ἐλεῆμον καὶ οἰκτίρμον § 60.

τοὺς πεπτωκότας ἔγειρον...τοὺς ἀσεβεῖς (ἀσθενεῖς) ἴασαι...λύτρωσαι τοὺς δεσμίους ἡμῶν, ἐξανάστησον τοὺς ἀσθενοῦντας § 59.

πιστὸς ἐν τοῖς πεποιθόσιν ἐπὶ σέ § 60.

τοῦ...ἀνεκδιηγήτου κράτους σου § 61.

τὸν ἀποκτείνοντα καὶ ζῆν ποιοῦντα § 59.

---

[1] The word מגן 'shield' is translated by ἀντιλήπτωρ in the LXX of Ps. cxix (cxviii). 114, from which Clement here borrows his expression.

faithful to bring the dead to life. Blessed art Thou, O Lord, who bringest the dead to life.

17. We confess unto Thee that Thou art He, the Lord our God and the God of our fathers for ever and ever, the Rock of our life, the Shield of our salvation, Thou art He from generation to generation. We will thank Thee and declare Thy praise. Blessed art Thou, O Lord; Goodness is Thy Name, and to Thee it is meet to give thanks.

σοὶ ἐξομολογούμεθα § 61.
ὅτι σὺ εἶ ὁ Θεὸς μόνος § 59.

εἰς τὸ σκεπασθῆναι τῇ χειρί σου κ.τ.λ. § 60.
ὁ πιστὸς ἐν πάσαις ταῖς γενεαῖς § 60.

τῷ παναρέτῳ ὀνόματί σου § 60.

18. Grant peace, goodness and blessing, grace and mercy and compassion unto us and to all Thy people Israel. Bless us, O our Father, all together with the light of Thy countenance. Thou hast given unto us, O Lord our God, the law of life, and loving-kindness and righteousness and blessing and compassion and life and peace. And may it seem good in Thy sight to bless Thy people Israel at all times and at every moment with Thy peace. Blessed art Thou, O Lord, who blessest Thy people Israel with peace.

δός, Κύριε, ὑγιείαν, εἰρήνην, ὁμόνοιαν, εὐστάθειαν § 61.
δὸς ὁμόνοιαν καὶ εἰρήνην ἡμῖν τε καὶ πᾶσιν τοῖς κατοικοῦσιν κ.τ.λ. § 60.
ἐπίφανον τὸ πρόσωπόν σου ἐφ' ἡμᾶς εἰς ἀγαθὰ ἐν εἰρήνῃ § 60.
[δῴη πίστιν, φόβον, εἰρήνην, ὑπομόνην, μακροθυμίαν, ἐγκράτειαν, ἁγνείαν καὶ σωφροσύνην § 64].

καλὸν καὶ εὐάρεστον ἐνώπιόν σου § 61.
ἡμεῖς λαός σου § 59.
[ὁ ἐκλεξάμενος...ἡμᾶς...εἰς λαὸν περιούσιον § 58].

These parallels are, I think, highly suggestive, and some others might be gathered from other parts of the *Shemoneh Esreh*: The resemblance however is perhaps greater in the general tenour of the thoughts and cast of the sentences than in the individual expressions. At the same time it is instructive to observe what topics are rejected as too purely Jewish, and what others are introduced to give expression to Christian ideas.

Jacobi (*Theol. Stud. u. Krit.* 1876, iv. p. 710 sq.) doubts whether this liturgical portion was any part of Clement's original letter, and suggests that it was inserted afterwards at Corinth. This theory seems to me quite impossible for many reasons.

(1) In the first place it is contained in both our authorities CS, and obviously was contained in A, before the missing leaf disappeared, as the space shows (see Harnack *Theolog. Literaturz.* Feb. 19, 1876). The combination of these three authorities points to a very early date (see above p. 247). Moreover the writer of the last two books of the *Apostolical Constitutions* obviously borrows indifferently from this prayer and from other parts of Clement's Epistle; and though he might have been indebted to two different sources for his obligations, the probability is that he derived them from the same.

(2) The expedient which Jacobi ascribes to the Corinthians would be extremely clumsy. He supposes that the reading of the letter in the Corinthian Church was followed by congregational prayer, and that, as Clement states it to be the intention of the Romans, if their appeal to the Corinthians should be disregarded, to betake themselves to prayer on behalf of Christendom generally (§ 59), it occurred to the Church at Corinth to interpolate their own form of prayer in the epistle at this point. When we remember that this prayer of Clement is followed immediately by special directions relating to individual persons who are mentioned by name, nothing could well be more incongruous than the gratuitous insertion of a liturgical service here.

(3) Jacobi remarks on the affinity to the type of prayer in the Greek Church. I have shown that the resemblances to pre-existing Jewish prayers are at least as great. Indeed the language is just what we might expect from a writer in the age of Clement, when the liturgy of the Synagogue was developing into the liturgy of the Church.

(4) Jacobi does not conceal a difficulty which occurs to him in the fact that, together with ἀρχιερεύς, the very unusual title προστάτης, 'Guardian' or 'Patron', which is given to our Lord in this prayer (§ 61), is found twice in other parts of the epistle, §§ 36, 58 (64); but he thinks this may have been adopted into the Corinthian form of prayer from Clement. If this had been the only coincidence, his explanation might possibly have been admitted. But in fact this prayer is interpenetrated with the language and thoughts of Clement, so far as the subject allowed and the frequent adoption of Old Testament phrases left room for them. Thus in § 59 for ἐλπίζειν ἐπὶ see §§ 11, 12; again ἀνοίξας τοὺς ὀφθαλμοὺς τῆς καρδίας ἡμῶν has a close parallel in § 36; εὐεργέτην applied to God is matched by εὐεργετεῖν, εὐεργεσία, in the same connexion §§ 19, 20, 21, 38; with the whole expression εὐεργέτην πνευ-

μάτων καὶ Θεὸν πάσης σαρκὸς...τὸν ἐπόπτην ἀνθρωπίνων ἔργων, compare § 58 ὁ παντεπόπτης Θεὸς καὶ δεσπότης τῶν πνευμάτων καὶ Κύριος πάσης σαρκός; for βοηθὸς see § 36; for κτιστής, §§ 19, 62; for ἐκλέγεσθαι, §§ 43, 58 (64), and the use of ἐκλεκτὸς elsewhere in this epistle; for ἀγαπῶντάς σε, § 29; for διὰ I. X. τοῦ ἠγαπημένου παιδός σου, § 59 διὰ τοῦ ἠγαπημένου παιδὸς αὐτοῦ I. X. in the same connexion; for ἀξιοῦμεν of prayer to God, §§ 51, 53, and with an accusative case, as here, § 55; for δεσπότης applied to God, the rest of the epistle *passim*. In § 60 for ἄέναος see § 20; for ὁ πιστὸς κ.τ.λ. compare a very similar expression § 27 τῷ πιστῷ ἐν ταῖς ἐπαγγελίαις καὶ τῷ δικαίῳ ἐν τοῖς κρίμασιν; for θαυμαστὸς, §§ 26, 35, [36], 43, 50; for ἐδράζειν of God's creative agency, § 33; for the repetition of the article τὰς ἀνομίας καὶ τὰς ἀδικίας κ.τ.λ., the rest of the epistle *passim*, and for the connexion of the two words, § 35; for παραπτώματα, §§ 2, 51, 56 (comp. παράπτωσις § 59); for πλημμελείας, § 41; for κατεύθυνον κ.τ.λ., § 48 κατευθύνοντες τὴν πορείαν αὐτῶν ἐν ὁσιότητι καὶ δικαιοσύνῃ; for πορεύεσθαι ἐν, § 3 (comp. § 4); for τὰ καλὰ καὶ εὐάρεστα ἐνώπιον (comp. § 61) see § 21, where the identical phrase appears, and compare also §§ 7, 35, 49; for the combination ὁμόνοιαν καὶ εἰρήνην (comp. § 61) see § 20 (twice), 63, 59 (65); for καθὼς ἔδωκας τοῖς πατράσιν ἡμῶν compare § 62 καθὼς καὶ οἱ προδεδηλωμένοι πατέρες ἡμῶν κ.τ.λ (see the whole context, and comp. § 30): for ὁσίως (omitted however in C), §§ 6, 21 (twice), 26, 40, 44, 62; for ὑπηκόους, §§ 10, 13, 14; for παντοκράτωρ, inscr., §§ 2, 32, 62; for πανάρετος, §§ 1, 2, 45, 57; for ἠγούμενοι, §§ 3, 3, 32, 37, 51, 55. In § 61 for μεγαλοπρεπὴς (comp. μεγαλοπρεπεία in § 60) see §§ 1, 9, 19, 45, 58 (64); for ἀνεκδιήγητος, §§ 20, 49; for ὑπὸ σοῦ... δεδομένην (see also twice below), § 58 ὑπὸ τοῦ Θεοῦ δεδομένα; for δόξαν καὶ τιμήν, § 45 (see below, and comp. § 59); for ὑποτάσσεσθαι, §§ 1, 2, 20, 34, 38, 57; for εὐστάθειαν, § 59 (65); for ἀπροσκόπως, § 20; for βασιλεῦ τῶν αἰώνων, see § 35 πατὴρ τῶν αἰώνων, § 55 Θεὸς τῶν αἰώνων; for ὑπαρχόντων, this epistle *passim*, where it occurs with more than average frequency; for διευθύνειν, §§ 20, 62, and for διέπειν...εὐσεβῶς, § 62 εὐσεβῶς καὶ δικαίως διευθύνειν; for ἵλεως, § 2; for ἐξομολογεῖσθαι, §§ 51, 52; for μεγαλωσύνη, §§ 16, 27, 36, 58, and more especially joined with δόξα in doxologies, as here, §§ 20, 58 (64), comp. § 59 (65); and for εἰς τοὺς αἰῶνας τῶν αἰώνων see the conclusion of Clement's doxologies generally.

Thus the linguistic argument is as strong as it well could be against Jacobi's theory.

The anonymous writer of the articles in the *Church Quarterly* (see above, p. 395), has collected parallels to Clement's prayer from the early Christian liturgies. My own text and notes were completed and in print, before I saw these articles, and therefore my investigations in this direction are altogether independent. Immediately after making myself acquainted with the new portions of Clement in the edition of Bryennios, I read the early liturgies through with a view to noting coincidences.

p. 273, note 1. A manuscript containing the Thebaic Version of these Egyptian *Apostolical Constitutions* was formerly in the possession of Tattam (see his preface, p. xiv)[1]. It was lent by him to Lagarde who transcribed it, and has given a very full account of it in his *Rel. Iur. Eccl. Ant.* p. ix sq. Lagarde describes it as 'codex recentissimus non bombycinus sed papyraceus.' It is now in the British Museum, where its class mark is *Orient.* 440. Unfortunately this copy is defective, and does not contain the proper 'Apostolical Canons' at all.

The MS mentioned in my note, which is also in the British Museum, *Orient.* 1320, supplies the deficiency. It is of large 4to or small folio size, written on parchment, and was recently acquired from Sir C. A. Murray's collection. It consists of two parts, apparently in the same hand-writing, but with separate paginations. At the end is the date ⲁⲛⲟ ⲇⲓⲟⲕⲗ . ⲯⲕⲃ̄ The year 722 of Diocletian is A.D. 1006.

The two parts, of which it consists, are as follows[2]:

(1) Paged ⲁ to ⲛⲁ, the reverse of ⲛⲁ being blank. This part begins

ⲡⲁⲓⲛⲉⲛⲕⲁⲛⲱⲛⲛ̄ⲛⲉⲛⲉⲓⲟⲧⲉⲉⲧⲟⲧⲁⲁⲃⲛⲁⲡⲟⲥⲧⲟⲗⲟⲥⲙ̄ⲡⲉⲛⲍⲟⲉⲓⲥⲓ̄ⲥ̄ⲡ̄ⲉⲭ̄ⲥ̄ⲛ̄ ⲧⲁⲧⲛⲁⲁⲧⲉⲅⲣⲁⲓⲅ̄ⲛ̄ⲡⲉⲛⲕⲕⲗⲏⲥⲓⲁ.

· Pⲁⲩⲉⲱⲡⲉⲛⲩⲕⲣⲉⲙ̄ⲛ̄ⲡⲉⲛⲩⲉⲉⲣⲉ etc. (see Tattam p. 2).

Its contents are the same as in the MS described by Lagarde (p. xi sq.), as far as the latter goes. The readings of the sections ⲁ—ⲟⲁ are also the same with slight variations of orthography, etc. At this point however the latter MS fails us (see Tattam p. xiv, Lagarde p. xv).

---

[1] Lagarde (p. ix.) is mistaken in saying that this Sahidic MS was given to Tattam by the Duke of Northumberland. He has transferred to the Sahidic MS the statement which Tattam makes of the Memphitic (p. xiv).

[2] In giving the extracts from this MS, I have copied the text exactly as I found it, without altering the pointing or correcting other errors.

The subsequent sections are as follows:

ⲟⲉ.   ⲉⲧⲃⲉⲛⲧⲉⲭⲛⲏ . ⲙⲡⲉⲓⲟⲡⲉ.

Παⲣⲟⲧϣⲓⲛⲉⲛⲥⲁⲡⲉⲧⲃⲓⲟⲥⲣⲛⲟⲧⲱⲣⲝ etc.

ⲟⲋ.   ⲉⲧⲃⲉⲝⲉⲁϣⲛⲉⲛⲉⲣⲟⲟⲧⲉⲧⲉϣϣⲉⲉⲁⲁⲧⲉⲧⲃⲉⲛⲉⲛⲧⲁⲧⲉⲛⲕⲟⲧⲕ.

Παⲣⲟⲧⲉⲣⲛϣⲟⲙⲛⲧⲛⲛⲉⲛⲧⲁⲧⲉⲛⲕⲟⲧⲕ etc.

ⲟⲍ.   ⲉⲧⲃⲉⲛⲉⲧⲟⲩⲁⲓⲱⲛⲉⲓⲙⲙⲟⲟⲧⲉⲧⲃⲉⲧⲡⲓⲥⲧⲓⲥ . ⲁⲧⲱⲛⲉⲧⲛⲏⲧⲣⲓⲟⲧⲥⲟⲛⲉⲃⲟⲗ-
ⲣⲙⲛⲡⲟⲗⲓⲥⲉⲛⲡⲟⲗⲓⲥⲉⲧⲃⲉⲧⲡⲓⲥⲧⲓⲥ . ⲣⲱⲥⲧⲉⲉⲧⲣⲉⲧⲃⲟⲛⲑⲉⲓⲉⲣⲟⲟⲧⲣⲓⲟⲧⲥⲟⲛ.

Ϣⲱⲡⲉⲣⲱⲧⲛⲛⲛⲉⲧⲟⲩⲁⲓⲱⲛⲉⲓⲙⲙⲟⲟⲧ etc.

ⲟⲏ is without any heading but begins,

Παⲓⲍⲉⲧⲉⲛⲡⲁⲣⲁⲅⲅⲉⲓⲗⲉⲙⲙⲟϥⲛⲏⲧⲛⲧⲏⲣⲧⲛⲣⲓⲟⲧⲥⲟⲛ,

and ends,

ⲡⲁⲣⲭⲓⲉⲣⲉⲧⲉⲓⲙⲉ . ⲡⲛⲟⲧⲧⲉⲉⲧⲉⲙⲛⲛⲁⲛⲉⲡⲟⲧⲧⲉⲧⲉⲛⲧⲱⲛⲉⲣⲟϥ,

followed by the colophon:

Ⲁⲧⲝⲱⲛⲉⲃⲟⲗⲛⲅⲓⲛⲕⲁⲛⲱⲛⲛⲛⲉⲛⲉⲓⲟⲧⲉⲉⲧⲟⲩⲁⲁⲃⲛⲁⲡⲟⲥⲧⲟⲗⲟⲥ . ⲕⲉ-
ⲫⲁⲗⲁⲓⲟⲛ . ⲟⲏ.

ⲉⲧⲱⲍⲁⲭⲁⲣⲓⲁⲥⲃⲟⲛⲑⲉⲓⲁⲙⲡ.

Comparing the Thebaic sections with the Memphitic as printed by
Tattam, we find that

    ⲟⲁ comprises ⲟⲃ, ⲟⲅ (Tattam pp. 130—136, but without the
        colophons etc.)

  ⲟⲃ corresponds to ⲟⲁ (*ib.* p. 136).

  ⲟⲅ ,, ,, ⲟⲉ (*ib.* p. 138).

  ⲟⲁ ,, ,, ⲟⲏ (*ib.* p. 166.)

  ⲟⲉ begins as ⲟⲋ (*ib.* p. 166). It contains the whole of ⲟⲋ
  (*ib.* p. 166—172), ending ⲛⲅⲧⲉⲛⲡⲣⲟⲫⲏⲧⲏⲥ, followed
  immediately by ⲡⲓⲥⲧⲟⲥⲁⲉⲛⲓⲙⲏⲡⲓⲥⲧⲛⲉⲧϣⲁⲛⲧⲱⲟⲧⲛ etc.
  (*ib.* p. 138) as far as ⲉⲃⲟⲗⲣⲛⲧⲉⲕⲕⲗⲏⲥⲓⲁ (*ib.* p. 146).

  ⲟⲅ corresponds to ⲟⲅ (*ib.* pp. 146—150).

  ⲟⲍ ,, ,, ⲟⲍ (*ib.* p. 150) as far as ⲛⲧⲉⲛⲧⲟⲗⲏ-
  ⲙⲡⲝⲟⲉⲓⲥ.

  ⲟⲏ, as described above, comprises *ib.* pp. 150—164.

(2) Paged ⲁ—ⲛⲁ. This part contains the *Apostolical Canons*,
properly so called, which are here so divided as to be 71 in number
(ⲟⲁ).

The heading (p. ⲁ) is :

ⲛ̄ⲕⲁⲛⲱⲛⲛ̄ⲧⲉⲕⲕⲗⲏⲥⲓⲁ . ⲛⲁⲓⲛ̄ⲧⲁⲛⲁⲡⲟⲥⲧⲟⲗⲟⲥⲧⲁⲁⲧⲣⲓⲧⲛ̄ⲕⲗⲏⲙⲏⲥ .
ⲡⲉⲛⲧⲁⲧⲧⲏⲡⲟⲟⲧⲩ . ⲋⲛⲟⲧⲉⲓⲣⲏⲛⲏⲛ̄ⲧⲉⲡⲛⲟⲧⲧⲉ . ⲋⲁⲙⲏⲛ.
Ⲉⲧⲉⲭⲓⲣⲟⲇⲱⲡⲉⲓⲙ̄ⲡⲉⲡⲓⲥⲕⲟⲡⲟⲥⲋⲓⲧⲛ̄ⲡⲛⲁⲧⲡⲉⲡⲓⲥⲕⲟⲡⲟⲥⲓϣⲟⲙⲛ̄ⲧ.

The ending (p. ⲕⲁ) is :

ⲁⲧⲱⲛ̄ⲋⲣⲟⲙⲟⲟⲧⲥⲓⲟⲛ . ϣⲁⲉⲡⲉⲋ . ⲡⲉⲛⲉⲣⲣⲁⲙⲏⲛ.
Ⲁⲧⲱⲕⲉⲃⲟⲗⲛ̄ϭⲓⲛ̄ⲕⲁⲛⲱⲡⲛ̄ⲕⲗⲏⲙⲏⲥ . ⲕⲁⲓⲫⲁⲗⲁⲓⲟⲛ . ⲟ̄ⲁ̄.

The remainder of this page, and the reverse, is taken up with
various colophons, including the date as already given.

The list of the O. T. books in Canon ⲟⲁ ends :

ⲧⲥⲟⲫⲓⲁⲙ̄ⲡϣⲏⲣⲉⲓⲥⲓⲣⲁⲭ . ⲉⲧⲟϣⲓ̄ⲛⲥⲃⲱ.

After which is the following list of the N. T. books.

Ⲛⲉⲡⲇⲱⲱⲙⲉⲇⲉⲣⲱⲱⲛⲁⲡⲟⲛⲛⲁⲡⲟⲥⲧⲟⲗⲟⲥ . ⲡⲉⲛⲁⲓ , ⲉⲧⲉⲡⲁⲧⲇⲓⲁⲟⲧ-
ⲕⲏⲛ̄ⲃⲣⲣⲉⲛⲉ . ⲡⲉⲩⲧⲟⲟⲧⲉⲧⲁⲅⲅⲉⲗⲓⲟⲛ . ⲕⲁⲧⲁⲫⲉⲛⲧⲁⲛ̄ϣⲣⲛ̄ⲇⲟⲟⲥ . ⲡⲕⲁⲧⲁ-
ⲙⲁⲑⲑⲁⲓⲟⲥ . ⲡⲕⲁⲧⲁⲙⲁⲣⲕⲟⲥ . ⲡⲕⲁⲧⲁⲗⲟⲧⲕⲁⲥ . ⲡⲕⲁⲧⲁⲓ̈ⲱⲣⲁⲛⲛⲏⲥ . ⲡⲉⲛ-
ⲡⲣⲁⲍⲓⲥⲁⲡⲟⲛⲛⲁⲡⲟⲥⲧⲟⲗⲟⲥ.

Ⲧⲥⲛ̄ⲧⲉⲡⲉⲡⲓⲥⲧⲟⲗⲏⲙ̄ⲡⲉⲧⲣⲟⲥ . ⲧϣⲟⲙⲧⲉⲛ̄ⲓ̈ⲱⲣⲁⲛⲛⲏⲥ . ⲧⲉⲡⲓⲥⲧⲟⲗⲏⲛ̄ⲓ̈ⲁ-
ⲕⲱⲃⲟⲥ . ⲙ̄ⲛ̄ⲧⲁⲓ̈ⲟⲧⲇⲁⲥ . ⲧⲙ̄ⲛ̄ⲧⲁⲩⲧⲉⲡⲉⲡⲓⲥⲧⲟⲗⲏⲙ̄ⲡⲁⲧⲗⲟⲥ . ⲧⲁⲡⲟⲕⲁⲗⲧⲙ-
ⲯⲓⲥⲛ̄ⲓ̈ⲱⲣⲁⲛⲛⲏⲥ . ⲧⲥⲛ̄ⲧⲉⲡⲉⲡⲓⲥⲧⲟⲗⲏⲛ̄ⲕⲗⲏⲙⲏⲥ . ⲉⲧⲉⲧⲛⲉⲟϣⲟⲧⲣⲓⲃⲟⲗ.

This part therefore corresponds to the Memphitic in Tattam, pp.
174—212.

The version in Tattam is stated in one of the concluding colophons
(p. 214) to have been translated from the language of upper Egypt (the
Thebaic) into that of lower Egypt (the Memphitic); and a very recent
date (Diocl 1520 = A.D. 1804) is given.

Comparing the Thebaic MS with the Memphitic we find that:

(1) Whereas in the former we have two distinct works, in the
latter they are thrown together and then divided into *eight* books[1], to
which special headings are prefixed. This division into eight books
was doubtless made in order to secure for them the sanction which was
accorded to the eight books of the Apostolical Constitutions, properly
so called.

(2) There seems to have been some displacement in the leaves

---

[1] Strictly speaking *seven* books, in the collection as it stands. But in the colophons the First Book is stated to be also the Second, the Second to be the Third,
and so forth.

of the Thebaic MS from which the Memphitic Version was taken, so that the portion, pp. 166—172, is placed after p. 164, instead of standing after ⲥⲉⲛⲟⲧⲧⲁⲅⲓⲥⲉⲛⲁⲡⲉϥ (p. 138) as in the Thebaic, which (as the connexion of the subjects suggests) is its original position.

The Ethiopic Version (see Tattam p. v sq., Lagarde p. x) seems to follow the Thebaic throughout, and was in all probability translated from it.

p. 279 note 1. In this note I have carelessly taken Adler's date without testing his arithmetic. The year 1503 of Alexander (i.e. of the Seleucidæ) is not A.D. 1212, as Adler gives it, but A.D. 1192. Thus this Paris MS is brought nearer in date to our Cambridge MS. A description of it is given in the *Catalogues des Manuscrits Syriaques* etc., p. 20, no. 54.

Another Paris MS (described above, p. 460 sq.) will probably prove an exception to what I have said here, for it may be expected to resemble closely our Cambridge MS in its arrangement of lessons, as in other respects.

p. 288 L 7 sq. See *Apost. Const.* i. 8 πάσης τε πνοῆς καὶ δυνάμεως δημιουργόν.

p. 289 L 15. See *Apost. Const.* ii. 6 τοὺς ἀγνοοῦντας διδάσκετε, τοὺς ἐπισταμένους στηρίζετε, τοὺς πεπλανημένους ἐπιστρέφετε.

p. 291 l. 11. See Hippol. p. 69 (Lagarde) τῆς τῶν ὁρωμένων ἀγαθῶν θέας ἀεὶ ἀπολαύοντες καὶ τῇ τῶν ἑκάστοτε καινῶν ὁρωμένων προσδοκίᾳ ἡδόμενοι κἀκεῖνα τούτων βελτίω ἡγούμενοι. Lipsius (*Jen. Lit.*, Jan. 13, 1877) would read σωζομένοις with Harnack.

p. 293 l. 11 sq. Lipsius (l. c.) would read ἐπικαλοῦμέν σε ῥῦσαι τοὺς ἐν πίστει καὶ ἀληθείᾳ ὑπηκόους γινομένους.

p. 293 l. 13 note. The expression παντοκρατορικὸν ὄνομα occurs in Macar. Magn. *Apocr.* iv. 30 (p. 225).

p. 304 note 1. Lipsius (l.c.) suggests reading μετὰ τὴν τῆς θείας ἀληθείας ἀνάγνωσιν ἀναγινώσκω.

p. 296 l. 2. Lipsius defends the reading of C and says, 'Die construction ist gut griechisch; übersetze "ad probam vitam iis qui volunt pie et juste dirigendam"'. This is to me quite unintelligible as a rendering of the Greek.

p. 314 note 3. I see that Lipsius also, finding fault with Gebhardt, says 'Ep. ii. 19... ist in Cod. φιλοσοφεῖν in φιλοποιεῖν, nicht φιλοπονεῖν corrigirt; lezteres ist emendation von Bryennios'. Both Lipsius and Hilgenfeld seem to have misunderstood the words of Bryennios, ἐκ διορθώσεως καὶ τοῦτο τοῦ ἀντιγραφέως, which must mean not 'my correction

31

of the scribe', but 'the scribe's correction of himself', as the rest of the note plainly shows. The καὶ τοῦτο apparently refers to μεταλήψεται § 14 (p. 135), where he speaks of τὴν λέξιν διωρθωμένην χειρὶ αὐτοῦ τοῦ ἀντιγραφέως.

p. 326 l. 4. Lipsius would supply λέγουσι μέλλειν καταβαίνειν after ἄνωθεν.

p. 340 l. 2. See Hippol. p. 69 (Lagarde) ἡ τῶν πατέρων δικαίων τε ὁρωμένη ὄψις πάντοτε μειδιᾷ ἀναμενόντων τὴν μετὰ τοῦτο τὸ χωρίον ἀνάπαυσιν καὶ αἰωνίαν ἀναβίωσιν...ἀλλὰ καὶ οὗτοι [οἱ ἄδικοι] τὸν τῶν πατέρων χορὸν καὶ τοὺς δικαίους ὁρῶσι, καὶ ἐπ' αὐτῷ τούτῳ κολαζόμενοι...καὶ τὸ σῶμα...δυνατὸς ὁ Θεὸς ἀναβιώσας ἀθάνατον ποιεῖν, and lower down ἀποφθέγξονται φωνὴν οὕτως λέγοντες, Δικαία σου ἡ κρίσις, and again τὸ πῦρ ἄσβεστον διαμένει...σκώληξ δέ τις ἔμπυρος κ.τ.λ. (comp. § 17). These resemblances suggest that our Clementine homily was known to this writer.

p. 413 l. 9, note on ἡ πόρνη (§ 12). In Heb. xi. 31 also ἡ ἐπιλεγομένη πόρνη is read for ἡ πόρνη by ℵ (first hand) and likewise (as Mr Bensly informs me) by the Harclean Syriac, this part being preserved only in the Cambridge MS (see above p. 233). Mr Bensly also calls my attention to a passage in Ephraem Syrus *Op. Graec.* I. p. 310 ὁμοίως δὲ καὶ Ῥαὰβ ἡ ἐπιλεγομένη πόρνη διὰ τῆς φιλοξενίας οὐ συναπώλετο τοῖς ἀπειθήσασι, δεξαμένη τοὺς κατασκόπους ἐν εἰρήνῃ. Immediately before, this father has mentioned Abraham and Lot as examples of persons rewarded for their φιλοξενία, so that he seems to have had the passage of S. Clement in view.

CAMBRIDGE: PRINTED BY C. J. CLAY, M.A. AT THE UNIVERSITY PRESS.

www.ingramcontent.com/pod-product-compliance
Lightning Source LLC
Chambersburg PA
CBHW031406020726
47499CB00005B/1483